MW00453529

THE STRANGEST FORMS

THE ADVENTURES OF HOLLOWAY HOLMES

BOOK 1

GREGORY ASHE

H&B

This is a work of fiction. Names, characters, places, and incidents either are the product of the author's imagination or are used fictitiously, and any resemblance to actual persons, living or dead, business establishments, events, or locales is entirely coincidental.

The Strangest Forms
Copyright © 2023 Gregory Ashe

All rights reserved. No part of this book may be reproduced in any form, stored in any retrieval system, or transmitted in any form by any means—electronic, mechanical, photocopy, recording, or otherwise—without prior written permission of the publisher, except as provided by United States of America copyright law. For permission requests and all other inquiries, contact: contact@hodgkinandblount.com

Published by Hodgkin & Blount
https://www.hodgkinandblount.com/
contact@hodgkinandblount.com

Published 2023
Printed in the United States of America

Version 1.04

Trade Paperback ISBN: 978-1-63621-045-2
eBook ISBN: 978-1-63621-044-5

My ancestors were country squires, who appear to have led much the same life as is natural to their class. But, none the less, my turn that way is in my veins, and may have come with my grandmother, who was the sister of Vernet, the French artist. Art in the blood is liable to take the strangest forms.

—"The Adventure of the Greek Interpreter," Sir Arthur Conan Doyle

Yes, it is an interesting instance of a throwback, which appears to be both physical and spiritual. A study of family portraits is enough to convert a man to the doctrine of reincarnation.

—*The Hound of the Baskervilles*, Sir Arthur Conan Doyle

You know, Watson, I don't mind confessing to you that I have always had an idea that I would have made a highly efficient criminal.

—"The Adventure of Charles Augustus Milverton," Sir Arthur Conan Doyle

Chapter 1

Empty All Receptacles

Watson was late.

I paced, planks creaking underfoot. The old boathouse was dark; starlight filtered through where boards had warped and no longer met and the tin roof sagged. The air smelled like waxed canvas, dust, dry wood. When I turned too fast, I bumped one of the boats racked on either side of me. I made my way to the south wall, bumping another boat in the process, and pressed my eye to one of the gaps in the wall.

On the other side, the twinkle of The Walker School's lights broke the mountain night. No movement. Me, and the murmur of the lake, and that was just about it. Then a golf cart whined, its shadow moving down the path less than a hundred yards off. A girl said something, and a boy laughed drunkenly, and then the golf cart was gone, the whine fading toward the glow between the trees. Friday night fun. Still no Watson.

I checked my jacket pocket. It was September, and down in the valley, it was still too warm to need another layer, but up here, on the back of Timp, the temperature dropped quickly. The zannies shifted under my touch; the plastic baggie rustled. I paced back the other way, toward the roll-up doors and the dock that pushed out into the lake. I told myself, For fuck's sake, stand still and stop making so much noise.

It wasn't always like this; it wasn't always Xanax. Sometimes it was beer. Well, more often it was rum or vodka or hard seltzer. Sometimes it was Ding Dongs or Twinkies or Doublemint, stuff you couldn't buy in the canteen. There was a manga girl who paid me a shitload to bring her a case of Milkis every month, covered in all that Korean writing I couldn't read, and then that little bit of English: *New feeling of soda beverage*. Sure, whatever. There was a wannabe tweaker, a little white boy, who wanted Sudafed. There was another white boy, not so little, who wanted live crickets, and I never asked why. One time, this real butch Mexican kid had wanted a Snuggie. So, you never knew.

It didn't matter what they wanted. They were stuck up here—that was the whole point of Walker, a place rich people could send their troubled teens to be kept neatly out of sight—and I wasn't. I knew what that meant; I hadn't read all those Wikipedia articles on economics for nothing. What mattered was that the rich kids paid, and some months they paid enough that Dad and I weren't completely underwater. Of course, that had been before I bought hundreds of dollars of zannies on credit from Shivers and Watson decided not to show.

Never again, I told myself. Never buy on credit again.

When I made my next loop, I pressed up against that gap in the boards, looking out again, and called myself every kind of stupid. Nothing. The boathouse was a good spot; it didn't get used much during the school year, and it was far enough from the rest of campus that people wouldn't stumble across you—with the exception of the occasional joyride or the kids who wanted a quick fuck. I had an excuse for being here if anybody spotted me: the raccoons dragged trash up this way sometimes. I always had an excuse. The rules were clear; any trouble, and Dad would be out of a job, and so I'd be out of a job, and what the hell would we do then?

I made one last loop of the boathouse and gave up on waiting any longer. I let myself out and locked the door behind me. I headed south, toward campus, the buildings faintly visible between the trees like the fairy lights Mom had hung on our Salt Lake porch. I fumbled the custodial cart out from where I'd hidden it behind some trash cans and wheeled it toward the maintenance building.

I pulled on my headphones, fired up Dad's old Discman, and turned up the volume as "Smells Like Teen Spirit" started. Kurt sang hello. How low. I tried to think. I'd finished my route for the night, so I could drop the garbage in the dumpster, put away the cart, and head home. But then what? I had almost five hundred dollars' worth of zannies, and we had bills that were due. Past due. I figured I could try to track down Watson, make her pay, but what if she'd changed her mind? Rich kids did that sometimes. I'd had a girl asking me for weeks to get her this skin cream, something Korean, and I did, only it took two weeks, and when it finally got here, she didn't want it anymore. *I changed my mind*, that's what she said. And who ate the eighty dollars? You're goddamn right I did. What was I going to do, tell Mr. Taylor or Headmaster Burrows?

And Watson wasn't some nobody first-year. She was a junior, and she was pretty and wore expensive clothes and was nice, I mean, as far as I could tell, and she had that family name. She was a prime candidate for missing white girl syndrome (thank you, Wikipedia); if she was more than ten minutes late, I was probably legally obligated to start a national news campaign. And, of course, Watson had Supercreep for a best friend. I'd sold to Holloway Holmes—aka Supercreep—a couple of times. Addys. And sure, he was pretty, if you were into white boys who looked like statues, and oh yeah, the statue was based on someone who had been a gaping dickhole in real life, like he hunted foxes and had a butler and stuff like that. But pretty or not, he was also scary as hell—didn't say anything, sometimes didn't even seem to breathe, just stared at you like he was waiting for you to turn around so he could suck your blood. And he was a Holmes. Like, related to that Holmes. I'd heard some of the kids talking— they didn't even seem to see me sometimes, like I was just another part of the background, picking up their trash, cleaning up their shit, literally— about how he'd asked a girl to Homecoming at his last school, and when she'd said no, he'd leaked all these nudes, and she ate like eight Tide pods and they had to put her in this special home in Switzerland or something. So, yeah, the short version: Watson and Supercreep were above my paygrade, no matter how badly Watson screwed me.

The edge of campus was quiet except for the night breeze coming off Timp's ass, making me shiver as I pushed the cart. The thing about Walker was that it was full of these rich, entitled assholes, full of teachers, full of staff like my dad—and, by extension, me—full of people, in other words, and you could still walk five yards this way, ten yards that way, and be the only person in the whole universe. The sky was thick with stars. The pines, the tall ones with their branches hanging down at their sides, made me think of crime-scene bodies, chalk outlines against the horizon.

My old, dumb, brick of a phone buzzed, and when I checked it, I saw a message from Shivers: *what up*

I put my phone back in my pocket and kept going. When I reached the little concrete slab bridge over the Toqueah, where the cottonwoods grew like someone had drawn them against the water with a Sharpie, I stopped and got my broom from the cart. I went down the sloping bank, bracing my foot on cottonwood roots, careful to keep from pitching into the water as I did a quick sweep. Kids liked to smoke and vape down there, and it smelled like that, like stale cigarette smoke mixing with old leaves and mud. Tonight I came up with some empty pods and a few butts. I dumped them in with the rest of the trash. Mr. Taylor didn't always check; he was like that, he wanted to catch you by surprise. When he knew I was covering for Dad, he did petty shit like that.

My phone buzzed again, another message from Shivers: *Jacky tough shit.*

Nothing but that—nothing but his stupid nickname for me.

As I pushed the cart across the bridge, the casters clattering over the slight unevenness of the concrete, the bad one still squeaking like crazy, I tried to think. I had other people who bought zannies, sure. Not this many at one time, but it's not like they were going to go bad. The real problem was the cash. I checked my phone; the messages, both of them, were still there on the screen, still marked unread. There was a girl, Lin, who bought Xanax from me sometimes. I pushed the cart a little faster. She always had extra cash. And there were a couple of guys in Anderson. They hadn't bought zannies before, but they were into chemsex—they wanted Viagra, MDMA, a couple of times coke. And, more importantly, they liked me. Hell, one time they'd gotten me halfway out of my pants, back when I'd just started hooking up with Ariana, and that had just been them messing around.

The maintenance building came into view ahead: a single-story brick structure, security lights cutting sharp corners out of the night. Using one elbow to steer the cart around back, I tapped out a message to Jonno, one of the Anderson boys. I needed the money, and I was single, right? And they were both cute if you were into twinks.

As I came around the corner, the cart hit something, and metal boomed. I looked up from my phone. Someone had wheeled one of the dumpsters out from the wall, and I'd run into it with the cart. Shaking my head, I shoved the phone into my pocket, took the headphones off, and pulled the cart back a few feet. I moved around to the dumpster to shove it back into position; the garbage truck drivers were assholes, and sometimes they wouldn't pick up a dumpster if it wasn't right where it was supposed to be. I stopped to grab a broken piece of plastic from the ground. Probably a stupid prank, I thought as I got to my feet. Or a dare. Or a challenge. Although what the hell kind of prank—

I stopped.

Watson—Sarah Elizabeth Watson—lay like a broken doll on top of the black garbage bags, dead.

Chapter 2

More than You Do

I stared at the dead girl in front of me. I was distantly aware of blood rushing to my head, the faint flecks of black at the edge of my vision, the sense of hanging in the air like I'd been cut in half at the waist.

She was dead. She had to be, lying there like that.

And then, on the heels of that thought: How the hell was I going to pay Shivers?

The shittiness of that thought brought me back to myself. I took a deep breath, tasting the garbage and a hint of piss in the air. My face was pins and needles. I took another deep breath. And then another. I was still holding on to the broken plastic in one hand, but I scrubbed my other hand on my thigh. Like I was trying to wipe something off, I thought. The security light buzzed. I took a step back, my ass connected with the cart, and one of the mops started to fall, clattering. I reached back, grabbing blindly, and caught it. My shadow, a little snippet cut out by the light over the door, twisted and turned. Then silence pressed in, silence like it had its fingers in my mouth.

This girl was dead. And someone had killed her. It wasn't the first time it had happened at Walker; the troubled teens were sometimes extremely troubled. There'd been a boy killed here twenty years ago, and people still told the story. But that was twenty years ago, and this was now. This was me. This was Watson.

My brain started working again, picking up details to fill in that conclusion. She was white and honey blond, her hair loosely curled. When I'd seen her—before—it had fallen to her shoulders, but now it followed the curves and bumps of the garbage bags, and it looked frizzy, flat, almost like a wig. But it wasn't, of course. It was her real hair, and some of it was pasted to the side of her head with blood. A scalp wound, I thought.

She already looked different. Part of that was death—I'd seen dead bodies before, and dead people never looked like how you remembered them. Part of it was the injuries. Her face was swollen, her eyes bulging. She looked like she had a rash, but after a moment, I realized it wasn't a rash, although I didn't know what it was—the skin around her eyes was red, and so were her ears. Her eyes looked bloodshot. Her neck had a shadow that I thought was probably the beginning of a bruise.

I shifted my weight; some of the broken asphalt underfoot clicked together, and the sound was huge in the stillness. The sound woke me up a little more, reminded me that there was a whole world around me—people coming and going all over campus, even at this hour. We didn't usually have students come to the maintenance building, but staff sometimes stopped by—they wanted to borrow a screwdriver, or a sink wasn't draining, or—no joke—they wanted somebody to kill a bug. And that meant someone could walk around the corner at any moment, and I'd be standing here, pocket full of zannies, with a dead girl who owed me money. Just lying there. Out in the open.

And that was strange, part of my brain told me. That was really weird because why hadn't somebody covered her? If you were going to kill a girl, if you were going to dump her and hope that they picked her up on trash day and nobody ever saw her, wouldn't you have, you know, tried a little harder? Or had they left her exposed on purpose? Had somebody wanted her to be found?

I didn't know. I didn't want to know. I was standing here with a corpse, alone, on the edge of campus, in a dark canyon, with miles and miles of woods where anybody could hide. The hair on the back of my neck stood up, and I reached for my phone, already planning. I'd ditch the pills, and then I'd call, and then I'd get home and shut the door and lock it. I was starting to think maybe I'd never take out the trash again. Then I had to stop because I was still holding that stupid piece of plastic I'd picked up, so I shoved it in my pocket and dug out my phone.

Before I could place the call, though, a phone rang—another phone, a different ringtone. It was a snippet of something, a pop melody that I didn't recognize. A moment later, the flashing screen caught my eye, and I saw it half-buried among the trash, hanging out of a little brown pouch that, to judge by the designer logo printed all over it, had been godawful expensive. The name on the screen was MM. After a moment, the call went to voicemail, and the screen went dark.

I stared at the phone. I stared at that little brown pouch, the kind of thing a girl would carry because she didn't want to lug around a purse but she wanted everyone to know she could afford—what? Louis Vuitton? And it had probably cost a couple of grand, right? And it was just lying there. And she owed me money.

Before I could reconsider, I shoved my phone back in my pocket and grabbed two garbage can liners, clean ones, from the cart. Fingerprints. I covered my hands with the plastic and eased the pouch, phone and all, out from under the trash. Then I stopped. I couldn't take the pouch. I couldn't sell it. People would remember that; people would be looking. But it was also a hell of a lot of money, money that I needed.

I tipped the pouch, and its contents spilled out: the phone, her keys, a tube of lip gloss, a crumpled tissue, a charging cable, all that stuff. And, of course, her wallet—a matching piece that went with the pouch. It was awkward, trying to do everything through the plastic, but I got it open. I skipped the cards and the license because that was stupid, and I got my fingers around a fat stack of bills. Girls like Watson didn't normally carry cash; they liked plastic. But this cash was for me. It was mine. And I needed it.

I stood there for another five seconds before my balls finally dropped, and I took the cash. I wadded it up in my pocket. Then I put everything back in her pouch, slid it back under the garbage, and took two quick steps back. I wadded up the liners. Then I buried them at the bottom of the custodial cart. I wiped my hands on my jeans. Then I wiped them again.

Abandoning the cart, I jogged over to the maintenance building and let myself inside. I followed the dark hall to the office, unlocked a filing cabinet, and dropped the pills and the cash behind all the 2018 invoices. I gave the drawer a few pushes and pulls to redistribute the hanging folders so everything would look normal, and then I locked the drawer again. Dropping into the chair behind Dad's desk, I picked up the phone—the landline—and called 911. It rang once, and in my mind, I saw Watson, baby-doll-broken on the trash, and I thought, I'm sorry, I'm really sorry, but I need it more than you do.

Chapter 3

Questions

"Why don't we go back to the beginning?" He was short—I bet I had six inches on him—but he was muscular, stocky like a wrestler, and he had one cauliflower ear that told me I was a pretty good guesser. His skin was darker than mine. He paid more than he should for his haircut; I could tell Detective Rivera wanted everybody to know it was expensive, but it was just a skin fade, spiked up in front, and what the hell was so great about that? "You left your house at—" He pretended to check his notepad. "Three?"

I nodded.

"And?"

"And I went to work." He didn't say anything, so I gestured to the Walker polo I was wearing. "Friday night, we do all the classrooms and bathrooms."

"Aren't you a little young to be a custodian?"

I tried not to groan. We'd been over this four times already. First, when deputies from the Utah County Sheriff's Office responded to my call—two white guys named Utley and Fitzgerald, Utley maybe forty, pouchy eyes, a plastic fork stuck behind his ear, and Fitzgerald closer to sixty, hair all but gone, skinny except for a potbelly and always hitching up his belt. They'd taken one look at Watson, and Utley had staggered behind the curtain wall and gotten sick. Fitzgerald had asked me all these questions, and then Rivera and his partner, a white lady named Yazzie, had asked them too. And then they'd asked them again. And now here we were, just Rivera and me, in the maintenance office, doing it again.

"Don't you need my dad to be here?" I asked.

"That depends. Are you an emancipated minor?"

"I told you: I'm home schooled, and I pick up shifts at the school sometimes."

"To help your dad," Rivera said, and there wasn't anything in his tone, but the way he said it was like it was bullshit, or maybe like we were telling a joke back and forth but he was getting sick of it.

I nodded again.

"This late?" He pretended to check his watch. "You found her at, let's see, you told the deputies it was almost midnight."

There it was: *you told the deputies.* This was the grown-up version of Mom and Dad trying to catch me in a lie. *You told your dad you were going to study. You told your mom you were spending the night at Nick's.*

Rivera spoke again before I responded: "You start a shift at three, I figure you're supposed to be done by eleven, maybe eleven-thirty. But come midnight, you still haven't dumped the trash. What's your supervisor going to tell me when I ask about your schedule? What's he going to say when I ask about your route? What am I going to see when I check the security cameras?"

I kept my eyes on his face; the filing cabinet to my right seemed like it had its own special gravity, trying to drag my gaze toward it. "I was supposed to be done at eleven-thirty. We get a half hour for dinner. But a raccoon dragged some trash up toward the boathouse, and I had to rake it up." And then, because sometimes Jack Moreno is an asshat, I added, "Sir."

An almost-invisible smile hooked the corner of Rivera's mouth. It was a hard smile. A tough guy smile. But it didn't look like an act; like I said, sometimes Jack Moreno is an asshat.

"Sure," Rivera said. "I'll write down raccoon."

But he didn't write it down. And he didn't look away. Sweat gathered along my hairline; September in the Wasatch Mountains was chilly, and the door was open, and down the hall, I could hear one of the deputies saying something, and then the woman named Yazzie saying something back, but in spite of all that, the inside of the maintenance office felt sweltering, my cheeks stinging with the heat.

"And you just happened to find a dead girl," Rivera said so quietly it was almost to himself.

I nodded. Some of the sweat started to run, and I reached up to wipe it away.

"Why'd you call on the landline?"

"Huh?"

Rivera tipped his head toward the phone on the desk.

"She was dead. It was, you know, an emergency." I wiped the side of my face on my shoulder. "The service is shit—it's bad up here."

Down the hall, the conversation had fallen silent. A door clapped shut. Someone moved—I could hear the creak of leather. But it was just movement like shifting your weight or something.

"What was your relationship with Sarah Watson?"

"I didn't have one." Rivera didn't speak, didn't blink, and it was like a tractor beam on Dad's *Star Trek* DVDs. "She's a student here, and—"

"Was," Rivera said quietly. "She was a student here."

I wiped more sweat away. "She was a student here. I just work here."

"So, if I ask around, nobody's going to tell me she's your girlfriend?"

"No."

"What was her problem?"

I blinked.

"School for troubled teens, right?" Rivera wore that tough guy smile, and it wasn't a game, and he wasn't playing, and I had a pretty good bullshit meter and figured Detective Rivera had fucked some people up in his life. "What was Sarah Watson's—what do they call it, her 'issue'?"

The filing cabinet might as well have been red hot. I swallowed, and my throat was so dry I had to swallow again. "I told you: I didn't know her."

"That's funny," Rivera said, "because you know what? The person who 'finds' the body—" He didn't draw the air quotes with his fingers, but I could hear them in his voice. "—is usually the killer. No idea why they do it; maybe they think it's going to clear them." He shifted in his seat. He cocked his head. His eyes were sharp; they made me think of the brass tips on darts, dead center, bullseye. Somebody had smashed up his ear really good, and I was starting to guess that hadn't stopped Detective Rivera, not even for a moment. "That red around her eyes? On her ears? Looks kind of like a rash? Those are called petechiae. Those, along with the damage to her neck, tell me I don't need the ME to say how she died. Somebody choked the life out of her. That takes a long time, longer than most people think. You really have to hate somebody to do that. Tell me, Jack, what do you think about that?"

"I want a lawyer," I said. "And my dad."

"This is a conversation—"

"I want a lawyer." When he didn't move, I stood; my leg hit the desk, and the sound was small in the silence between us. I took a step toward the door. "I want a lawyer—"

Rivera was out of his seat faster than I could believe, moving into my path. The smile was sharper. I could see all of it now, the long, bright edge.

"All right." Yazzie stood in the doorway. She probably came up to my shoulder, and with her Wayfarer glasses and her red hair out of a box and her suit, she looked more like a depressed realtor than a detective. Than any detective I'd seen on TV, anyway. "Detective Rivera, could I talk to you for a minute? Mr. Moreno, hold on a second, please."

Rivera stayed where he was. He'd tucked the smile away, but his eyes were still dark darts.

"Now," Yazzie said.

In a smooth movement, Rivera turned away from me, and then both detectives were moving down the hall. A moment later, the door at the end of the hall clapped shut. I moved to the doorway and checked to see if they were really gone. A length of shadowed, empty linoleum stretched toward the door. I was alone.

How long did I have? A minute? Maybe two? I had two competing thoughts: they might search me again—the deputies had already patted me down once; but, even worse, they'd definitely search the maintenance office. What were they going to do when they found cash and pills in the filing cabinet? Who were they going to blame?

The keys jingled when I pulled them out of my pocket, so loud that they sent my pulse racing. As I unlocked the top drawer, I kicked off my Vans. I pulled out the drawer, wincing at the squeak of the metal runners, and fumbled around behind the folders until my fingers closed over the cash. I couldn't find the pills, and it took what felt like forever, reaching around blindly, until plastic crinkled under my touch. I bent and shoved the cash into one shoe and the pills into another. Five hundred dollars' worth of zannies might sound like a lot, but it's really not, and anyway, I was highly motivated. As I slid the Vans back on, I shouldered the drawer shut. It squealed again. I bumped the lock shut with the heel of my hand just as the door opened at the end of the hall.

A single set of footsteps came toward me. Rivera appeared in the doorway, hands on his hips.

I watched him. Distantly, from outside, came raised voices and the beep of a truck backing up.

"Can I go?"

He nodded. But he didn't move.

A second limped past, and then another, and then I decided to hell with it. I headed toward the hall, and when I reached Rivera, I decided no macho shit, and I twisted to slide past him.

Rivera's hand snaked out to grab my arm. A moment later, I was pressed against the wall, my cheek flattened against the plaster. The detective began patting me down.

"You didn't forget to tell me something, did you, Jack? There isn't anything you want to say?"

"Get off me." I pushed back against the hold, but all it did was send pain lancing up my arm. "I said get off!"

"Rivera!" Yazzie was a silhouette in the doorway at the end of the hall. "What's going on in here?"

"Just telling Jack goodnight." Rivera released me, and he pivoted, backing into the office. "Sleep tight. Don't let the bedbugs bite."

I looked over my shoulder at Yazzie, but her face was lost in shadow. Trying to make my voice normal, I said, "It's like he thinks he's on TV."

Yazzie's silence had a strummed, vibrating quality. Then, out of the darkness where her face should have been, she said, "Mr. Moreno, I think you should go home now. We'll be in touch if we need anything else."

I cast a last look at Rivera, and I thought that in spite of the bad dialogue, the over-the-top bad cop performance, there was something there, something I didn't like. I turned, passed Yazzie, and headed out of the building. The pills and the wad of cash made every step unnatural, and I waited for them to call me back, to tell me to take off my shoes. Then I was pushing out into the night, the air like cold velvet, the taste of diesel exhaust and pine resin coming in and making me cough, and a rush of something a lot better than Xanax shot straight to my head — cold and clear and darkly running. Like the Toqueah.

I headed toward the cottage, which wasn't far — just on the other side of a scrubby line of spruce. And I looked back. Once. Two guys in uniforms — not police, something else — were loading a gurney into a van marked UTAH OFFICE OF THE MEDICAL EXAMINER. And then I saw Rivera, action-figure sized now, all the way down to his cauliflower ear. Watching me. And then he threw me the peace sign, or maybe it was V for victory, and I was sure he smiled.

Chapter 4

$1010.09

I let myself into the cottage silently. Our first weekend, I'd gone around and WD-40'd the hinges on all the doors. And I didn't have to worry about the locks; we never set them. It's not like we had anything worth stealing. Dad had trouble sleeping—since the accident, Dad had trouble with just about everything—and I didn't want to wake him when I came home late. Besides, it was better if he didn't know; he worried enough already.

I stood in the combined space at the front of the house, a tiny kitchen mashed together with a tiny living room. It wasn't anything like our Salt Lake house: battered, particle-board cabinets; a laminate countertop bloated with water damage; ancient linoleum with a parquet pattern peeling at the corners. We cleaned—I cleaned—every Sunday, but the place had that rubbed-in kind of grime that meant it always looked dirty, and even with the windows open to catch the cool breeze, the house felt hot, and the three-quarters fridge smelled like the motor was about to catch fire. But the cottage came with the job, which was one of the reasons, maybe the main reason, Dad had taken it. We had to live somewhere, right?

As quietly as I could, I shut the door. In the living room, we'd hung the TV from our Salt Lake house, and it took up almost a whole wall. Dad had it on KUTV, and it was a replay of *2 News at 10*. I guess in case you missed it the first time. They wouldn't have anything about Watson—hell, I hadn't found her until after ten—but I still had this weird tightness in my chest, like any minute they might cut to helicopter footage of the school, a spotlight picking me out by the dumpsters behind the maintenance building. I took a step toward the hall.

Dad's voice came from the recliner: "Buddy?"

I started. Then I took a deep breath. I pressed my hands against my eyes. A prickling flush, the aftermath of the shock, crawled up my chest. When I trusted my voice, I said, "Hey, Dad. How're you feeling?"

"All right." He struggled to sit up, and then his head appeared above the back of the recliner. For a moment, he tried to turn around. We'd paid for as much PT as we could afford, which wasn't much, and sometimes, at night, I thought the mobility issues were getting worse. "Come over here. What's wrong?"

I thought about my room. I thought about running down that short hall and slamming the door. Instead, I took another deep breath and sat on the couch.

He was dressed for work, which he shouldn't have been, and in the faint light from the TV, he looked older than he was. His hair was almost completely gray, which didn't help, and he kept it buzzed short because he hated it. Over the summer, I'd gained half an inch on him, and on good days, when he was like my old dad, he'd put his hand on my head and press down, laughing like crazy at his own dumb joke. He'd always been strong, but since the accident he'd put on weight, and weirdly, it made him look smaller. People said we looked alike, and I could see it in our jaws, but he told everyone I looked like my mom. Up close, I could smell a faint hint of urine.

It must have shown on my face. The weak light from the TV stole the color from everything, and Dad's blush looked gray. "Sorry. I meant to change and shower, but I was so wiped out after I seized that by the time I got back..." He trailed off and shrugged.

"What do you mean, you seized?"

He didn't flinch, not exactly, but I could see it in his eyes: he knew he'd made a mistake.

"Have you been taking your medicine?"

"Jack—"

I crossed to the kitchen and opened the cabinet where we kept his pills. The brown plastic vials stood in a row, and the one for his Aptiom was empty. When I checked the fill date, it was from June. I carried it back, held it out, and said, "Dad?"

He looked away. "It's expensive, buddy. And I'm fine most of the time."

For a moment, I didn't have anything to say to that. I went with: "I told you I was going to cover the shift. You had a migraine; you were supposed to be resting."

"I know, but I thought I could help with a little—"

"That's not how this works. You're not back to a hundred yet. You need to rest."

"I shouldn't be sitting around on my fat ass while my son does my job."

"The doctor said—"

"I don't care what the doctor said! It's my job!"

I breathed sharply through my nose, trying not to respond. After a moment, I took a step toward the hall. Dad held up a hand to stop me.

On TV, an attorney with an eyepatch was promising big cash settlements. He was in his office. Then he was somewhere else—just a blue screen—with his arm around a girl with enormous boobs. She was holding a stack of paperwork. I figured hell, put her on the case. Not that she could get us any money. To get a big cash settlement, first you had to find the asshole who hit you.

"Sorry," Dad said. He was looking down.

"It's all right," I mumbled. "Your head—"

"Yeah, my head." Dad made a noise that wasn't really a laugh and touched his temple. "I'm grateful, Jack. I really am. It just—it makes me feel—" He let out a breath. "I went out, I don't even remember why, and I must have had a seizure because the next thing I knew, I was dragging my sorry butt back inside, so tired I barely made it to my chair."

The blackouts were pretty common, extending on either side of a seizure. I didn't know if they were because of the seizure, or if they were another side effect from the accident. They called this stuff *long-term symptoms*. They called what happened a *traumatic brain injury*. Who gets paid, I wanted to know, to come up with these names?

"Sit down," Dad said. "Tell me what's wrong."

"Nothing's wrong." But I sat. I wanted to kick off the Vans—the shit in my shoes was starting to hurt my feet. I flopped back, and the resale-shop smell of the upholstery wafted up around me. "Something happened to a girl. The police are up here. The deputies, I mean. One of them's an asshole."

"What?" Dad asked.

Then I had to tell him all of it—or enough, anyway, that he could stop worrying: how I found Watson, Rivera, the likelihood that they'd want to talk to me again.

"They should be grateful," Dad said when I finished. "Somebody else might have tried to walk away, pretend they didn't see anything."

"It's fine," I said. "I think that guy, Rivera, has seen too many cop movies, is all. Come on. Let's get you to bed."

"I think I'll stay up for a while."

"The doctor said you need to try sleeping in your bed. Sitting out here in front of the TV isn't good for you."

He grumbled about it, and I heard a few swears thrown in here and there, but eventually he let me help him up, and I got him in the bathroom. There was only one, and it was located off the main hall. At the end of the hall, we each had a bedroom—the same size, which meant identically cramped. When I heard the water start to run, I went back and checked the recliner. It was dry, and I didn't smell anything, so I didn't bother spraying it down. When the sound of the water changed, and I knew Dad was showering, I opened the top kitchen drawer, took out the stack of bills to be paid, and carried them to my room.

It was a small room, so it was easy, even in the dark, to find my desk and click on the lamp. The only other furniture was the twin bed. In theory, my clothes went in the closet, but most of them were on the floor. I spent enough of my life cleaning up; I figured it was my room, and I could put my clothes wherever I wanted. And anyway, I knew which ones were clean and which ones weren't. Most of the time.

Kicking off the ancient Vans, I unbuttoned my jeans. I kicked my way out of those too. Then I dropped onto the chair and set the bundle of papers on the desk. I was too wired to sleep, so I might as well be productive. Old me, the one who lived in Salt Lake, would have laughed at that.

The checkbook was buried in the stack of papers. I fished it out and checked the balance in the register. I hadn't written a check—heck, I hadn't looked at a checkbook—until about six months ago. That's when the repo guy showed up and took my car. After that, I figured I'd better learn.

First order of business: the balance in Dad's checking account was depressingly low. I could have gotten on his old iPad and made sure the funds were right, but I didn't need to; it was always low.

Second order of business: triage, like they did in *Band of Brothers* and *Saving Private Ryan* and all the other war movies Dad clicked through on Sunday afternoons. I went through the envelopes, opening the new ones, checking the amounts, and then setting them in stacks: credit cards went into one, hospital bills went into another, insurance documents that I didn't understand (what the hell was an Explanation of Benefits? It didn't explain anything, as far as I could tell) went into another, physical therapy bills in another, and, of course, collection agency notifications. Some of those were for utilities, gas and electric from the Salt Lake house, but since we didn't live there anymore, I just put those straight into the trash.

Walker didn't pay Dad much, and they didn't pay me at all. I was strictly unofficial—pinch hitter for Dad's bad days. That's why I wasn't in school anymore. It hadn't been hard; Shivers knew a white lady who couldn't afford what she wanted, but she had one of those notary stamps, so all I had to do was write a letter and give her a hundred bucks to say it was Dad's signature. So, now I was home-schooled, which meant when I wanted to know something, I read about it on Wikipedia. Or I watched YouTube videos. But most of the time, I covered for Dad so Mr. Taylor wouldn't fire him. Mr. Taylor complained, but the greedy motherfucker secretly loved it, I was pretty sure, since I worked twice as many hours as were in Dad's contract.

The big plus of this job was the cottage, and I guess in theory, it made sense: if we didn't need to pay for housing, we didn't need as big of a salary. Of course, most people probably didn't have a mountain of bills from an accident. And while collection agencies couldn't force us out onto the street—at least, not from what I understood, since The Walker School technically owned the cottage—they sure could be assholes, calling Dad all the time, yelling at him, threatening him.

I didn't understand the hospital bills, and the numbers on those were way too big for me to do anything about, so instead, I paid the minimum on the credit cards, and I ignored the PT bills and the collection agency notices. I signed the checks—I'd gotten better at Dad's signature since the home-school letter—and I stamped the envelopes. Then I stacked them up. Bigger, I thought. It was definitely bigger than last month.

I picked up my phone, and before I could stop myself, I texted Mom: *Am I too young to declare bankruptcy?* The screen was full of one-line messages like that from me. I sent another one right away: *jk*

After a couple of minutes, the screen timed out.

I grabbed my Vans and shook them out over the desk. The wad of cash looked smaller than it had felt when it had been trapped under my sole. The pills looked all right—only a couple had been broken, and people would still pay for those. I thought about Rivera, and I pulled the box fan down from the window and got a screwdriver from the desk. In the bathroom, the water shut off, and I could hear Dad moving around. I worked the screws out, and then I pulled the back of the case off. Then I rolled up the baggie of pills, making it as small and tight as I could, and taped it to the inside corner of the case. I reattached it to the fan and returned it to the window.

Dad's steps lumbered down the hall. I heard him hesitate outside my door. The room would have looked dark; I'd tested it before, what it looked like from the hall with only the lamp on. The lights in the hall clicked off, and Dad's door opened and shut, and a moment later, the springs of his bed creaked.

I counted Watson's money. It was mostly twenties, with some fifties and hundreds mixed in—the kind of casual disorder that told you she didn't care how much she had because she always had enough. The outer bills felt a little damp—and smelled a little shoe-y—but after that, they were fine. The beautiful thing about cash, I thought, was that nobody knew how much you had of it. Collection agencies couldn't point to it and demand it. Hospitals couldn't insist you shell out. My girl had been carrying seven hundred and twenty-one dollars. Enough to cover what I owed Shivers, plus some extra. If I stretched it, that would be groceries for a month. Or I could put some of it toward new brakes for the truck. Or I could buy myself a phone, a smart one, and not feel like I was living in the Stone Age. I gave a mental snort. What was I going to do? Post selfies of me auguring some asshat's underwear out of a toilet? Maybe me flipping off the camera to look bad ass while I drilled through human shit? Yep, that would get me a lot of likes. But it was almost enough money for—

For the Aptiom, I realized. For Dad's anticonvulsant. It wouldn't cover all of it, but it put me a hell of a lot closer—it was over a grand for thirty days' worth of the stuff. $1010.09 for thirty little pills.

As I started organizing the money by denomination, counting it more slowly, something fell out from between two of the bills and landed on the desk. I stared at it. It was a scrap of paper, like something torn from the corner of a notebook, and it had something written on it. I set down the cash and picked it up. *Vonkramm*. It didn't mean anything to me. But it looked like it meant something to somebody. It looked like it might even be important. She had been carrying it in her wallet the night she got killed, and it didn't look like the kind of thing a girl—especially a girl like Watson—carried normally. If she'd had it in her pocket, or if it had been lying at the bottom of her purse, I might have thought it was just scrap—a piece of paper she meant to trash—

That thought stopped me. Then I bent, hooked my jeans, and dragged them toward me. I dug around in my pockets until I found the piece of plastic that I'd picked up by the dumpster, in those last moments before my life had gone to shit. When I found it, I held it under the lamp and examined it more carefully.

It was maybe half an inch of plastic, uneven on one side where it had been broken, and now that I looked at it with some decent light, I thought I knew what it was: part of a flash drive. The lamplight made it easy to see a rust-colored smear on the edge of the plastic, and I remembered the side of Watson's head, the scalp wound, her hair matted with blood. I tried to play it back in my mind, like those guys do on TV—I want to say the show is called *Criminal Minds*. Watson goes to meet somebody. But it's not me. Maybe she thinks it's going to be quick, and she'll still be able to get to the boathouse in time. Or maybe it's important, so she blows me off. And then—what? I had no idea. I had this image in my head of a hand—it looked like Detective Rivera's hand, for some reason—clutching a flash drive, clubbing Watson on the side of the head. The plastic cuts her. The drive breaks. She starts to scream, but he can't have that, so he grabs her by the throat, and—

My heart was pounding, and sweat stung under my arms, ran in a hot line from my chest to my belly. I dropped the piece of the flash drive, and it clattered against the wood. Then I stared at it, a single thought working its way through the chaos in my brain: my fingerprints. My prints were all over it now. And Rivera already thought I was hiding something. I couldn't walk over to the maintenance building and say, *Hey guys, remember how I told you I just happened to find her, and that's all? Well, really, I was going to sell her drugs, and then I found this broken flash drive that might be evidence, and then I found her body, and instead of calling the police right away like a normal human being, I stole all her cash, and, oh, she had this piece of paper mixed in with everything, and yeah, don't worry, I've still got the drugs, but don't arrest me, 'k, because if you do there won't be anybody to take care of my dad.*

Sure, I thought. Sure, dumbfuck. That sounds great.

I took a deep breath. And another. Ignoring the broken flash drive for now, I finished organizing the bills. Then I stuffed the money in my wallet, picked up the scrap of paper, and switched off the lamp. I dragged myself into bed. The darkness felt like something on my face, like gauze or like whatever they made tutus out of. Not enough to keep me from breathing, but enough anyway.

My phone buzzed in the dark. I checked the screen. It was almost two, and the message was from Shivers: *wtf*

I clicked the button on the side of the phone, and the screen went dark.

It buzzed again almost immediately, and this time, the message was from Ariana: *heyy*

I thought about it. I really did. That extra y almost got me. I could drive into Provo. She'd be at her sister's place, alone, because Joslyn would be with her latest boyfriend. She always had weed, or at least a dab pen. She always had condoms. She was hot, and she laughed at my dumb jokes, and she didn't care that I wasn't in school and that I cleaned toilets for a living, which, let me tell you, is hard to find in girls my age.

And then I thought about the timing, and I thought maybe Joslyn was having a party, and maybe Shivers was there, and maybe he found Ariana and said, real casual, *Is Jacky tough shit coming*? And she was drunk, and he said, *Ask him if he's coming*, and I knew that's how it happened. It made my chest feel tight, like someone had stitched a zipper there and was pulling on that little tab.

I hit the button again, and the screen went dark. I lay there. I closed my eyes. My heartbeat sounded louder then. Faster. I opened my eyes, and a thin, faint glow came through the windows, drifting in from the security lights that studded the campus. It was like sand. We'd gone to California last year. No, it was two years ago. Three days at Disney, two days at the beach. Mom bitched the whole trip home. Sand everywhere. My eyes roved the ceiling. Yeah, I thought. Light just like that.

I thought about Mom for a while. And then, clear as day, I thought about Watson. Someone had killed Sarah Watson. And I was pretty sure it wasn't an accident, and it wasn't that something had gone terribly wrong. And now, because I was a fucking moron, I was holding not one piece of evidence but two. Two pieces of evidence that might be important—that might be crucial—to finding who had done it. I tried to breathe slowly. The scrap of paper lay on my chest, a shadow rising and falling.

Swearing silently, I rolled off the bed. I grabbed my filthy jeans and the disgusting Vans, and I got my keys—technically Dad's keys—and my phone and my wallet. Then I crept to the door, glad once again that I'd gone WD-40 all over that shit, and told myself I was being an idiot, and let myself out into the hall.

Chapter 5

Cross Campus

The night felt downright cold when I left the cottage, but I blew an experimental breath, and I couldn't see anything, so it must have been in my head. Friday nights, campus was quiet, but it wasn't dead; one of the porch boards creaked when I settled my weight, and behind a line of aspens, I could hear a couple of boys talking in what they probably thought were quiet tones. This part of campus was darker than the main portion—the cottage and the maintenance building and the other staff housing (which was different, by the way, from faculty housing) was all kept behind neat screens of haw and pine and scrub oak. It was one thing for the Walker kids to know that poor people existed—after all, somebody had to make their avocado toast every morning. It was another thing entirely for those poor Walker kids to have to see poor people, you know, actually living their lives.

That darkness saved me. I was about to step off the cottage's porch when light bloomed ahead of me, less than twenty yards away. It was the blue-white light from a phone, and in the darkness, it cast enough of a glow for me to make out a face and a hint of a deputy's uniform. I didn't recognize the man, but that didn't mean anything. He was standing there, in the dark, watching my house. And he was doing it, I knew in a flash, because Rivera had put him there. The moron was still staring at his phone, probably bored out of his mind. I considered going back inside and leaving through the door that led out to the carport. Instead, though, I eased my weight onto the next board, moving sideways across the porch. When I reached the rail, I swung a leg over, wincing when one of the posts shifted and made a sharp squeak of wood forced against wood. I glanced over; I couldn't have stopped myself if I wanted to. But the deputy was still staring at his phone, his face painted with its light, and I swung my other leg over the railing and dropped down on the other side.

As I pushed my way through a clump of scrub oak, the smell of their leaves filling my nose, I tried to make sense of what was going on. Rivera wasn't just a little bit suspicious of me. Rivera didn't just not like me. Rivera had put somebody on the house to watch me because he thought I was going to do something stupid. Which, ok, fair, I was doing. When I caught a branch in the mouth, I winced and spat leaves. I wiped the stinging corner of my lip, but I didn't find blood. Yes, all right, technically, I was doing something incredibly fucking stupid, but—and that was a big but—I was doing it for a good reason.

Right?

Watson lived in Butters Hall. It was one of the oldest girls' residence halls—and, of course, one of the fanciest—and it was located on the west side of campus, not far from Walker Hall and the quad and all that good stuff. The problem was that I was on the east side, and I had to cross almost the whole length of campus to get to her hall. Once I got there, all I had to do was wipe down the paper and the flash drive and hide them somewhere the detectives would find them. Then my part in this would be over. Easy. Sure, I thought. Nice fucking try.

So, problem one: cross campus without any of the deputies seeing me—the same deputies, of course, who were swarming campus, looking for evidence.

Solution one: the tunnels.

The Walker School actually wasn't that old. It had been built in the '50s or '60s, I think. Then, in the '70s—this was according to Mr. Taylor, who was the kind of person who liked telling you stuff that you didn't want to know, just to prove he knew something that you didn't—they'd done a lot of major structural work and told everyone that they were trying to make the buildings earthquake-proof. Or something like that. But, really, because this is crazy Mormon country and because the school was started and run by crazy Mormons, they were building these fallout shelters underground, along with food storage—Morms—and, of course, tunnels to get around. Mr. Taylor said it was part of the Cold War, which, yeah, I'd seen the ads for the new *Call of Duty*, and I think Reagan was involved, but that was about the extent of what I knew.

The important part—the only thing I needed to know—was the tunnels. And one of the entrances was at the maintenance building, of course.

I crept through the trees; ahead, halogen lights broke up the night, and men and women called back and forth, not even trying to lower their voices. I moved slower, and then even slower, and then, as I was passing through another stand of aspens, I stopped. I could see the steel door that marked the entrance to the tunnels; it was set into the side of the maintenance building. But less than ten feet ahead of me, a woman wearing a deputy's hat swaggered past, shining her flashlight back and forth. I held still. My face felt greasy, and I had the sudden, intense thought that my face was shiny, that I needed to wipe my face right that moment or someone would see the light reflecting off it. Standing still, keeping my arms at my sides, was one of the hardest things I'd ever done.

And then she passed me, the light moving away, my eyes readjusting to the dark, and she was singing "A Mighty Fortress is Our God," and a giggle threatened to burst free from me. Crazy Morms, I thought. Crazy fucking Morms.

I made it to the edge of the aspens before I had to stop again as two men came around the building.

"—get it open." That was Rivera, and he sounded pissed. "I don't care if it's not your policy; this is a police investigation."

The breeze shifted, carrying the tang of rust and sour onion to where I hid. I didn't have to see the face of the man with Rivera to recognize Nuz—Jerry Nuzman—one of the security guards. He was, as far as I could tell, a Walker lifer; he'd been here for something like twenty years, apparently because this was a job where he could get away with not showering for days at a time.

As I watched from the oaks, Nuz unlocked the door to the tunnels and hauled it open. Steel screeched across the cement pad. Then Rivera leaned forward, playing the beam of his flashlight down the steps, and shouted, "Yaz?"

Ducking back into the trees, I reversed course, my mind racing. I'd expected them to be busy at the crime scene. Hell, I'd expected them to find the tunnels. But I hadn't expected them to find the tunnels that quickly, and that messed up my plans. I crouched at the edge of the thicket, where some of the tall canyon grass helped hide me, and scanned the darkness ahead. For a moment, I was by myself, but lights in the distance marked what had to be deputies roaming campus. Some of them were clearly following the service road that hugged the backside of campus. Others had to have been on the main footpaths that connected maintenance—and my house—with the main portion of campus. I tried to think of another way to get to Butters, but if the tunnels weren't an option, then I only had one route left.

After a quick glance to make sure I was alone, I pushed through the dry stalks of blue grama, the dusty blades rustling where they dragged against my thighs. Jogging west, I tried to stick to open ground. I wasn't sure how good Rivera would be at following tracks—he didn't look like he spent much time hoofing it up the canyons—but somebody in the Sheriff's Office would be, and I didn't want to make it too easy for them.

A moment later, I reached the cottonwoods lining the Toqueah. The darkness was deeper here, and I trampled a path through grandfather sage, the smell of the crushed leaves wafting up to me. The undersides of the leaves were silver, and they caught the little light that made its way through the trees, tiny glimmers against the darkness. It made me think of ninth grade, photography elective, making a black-and-white print. Ms. Eldridge had made us try all sorts of different experiments with exposure and different amounts of light. You slide the print in the developer, and then it starts to happen, and yeah, it's the dark stuff showing up, but in a weird way, that lets you see the bright stuff too.

My foot slipped on a muddy root, and I caught myself on a cottonwood's trunk. The bark scraped my palm. I imagined falling into the creek, the splash, all the deputies coming to see what happened. Great, I told myself. You're doing really great.

More carefully, I lowered myself down the bank until I was standing on the rocks that lined the creek. I moved faster, picking a path as quickly as I could in the darkness, the murmur of the water keeping time with the scrape of my Vans against stone. I had to follow the creek until I reached the main road into campus. Then, if I were lucky, I could sprint across the street and lose myself in the athletic fields on the other side. I'd buttonhook back toward the center of campus, coming at Butters from the opposite direction. There was no chance Rivera would have people over there. Not yet, anyway.

Splashing stopped me. I froze, listening to the sound. Then I dropped down, trying to make myself smaller. That wasn't a natural sound; that was the sound of someone—something—moving in the water. On the bank, a light was moving maybe thirty yards away. I glanced right and considered whether I could make it across the creek without drawing too much attention. Then something moved in the corner of my eye.

As slowly as I could, I brought my head forward to look at it. My first thought was that it was an animal. Then my brain decoded the shape in front of me: a person, crouched and crabbing from rock to rock, reaching down to splash in the creek and then straightening up again. Light flooded the space in front of me—a phone. Not the screen, but the phone's flashlight. There was a click as the person—I was pretty sure it was a guy—set the phone on a rock, and then he shifted around, holding up his hands. Checking himself like he'd been washing something off.

The light caught his face, and I recognized him: Aston something. No joke, Aston. Someone had seriously decided to name him that, presumably with a straight face. He had a messy blond side part, and he was tan the way these rich white boys always were, and tonight he was shirtless in a pair of cotton shorts that looked like they'd gotten soaked in the creek. He had a nice chest, mostly flat but with a hint of definition, and whiskery hair under his arms. When he bought from me, it was almost always condoms. And if I wasn't totally blind, his neck and chest were covered in hickeys and bite marks, which meant Aston what's-his-name looked like he'd just done some serious making out and—what? Rushed down to the Toqueah to freshen up?

Before I could finish thinking about what I was seeing, Aston glanced up, and he saw me. Shock painted his face. Then he half-stood out of his crouch like he was going to rush me.

I was so surprised that I took a step back. I missed the rock, and I went into the creek. I didn't go all the way down, fortunately; my feet found bottom, and the water was only up to my calves. But the splash was unmistakable.

Fury replaced the shock in Aston's face, and he rose to his full height.

Then a shout came from the left: "Who's there?"

Aston turned and sprinted downstream.

The light bobbed toward me, suggesting a run, so I turned and splashed across the creek. The guy was still shouting—now he was adding, "Stop! Don't move!" which was a pretty stupid thing to count on, because I planned on running like hell. I reached the rocks on the other side, climbed up, and started racing downstream.

For the first ten yards, Aston was a glimmer of water-dappled skin and hair ahead of me. Then he jinked up the bank and was gone. I kept running. When I risked a glance, I could see the light behind me; the deputy had stopped, and I thought I could hear the crackle of his radio—although, to be fair, all I could really hear was the slap of my Vans and my pulse pounding in my ears and the roar of my breath. Fifty yards, I told myself, scrambling to pick a path that wouldn't end with me ass-up in the creek. Forty yards. Please, God, let them catch Aston.

Thirty yards. Twenty. I stumbled, caught myself on a rock, and hissed as it scraped my already raw palm. Ahead, security lights showed the culvert where the Toqueah passed under the embankment and the main campus road. Trash collected at the mouth of the culvert—plastic bags, soda cans, sometimes beer bottles, which shouldn't have been a surprise but everyone always acted so shocked about. Tonight, I could see a half-flattened soccer ball caught against the side of the culvert, bobbing in the creek's flow. Dad and I were supposed to clean the place out once a month, but it looked like it needed it more frequently. Maybe Mr. Taylor would like that, a little show of initiative. I made a mental note as I staggered up the slope, the night air freezing my soaking legs and feet. Aspens grew here, a line of them shivering in the canyon breeze, and I wriggled between them toward the road. On the opposite side, the athletic fields opened up—the soccer field was directly across from me, which, I was realizing, explained the ball in the creek. I inched forward.

A flash of light from my right stopped me. Another deputy with a flashlight, prowling the street. Fuck, I thought. Fuck, fuck, fuck. Can I catch one fucking break?

For a moment, I considered it: turning around, trying to get back home and forgetting all of this. Dump the scrap of paper. Burn it, hell. Drop the broken flash drive in the creek. Be done.

I remembered her face, swollen in death, and thought that someone had done that to her. She smiled when she talked to me, which a lot of these kids didn't. She had a way of pulling her hair back, exposing the line of her neck, and it made me think of my mom opening the curtains.

Shouts came from the field across from me, and I saw a group of boys emerge from the shadows between two of the residence halls. They came across the grass, clumped together, laughing and shoving each other. First-years, I guessed. Some sort of pickup game, or maybe a competition between the residence halls. Walker had a curfew, but it was Friday night, the beginning of the semester, and a lot of these kids were living away from home for the first time. By the end of October, they'd have figured out better—and less obvious—ways to break the rules on weekends.

And then I realized: thank God for idiot first-years.

I scrambled back down the slope. It took me two tries to hook the soccer ball with a stick and float it over to the bank. I picked it up; one side was slimy with algae, and I grimaced as I carried it back up the hill. I jogged across the street toward the soccer field, and immediately from my right came a shout from the deputy.

"Hey! Stop right there!"

I kept moving—an easy, dumbass lope, holding the soccer ball overhead and letting out an excited whoop as I headed toward the boys. I made sure to keep the ball turned so that the deputy couldn't see where it had been flattened and soaked in creek water. I was just another stupid first-year, and I'd found the ball we'd lost, and now we were going to play. Never mind that I had, I don't know, a minimum of four inches on most of the boys on the field and maybe forty pounds.

"Hey!" The deputy shouted again.

But by then, I was crossing the field, and the boys were turning to look at me. I kept my body loose, eager, as I joined them. Twelve sets of wary first-year eyes swiveled toward me.

"Hey," I said, tone light; even if the deputy couldn't pick out my words, I didn't want him catching the tone, realizing something was wrong. "You guys know there's curfew, right?"

"Who are you?" one of the boys asked. He had on a puka shell necklace that his dad had probably given him, and he looked like the type that his mom still wrote his name in his underwear — or whatever the prep school equivalent of that was.

"He's, like, a janitor," another one said.

"How old are you?" the first one asked. "Shouldn't you be in, uh, school?"

"Tonight," I said, "I'm either, uh, your best friend or, uh, your worst fucking nightmare. You tell me: does that sound like a janitor?"

"Hey!" The shout came from the road, where the deputy was staring at us. "What's going on over there?"

"I've had a shitty night," I said to the boys in a low, cheery voice. "And part of that shittiness is having to pick up after the soccer bros who can't bother to keep track of their equipment." I tossed the algae-covered ball at the first boy, who obviously wanted to be the leader. He caught it by reflex as I continued, "But I'm a nice guy, all around, and you're first-years, and you don't know how this works. Yet. So I'm going to cut you a break: either you turn around, and I walk you back to your res, and that's the end of this, or I call that deputy over, and I tell him I saw you vaping, and then he gets to pat you down because I gave him probable cause. How does that sound?"

The leader, holding the soccer ball like he wanted to drop it, stared at me. His mouth made a tiny, dismayed moue. Translation: this is so unfair.

"Five seconds," I said.

"You boys need to get back to your rooms," the deputy shouted. "Do I need to come over there?"

"Fine," the second boy said. "Whatever. Come on, Payton."

The group turned, and I trailed after them toward the boys' residence halls. I'd been wrong about a competition between residence halls — or maybe they were planning on sneaking out again later — because they all filed into Snow. The first one lingered to glare at me. I figured he thought a hundred and fifteen pounds of sackless white boy with a trust fund was supposed to be intimidating. Then he threw the soccer ball at me. I caught it and tossed it back, and it smacked him in the face. His head snapped back, clipped the brick behind him, and then whipped forward again. He covered his nose, his eyes shocked. And then, starting to cry, he rushed into the residence hall.

For fuck's sake, I thought, as I kicked the ball under a boxwood and headed into the darkness. How many years of this was I supposed to do?

After that, things went smoothly: I looped around and came up on Butters from the back, avoiding the security lights—and the cameras—until I reached the exterior stairs that led to the basement. I let myself into the building, locked the door behind me, and navigated the boiler room in the dark. Most of these buildings had the same floor plan, and I spent a lot of time in the basements. I found the door to the stairwell, and I went up to the ground floor. I ducked out to the lobby, which was lit only by a single lamp at this hour. On a bulletin board near the front door, someone had decorated with an autumn motif—FALL INTO NEW FRIENDSHIPS—and then photos of the girls who lived at Butters were posted with their first names and room numbers. Sarah Watson was in 307.

I was excited, and I was hurrying, and I got careless. I pushed into the stairwell and ran into someone. I didn't fall down, but I did hit my nose hard enough to make my eyes water, and I took a step back and pressed a hand to my face. I felt slightly—but surprisingly—bad for the first-year I'd bopped with the soccer ball. The woman I'd run into was doing better; she was rubbing the side of her head, and as my eyes cleared, I could tell she was scowling.

"What do you think you're—" She cut off. "Who are you? This is a girls' residence hall."

For a moment, all I could do was stare, still rubbing my nose. She was tall, especially for a woman, with skin darker than mine and her hair in pink and purple and red spikes that, admittedly, looked a little flat at this hour. She had a tattoo on her neck that made me think of a pirate's map, and I decided I'd been right: she was definitely scowling. Her name was Soares, and she was an instructor—biology, I thought—and, more importantly, she was the resident master of Butters. Because it was Walker and they couldn't just say dorm mom; they called it something fucked like resident master instead.

"Well?" she snapped.

"Sorry." I managed a smile and pointed to my nose for explanation. "Conked me. Um, we had a water sensor go off. Basement is flooded."

Instead of irritation or surprise, her expression was one of pure horror: she literally went pale, and she shifted her weight like the news had staggered her. The movement drew my attention to what I now realized she'd been trying to hide: a black garbage bag, full, that she was trying to block from sight by keeping it behind her body.

She recovered after a moment and asked, "How bad—I didn't—why didn't anyone say anything to me?"

"Not too bad." I lifted one sodden foot, and I thanked the cold, heartless universe for cutting me some slack on this one. "Like I said, the sensor went off, and I just got here."

She was nodding. Then her eyes went to the door behind me, and I understood the question she was asking herself: if I was here to deal with water in the basement, why had I been in the lobby?

"Gotta turn the water off on every floor," I said. "I'll try not to bother the girls." When she didn't say anything, I glanced at the stairs and then back at her.

"Yes," she finally said. "Yes, of course. I'll just—" The bag rustled as she adjusted her grip around it.

"Do you want me to take that for you? You don't want to go down there right now."

"No!" The word echoed in the stairwell. She tried to smile; it reminded me of trout flopping on the bank of the Provo. "No," she repeated in what was a strained attempt at normal. "I'll just—I'll deal with it tomorrow. You need to shut off the water, right? Yeah, you probably need to do that."

I nodded and gave the bag of trash one last glance, and then I started up the stairs. My Vans squished against the thin carpet on the concrete steps. Below me, a door boomed, and I shot a look after Ms. Soares as she hurried out into the lobby. I got one last glimpse of the garbage bag swinging behind her, and then she was gone, and the door fell shut.

Skipping the second floor, I made my way to the third. My steps— and my squishing—were the only noises in the stairwell now. The door to the third floor opened easily, and I found myself standing in the long hallway that ran the length of the building. I glanced at the numbered doors opposite me, figured out which way the numbers ran, and turned toward 307.

Then I stopped. Less than ten yards down the hall, a deputy was leaning against the wall, eyes glued to his phone. To judge from the chimes and dings, he was playing some sort of game. I slipped back into the stairwell and eased the door most of the way shut. Then I stood there, listening to the tinny sound effects, and tried to think.

Of course they'd put someone on her room. It was probably the first thing Yazzie and Rivera had done when they got to campus—they secured the crime scene, and then they sent someone to secure Watson's room. So what was I supposed to do now? I didn't think this guy would care one way or another about some minor flooding in the basement. Worse, Rivera might have already contacted him and told him to keep an eye out for me. Rivera seemed like that kind of guy, suspicious and covering his bases. Maybe I could pull the fire alarm—

A radio crackled, and then a hard voice came over the air: "Who's on Watson's room?"

A man's voice came from the hallway. "Eddy here. What's—"

"Jesus Christ, you're still there? Who's down at the athletic center?"

"Rivera said to stay on the room—"

"Is her door locked?"

"Well, yeah, but—"

"Then get your ass down to the athletic center and find her goddamn locker."

"Who is this?"

"This is Evan Reilly with the fucking FBI, and if you waste one more second of my time, I'm going to have your ass in a sling. Go secure that locker!"

From the hallway came the sound of a handle being jiggled, and then steps jogged toward the stairwell. I pulled back to stand behind the door, which opened a moment later. Deputy Eddy sprinted down the stairs, clutching his service cap in one hand, the other braced on his sidearm. The lobby door slammed open, and then the sound of his steps faded.

That, I decided, was my second piece of good luck tonight.

I yanked open the door and hurried down the hallway. 307 was on the right, and when I tried it, it was locked. But that was the beauty of working in maintenance—I had keys to just about everything. I found the residence hall master on the key ring, slipped it into the lock, and let myself into the room. Then I shut the door behind me and locked it.

For a moment, I stood there, my back to the door, my heart hammering in my ears. Watson's room definitely belonged to a girl, even though it looked like someone had accidentally transplanted it to a prison: the fringe hangings softening the cinderblock walls; the pink rosette quilt on the bed with piles of rosette pillows, pink and gray, on top of it; a floor-length mirror with marquee lights. They provided the only illumination in the room, a soft, electric glow, and it was strange, seeing myself framed like I was on a Hollywood billboard, a ghost behind those fragile incandescent filaments. It even smelled like a girl's room, some sort of air freshener that made me think of flowers. The only other piece of furniture was a desk that had been pushed into the corner. A closet door stood shut on the wall to my right.

I needed somewhere I could stash the broken flash drive and the scrap of paper so that Yazzie and Rivera would find them—not too obvious, so they'd be suspicious, but not too hard to find either. I started with the desk, pulling open the top drawer. It had the usual desk clutters: gel pens, paperclips, a stapler, sticky notes with curling corners. But my eyes settled on the envelope that had been wedged into the drawer at an angle.

It was a standard size envelope, and it was face down, its flap open. It also happened to be stuffed with cash.

I worked it out of the drawer and thumbed through the bills. They were twenties, three hundred dollars total. My first thought wasn't that a girl had died. My first thought wasn't that I was here to hide that scrap of paper and then get the hell out. My first thought wasn't even that I might not have much time. My first thought as I looked at that cash was that if I added this to what I'd taken from Watson's purse, I'd have enough for Dad's Aptiom, and that felt like a sign. It couldn't be a coincidence, right?

This time, the note was tucked inside the envelope, and I spotted it right away. It was written in a script that made me think it was a woman's handwriting, but when I glanced at the pad of sticky notes, where Watson had scribbled a reminder about her Social Studies textbook, I didn't think it belonged to the same person. Someone else had written this note. And someone had given it to Watson.

I'll buy any other stories you have.

And then a name, signed in cursive: Lissa.

The door handle rattled. It was locked, but then it rattled again, and then I heard metal click against the lock.

I glanced around the room: the mirror, the bed, the closet. Shoving the envelope behind my waistband at the small of my back, I got down on my knees. Then I flattened myself and squirmed under the bed. I had barely pulled the rosette quilt back into place, leaving a tiny opening for me to look out, when I heard the lock disengage, and the door swung open.

Through the tiny gap I'd left myself, I stared, trying to make sense of what I was seeing. I recognized him, of course. Everyone knew him. Blond hair in an Ivy League cut, features so perfect he looked cold chiseled. In seventh-grade art, Ms. Prinze had taken us to the U, and we'd gone to the art museum, and there'd been all these old oil paintings of frozen angelic faces, and that was what I thought of when I saw Holloway Holmes, Supercreep.

And then he stepped into the room, shut the door, and locked it.

Chapter 6

Supercreep

From my hiding spot under Watson's bed, all I could do was watch as Holmes moved farther into the room. He was tall and slender, and he moved silently. His head swiveled restlessly. He had gray eyes, and in the light from the marquee bulbs, they looked like they had tiny fires burning at the back.

He went to the desk first, opening each drawer in turn, and I was suddenly aware of the envelope at the small of my back, the sweat gathering there, gluing the paper to my skin. But if Holmes had been looking for the envelope, he didn't give any sign that he was disappointed not to find it. He rifled each drawer quickly and thoroughly. Then he pulled them out and checked the undersides and backs. Then he returned them. His movements were jittery, almost agitated. The drawers rattled when he placed them back on their slides.

When he'd finished with the desk, he came over to the bed. His shoes filled my vision: chukkas that looked like they'd never been worn, the leather without a single scuff, filling my nose with its scent. It sounded like he was moving the pillows. Then he wasn't doing anything. He stood there, completely still, and I knew he'd figured out I was there—I'd given myself away somehow, and Holloway Holmes, who was searching his dead friend's room in a way that was suspicious as hell, was going to deal with me. I realized, heat flashing in my face, how stupid I'd been. It hadn't been good luck that Deputy Eddy had been pulled away; it had been Holmes, drawing him away with that bogus call on the walkie so that he could get in here and —

What? Why was Holmes in here?

Well, that was the question, wasn't it?

Then he moved again, the chukkas silent as he slipped away from the bed. I let out a breath. My pulse was hammering in my head so loudly that for a moment, I couldn't hear anything else—all I could do was breathe in the dust under the bed, sweat prickling across my chest and back.

Holmes had left the narrow field of my vision, but I heard the closet door open, and then I heard something thunk. I told myself it didn't matter. I told myself it was none of my business. Five seconds ago, I'd been sure he'd caught me, and I didn't need to do anything stupid now. But it didn't matter. I wriggled forward, trying to adjust my angle so that I could see him again.

He was crouched in the closet doorway. I heard that thunk again—it sounded like steel hitting steel. Then Holmes shifted his weight and reached back to pull a small, leather-bound notebook from his back pocket. The slight torsion of his body gave me a glimpse of the closet itself, and I saw what he was doing: trying to open a safe bolted to the floor. Holmes flipped to a page in his notebook, and then he turned back to the safe. The dial clicked as it spun. And then something thunked again, a different kind of sound, and Holmes opened the safe. He took a moment, moving things around. Then he drew out a laptop and set it on the floor next to him. He searched the safe for another minute, and then he swung the door shut, and the lock clicked as it set itself. He was busy for a moment, wiping down the surfaces that he'd touched. Then he turned to open the laptop.

A password screen appeared, and this time, Holmes tapped out something without any hesitation. The screen changed. He spent a few moments, looking at different files, clicking and clicking again. I wasn't exactly a computer whiz, but it didn't look like he was doing anything special—mostly, it looked like he was browsing what was on the computer, trying to figure out what she had on there. He couldn't seem to keep his hands still. If he wasn't clicking or typing, he was rubbing one hand along the dark chinos, or playing with the button of his oxford, or digging his nails into the thin carpet. This was the boy who bought Adderall, I remembered. And he was flying on something tonight.

With a sound of disgust, he shut the laptop. Then he got to his feet, all smooth elegance, tucking the computer under his arm. He cocked his head, as though listening to something, and hurried to the door. He stepped out into the hall, pulled the door shut behind him, and was gone.

I sagged, my forehead resting against the carpet, and let out a slow breath. My heart still pounded in my ears. I counted to thirty, and then I crawled out from under the bed. I got to my feet, checked the envelope tucked into my waistband, and hurried over to the desk. My legs felt noodly. I opened the top drawer, fished out the slip of paper I'd found mixed in with Watson's cash, and tried to wipe it down the way I'd seen

Holmes do, smudging any prints I might have left. I did the same with the broken flash drive. Then I shut the drawer, wiped it down too, and let myself out into the hall.

He grabbed me as soon as I stepped through the door, and my brain told me two things: Holloway Holmes had been waiting for me, and he was a lot stronger than his skinny white ass looked. I spun away, breaking free of his grip. My breathing sounded like a tornado, and I was suddenly, intensely aware that there were girls sleeping in the rooms around us, that any noise might wake them, and the first thing they'd do is call campus security.

Holmes, for his part, hadn't made a sound. He came toward me again, silent, his movements almost liquid. I took a swing.

He pivoted, and the punch caught only air. Then, somehow, he got hold of my arm and twisted my wrist. The pain was so intense that all I could do was move into the hold, trying to reduce the tension he was placing on my joints, giving him total control over me. He didn't even seem to be trying; all he did was shift how he applied the pressure, and the next thing I knew, the door jamb was biting into my cheek, and I was making a high-pitched noise that I couldn't get under control.

"Be quiet," he said.

I took a deep breath and managed to stop sounding like a sick cat.

"Inside."

He forced me back through the door into Watson's room. When he turned to shut the door behind us, he relaxed his grip, and the pain in my shoulder and elbow ebbed. I tried to twist free, and he made a disgruntled noise and snapped my wrist back into the hold. I let out a sharp, punched-out sound.

"Stop it," he said. "You're not going to get away, not until I'm ready to let you, and you're making this much more difficult for yourself."

"Get off me," I said.

He made that annoyed sound again and forced me toward the wall. My face came to rest against the cinderblocks. The paint was textured — grit and dirt that had gotten trapped in it because somebody was lazy or because they used a cheap roller. Holmes kept up the pressure on my wrist, and although I'd managed to get hold of that noise in my throat, I couldn't keep myself from gasping every time he adjusted his grip on me.

"You telegraph your punches, by the way," he said. "And you didn't generate any power from your hips."

I couldn't help it; it was so surreal that a jagged laugh tore free. "Thanks for the tip. Maybe I'll do better next time."

"Maybe. Hello, janitor boy. Why were you hiding in Watson's room?"

I tried to think of an answer.

Holmes did something, and the pain in my arm doubled. My breath caught in my throat, and for a moment, I thought I was going to be sick. I had a vision of me puking all over myself while Holmes broke my arm.

"Well?" Holmes said.

"Jack. My name is Jack Moreno, not janitor boy."

"What were you doing?"

"Nothing! I swear to God, I wasn't doing anything."

Whatever he did, it hurt so bad I went up onto my tiptoes, the rough paint scraping the side of my face. Tears welled in my eyes. I couldn't seem to get any air.

"I don't like liars," Holmes said. "And, if you haven't noticed, I don't have any qualms about hurting you. I want answers, and I intend to have them."

Gritting my teeth, I sucked air and tried to breathe through the pain.

"Do you know how difficult it is to repair the wrist, the elbow, and the shoulder?" He applied more pressure, and I gasped. "They're each incredibly complicated. You'd have to have a number of surgeries. The recovery time would be, well, tremendous." He leaned into me, and I made a shattered sound, sliding along the cinderblock as I tried to get free. He moved easily with me, keeping up the pressure. "I asked you a question: what were you doing here?"

I blinked my eyes clear—or I tried to, anyway. They flooded again almost immediately. "Just grabbing the trash. Do you—" I had to stop. Black fuzz crawled at the edge of my visions. "Do you need me to—" I got the rest out on a final burst of breath. "—to take anything out for you?"

For a moment, the pain rode a knife's edge. And then Holmes made that same sound of disgust and relaxed his hold on me. Not all the way, but enough that I could drop down onto my heels. I was shaking. If he hadn't been holding me like that, I wasn't sure I'd have been able to stay on my feet.

"You're being stubborn." The words were too fast, tumbling over each other, and they carried a note of childlike frustration. "Why won't you tell me?"

"I've got this weird thing about bullies."

"I could hurt you some more."

"Not much I can do to stop you."

"I could call the police."

I coughed, and I surprised myself when I realized that sound was a borderline laugh. "You're not going to do that."

"I could—I could get you fired."

I closed my eyes. The cinderblock was cool; my face was hot. After a moment, when I trusted myself, I said, "Let go of me, would you?"

For whatever reason, Holmes did, and he stepped back. Massaging my arm and shoulder, I turned to face him. His pupils were huge. He kept turning his head, as though trying to catch a sound. He was speed-skating pretty bad, I figured.

"Your father is an employee here," Holmes said in those skittering words. "Juan Cano Moreno Garcia. Custodian. I could get him fired. And I will, if you don't tell me what I want to know."

"Isn't that your party trick? Isn't a Holmes supposed to be able to look at my shoes or my fingernails or something and tell me everything about me, down to the presents I got when I turned five?"

"My party trick." The corner of his mouth twitched. Then a short, stifled laugh escaped him, and he wiped a trembling hand across his lips. "Yes. Yes, my party trick." That laugh screwdrivered out of him again. It had a frayed, helpless edge to it. "She's dead, and you want—" He stopped. He was obviously trying to take a deep breath, but all he seemed capable of was shallow panting. "You want—" He wiped his mouth again. There was that laugh again. His eyes were huge. "You want—" The laugh tore free from him, and he clapped both hands over his mouth, fingers tented above his nose. He sounded like he was hyperventilating.

"Ok," I said. "Chill. I just meant, that's how it is in the movies, Holmes and Watson—"

A noise that wasn't quite a sob tore free from his throat. "She's dead. She's—she's dead. She's—"

"Be quiet." I glanced toward the hallway. No sound made its way through the door, no sound to suggest that he'd woken anyone up, but that didn't mean anything. They could be lying awake right now, listening, trying to figure out if they'd really heard something or if it had been a dream. "You need to calm down." He was still sucking in those sickly, shallow breaths. "One slow breath; count to four." After the accident, when the paramedics had fished me out of the scrub brush, they'd made me do this. Holmes still had his hands over his mouth, and as slowly as I could, I reached up. His hands were surprisingly cool under mine. I peeled them away. "Breathe in, and I'm going to count to four." He did. His hands were shaking in mine, but he wasn't pulling away or trying to break my shoulder, so I figured this was a win. "Now you hold it—one, two three, four. Now you let it out through your mouth—two, three, four. Let's do it again."

It took a couple more rounds before he didn't sound like he was having a panic attack. For a moment, he was staring at me, wide eyed and helpless, the side of his face bathed in the marquee lights, picking out gold highlights in that neat blond hair. I had seen that look before, on my own face, when the bills kept rolling in, when Dad couldn't get out of bed for a week straight.

Then, the next moment, a mask dropped down. I didn't know any other way to describe it; one minute, he was terrified and alone and desperately needing—me?—someone, and the next, his face was blank and cold. His hands were still trembling, but he turned his wrists and broke my hold. The movement was controlled and practiced—we'd learned it in eighth-grade PE, part of the same four-week self-defense unit when Maddyx Johnson had broken Mr. Sorenson's nose by accident.

"Ok?"

His eyes slid away, and he rubbed his hand. "Of course."

"Did I hurt you?"

His gaze came back and flicked up and down me. "The fact that you're in Watson's room, and that you took advantage of the deputy's departure to enter secretly, and that you hid when I approached—these facts suggest that you know Watson is dead and that you urgently wanted something in this room. It wasn't simple theft because you hadn't touched any of her jewelry, which means it was something more complicated. And it wasn't a romantic entanglement. You aren't Watson's type—"

"Hold on," I said with a crooked smile, "you haven't seen me with my shirt off yet."

For some reason, that made him blush, and he stumbled over his next words. "You—that is—she—" He drew a breath. "All of this suggests that your purpose here is connected to Watson's murder. The most obvious conclusion is that you killed her and need to remove something incriminating."

The sentence dangled, and when he didn't say anything else, I asked, "But?"

"But," he tore off the word, "I do not like making conclusions without all the necessary facts. And you do not seem like a killer."

"Gee, are you sure?"

"Yes, you see—"

"God, no, don't. I do not want to hear about how you figured it out because I shift my weight to my right foot or something like that."

His blush got hotter, but he met my gaze. "Well?"

I thought about this strange, hard-eyed boy standing in front of me. We were about the same height, although I had to have thirty pounds on him, which would have seemed important until Life Lesson #73, Holloway Holmes could kick my ass. I thought about not telling him, but he was clearly freaking out, and it was hard to stay mad at someone when they were losing their shit right in front of you. "I found her. Sarah, I mean. I was supposed to meet her for a deal, and instead —" I told him what had happened, and to my surprise, he didn't object or complain or make outraged noises when I admitted to taking Watson's cash. I filled in the rest of it, and then I pointed to the top drawer of the desk. "After you left, I put it in there."

"Aston Young was cleaning his hands in the creek?"

I nodded. "Freaked the hell out when he saw me, too."

Holmes made a considering noise. Then he turned and opened the drawer. After removing the slip of paper and the broken piece of the flash drive, he considered each in turn.

"The police need those," I said.

If he heard me, he gave no response. He laid the items on the desk, took out his phone, and snapped pictures of each. Then he rummaged an eraser out of Watson's desk and went over the paper with it, applying pressure so that the paper looked close to tearing. He flipped it over and continued the process. It didn't affect the word, *vonkramm*, which was written in ink, but he went over every inch of the paper anyway.

"Can't you just wipe it down?" I asked.

"If you prefer, I can. Would you like to spend a substantial amount of your life in prison? Your fingers deposit oil; wiping it down might not be sufficient. Abrading the paper itself is preferable."

"You know, you could have started with that and left out the snark."

Holmes made a considering noise as he leaned back, examined the paper, and used the plastic flash drive to nudge it into the drawer. Then he wiped down the drive and dropped it in as well.

"Don't you need that?"

"No. Do you need a broken piece of plastic? If so, you're welcome to it; it's a piece of the case, not the drive itself."

"Again, the snark."

"They're observations."

"Fantastic," I murmured. "He's cute and a smartass."

Holmes's face was already red; now it caught fire, and he mumbled something, broken syllables strung together without any meaning. He turned away to set Watson's laptop on the desk, opened it, and signed in.

"How did you know her password?" I asked.

He clicked through several folders.

"And how did you know the combination to the safe?"

He stopped on a folder marked *Zodiac*. When he clicked this one, it demanded a password. I followed his fingers as he typed in *vonkramm*, the word from the paper I'd found in Watson's wallet.

"What's in that folder?" I asked.

The password box blinked, and red letters appeared, prompting him to try again.

He tried again, this time with four numbers at the end—what I guessed was Watson's birthday. The box blinked at us again. Then he tried again with a different string of numbers. By now, the password box was starting to look a little annoyed.

"Can't you just hack it?"

He inhaled and leaned back, his hands tightening at his sides. "Do you even know what hacking is?"

"Sure. You type in, like, these different commands, and nothing is working, and then I say, 'If I reroute the back-end TCP hard drive, maybe you can override their array,' and then it works."

Holmes blinked. "Those words don't mean anything. At least, not the way you're using them."

"But they sounded good, right?"

"No." He studied the computer for a moment. Then he clicked on her browser. It opened to her school email account, and he scrolled through it quickly. I didn't see anything interesting, and apparently, neither did he. Then he opened a new tab and checked her history. He made a satisfied noise, clicked on one of the many entries, and another tab opened. This site was called Mailbluff. Aside from the name printed at the top of the screen, the only other thing I could see was an empty box in the center of the page.

"What is this?" I asked.

"An anonymous email service." He clicked in the box and typed *vonkramm*. When he hit enter, the page went blank. "They're low security, usually meant to provide a temporary email address. But—"

The screen loaded. It looked like any other email that I'd seen, with the inbox and a preview of the email's contents. There was only one message, and it was from a random string of numbers and letters. Holmes clicked on it. The message was short enough to read in the preview pane.

Meet at the maintenance building. Ten-thirty tonight. Cash for the flash drive.

"That's from the killer," I said. "Right? That has to be from the killer."

Holmes's expression was blank. He shut the laptop.

"You need to tell the police," I said. "If the killer contacted Watson, they need to know."

"Goodnight, Jack. For your own sake, I'll advise you not to tell anyone about this. It will only make your situation worse."

He took a step toward the door, and I grabbed his arm. "Hey—"

Somehow, he got one of my fingers and bent it back. I danced sideways, trying to relieve the pressure, and let him go.

"Don't touch me."

Shaking out my hand, I said, "Yeah? Well, fuck you too. Fucking rich, spoiled assholes, all of you. You think this is a game? You think you're going to play Sherlock Holmes and find who killed your girlfriend?" I wasn't sure why I picked that word, but I was too angry to stop. "This is a police investigation, and I'm sure as fuck going to tell them everything I saw tonight."

His lip curled, and he turned toward the door.

My phone buzzed.

Finger aching, I eased it out of my pocket. Dad's name flashed on the screen, and I realized it was almost three o'clock in the morning.

"I just went out for a walk," I said, trying to smooth out my voice. Holmes had stopped to study me, and I gave him the finger and turned my back on him. "I'll be home in a few—"

"Jack, why are the police here?" Dad sounded muzzy, almost asleep, the way he did when the migraines were so bad that he could barely make sense. "Why are they asking me all these questions?"

"Don't say anything. I'll be right there."

I disconnected and turned to run.

The door stood open. Holloway Holmes was gone.

Chapter 7

The Net

When I got home, a deputy stood on the porch. Fitzgerald, I was pretty sure. The string bean. He hitched up his belt when he saw me. The gun holstered there drew my eye, but he didn't try to stop me when I pushed open the door.

Yazzie sat in the living room, her face waxy in the light from the fluorescents. Movement in the kitchen made me peer around the door; Rivera was spinning a piece of mail on the countertop. Not just any piece of mail. A bill from the hospital. He had the corner pinned with one finger, and he spun it round and round. He smiled when he saw me and gave me a thumbs-up with his free hand. "Heya, tiger."

"Dad, are you all right?"

He was sitting in his recliner, his face drawn with pain, a slight tremor in his jaw telling me how hard he was trying to master it. I found his hand, and he squeezed back. Hard.

"He's not well," I said. "He can't talk to you right now."

"Jack, it's a few routine questions," Rivera said. He let the bill come to a halt, and then he tapped it once, like he was putting a pin in it. "I'm sorry your dad has a headache —"

"He doesn't have a headache. He has a migraine, and they're really, really bad. He needs to take his medicine, and then he needs to sleep."

Rivera's eyebrows went up, and he continued as if I hadn't spoken. " —but we need to talk to him, and, of course, we were all worried when you weren't in your room." He paused. "Where you said you'd be."

The question was in his eyes, bright and amused.

"I went for a walk," I said. "To clear my head. It's been a bad night."

"Makes sense," Rivera said. "We've got deputies all over campus. I bet you ran into a few of them on your walk."

I glared at him.

Yazzie scrubbed her hands on her knees. She had a nice voice; in choir, I bet Ms. Quincy would have put her with the sopranos. "Mr. Moreno, now that your son is here, we'd like to ask you some questions. Then we'll let you get back to sleep."

Dad nodded and cracked an eye. He was still clutching my hand hard enough to hurt.

"As we told you before you called your son," Yazzie began, "a young woman was found dead tonight behind the maintenance building. Could you tell us who has access to that building?"

"Jack and I," he said. "Olin and his guys. There are some day-shift custodians."

Yazzie glanced at me.

"Dad and I are the only on-campus maintenance. People come in during the day, otherwise we couldn't keep up, but we're the only ones here nights and weekends. The schedule's hanging in the office if you want their names and shifts for the last month." I shifted in my seat, fighting a backward glance at Rivera, and lost. The detective had wandered over to the fridge. He was leafing through a calendar, the free kind that comes in the mail with a million coupons. I looked back at Yazzie. "Why does it matter who has access to the building? She was in the dumpster, not inside."

After considering me for a moment, Yazzie spoke to Dad. "Mr. Moreno, do you know when the security camera on the back of the maintenance building stopped working?"

Dad shook his head. "Don't look at the security footage. Never need to. That's Olin's job."

"Why aren't you asking Mr. Campbell?" I said. "Olin Campbell? He's head of campus safety."

"We've spoken to Mr. Campbell," Yazzie said. To Dad, she said, "You don't have any idea, Mr. Moreno? I understand that you might not have reviewed the security footage, but you never noticed anything that suggested the camera might not be working? You know how it is—you're in a space long enough, you start to notice all the little details that nobody else would catch. My wife is like that; she can read you chapter and verse about everything we need to update in the kitchen."

Dad shook his head.

"Are you sure—" Yazzie began.

"He told you he doesn't know."

Yazzie shifted to face me. "What about you, Jack?"

"What? The camera?" I shook my head. "It's just there. Olin said people used to come up and pick through the garbage; that's why they had to put up the camera. We've never had any problems."

"No problems," Rivera said. He moved into the living room, his cauliflower ear turned toward me. He stopped at the side table and examined one of my Little League trophies. He put a finger on the plastic bat and pushed until the trophy canted sideways. Just when it was about to fall, he pulled back and let it settle onto its base. Then he picked up a photograph of me and dad. He looked at it for a long time, and I wondered if he could see where I'd folded Mom out of it, the uneven edge visible against one side of the frame. "Like you walked past that camera two, three, five, ten times a day, and you never noticed that someone had cut the power to it?"

"What do you mean?"

"Someone cut the wires," Yazzie said. "It looks relatively fresh, but we're trying to hammer down the timeline. That's why we decided to wake up you and your dad tonight."

"But you weren't asleep," Rivera said, flashing me a smile over his shoulder as he moved through the tiny living room. "You were on a walk, remember?"

"Ok, well—" I fumbled for the next word and settled on, "If that's all you need, my dad—"

"Mr. Moreno," Rivera said over me, "where were you tonight?"

"What?" I asked.

Rivera didn't look at me; he stared at Dad, waiting.

"Here," Dad said. "Home. All night."

"Are you sure about that?"

Dad shook his head, fingertips white where he pressed them against his temple. "I've had this migraine, and then—I get these seizures, see..."

He trailed off, and the silence that followed vacuumed all the air out of the room.

"Can anyone verify that?" Rivera asked.

"I can," I said. "He was sick. He stayed home. I covered his shift."

That smile was in Rivera's eyes again. When he spoke, he sounded confused. "But you were working, Jack. Right? So, you can't verify that your dad was home all night, can you?"

I folded my arms and tried to meet his gaze, but I looked away first.

"Who else uses those dumpsters?" Yazzie asked.

"The other custodians."

"That's all?"

"The only ones I can think of. There's no reason for anybody else to go over there; each building has its own collection point, but campus wasn't designed for those garbage trucks, so we have to transport the waste to the maintenance building where the trucks can pick it up."

"When was the last time you were at the maintenance building?"

"Yesterday, I guess. Thursday. I was laid up all day Friday."

"And how frequently are those dumpsters emptied?"

"Once a week. Mondays."

"So," Rivera said, "whoever dumped that girl only had to wait a couple of days before she was gone for good. Two days when the only people who might stumble across her were you and your son."

Dad stopped rubbing his temple. He was still squinting—any amount of light was killer when he had a migraine this bad—but now it looked like he was trying to fix Rivera in his vision. "What are you trying to say?"

"What is your relationship like with the students on campus, Mr. Moreno?"

"I don't have a relationship with the students." Dad's voice was even, but I could hear the anger under it. "I'm not student-facing staff."

"Are you sure about that?"

"Excuse me?"

"Well, I mean, a place like this, all these rich kids trapped up here, plenty of money to burn but nowhere to spend it—I figure a guy like you, a guy who can run into town and get them whatever they need—that guy could make some good money."

"What are you talking about?" I asked.

Dad held up a hand to stop me. "I don't have any kind of relationship with the students here, Detective. I understand what you're implying, but that's not the case."

"Mr. Moreno," Yazzie said, hands on her knees, "the best thing any of us can do right now is be completely honest. It took us five minutes to learn about your accident last year, and it's—"

"What?" I asked. "You looked us up?"

"And," she repeated, "it's not hard to figure that you and your son must be in an extremely difficult financial position."

"Add to that," Rivera said, "the fact that you're not doing your job—"

"He's sick," I said. It was more of a shout, to judge by how Yazzie's gaze swiveled toward me.

"—and, of course, you're a single man, up here all alone, with all these girls who are far away from their parents…"

The suggestion hung in the air.

When no one said anything, Rivera snatched up a Dodgers cap, a novelty one, the kind made out of foam. He slapped it against his open hand. "Like my partner said: the best thing you can do right now is be totally honest."

"I'd like you to leave," Dad said quietly.

"Maybe it was an accident."

Dad massaged his temple.

"Maybe you had an argument and things got out of hand."

Planting one hand on the recliner, Dad got to his feet. His face was chalky, and when he pointed at the door, his hand shook. "Get out of my house."

Rivera raised an eyebrow, but he glanced at Yazzie, and she nodded. The woman stood, and they made their way to the door. I followed them, and when Rivera cocked his head at me, I stepped out onto the porch and pulled the door mostly shut. Rivera waved off the deputy, and then it was the three of us.

"You've got a choice, Jack," Rivera said in a low voice. "You can tell me what you're holding back, tell me what you went digging around for in that filing cabinet after I left you alone in the office, or I'll get it by tearing your life apart. How do you think your dad would do in an interview room, twelve hours under fluorescent lights, while I ask him again and again and again?"

My face felt tight, the skin too small. Off in the distance, a breeze stirred the aspens, and branches clacked together. Rivera watched me. He was still holding the foam cap, compressing it between his hands and then shaking it out again to let it expand.

"May I please have that back?" I asked. "You're going to tear it."

For a moment, the shock in Rivera's face was worth it. Then it was gone, his face empty except the smile at the back of his eyes. He tossed me the cap, and I caught it one-handed against my chest.

"Jack," Yazzie said, "we want what's best for everybody, believe me."

I nodded, but I didn't look away from Rivera.

This time, he turned away first, and the two detectives clumped down the steps.

I let myself back into the house and shut the door behind me.

Dad was still standing, leaning heavily against the recliner, the back of his hand pressed against his mouth. He got sick a lot of the time when the migraines were too bad. I slipped past him into the tiny living room. I adjusted the Little League trophy that Rivera had disturbed. I shifted the photo until I thought it was back in its original place. Dad's eyes followed me, and then I ran out of things to do, and I had to look up.

We did look the same, I thought. In some ways, at least. Because that was how I looked, I was pretty sure, when I was pissed.

"Where were you?"

"I went for a walk."

Dad opened his mouth. Then, with what looked like a tremendous effort of will, he closed it again. He breathed through his nose. Then he said, his voice quaking, "Where were you?"

"I went—"

"Don't lie to me!"

The shout echoed through the cottage. Then silence zoomed in behind it, the clanking hum of the fridge's motor, the creak of a rafter as the house settled. I looked down at my Vans, but my hands curled into fists at my side.

"Go to your room."

"Did you take—"

"Go to your room!"

I slipped past him to head down the hallway. He was shaking, barely able to stay upright even with the recliner supporting most of his weight, and he smelled like sour sweat. Then I was past, and I hurried toward my room. I shut the door and fell onto the bed. For a while, my brain chased its own tail, replaying everything with Rivera—round one and round two—and my frantic, scrabbling trip cross-campus, and Holloway Holmes. And the last thing before I slept, the thing that made my brain turn circles faster and faster, was the terror on his face, the heat of his skin, the surprising cool of his hands. He had gray eyes, I thought as the net of sleep pulled tight around me. And then, so diffuse that it was barely words at all, the thought: He must be lonely.

Chapter 8

Green Out

By Saturday night, I was wound so tight that I couldn't breathe, so I took the truck and drove into town.

I'd woken at six to the squawk and static from the radio in the kitchen. It was Taylor, and he was pissed because nobody had bothered to tell him what had happened, and it hurt his sense of self-importance. He wanted to talk to Dad, but I finally begged him off; the vial of sumatriptan was out on the counter, and it hadn't been there before, which meant at some point, Dad had gotten up in the night to take more medicine.

I met with Taylor and talked him through everything—between huge yawns. He wasn't what you'd expect, not the little tyrant or anything like that. He was taller than me, and he was heavy, his gut spilling over the waistband of his jeans, his arms big and soft. He kept an article from the *Daily Herald* in his office, something about him playing football for BYU. He'd tell anyone who listened about how he hurt his back, and God help you if you didn't act like that was the greatest tragedy ever to happen to college sports.

After answering the same questions three or four times, I managed to get out of the meeting by telling Taylor I needed to cover Dad's shift. It was the truth—there was no way Dad was going to be able to work today—and most of the time, Taylor liked it because he could be a hard-ass with me in ways he wouldn't have tried with Dad. So, I worked Dad's shift, deep-cleaning classrooms and offices, doing all the stuff we didn't have time for during the week. I caught a couple of hours of sleep in the library utility room because it was the cleanest one on campus and because I'd barely slept three hours the night before. Throughout the day, I'd seen signs that word of Watson's death had spread through campus—a flyer announcing a candlelight vigil, two girls crying on a bench in the quad, black crepe hung above the doors of Butters Hall. But mostly, everyone seemed to be going on with their lives as though nothing had happened. I don't know which one made me more tired. When I got home, I showered and ate dinner with dad—tonight, like most nights, it was noodles and a jar of red sauce.

He said two words to me: "Any problems?"

I shook my head, and we finished the meal in silence.

Dad must have been feeling better because the prescription vials were all put away, and we watched the news, and he fell asleep in the recliner. A few bad days in a row like this wore him out every time; he'd sleep until the morning, and for a few days—or two, or maybe just one—he'd be normal. Or as close to normal as we were ever going to get again.

That was when I took the keys and drove into town, the Stone Temple Pilots singing to me about falling. It was all about falling faster.

My first order of business, before I could stop myself, was to pull into the CVS where Dad had all his prescriptions and pick up his Aptiom. It was physically painful, counting out the bills. But it was bad enough that Dad had the migraines, that he still had some mobility issues, and everything with his memory. Add in the seizures, and you had a real disaster. What if he seized while he was driving? What if he seized while he was using the band saw? I played out a dozen different disasters, most of them having to do with work, and by then I'd finished laying the bills on the counter. When the tech came back, I had thirty pills. I locked them in the glove box—the truck was ancient, a 2000 Dodge Dakota, the quad cab model, its red paint salt-bleached and stripped until it looked almost white in places, so it wasn't exactly the kind of vehicle people broke into, but I figured the way things were going, that would be just my luck.

It was a Saturday night, which meant Joslyn was having people over and—if I were lucky—Ariana would be there. Their parents were shit, but Ariana was only a year older than me, and because she was seventeen, she couldn't get her own place. So, whenever she could, she stayed with her sister. Joslyn's place was on the south side of Provo, and I found a spot to park under a streetlight a block up from the railroad tracks. I double-checked that the glove box was locked, and then I got out of the truck and walked north.

Provo nights in September could be cool, but they weren't as cold as the nights up at Walker. I had on my favorite Dodgers tee and my good pair of jeans and, of course, my Nikes. The Cortez, in case you're wondering. White leather with the red swoosh. Mom gave them to me, and Dad had only asked once if I'd be willing to sell them.

I made my way toward Joslyn's apartment, which was on the third floor of a brown box of a building. The night sky was clear, the way it always was this time of year, but the stars looked washed out compared to what I usually saw at Walker. The air smelled like asphalt, a little bit like the dust-and-rust of the tracks when a breeze picked up behind me. Someone had their windows open, and I could hear a woman on the phone saying, "Yeah, Ma, yeah, I know."

I took the stairs up to Joslyn's two at a time, the music loud enough that I could hear the bass as soon as I reached the stairwell. Joslyn's neighbors had complained about the noise a few times, and I figured tonight, they were going to complain again. It didn't seem to faze Joslyn, though, and when Ariana talked about it, she just laughed.

The door was propped open, a wall of light and sound and heat waiting on the other side. Air that was overly warm from too many bodies, stinking of sweat and perfume and weed, met me, along with the thump of the bass and the buzz of a subwoofer that had blown. Then the music changed, and Lil Nas X came on—the guitar, the mumbled words, and then his voice coming in clear and strong. The apartment was tiny: a combined living space and kitchen, and then a single bedroom and bathroom. Bodies were packed inside, and only the occasional shift in position revealed the oatmeal-colored carpet. A guy with a stringy billy goat beard had his head back, laughing. A girl with pigtails and smoky eye makeup was blowing vapor out of the side of her mouth. A pretty boy in a ripped tank that said *Dumpster Slut* kept trying to catch my eye; we'd made out one night when Ariana was gone, and I couldn't remember his name.

"Jacky tough shit." I had a moment to recognize Shivers's voice before a hand fell on my shoulder and spun me toward the kitchen.

Shivers was pretty much the definition of white trash. He wore his dark hair in a mullet, and his cheeks were pitted with acne scars, but the thing you remembered when you looked at him was that his jaw wasn't symmetrical—like a cartoon character, face rippling after he'd taken a punch. In jeans and a Jazz jersey, he looked like he thought he was the shit, which was kind of funny considering he was one step up from dealing on a corner. His hand felt hot through the cotton of my tee.

"Where's the love, Jacky? Why you been avoiding me?"

"I haven't been avoiding you; I've been dealing with shit." I sketched out in a few sentences what had happened with Watson.

"Shit." Shivers's eyes were huge. "You didn't tell the cops—"

"Jesus, no."

Shivers took a breath. He laughed, and it was a little too high pitched. "Right. I had to ask, you know."

I took a page out of Rivera's book and raised my eyebrows.

"So," Shivers said, his smile back now. "What about my money, Jacky tough shit?"

"I've got your money."

Shivers waited. His eyes got a little wider, like he was in on the joke. The apartment was fucking hot, and sweat trickled down my nape.

"I left it at home," I said. "I've been so messed up about this girl, I totally spaced it."

The slow strum of the guitar was fading out at the end of "Old Town Road." Then something synthesized came on. A vocoder. That was the beauty of homeschool; if you wanted to know what that weird noise was at the beginning of an Ariana Grande song, you just googled it, and then you read the Wikipedia article on "vocoder," and then class dismissed. The first drop of sweat slid between my shoulder blades.

"So," Shivers said, and he was still grinning like a jackass, but it didn't come near his eyes. "You don't have my money?"

I kept eye contact, and I kept my shoulders back, and I kept my voice even. With guys like Shivers, that's the only thing you can do. "I've had a couple of fucked-up days, Shiv. I told you I've got the money."

"This isn't some payday loan shit."

I waited. Ariana was really hammering it now, the music swallowing up the rest of the party.

Shivers's smile got bigger. "Jacky tough shit," he said, mostly to himself and so quiet I could barely hear him. In a louder voice, he said, "I want my money tomorrow."

"I said I'd pay you. You got some kind of question about that?"

He shook his head slowly. I counted to ten, my eyes locked on his. Then I turned, and when he didn't grab me, I pushed my way into the mass of bodies. Joslyn had a card table set up in the corner, with gin and whiskey and rum bottles lined up in front of her, and there was a keg and a stack of red plastic cups, but I didn't have any cash. She had hair extensions that went to her waist, lots of beaded braids, and she was doing what she always did when she had a new guy—laughing at his jokes, touching his arm, arching her back because she always dated guys who couldn't keep their eyes off her chest. She might have given me a freebie, but I didn't want that, not in front of Shivers. I squeezed behind a white guy who looked, God, forty, and he was grinding so hard on Joslyn's cousin that he looked like he was about to squirt. The pretty boy—

Dumpster Slut—was trying to angle his way through the crowd toward me, so I changed directions and headed for the slider that stood open to let in the cooler air off the balcony, the vanes of the vertical blinds drifting on tiny eddies.

A hand on my arm stopped me, and I glanced over my shoulder. Ariana barely came up to my shoulder, and she was darker than me, a deep brown that got lighter on her breasts and between her legs. Her hair was long like Joslyn's, falling to the small of her back, and she had coppery highlights throughout it. She was curvy in all the right places, and tonight, she was showing it off in a dark red cocktail dress. Like Joslyn, the girl had some serious boobs.

"Hey," she said.

"Hey."

We'd met the week after Dad and I moved to Walker. I was picking up some of his meds at the CVS, and when I flipped a u-ey, she was right there, walking toward the Sinclair in jeans and a spangly top and these heels that looked about a mile high. I pulled onto the curb and leaned over to crank the window down, and it took me so long that she walked right past me. Didn't even look at me. So then I had to creep up on her, and when I offered her a ride, she rolled her eyes and kept walking.

"It's not you," I'd told her as I rolled alongside. "It's those heels. I hate to see somebody ruin a good pair of stilettos."

That made her laugh, and after that everything else fell into place. Not all at once—it took some time and effort on my part—but eventually.

Now, looking up at me, she lifted a blunt and took a long hit. She held it, let her head fall back, and shook her head so that the copper seemed to snake through her hair. When she exhaled, the mingled smoke of tobacco leaves and weed drifted around me. She held up the blunt.

I took it and hit it, and while I was doing that, she caught my free hand and towed me toward the loveseat, which was now empty. She pulled me down next to her as I jetted smoke out the side of my mouth. The rush made me dizzy, but in a good way. It made me think of Holloway Holmes and his pale, slender fingers spinning the dial on Watson's safe. All the dials were spinning inside me now, the locks undoing themselves one by one. I hit the blunt again and knew I was going too fast.

When I sank back against the loveseat, Ariana took the joint. Everything seemed more mellow after the weed, but also more intimate: the dampness starting on my chest, the smell of sweaty dudes and summery body sprays. The noise of the party was like water, splashing against me on every side, lifting me up so I was floating. I don't know how long I was like that, but it must not have been too long, because when I opened my eyes, Ariana was still sitting next to me, stubbing out the joint in a mug with a beehive on it.

"Where you been?" she asked.

I rubbed my eyes.

"I texted you."

I nodded.

"Shivers is looking for you."

It was hard, competing with the shouts and the laughter, the music and the drunken sing-along, but I told her. Enough, anyway. Not about Holmes.

"You poor baby," Ariana said, stroking my arm. "Are you ok?"

I motioned for the joint, and a little line appeared between her eyebrows, but she got a lighter from the coffee table, got the blunt going, and took a long drag. Then she passed it to me, waving the air in front of her face, her eyes red.

After another hit, more of those locks spun loose—they were in my shoulders, my elbows, my wrists, tight at first and then relaxed. It made me think of him again, the electric zigzag of pain up my arm, the rough texture of paint and cinderblock under my cheek. The unsettling coolness of his hands. When I exhaled, some of the heat stayed with me, embers stirring low in my belly.

"You need a lawyer," Ariana was saying. "I think Joslyn knows a guy."

I snorted. "You mean one of her fuckboys?"

"He's still a real lawyer." When I laughed, Ariana plucked the blunt away and stubbed it out again. "Don't be an ass."

I laughed some more, trying to shield myself as she pretended to slap me on the back of the head. But she wasn't wrong. All day, I'd managed to avoid thinking about Rivera, about the questions, about Dad. And now that she'd reminded me, I couldn't ignore it any longer. Rivera thought I had something to do with Watson's death. He already had an idea I was dealing, and if he spent more than five minutes questioning Walker kids, he'd find one of them who'd tell him anything he wanted to know. Worse, Rivera had some kind of hard-on for Dad. I couldn't tell if it was because he was using Dad as leverage, trying to scare me into talking, or if he genuinely thought Dad was involved somehow. Either way, it was bad. Dad under fluorescent lights for twelve hours. Dad without his medicine, without a chance to lie down when the headaches got really bad. Or what if he had one of his dizzy spells, when he couldn't walk? Or he seized? And the whole time, Rivera would be there, right in Dad's face, asking and asking and asking until—

"Ariana!" That was Joslyn, and Ariana and I both glanced over at the card table. Joslyn was waving at a skinny white girl—one of Ariana's friends; I thought her name was Morgan. Ariana sighed. She set the blunt, still resting in the beehive mug, on the coffee table with the lighter, and stood. "I'll be right back."

After Ariana had slipped into the crowd—I figured she was going to make sure Morgan puked into the toilet and not anywhere else—I took out the blunt and lit up again. I knew this was dumb. When I'd been going to see Dr. Wadley, the first few months after the accident, I'd been honest about everything because I didn't care what she thought, and she'd told me this was called high-risk behavior, and that it was common in men after a traumatic event. So, I thought, blowing out smoke, great. I've got a name for it.

On the other side of the room, where the fridge and the tiny sink and stove were all crammed together, Shivers was watching me and not bothering to hide it. He had two of his buddies with him. I'd met them before; I'd bought from one of them a couple of times, when Shivers wasn't around. Alma was a round-faced, heavyset Latino guy. It was hard to tell how old he was; part of it was his size, and part of it was his haircut, which made him look like one of the Beatles. I put him in his early twenties, but he might have been younger. Vearl, on the other hand, was probably older than he looked—he was a skinny white kid with a high forehead and raw lips. He always had one hand in his pocket because he thought it made him look tough. I'd told him one time, when he got in my face, that it just made him look like he was playing pocket pool.

I pretended not to notice the three of them looking at me, which was easy because I was getting blazed. Shivers's money was another problem. I might be able to put him off a few more days. But then again, I might not. Shivers was a lot of things, but he wasn't stupid, and he wasn't a coward, and—this time, at least—he wasn't wrong. I owed him, and I'd been stupid to buy the zannies on credit. He'd just have to wait until I could figure something out, though. I wasn't a rich kid with an envelope of cash sitting around—

The thought startled me out of my haze for a moment. The woman's name in the envelope, the one I'd found in Watson's desk. She'd said she'd buy more stories—that's what she'd written on the note, right? What kind of stories? Stories about Walker? If she was willing to buy, I'd be willing to sell.

I got up and made my way to the bathroom, where Ariana was holding Morgan's hair while the girl upchucked. Ariana rolled her eyes when she saw me, but she smiled too.

"Great," she said. "You're going to be in a weed coma by the time I clean her up."

"I can hold my shit. Hey, can I borrow your phone? I want to look something up."

Ariana made a face, but she passed me her phone. "If you didn't have a brick…"

I made a noise that was kind of *yeah, yeah* and kind of a good-natured *fuck off,* and then I opened the browser on her phone and typed in the name from the envelope: Lissa. Then I added stories. I hit search, and I got a lot of stories. They were all over the place—Wattpad stories about bonding with someone (something?) called Lissa, rehab center videos on YouTube about girls named Lissa, an actual woman named Lissa Story on the East Coast. I tried adding Utah to the search, and I got more results— stories about Lisas, Lissas, and M'lissas, all of them in Utah, but none of them having anything to do with Watson or Walker, as far as I could tell. One of them was about a high school football game. One of them was a U of U profile. One of them was about forest bathing, whatever the hell that was. I added Watson to the search, and the results became meaningless.

It wasn't something that I thought of consciously; it swam up to me through the smoke, coming from that hot-coal place deep in my gut. I deleted Watson and added Holmes. And there they were: story after story on Lissa Keahi's blog about Holloway Holmes. Her picture was on the homepage: a woman who might have been Latina or Polynesian, her dark hair held up in a hibiscus flower clip, chunky black glasses, an underbite. For the most part, the articles read like celebrity gossip pieces: Holloway's awkward encounter with a girl in the dining hall; Holloway's B- on a psychology paper; a whole article describing Holloway's clothes—it sounded like he exclusively wore variations on what I'd seen him in—an oxford, chinos, chukkas. Breaking news was that apparently he occasionally wore cardigans.

Then, as I was scrolling, my thumb paused, pinning in place an article from a few weeks ago: "Is Holmes Gay? Our Sources Weigh In."

"All right," Ariana said, "rinse your mouth out, and I'll get David to drive you home." As she passed me, she took the phone back, smiled, and whispered, "Two minutes."

I eased away from the doorway, giving Morgan space as she splashed water on her face, and I tried not to think about—well, something. Instead, I tried to think about the facts. Watson had been selling information about Holmes. She'd been selling personal information about him. Is that what was in those encrypted files that he had been trying to access on her laptop? Holmes had suggested that the broken flash drive was evidence that Watson had been selling information when she'd met her killer— could it have been this woman, this Lissa Keahi? Or someone else who wanted information on Holmes?

It was hard; my brain was getting foggy, and on top of that, I was having a seriously hard time not thinking about those gray eyes, about the cold-chiseled perfection of his features, about the way his hands had trembled when I'd caught them, and the slight, reflexive movement as he clutched my fingers, like someone trying to hold on.

"Hey," Ariana said; I hadn't noticed her come back, and I hadn't noticed Morgan leave, and then Ariana was leaning into me, her face turned up, and she kissed me. The kiss was soft at first, and then her tongue slid inside my mouth, and I forgot all about Holmes's skinny white ass. When she pulled away, she rolled her eyes at whatever she saw on my face, and she laughed, and she took my arm and said, "It's too loud out here."

Joslyn's bedroom was quiet; it felt like dropping into darkness. The only light came from the street, bumping along the wall in waves as the blinds stirred in the breeze. The heat in my belly was waking up, something stirring the coals. I kicked something in my path—a basketball, left behind by another of Joslyn's boos—and it clunked when it bounced off the wall. Ariana laughed again. When we got to the bed, I lost my balance, and trying to sit turned into a fall. Ariana lay on top of me. She was still laughing. Then she was kissing me. Then my hands were under her skirt, and she was undoing the waistband of my jeans.

The other nice thing about Joslyn's place? She always has condoms.

When we were done, it felt like in a movie, like the camera pulling back, everything seeming to rush away all at once. The thumping bass and the mingled voices from the party dwindled. The feel of Ariana curled under my arm became detached. I was floating. A little part of me was still telling me I was a dumbass because I'd kept my shoes on, and then even that was too far away to hear.

"Hey Jack?"

I couldn't quite reach my words, but I managed a noise.

"I really like you," she whispered.

"I like you too," I said.

"Do you think—"

But whatever she asked, I missed it, because sleep hooked me and pulled me down. For a while, there was nothing. And then it was the same old dream: the pain in my head and in my ankle, the smell of gasoline and burned rubber, someone crying. That was me. I understood, because it was a dream, that the car had flipped twice and somehow, miraculously, landed right-side-up. But at the time, I hadn't understood anything; I'd been too shaken, and later, they'd told me I'd had a concussion.

It happened the way it always happened. I saw them, Mom and Dad, in the front seat, neither of them moving. I called out to them. I couldn't reach Mom—it didn't occur to me that I was still belted in—but I shook Dad's shoulder.

And then I saw him: just a shadow on the other side of the glass, growing as he came toward us, and terror crystallized in my gut.

I woke up covered in sweat, my breathing shallow and too fast. For a moment, I didn't know where I was. The darkness. The ripple of light on the wall. The weight on my arm. I sat up, sucking in air, and someone made an annoyed noise. Ariana, part of my brain told me.

"Jack?"

I got to my feet. My jeans were still unbuttoned, and they started to slide down. I yanked them back up, trying to get the button done, my hands shaking too bad to do it. I gave up and settled for drawing up the zipper. My shoes were still on. Part of me wanted to laugh. Thank God, that part of me was saying. Thank God you are such a fuckboy piece of shit that you kept your shoes on. I stumbled to the door, still trying to get enough air.

"Jack? Hey, is something wrong—"

But by then I was out the door, plunging into the dregs of the party—*Dumpster Slut* doing shots with Joslyn, a black girl with curly hair dancing while two Latino guys watched from the sofa, a white kid trying to tie his Chucks and laughing as the laces slipped through his fingers. I hauled open the door and threw myself out into the night.

When I got to the truck, I drove without seeing until I finally stopped on the shoulder just before the canyon. Adrenaline drained out of me, and I slumped over the steering wheel and pressed the heels of my hands against my eyes. The green out or the panic attack or whatever it had been was shrinking in the rearview mirror. I counted my breaths like they'd taught me that night in the ambulance. Then I got out my phone and texted Ariana.

Sorry. The weed messed me up.

My screen timed out. I closed my eyes. Then the phone buzzed, and I checked her text.

R u ok?

Yeah, I typed back. *I'm really sorry. Make it up to you?*

This time, the reply came faster: *I only accept diamonds.*

I sent her back an eggplant emoji.

You wish. Then, before I could respond, another message came through: *Jack, are you really ok?*

Fine, thanks. I'll talk to you tomorrow.

She sent a kissy face, and I sent one back, and I shifted into drive.

As I headed up the canyon, though, the moon painting the rock walls blue-white, I thought about the dream. It makes sense, I told myself. It's a stress dream. You're stressed.

But it had also made one thing perfectly clear: I wasn't going to let Rivera hurt my dad. And the only way to keep that from happening was to find who killed Watson; God knew Rivera wasn't going to do it, not with all his attention focused on me and Dad.

The bitch of it, though? I was pretty sure I was going to need Holloway Holmes's help.

Chapter 9

Let Your Friendship Take Flight

The next morning, Dad woke me up when he fell in the hall.

I stumbled out of my room, hitching my boxers up with one thumb, rubbing my itchy eyes with my other hand. Dad lay on the floor, a hand pressed to the side of his head, his eyes squeezed shut.

"Are you—" A huge yawn interrupted me as I crouched next to him. "—ok?"

Dad nodded, but he didn't open his eyes. "Get me my meds, buddy? I just need the sumatriptan, and I'll be good to go."

I yawned again, and my jaw cracked. "Come on," I said, getting a hand under his arm. "Let's get you some food."

"I can't spend another day sitting around, Jack. I've got work—" He stopped as I sat him up, and he gagged, obviously trying not to puke.

"Breakfast," I said, and this time I managed not to yawn. "You can work when you can walk a straight line."

I got him into his recliner, and then I popped two frozen waffles in the toaster. Outside, the sun still hadn't cleared the mountains, so the canyon lay buried in deep morning shadow. I said a silent prayer of thanks because my head was pounding, and I didn't think I could handle sunshine yet.

After passing Dad a glass of water with an electrolyte packet mixed in, I ducked into the bathroom. I couldn't smell the weed on me, but that was probably because I'd been marinating in it for the last six hours. I washed my face. My eyes were still itchy, and it might have been the weak light, but I was pretty sure they were red. For a moment, all I could do was stand there, the moments slipping away from me. Not even thinking. Just graying out. Or, if I were being honest, probably still greening out. A little, anyway.

The pop of the toaster called me back. I shambled into my room, pulled on a pair of work jeans and a Walker polo that definitely wasn't fresh, and found mismatched socks to go with the Vans. I needed to do laundry. But, of course, to do laundry, I needed a day off, and to get a day off, Dad needed to, you know, actually be able to do his job every once in a while—

The crash from the kitchen pulled me out of my room. When I got to the front of the cottage, Dad was steadying himself with a hand on the kitchen counter, his face red, shaking his head. A hole in the plaster showed where he had taken another dive.

"They were getting cold," he mumbled and waved at the toaster.

"Sorry."

"For heaven's sake, Jack, don't say sorry." He rubbed his head. His hair was growing out; he'd want me to buzz it again soon. As he ran his fingers over it, all that gray made a soft rasping noise in the kitchen's silence. "Where'd you go last night?"

"To pick up your medicine," I said. I spread margarine on the waffles, then syrup. "Aptiom is in the cabinet. Do you want a fruit cup?"

Dad shook his head, so I carried the food over to the side table next to his recliner.

"How did you get that?"

I picked up an empty bag of store-brand potato chips, a sock I'd lost, and a couple of Walker ballpoints that were laying on the side table. "I did some extra stuff for Mr. Taylor."

"Jack Sixsmith Moreno."

The sharpness in his voice made me look up.

"Don't lie to me."

"I'm not lying!"

"What kind of jobs did you do for Mr. Taylor?"

"I don't know, Dad. Stuff."

"And you were gone until four in the morning to get medicine? In my truck? When you only have a learner's permit?"

I pitched the bonus sock toward my room and shoved the empty chip bag into the trash, which needed to be taken out—it was starting to smell. I tucked the Walker pens into my pocket and stepped into my Vans. "Food," I said. "Then medicine. Then rest."

"I asked you a question."

"I want you to take the Aptiom every day. When it runs out, we'll get more."

"Jack!"

"So ground me," I said. I yanked open the door, and the force made it wobble, the glass rattling where it was loose in its frame. "How about that? I don't get to leave the house except for work and school. Big fucking change."

"Get back here," Dad said.

I slammed the door shut and went down the steps. Half of me wanted him to follow, to keep up the fight, because at least that meant he cared. But that was a little-kid thing, and anyway, he didn't.

By day, especially in autumn, the Walker School was beautiful. Part of that was because of its location—I'd lived in Utah my whole life, but before the accident, we'd traveled, and I'd seen some amazing places: San Francisco, New York, even London the summer I turned twelve. But nothing could compete with the Wasatch Mountains. The light was different here, brighter, the air clearer like a film had been peeled away. The color of the stone changed hourly: now it was dark gray, purple, in places a smoky blue that seemed to wisp away until I couldn't tell where the stone ended and the shadows began. But later, it would be gray and white, whetted like a scalpel's edge, every line crisp and clear. Today, the scrub oak was scarlet on the slopes, and the aspens were starting to turn gold. The air was cold enough to raise goose bumps on my bare arms, but it was a nice kind of cold, waking me up, tasting like pine and a hint of wood smoke. So, like I said, the Walker School had an advantage: throw in some redbrick buildings, with the kind of detail in the stonework that (after an hour of searching *old brick houses beautiful* and then googling different search terms) I was pretty sure were Victorian, and you had a beautiful campus.

On Sundays, the campus was even quieter than on Saturdays. Kids slept in. The dining hall served breakfast later than usual. Dad (and I) were supposed to do the weekly deep cleaning for Walker Hall, the administrative annex, the library—basically anywhere we hadn't done Saturday. In theory, it was a shorter day. And, in theory, Dad got two floating days off during the week to make up for covering the weekends. At first, that had seemed ideal—at the beginning, especially, we had needed to go to a lot of doctors' appointments and PT and specialists and then more specialists, so it worked out well, having two days off like that. Then, when people started realizing we couldn't pay, we had fewer appointments. And then Mr. Taylor needed Dad (me) to cover a shift "just this once." And then it wasn't "just this once" anymore.

I stopped at the maintenance building to get a custodial cart, and I checked it over to make sure I had everything—all the sprays and mops and buckets and rags. And toilet paper. God, people at this school went through so much toilet paper. Then I headed toward the academic buildings at the center of campus.

Finding Holmes actually shouldn't be too hard on a Sunday. Most of the classroom buildings were closed, and so were the administrative offices. Students at Walker weren't allowed their own vehicles, and there wasn't any public transit. That was kind of the whole point of a place like Walker: keep the rich kids safe and quiet and out of view because they'd already caused their parents enough problems. Sure, kids found ways to sneak into town—usually by paying someone to drive out to the ass-end of Timp and pick them up—but I didn't think Holmes had done that. Which left only a few options: his residence hall, the library, the athletic center, or the dining hall.

I started with Holmes's residence hall. I knew he was in Baker House, so I headed south, toward the mouth of the canyon. When they'd built Walker, they'd set the boys' housing about as far from the girls' as they could. The boys all lived southeast of the campus center, near the old athletic fields—what they'd used before some donor had donated who-knew-how-many millions of dollars for Walker to build a brand-new athletic center and even better fields on the north end of campus. They called these the practice fields, and that included the soccer field where I'd stumbled on that group of first-years a couple of nights before. Baker House fit the Walker mold: the dark red brick, the granite accents, the steep slate roof, the weird little turret poking out the back—I guess how people built things back before everything got streamlined.

The theme for their bulletin board was LET YOUR FRIENDSHIPS TAKE FLIGHT, and it featured paper rocket ships and shooting stars, which seemed kind of...a lot. Holloway Holmes stared back at the camera with cold indifference. He wasn't that cute, I decided. Yeah, my God, that jaw. Ok, hell, those cheekbones. But his mouth was a thin, hard line. And his eyes were blah. Gray, who cares? So yeah, I thought, like I was hyping myself up, yeah, he's got a dumb face.

The number printed below was 221.

I left the cart and went upstairs and listened at the door of 221. I checked in both directions. The daylight coming in at the end of the hall was the color of the sponges we bought in bulk. When I ran through the keys, they jingled because I couldn't keep my hands steady. Then I found the right one, inserted it, and let myself into Holloway Holmes's lair.

At first glance, it could have passed for uninhabited: the cinderblock walls were bare, and the white bedding and white pillows blended in with the paint. The closet door was shut, the blinds were down, the carpet was clean, and the whole place smelled faintly like the school laundry detergent. It might have been a guest room, somewhere they kept clean and ready in case someone needed to spend the night. There was nothing personal, nothing that suggested someone actually lived there—not someone who farted and dropped lint from his pockets and maybe picked his nose sometimes, maybe rocked out when nobody was looking. The closest thing to decoration was a week's worth of dust on the mirror.

The only thing approaching personal was the laptop on the desk. It wasn't Watson's, so it had to belong to Holmes. I opened it; the login showed a single initial, H, and a space for a password. Ok, I thought, cracking my knuckles for my invisible audience—and for my own amusement. Let's see if Janitor Boy can outsmart Boy Genius. I tried *holmes, hollowayholmes, password, 1234*. It said I had one last attempt, so I smirked and tried *cutebutt*, all one word, lower case.

It told me my account had been locked for security reasons, so I shut the lid on the laptop. I didn't bother wiping it down. If Holmes cared, he'd be able to figure out it was me.

I moved to the closet next. I found what appeared to be the Holloway Holmes Official Robot Dress-up Kit™. Oxford after oxford after oxford. Light blue, gray, and white. Chinos—navy, gray, and black. And seven pairs of chukkas, none of which appeared to have a single scratch on them. I thought about scratching them, but I figured I wouldn't be here to see him short circuit, so what would be the point?

After shutting the closet door, I moved back to the desk. The drawers on the side opened, and they showed me office supplies similar to what I'd seen in Watson's desk—albeit a lot more organized. Hell, this boy had four different kinds of tape. I moved them around just to screw with him. Then I grabbed the top pad of sticky notes and took a blue pen—they were organized by color, of course. I drew a happy janitor blowing a kiss, just a few quick lines. I stuck it to the top of the desk. I put the blue pen with the reds, wondered if I was being too much of an ass, and closed the drawers.

I was about to give up when I tugged on the long, skinny center drawer and discovered it was locked. I thought about that for a moment. It seemed unlikely that Holmes would be dumb enough to leave anything too important in a desk drawer, locked or not. But it also made me curious. I flipped a coin in my head, and then I realized I was kidding myself— heads or tails, I was going to open the drawer.

I ran down to the custodial cart and grabbed a screwdriver. Once I got the screwdriver between the drawer and the top of the desk, all I had to do was apply pressure, and the bolt slipped free. The drawer skidded out an inch. I eased the screwdriver out, tucked it into my back pocket, and opened the drawer the rest of the way.

A notebook—the one he'd had with him Friday night—lay inside. I opened it, flipping through page after page. The entire notebook had been filled, and several pages at the end had been torn out. It looked like something a crazy person had done, like the kind of thing you see in a movie, when the conspiracy guy has taped pictures to the walls and hung string everywhere. Every page in the notebook was covered in frenzied writing, words and phrases, some of them circled, others crossed out, arrows suggesting connections. In some ways, the pages were different from each other—the arrows connecting different words, for example—but some elements repeated. Watson was one of the words that showed up over and over again. And I recognized (how could I not?) the name Moriarty, although I'd never heard of a Margaret Moriarty before. Blackfriar appeared on almost every page. Zodiac. And IPO. Hewdenhouse. Holmes's own name appeared. And towards the back of the notebook, where the writing became scribbles and the arrows were deep lines that gouged the paper, Jack. My name.

I returned the notebook to the drawer. I couldn't seem to do anything right; the notebook thumped when I released it too early, and my hand jostled the drawer, making it rattle. I slid it shut and used the screwdriver to pop the tiny bolt back into place. There was a spot on the front of the drawer where the shaft of the screwdriver had scuffed the paint. If Holmes were anything like the guy in the movies, he'd notice. Five minutes ago, that wouldn't have bothered me. Now I kept seeing *Jack* in those furious, deep scratches.

Letting myself out into the hall, I did a too-late check. I'd been lucky; no one was there to spot me. I shut the door, locked it, and hurried downstairs.

I didn't find Holmes at the dining hall, and then I had to stop because Katja, the food services weekend team lead, spotted me. They had water pouring out from under a sink. I thought a pipe had burst, which was way above my pay grade—and skill—but it turned out that the slip nut between the drainpipe and the trap had come loose. I tightened it, made a note to check it tomorrow to see if it was starting to come loose again, and mopped up the mess. It didn't take long, and I did manage to get soaked from the waist down in the process, but Katja gave me coffee and a paper lunch sack full of breakfast pastries, so it was worth it.

By that point, I was starting to drag, so I put on my headphones. I couldn't remember if I'd changed the CD in Dad's old Discman, but Rage Against the Machine came on, and I shit you not, "Wake Up" was the first song. It helped, and so did the coffee, and between the two of them I managed to feel slightly more human.

After a quick check of the library (I escaped before Ms. Roxy, the weekend library assistant, could stop me), I found him in the athletic center. It was chance, more than anything; I was still coming up the walk, the cart's casters rattling on the uneven concrete, when I saw him through one of the athletic center's lower windows. It looked in on a weight room, and with the sun still struggling to get above the mountains, there was no glare on the glass. Holmes had on a gray athletic tee and gray shorts; they looked like they'd come as an expensive set. He was facing the window, although I'm not sure he saw me. His gaze was a strange combination of ferocity and emptiness—a tremendous focus bearing down on something nobody else could see. His hair was damp with sweat, shaggy out of its usual Ivy League part. He had a barbell across his shoulders, his feet planted, and as I watched, he dropped into a squat and came back up again. The shorts and the squats were making some convincing arguments that I needed to rethink my whole skinny-white-ass first impression.

I sped up, the cart practically bouncing along the walk. Then I slowed down. I'd had some trouble with the athletic center; when Dad and I had first moved here, I'd assumed that I was allowed to use the indoor track, the weight room, the pool—all of it, because I was staff. It turned out, though, that although we were all part of the Walker family, we weren't all equal parts of the family. From the details I could pick up, it sounded like it hadn't even been a student who had complained—I was pretty sure it was one of the staff. Anyway, word came down: I was welcome to use all Walker facilities, but only when they were closed. I'm pretty sure the exact words were: "for the comfort of everyone involved." Sure, got it. It must be fucking awful to be reminded that there are real, breathing poor people around you. Like cockroaches. We're everywhere.

While it wouldn't be an issue for me to go into the athletic center and do a quick walk-through, if I lingered, there was a good chance someone would report me. I figured I'd better have a decent excuse. Instead of the walkie, I took out my phone, and I placed a call to Walker's twenty-four-hour emergency line.

"This is Melissa with The Walker School, we are Walker, how may I help—"

"You can start," I said, pitching my voice higher and harder than it normally was, "by explaining to me why I'm paying sixty grand a year so my son can step through shit puddles in the locker room. That's a biohazard, get it? That's negligence. He's got to get tested. And what if he'd slipped?"

Melissa's silence had a hunkered-down quality that made me think of those World War I movies Dad liked, everybody huddled in the trenches. Somebody had done a hell of a job writing her script, though, because all she said was, "That sounds like something I can help you with. Why don't we start with your name and your son's name?"

I decided to go with Aston; his was the first name to come to mind. After that, it was easy, and I disconnected when Melissa started talking about follow-ups and parent satisfaction consultations. When I checked the window, I'd lost sight of Holmes. The sun was clearing the mountains, making it harder to see into the gym, but I could make out other shapes at the back of the weight room. I wheeled my cart along the side of the building and let myself in through the service entrance.

Passing through a cinderblock room that held the water heater and the furnace, I found the door that connected with the public area of the gym. The locker rooms were to my right, and the weight room was to my left. I went left. The familiar gym smell met me: sweat, Fabuloso, recirculated air. Speakers mounted throughout the building looped the top forty—you couldn't get away from the music if you tried. A couple of boys shouted behind me, and then the locker room door hit the wall with a crack. The boys' voices faded, and I winced. I knew who would be fixing the scuffed paint.

Then a voice behind me said, "Jack?"

I turned and saw Headmaster Burrows. He was standing in the locker room doorway, holding it open with one hand, and it looked like he'd started to go after the noisy boys and then stopped when he saw me. He was a nice-looking guy. A familiar face, the kind some people have. Ok, he was more than nice looking. More than a familiar face. He was hot, and he looked way too young to be a headmaster, especially at a place like Walker. With creamy skin, a crewcut, a slightly crooked nose, and a Super Bowl smile, he looked like he might have been a few years out of college, not at a point in his career that a lot of administrators with twice his experience would have envied. Not that I knew how old he was. Not that I cared. At all.

"I thought that was you," he said, like he had other teenagers around here pushing custodial carts. "I wanted to talk to you." Letting the door fall shut, he closed the distance between us. "How are you doing? After everything on Friday, I mean."

Everything on Friday. Sure, that was one way of putting it. "All right, I guess."

"Are you sure?" I hadn't realized until now that he was wearing gym clothes: Adidas, mesh shorts that hit him above the knee, a tank top dark with sweat where it clung to his chest. "That must have been horrible. Do you need to talk to someone?"

I shrugged. "I'm fine, really." Burrows's eyebrows twitched, and I realized how that sounded. "It was bad, yeah. But I talked to someone, you know, after the accident. It didn't really help. So..." It was one of those conversational moves that usually worked—bringing up something that nobody wanted to talk about, dangling an unfinished phrase, letting that line of discussion unwind into the silence.

Burrows, however, frowned, and his eyebrows did their twitch again. "Jack, if you're upset, you need to talk to someone." He held up a hand. "I'm not saying a therapist, although you're welcome to make an appointment with the school counselor—that's the least we could do. But I'm talking more generally. Have you talked to your dad? An aunt or uncle? Maybe a grandparent?"

"It's just me and my dad now," I said.

He made a soft, understanding noise. Then he smiled; it was knowing, and it made him look even younger. "You do that a little too well, Jack—dodging questions like that. I'm not going to keep pressing you. Just—think about it, all right? If you need something—anything— drop by my office. Open-door policy, you know."

"Yes, Mr. Burrows."

Tipping his head at the locker room door, he said, "I suppose those yahoos aren't going to cause any more trouble, so I can get back to my run. When I was your age, I could eat whatever I wanted, but now I've got to sweat it out." For some reason, that made him look at me again, like he was seeing me for the first time. "Jack, what are you doing—"

The walkie on the cart squawked, and Mr. Taylor's voice came on the air. "Moreno? Melissa just called me. I need you to get over to the athletic center. I asked her why she didn't call you directly, and she said you didn't answer your phone."

I grabbed the walkie and pressed the talk button. "On it. I was just telling Mr. Burrows that a student flagged me down outside the building."

"Mr. Burrows?" Taylor's voice shrilled into imitation pleasantry. "Well, if the headmaster is concerned—"

Rolling my eyes, I turned down the volume. Burrows laughed, clapped me on the shoulder, and headed back toward the room that held the treadmills and ellipticals—opposite the direction I was going, toward the weight rooms. I pushed the cart slowly, casting backward glances over my shoulder. When I was sure Burrows wasn't going to reappear, I opened the door to the weight room and pushed the cart inside.

It was like the weight rooms you saw on TV: two walls of windows, two walls of mirrors, lots of natural light. Neatly racked weights. Every machine you could imagine. Benches, barbells, kettlebells, bumper plates, power racks. The tang of iron hung in the air, along with a hint of rubber— that was the floor, which gave softly under my old Vans.

Holmes was doing bent-over rows. I guessed he was using twenties. His arms came back, the form perfect—of course, why wouldn't it be?— and through the thin athletic shirt, the muscles in his back were visible as outlines. His blond hair was dark at his nape. When he lowered the weights, his shirt rode up, exposing a hint of shockingly white skin and the nub of a vertebra.

A snort of laughter pulled my attention away from the show, and I saw, to my right, five boys. Not just any five boys. This was the Boy Band. Whether it was true or not, they considered themselves the hottest shit at Walker and, by extension, on the planet. They were good customers, of course, like you'd expect from a boy band. First up was Riker (weed), then Jaxon (vape pens and juice), then Dawson (condoms and, interestingly, lube), then Axle (coke, but only occasionally), and last of all, my buddy from the creek, Aston (condoms). They all had the kind of family money that had, for a while, allowed them to get away with bad behavior and, then, had allowed their parents to lock them away at Walker. Jaxon's dad had developed some sort of proprietary code that had made him millions. Dawson's mom was tied into the Waltons somehow. Aston's grandfather was one of the leaders of the Mormon church—an apostle, they called them. They were all people like that. And they loved making sure everyone knew it.

I didn't mind dealing with them one on one, but they were like any pack animal—nastier in a group. I eased the cart to the side of the doorway, trying to be as quiet as possible. Dawson had noticed me, his bushy eyebrows lifting in recognition and, maybe, acknowledgment. The other four were crowded around Aston's phone, laughing at something. The clip must have been short because they were laughing at regular intervals, braying like jackasses at the exact same moment.

Holmes must have heard them; aside from him, the room was empty, and there was no way he could have missed the noise. But he finished his set, racked the weights, and grabbed his phone from the floor. He carried it past the Boy Band, ignoring looks from Riker and Axle, and set his phone next to a weight bench. Then he grabbed a barbell, racked it, and began adding weights. Not too much, I noticed. I added it to my list of things about Holloway Holmes: he apparently felt absolutely no need to show off.

I watched him, trying to figure out what to do; I couldn't talk to him in front of the Boy Band, although talking to him alone didn't exactly seem like a great idea either.

Before I could make a decision, Axle said something that made the rest of the Boy Band burst out laughing. Then he turned and strutted over to the bench where Holmes was securing the bumper plates on the bar.

"Hey," Axle said. He had dark hair worn just long enough for it to look tousled, and his skin had a red undertone to it. A sore marked the corner of his mouth. "I want to use this bench. Fuck off."

Holmes didn't look over at him. He finished securing the weights, and then he straddled the bench. He messed with his phone for a moment and then set it back on the rubber tiles.

"Did you hear me?"

"There are other benches," Holmes said as he lay back, wrapping his hands around the bar.

"I want to use this one." He leaned closer. "So: Fuck. Off."

"Too bad," Holmes said. With one clean movement, he cleared the bar from the rack and began to do a set.

Axle stared at him. It was obvious he hadn't expected that answer, and it was obvious, too, that he didn't know what to do with someone who wasn't immediately willing to do what he wanted. He cast a glance over his shoulder.

Dawson smirked and lifted one shoulder. He was one of those guys with huge, bushy eyebrows and sunken eyes, and he could pull it off—a kind of caveman rugged that definitely had an appeal. Riker and Jaxon laughed.

Phone in hand, Aston moved toward the bench. "You're doing it wrong." He walked a circle to stand at Holmes's head; Holmes was breathing out in controlled bursts as he raised the weights. "See, Supercreep here doesn't understand how normal humans talk to each other. So, you've got to talk to him in his language." He leaned over

Holmes, displayed his phone, and in a too loud voice, said into his face, "I'm sorry for your loss."

Holmes made a noise that didn't sound like anything I'd heard a human make before. It sounded animalistic, savage, uncontrolled. He extended both arms, and the barbell shot up and struck Aston in the chin before he could pull back. Aston yelped and fell onto the floor. His phone hit the rubber tiles, bounced, and came to rest a few feet away from me. On the screen, I could see what Aston had been showing everyone: it was an animated GIF, the silent video looped. It showed a nude of Watson, her arms behind her head, legs spread. The words EVERYONE IS WELCOME flashed at the top of the screen. And then, in the final second, a crudely photoshopped image of a naked man with Holmes's head pasted onto his body appeared to penetrate her. Then the video started again.

I barely had time to process what looked like a sixth-grader's attempt at cyberbullying when Holmes launched himself up from the bench. He came around the bar as Aston scooted backward, hand pressed to his chin. Blood seeped between Aston's fingers. Holmes was silent. After that one wild noise, he hadn't said anything. But as he came toward Aston, he threw a hard kick at the other boy's head. It only missed because Aston dropped flat onto the rubber tiles and rolled away.

"Hey!" Riker shouted. He grabbed Holmes's shirt, and Holmes pivoted, striking Riker's hand. The boy let out a startled cry and stumbled back, shaking out his fingers.

Holmes had already turned back to Aston, and Aston was trying to crab backward. He'd dropped his hand from his chin, and blood stained his black-and-white Nike swoosh tee.

"Cut it out," Jaxon said. He looked like he had Middle Eastern blood in his family: silky black hair that fell to his jaw, olive-colored skin, a chin that verged on too strong. "Holmes, you freak, stop!"

"Dude," Dawson said almost apologetically, although he was talking to Holmes's back, "there are five of us. We're going to beat your ass."

Holmes stalked toward Aston. I figured Aston had it coming, and I also figured dear old Supercreep obviously knew how to take care of himself. But, at the same time, it didn't matter how good Holmes was at karate—or whatever the hell he was doing. Five against one meant that only one of them had to get lucky, and then they really would beat his ass—or worse, depending on how far things had gone by then.

"Uh, guys," I called.

Holmes had brought his sneaker up, obviously intending on face-stomping Aston. He lowered his foot now and glanced over his shoulder.

Aston looked at me with something like begging in his eyes. The rest of the Boy Band stared at me.

"What do you want, Abercrombie?" Riker asked.

It's a hoodie, I wanted to say. It's a hoodie from a store you don't think is cool, but my dad got it for me for Christmas when he should have spent the money on PT, because when he was a kid, that brand was fire, and you want to dog me for it because you've got a micropenis. That's what I wanted to say. But I didn't say anything; the Boy Band had been calling me Abercrombie since the first time they'd seen me in that hoodie, and anything I said would only make it worse.

I thumbed at the door. "Hate to break up the dance, but I thought you'd like to know that Burrows asked me for a pair of bolt-cutters."

It took a moment. Dawson got it first. "What? When?"

"I saw him headed toward the maintenance building about five minutes ago."

"Jesus fuck," Dawson said. He cast a glance at Holmes and Aston.

"What?" Riker asked.

"He's going to search the lockers," Axle said with a note of panic.

"I think technically it's called an inspection," I said.

"He can't do that!" Jaxon said.

"Well, I called the Supreme Court, but they're pretty busy today."

Dawson actually rolled his eyes at that one. When he spoke, he pitched the words toward Holmes, but his eyes were still on me. "What about Aston?"

"I think he's learned his lesson," I said. "Don't you, H?"

It just happened. It just came out of my mouth like that. And I saw the shock of it on Holmes's face, the look of somebody who's just swallowed a fly. After a moment, though, he nodded, and he stepped away, giving Aston room to haul himself to his feet. One hand to his chin, Aston limped toward the door. The Boy Band trailed after him. Dawson kept looking at me. It wasn't a tough guy look. But it wasn't exactly friendly. As they passed out into the hall, they burst into jabbering conversation.

"—fucking psycho—"

"—tell my parents—"

And then, the words muffled by the hand to his chin, Aston saying, "He killed her; I know he did."

The door shut silently on its pneumatic closer. Holmes watched me. We hit the end of this Top 40, and the next song picked up, something closer to a ballad than the pounding beat of the last one. He folded his arms.

"You could say thank you," I said.

Shock flashed across Holmes's face again. Then his cheeks reddened. His arms dropped to his sides, and he returned to the bench and began to add more weight to the bar.

"That's it?" I asked as I came across the room. "I just saved your ass, and you're going to ignore me."

Another weight rattled down the bar, clinking when it slid into place. "I was handling that."

"Right, you were handling five guys who wanted to tear you apart. I must have gotten something in my eye because it didn't look like you were handling anything."

"Then you should rinse out your eye," Holmes said. He secured the weights and dropped back onto the bench. He wrapped his hands around the knurled steel. He did not have pretty hands, I realized. The rest of him, sure, pretty as an ice sculpture. He was white everywhere, but his knuckles were pink. His middle finger on his left hand was wonky. The closest thing to pretty was the tracing of blue veins on the undersides of his wrists. In seventh-grade art, Ms. Prinze told us some Japanese artists included deliberate imperfections in their work. The Navajos, too. So the soul didn't get trapped in perfection. Sure, I thought, looking at him. I get it.

It was hotter in the weight room than I'd realized. I pulled on the Walker polo, trying to get some air. I watched him lift the bar. He must have been close to his max; he struggled to get the bar clear from the rack, and his chest and biceps swelled as he tried to press this much weight.

"You should have a spotter," I told him.

His answer was a white-hot burst of breath as he forced the bar up again.

"Could you cut it out? I need to talk to you."

Another sharp breath.

"About Watson."

"Go. Away."

His face was bright red now. Some of the blond hair was plastered to his forehead. I moved around the bench to stand where Aston had been. I was painfully aware of the vee of my legs bracketing Holmes's head. Sweat dampened the cotton under my arms. I wished I'd worn a different shirt. I wished I'd worn more, uh, discreet underwear.

I spotted him, my hands hovering under the bar, ready to catch it if he needed me. He scowled up at me, furious. Here he was, Holloway Holmes, and all he wanted was for me to leave him alone. I figured this kid got just about everything he wanted, so I figured I was doing him a service. And then, just to be a prick, I curled my thumbs over the bar and began to press down. Not hard. And not all at once. Just enough that it was harder for him to press the additional weight. His chest heaved. When his breath exploded, spittle flecked the back of my hand.

"I came in here," I said, my voice low, "to talk to you, and in the process, I saved your butt. What do I get? You've been rude to me and won't take five seconds to hear what I have to say. So, I'm going to give you a choice: you can either say thanks, or you can tell me you're sorry. And then I'll help you rack this, and we can talk."

I'd seen hatred before, and right then, hatred and fury shone up at me from those gray eyes as Holmes struggled to lift the bar, fighting the additional weight I was adding. He arched his back. One of his hands slid a half-inch along the steel. His cheeks almost looked purple, and when he breathed, it sounded like gunshots.

"Motherfucker," I whispered, "I am just as stubborn as you."

For one more moment, he strained against the weight. Then he jerked his head in a nod. I straightened, caught the bar, and racked it. Where my arm brushed his, I could tell he was shaking. He didn't sit up right away. He closed his eyes, taking frantic, furious breaths.

"Slower," I said. "And deeper."

Even with his eyes closed, he could snarl pretty well, but he did what I said. The color in his face got better. His arms hung off the sides of the bench, and he opened and closed his fingers. I could see where the knurled pattern of the steel had left its mark on his palms.

Then his eyes opened, and he sat up.

"Well?" I said.

His voice was hoarse. I hadn't noticed it on our first encounter, but he didn't have an accent. At least, not one that was distinctly English. He sounded different, but that could have been because he was a robot. Or maybe just because he was smart. "It's good that things did not escalate further."

I rolled the barbell in the rack, grinning as the metal chimed. "That is the worst thank you I've ever heard."

He blinked. "That was an apology."

I couldn't help it; I burst out laughing. "Have you ever heard an apology before?"

He was still red from the exertion, but I thought he was blushing now too. "I'm familiar with the concept."

"God, we're going to have to work on that." I watched him. "Those detectives think I had something to do with Watson's death."

For a moment, I saw it—what they said in the books about his ancestor, what was in the movies, the flurry of analysis and consideration. Then he said, "That's ridiculous."

"Well, it's true."

"Yes, I'm sure you look very appealing to them as a suspect. And they're looking at your father closely too, aren't they?"

"Yeah, but—" I couldn't help it; I grinned. "Yes, exactly. That's why I need your help. I've got to figure out who killed Watson. And I've got to be able to prove it to the police so they'll leave me and my dad alone."

He shook his head. "No."

"What do you mean, no?"

"I'm handling it."

"Like you handled the Boy Band?"

"Who is—"

"Because it sure as hell doesn't look like you're handling it. I don't think you can handle jack shit on your own."

"It may surprise you to learn that I don't care what you think." He wiped his face with the hem of his shirt and looked up again. "I'd like to finish my workout."

"I don't think you heard me—"

"I heard you, and I don't care. For now, it is convenient for me that the police are interested in you and your father. I am conducting my own inquiries into Watson's death. I do not require your assistance. I do not want your assistance. You would be a liability. More likely, you would be dead weight."

I stared at him.

"Was something unclear?" he asked.

His phone buzzed. He moved for it, and before I could think about it, I swept it up from the rubber tile.

He looked up at me, his eyes narrowing. "Give that to me."

"Or what?"

"Give that to me right now."

"It may surprise you to learn that I don't care what you want," I said, trying to copy his emotionless tone. "I need help, and you're going to help me."

He was clutching the bench with both hands. His fingers were white from pressure. "Give me my phone, Jack."

"Oh, you know my name now? Tell you what: you agree to help me, and I'll give you information that even the cops don't have. I'll even give you your phone back so you can talk to—" I glanced at the screen. "Who the hell is Blackfriar?"

It had been a mistake to look at the screen. I was still turning my head to look at Holmes when he launched himself up from the bench. The heel of his hand caught me in the solar plexus, and the breath whooshed from my lungs. He twisted my wrist, pain shot up my arm, and the phone fell from my hand. Then, with his other hand, he shoved me. I landed on my ass and rolled backward, trying to get air.

Through the roaring in my ears, I barely made out the sound of a door opening, and then a man's face swam into view as I tried to convince my lungs to work. He was black, his hair shorn to the scalp, and his skin was so dark that it gleamed. He looked down at me, upside down in my vision, and shook his head.

"I'm sorry he was bothering you, Mr. Holmes," Olin Campbell, head of security for Walker, said. Then, to me, he added, "Get up, Jack. I think we need to have a talk with Mr. Taylor."

Chapter 10

Say Thank You, Jack

The maintenance building office was technically Dad's office, although you couldn't tell it from the way Taylor sat behind the desk. Campbell had brought me here after hauling me out of the gym. Here, instead of Taylor's office in Walker Hall. At the time, I'd been too busy massaging my chest and trying to get air into my lungs to wonder why he'd escorted me back to the maintenance building. Now, though, in the silent seconds that were threatening to bury me like a snowdrift, I was starting to wonder, still working the heel of my hand against the tender spot where Holmes had hit me.

The office didn't look like much: a steel desk, old chairs with split vinyl upholstery, battered filing cabinets—the same ones where I'd hid Watson's cash a couple of nights before—a dart board with its darts clustered in the inner red circle of the bullseye. Dad's only addition had been a 2017 Dodgers calendar. We hadn't lived here in 2017; we'd still been in Salt Lake, in our old house. Things had still made sense in 2017. But he liked the pictures from that year. The first week we'd been here, he'd put a picture of me and Mom on his desk in a frame we'd bought at Walmart, but at some point, he'd moved it or thrown it away. It was gone, anyway.

I was sitting where Campbell had left me, in one of the chairs in front of the desk, when the door opened and Taylor came into the room. His hair was military short and thinning, and he'd gone with a Walker polo today that left his flabby arms bare to the world. He looked at me, and even though he wasn't smiling, he wore that kind of satisfaction that adults get when they think they've got your ass on a hook. When he lowered himself into Dad's chair, he wrapped his hands around the armrests and rocked for a few moments.

"Jack, did somebody say you could sit?"

"Huh?" I glanced down at the chair, then back at Taylor. "Mr. Campbell—"

"Because that's bad manners, being in someone else's space and sitting without an invitation."

I stared at him. He rocked and rocked and rocked. My face started to heat, and I stood. He gave a little nod, still not smiling. This was Taylor all over, the passive-aggressive power plays, the need to control. He'd probably spank it to this memory for the next month.

"Mr. Taylor—"

He sucked his teeth and shook his head. "Now, Jack, I think the polite thing to do would be to wait and speak when you're spoken to. I've busted my butt this morning trying to keep Mr. Burrows from sending you and your dad packing, and the last thing I need is back talk." His hands slid along the armrests, his thumbs tracing the ends of the wood. "Don't you think the polite thing would be to keep quiet?"

Pins and needles ran through my face, down my chest. I nodded.

"Jack." He said my name with drawn-out embarrassment, like I was the one making this harder. "That was a direct question."

"Yes." When he raised his eyebrows, I added, "Mr. Taylor."

He nodded. He rocked for a few more moments. When I'd been twelve, Preston Gregory had dared me to slash Mr. Oveson's tires. He lived at the end of the street, and he lived alone, and he was an all-purpose asshole. He'd run over our frisbee on purpose, cracking it, when it flew into the street one day. And because I was twelve and because Preston had dimples, I did it. I got busted, of course. And when Dad found out, he'd given me ten with his belt, which was the only time in my whole life he hit me. Then he marched me down to Mr. Oveson's house, and he made me apologize in person, and I'd started sobbing, and my face had been like this, so hot it felt like I had ants crawling all over it. And then Dad had sent me to my room, and that night, he'd come in and given me a huge hug, and I'd started crying all over again. That time, though, it had been because I knew things were going to be all right eventually. I stared at a spot on the floor, trying not to meet Taylor's eyes, and thought about that. It's weird, the things you remember. And at the weirdest times.

"I understand," Taylor said, "there was an incident."

He paused long enough that I figured it was a question, so I shook my head. "No, Mr. Taylor."

"No, there wasn't an incident?"

I shook my head again. "I tripped."

Taylor's silence stretched out. "What are you talking about?"

I risked a glance up. "Uh, what are you talking about, sir?"

"The fight between Holmes and Aston Young."

It only took an instant to make the decision. I shook my head. "I didn't see a fight, Mr. Taylor."

"What do you mean, you didn't see a fight? Aston says you were there. He says you saw the whole thing. They all do."

"Nothing happened. There was no fight."

"Are you calling those boys liars?"

Direct question or not, I wasn't going to engage with that one, so I stared at an uneven spot on the desk, where someone had spilled water or soda and the laminate top had warped.

When Taylor spoke again, I didn't recognize his tone; it took me a minute to realize he was trying to sound friendly. "Jack, I understand that the Holmes family, their legacy, it can be very intimidating. But if you're worried about reprisals, I give you my personal assurance that you don't have anything to be afraid of. Blackfriar Holmes is very supportive of school discipline. He's made it clear to all the staff that he will reward full, unvarnished accounts about his son's behavior."

Two realizations: first, Blackfriar was Holmes's dad; second, that's why we were here instead of Taylor's office in Walker Hall. Taylor didn't want to risk a run-in with Burrows. Not when he could get the story first and—what? Sell it to Holmes's dad? I realized the silence had stretched out too long, so I shook my head. "Mr. Taylor, I don't know what happened before I got there, but I didn't see a fight. Those boys wanted something from Holmes. When he didn't give it to them, they said they were going to tell a teacher that he'd attacked them. He ignored them, and they left."

I risked another look. Taylor's eyebrows had climbed to his thinning hair. "So, Holmes didn't attack Aston Young?"

I shook my head.

"And what is Aston going to say if I ask him to join us?"

But he wouldn't; I knew he wouldn't, now that I understood Taylor's game. Burrows might call me in. Burrows might make me sit down with Aston. But Taylor wouldn't. Couldn't. Because the only person Taylor had authority over was me, and if Burrows got a whiff that Taylor was messing with student discipline, he wouldn't be happy.

I shook my head again. "I don't know, Mr. Taylor."

The silence was taut, tuned so tight it felt like it might snap if either of us breathed. Then Taylor said, "I see." The friendly tone had dropped away. The words were hard and flat. "And what were you doing in the athletic center, Mr. Moreno? That's not part of your Sunday duties." His volume went up. "And you might explain why you were in the weight room when the callout was for a clogged toilet, if I remember correctly."

"Nobody said anything to me about a clogged toilet," I said. "A student stopped me and said someone had spilled Gatorade in the weight room. When you got me on the walkie, I thought that's what you were talking about."

This time, the words landed like two slaps. "I see." He seemed to struggle to take a breath. "Then I don't need to remind you about the policies regarding fraternizing with the students or about using student facilities?"

"No, Mr. Taylor."

He sat forward heavily, the chair thunking under him. He propped his elbows on the desk. I was having a hard time telling what color his eyes were; blue or green, I guess, but so washed out they looked colorless. His collar was a little too tight; maybe that's what was making his face so red.

"All right," he said. "If you're not interested in helping maintain a safe and respectful campus at Walker, then I suppose that's the end of that conversation. Why are you covering your dad's shift today?"

The change in topic caught me off guard, and I had to take a moment. "He's got a migraine."

"I thought he had medication for those."

"He does, but it doesn't always work, and—" I stopped myself, but it was too late.

Taylor rolled the chair forward. "In his interview, he told me he had it all under control. He said the doctors had cleared him for work."

What would you have said, I wanted to ask him. What would you have told people after the third week you'd been living out of the truck, showering at the gym, both of us doing pickup landscaping work that most days Dad was too sick to do anyway?

"He does," I said. "Today's the exception."

"I thought Friday was the exception. Or Saturday. Or last Wednesday. Or Thursday and Friday of the week before."

"Yeah, but—"

"We hired your dad as a full-time custodian, Mr. Moreno. Now, I've turned a blind eye to how much you compensate for your dad's...disabilities, but I don't want you to think I haven't noticed. Nothing happens on this campus that I don't know about." He paused, probably to let that sink in. You missed your calling, I thought. Instead of a washed-up football player, you should have been a washed-up actor. The baddie of the week. That kind of thing. "Walker needs—no, Walker deserves—a full-time custodian who can do his job."

"My dad is doing his job, and anyway, when I cover for him, you know I do twice as much as anybody else—"

"Are you raising your voice, Mr. Moreno?" Taylor shouted over me.

I managed to bite off my answer. I stared down at the linoleum between my feet.

"Mr. Moreno, that was a question."

"No."

"I think you were. I think you were being tremendously disrespectful."

"No." I had to grit the words out between my teeth. "No, Mr. Taylor."

"Yes, I think you were. I think you owe me an apology."

My heart was pounding so hard that I could feel it in my ears—it was more than hearing it; it was physical, a sensation of pressure. Taylor shifted his weight. The chair creaked.

"I'm sorry, Mr. Taylor."

"For raising my voice."

"For raising my voice."

"And for being an ungrateful brat."

"And for being—" I had to stop and swallow. The linoleum was speckled, a pattern meant to hide dirt. I tried to follow it with my eyes. "—an ungrateful brat."

"Because, Jack," Taylor said, his voice low and sounding weirdly thrilled, "not everyone would put up with this nonsense. Not everyone would be as understanding as I have. I could snap my fingers, and you and your father would be out on your rears. Did you think about that?"

I nodded.

Taylor shifted some more. His elbows made faintly sticky noises as he lifted his arms from the desk. "In light of everything," he said. "I believe it would be best for you to end your shift early today. Your pay will be docked accordingly. And I'll be adding a written warning to your father's file." When I opened my mouth, he spoke over me. "I'm doing you a favor, Jack; I could have him suspended if I wanted to. You can spend the afternoon thinking about how you can show your gratitude for my incredible generosity. The next time I ask about Holloway Holmes, for example."

I shivered. It was like having a fever, this heat that was also a kind of chill.

"You're dismissed, Jack."

I made it to the door before Taylor clicked his tongue.

"Say thank you, Jack."

"Thank you, Mr. Taylor."

"Good boy," he said, leaning back in the chair again. "Tell your dad I hope he feels better soon."

Chapter 11

cutebutt

I stood in the hallway outside the office, my hand still on the knob, the brass cold but warming under my touch. I couldn't go home, not yet. If I went home, I'd have to tell Dad why I wasn't at work, and he'd freak out about the hours Taylor had cut. I'd have to make up some kind of excuse about what had happened eventually; I couldn't tell him the truth because if I did, Dad would go apeshit. He'd make us leave. He'd say it wasn't worth it. And he'd be wrong. Because here, at least, we had a roof, and we had food, we could pay for his medicine, and when he had really bad days, he didn't have to spend them folded up double in the cab of the truck.

So, instead, I went to the garage.

It was a big, three-bay cinderblock addition to the maintenance building. It had glass-block windows that let in a lot of light while still making the space feel secluded, and it smelled like two-stroke oil and cold concrete. Against one wall, the last custodian had stacked Duralast batteries, the terminals fuzzed blue-white with corrosion. There was a dinged-up rolling tool chest, a pegboard full of tools, and a good-sized workbench. Dad had left out an old multimeter he was trying to get working—it had a greasy thumbprint on the display. Above the workbench, someone had hung a Tabernacle Choir calendar from 1998 and a picture of Salma Hayek cut out of a magazine. Someone had traced her boobs with blue ballpoint. The same person had apparently tried to do it with the Tabernacle Choir gals, but you couldn't really see much under those dresses.

My bike—Dad's old mountain bike—was upside down, resting on the handlebars and seat. I liked riding it when I had time, although it seemed like that was less and less often; there were great trails all over Timp, and Walker was in a prime location to take advantage of them. The bike needed constant work. On my last ride, the brakes had given out completely, and I'd had to steer into a shrubby cedar to stop myself.

I pulled out a stool and sat, my back against the work bench, wiping my hands on my knees. I thought about Taylor, replaying the whole thing and then doing it all over again. I stared at the bike. I thought, for a minute, about how good it might feel to pick up a framing hammer and just beat the hell out of the stupid thing. It wouldn't help anything, though. I'd still be stuck at Walker. Maybe forever. Sure, I could get my GED. And I could probably get into a school somewhere. But what was I supposed to do about Dad? I let my head hang back, staring up at the heater mounted up on the ceiling. I thought about Dad, how happy he'd been about that heater. He'd had big plans. He'd do all the oil changes on the Walker vehicles. He'd be able to fix some stuff on the truck that had been bothering him. He'd have all winter to do it, warm in here. I felt tired, and it was a kind of tired that was new to me, although I was feeling it more and more these days. It was tired like feeling empty, like someone had pulled a stopper and let everything drain out.

After enough of that, I got to my feet and went over to the bike. I found the release lever on the axle, pushed it to open, and turned it counterclockwise. It got stuck a couple of times because the threads were starting to wear down, which made it feel weirdly loose at times and, other times, made the whole thing a pain in the ass to disassemble. I had to get down on my knees and put my shoulder into it. Finally, the axle came free. I lifted the wheel out of the fork, being careful not to mess up the brakes, and leaned it against one cinderblock wall. When I straightened and turned, Holmes was standing in the doorway.

He'd changed into oxford and chinos and chukkas again. Today, he was wearing light blue and gray. The daylight silhouetted him, picking out the perfect lines on one side of his face. Ok, I thought. Ok, he's got muscles, even if you can't see them. And he's handed you your ass twice without having to work for it. But reminding myself didn't help; he was just so damn skinny.

"What?" I asked as I moved back to the bike.

He stepped forward, letting the door fall shut, and for a moment, my eyes had to adjust to the relative darkness. His chukkas were silent as he came across the concrete. When he stopped next to me, I could smell leather, and something else. My brain seemed to have switched off, so I crouched next to the bike, examining the brake pads. Well, pretending to examine them. I was so attuned to him standing next to me that I wasn't really registering anything else. Maybe he's going to break your neck, I told myself. Maybe he's tired of half-assing it.

"Mr. Campbell wanted to talk about Aston and the others," he said. His voice was flat, almost expressionless. "They reported me."

"Yeah, well, you tried to hand the Boy Band their collective ass, and you handed Aston his ass in particular. I guess they weren't too happy about that."

He was silent for a moment. I bent down, inspecting the chain, smelling the sweetness of the bike chain's lube. "The Boy Band?"

"Really?" I asked. I stood up too fast, jostling the bike, and it threatened to topple. I caught it. The rear wheel spun lazily, the sound of its movement filling the silent garage. "That's what you want to talk about? You don't want to, I don't know, apologize? And maybe say thank you?"

He blinked.

After a moment, when I realized he wasn't going to say anything, I said, "Could you get the hell out of here, please?"

"You took my phone."

"Are you not hearing me? Get lost."

"I was simply recovering my personal property."

"Don't give me that. You were worried because your dad was calling and you didn't want to get in trouble. You know I wouldn't have answered that call. I wanted to talk to you is all, and you were being a dick."

Holmes's face flushed. He even turned red prettily, not a whole-face blush, but these bright spots in his cheeks that made him look—I suddenly had a very clear image of what Holloway Holmes might look like during sex, and then my face was hot. He took a step toward me. His hands curled into fists.

"Yeah," I said, grateful for the distraction from my own messed-up thoughts. "What's it going to be this time? You're mad I called you out, so you're going to break my knee, and I'll walk on a cane the rest of my life? You're going to break my ankle so they'll have to put a million pins in it?" I shook my head and crouched next to the bike again. The rear wheel was still spinning, so I stopped it with one hand, the textured rubber scraping the pads of my fingers. I tried to look like I was really interested in the brake pads again.

He didn't take another step. When I couldn't stand the silence, I looked up. The corner of his mouth was twitching. It didn't look like a laugh or a smile. It looked like a nervous tic, like something he couldn't control, and something told me Holmes liked to control everything.

As clearly as I could, I enunciated, "Fuck. Off."

For another moment, he stared at me. Then he turned and left.

I had to leave the bike, stand up, walk around. Then I stopped, bending over, my stomach churning so badly I had to rest my hands on my knees. Who the hell did he think he was, coming in here, like he could get whatever he wanted? Then I stood up, laughed a little, shocking myself when the sound broke the stillness. He was a Holmes. Worse, he was a Walker kid. They were all like that—they all wanted something, and they didn't care who they hurt to get it. No wonder Watson had hated him enough to rat him out to the paparazzi.

Before I could think about it, I headed into the maintenance building. The lights were off, and the office was dark, so I let myself inside. Taylor was gone. I powered up the computer, logged in with Dad's credentials, and opened Gmail. I was doing everything fast. At the back of my brain, I had the feeling that if I slowed down, I'd fall off this tightrope. I found Lissa Keahi's contact information and typed out a short email: *I can tell you about Holloway Holmes. Cash only.* I included my phone number and clicked send.

Then I sat, staring at the computer. It was like something had blown through me, one of the big canyon winds that comes down at night, snuffing out the fire. I sank down in the chair and I realized I could smell Taylor's drugstore body spray lingering in the room, and that made my stomach do flips. I stared at the screen, my Gmail account blurring in my vision. What the fuck, I asked myself, is wrong with you?

I leaned forward, shut the browser, and dragged my mouse over to power down the computer. I stopped before I clicked it. I wasn't a Walker kid, and I wasn't going to sell information about somebody's private life— no matter how huge of an asshole he was. And anyway, I needed to be focused on something much more important: figuring out who killed Watson so that Rivera and Yazzie would stop looking at me and, more importantly, my dad. But I didn't have any idea where to start. I mean, I'd seen the body for a total of, what? Maybe five minutes? And I'd already tried to help the police by placing the scrap of paper from her wallet in her room along with the broken flash drive, but I hadn't seen any sign that the detectives had found them—or that they cared.

Had there been something else that night? Another clue? Something I'd missed that might point to whoever had done this? I tried to run through the events in my head. Picking up the broken flash drive. Seeing

Watson, the trash bags piled up around her. I paused here. I still thought that was strange; why hadn't the killer covered her? But it didn't get me anywhere, so I kept going. I'd been worried because I was holding, and I needed to call the police, but for some reason I went through her purse—

No, I thought, and a rush of excitement made the hair on my arms stand up. No, that wasn't how it had happened. I'd been about to call the police, only her phone rang. Watson's phone. And that had made me notice her little black pouch, and then I'd decided to look inside.

The phone.

The caller ID hadn't shown a name. It had shown two initials: MM.

I don't know how I missed it the first time, but now I connected it to what I'd seen in Holmes's notebook, the one I'd found in his desk. Margaret Moriarty. MM. That made sense, right? The Moriartys were the Holmes' enemies. Holmes had already suspected her, even though I hadn't told him about the phone call.

Slow down, I told myself. I could hear myself breathing too fast. Slow down. Margaret Moriarty called Watson after she was dead, not before.

But, another part of me argued, wouldn't that be genius? Wouldn't that be a great alibi? If what I'd seen in the movies was any indicator, wouldn't that be exactly what a Moriarty would do? Kill Watson and then place a phone call that's been routed from Paris or Tokyo so it looks like you were thousands of miles away?

I opened the browser again and typed in Margaret Moriarty.

Every result on the first page was about her. I started with the pictures: she looked petite, with glossy dark hair that hung to her waist— although in most pictures, she wore it up. She had some sort of Asian heritage; in close-ups, the epicanthic folds of her eyes were visible. But what really interested me was her clothing. She wore a studded leather jacket and ripped black jeans and knee-high boots with more studs. Her nails were painted black. Her eyeshadow and lipstick were black. She looked like the walking intersection of Goth and Punk.

As I read more, I learned that she was half-Chinese; her mother had allegedly been, according to the Wikipedia article I was digging into, a spy for the Chinese government at one point. Her father, of course, was English, an economics professor at Cambridge. Margaret Moriarty was currently Chief AI Scientist for a company called Zodiac.

I clicked on Zodiac and then froze at the first sentence: *Zodiac is an American multinational technology conglomerate based in Lehi, UT.*

Which was, oh, all of thirty minutes away from Walker. And Zodiac had been the name of the encrypted folder Holmes had been trying to open on Watson's laptop.

Thirty minutes. Maybe longer if you took the roads on the back of Timp, but not by much. On the back roads, late at night, you might not pass anybody. Nobody to remember you coming or going.

I scanned the rest of the article about Zodiac, but I was too excited to make sense of the technobabble that described what Zodiac actually did. Then I went back and finished reading the Margaret Moriarty article, although the rest of it was a quick sketch of her education—Yale, which was kind of a surprise—and her AI career, which the article called *meteoric* twice in the same sentence. If they'd tried that in eighth-grade Language Arts, Mr. Scholz would have shat himself.

After another twenty minutes of reading about Moriarty, I gave up. The rest of the articles were either press releases that identified her in connection with some sort of corporate development (most of the articles were about Zodiac, although a few were other big tech names that I recognized) or they were quick bio pieces that didn't add anything to what I'd already read on Wikipedia. Nobody else mentioned the possibility that her mother had been a Chinese spy, and I wondered if that was just a prank—something a bored intern at Zodiac had slipped into the Wikipedia page that nobody had vetted yet.

When I'd finished, I shut down the computer. I tried to run through facts, but all I could come up with were two: Margaret Moriarty had some kind of link to Watson, and Taylor had told me to screw off for the afternoon.

Eventually, I stopped thinking about it. I locked up the maintenance building and jogged over to the cottage. I picked the right spots on the steps and the porch, making sure to choose the boards that wouldn't squeak. I eased the front door open an inch and stopped to listen. TV voices came back to me—a lady who sounded kind of like a donkey was lecturing someone about personal responsibility. Then Dad snored, and I slipped into the house. He'd fallen asleep in his recliner; the judge lady on TV was really letting this white girl have it. I plucked the keys from the ring near the door, and then I hurried to the truck.

I stopped when I got there, and I did some swearing. In the back seat of the cab, someone—obviously Dad—had packed a tarp. Even though I'd told him not to, he'd clearly tried to do some work after I'd left the house. I thought about pulling the tarp out, putting it away. But I was too amped up from my discovery. I got behind the wheel, started the truck—which took longer than I liked, with a lot more chugging and whining than it used to—and grabbed one of Dad's CDs at random from the visor holder. Foo Fighters. "This is a Call." I turned it all the way up and started down the canyon.

Utah (in general), and Utah Valley (in particular), didn't make sense to people who weren't from here; Moeka Ishii had moved to Salt Lake with her family in sixth grade, and I still remembered all the questions. Why is everything closed on Sundays? Which church are they talking about? Why does everyone spend so much time in their yard? I'd grown up there, so a lot of it just made sense, the way it does when you take things for granted. But after Moeka started asking questions, then I started asking questions too. I wondered about the yards too. Here we were, on the geographic border of a desert where people hadn't stopped killing each other over water rights all that long ago, and everybody had a bright green lawn like you saw in pictures of England or Ireland or, I don't know, Vermont. And the driving, that was another thing. Everybody was friendly in person, but once you got in a vehicle, God help you—every happy Mormon family was determined to get wherever they were going fast, maybe even get there first, and they wouldn't mind running you over if you got in their way.

I asked Dad about it one time.

"People are complicated," he said. He was trying to fix the lawn mower, which Mom hated; she wanted him to just take it to the shop. And when I pressed him, he said, "Jack, they're nice people; that doesn't make them perfect." Then he'd grinned. "But they sure do drive like assholes."

And they did. All the way up I-15.

For the most part, Utah Valley consisted of miles and miles of dirt and scrub. The east side of the valley, pretty much everything between the mountains and the lake, had been plowed under and paved over and turned into strip malls and subdivisions. Everything was built low, everything sprawling. For a long time, land had been cheap and plentiful, and nobody had bothered to plan for the fact that sooner or later, things would start to get crowded. The sun was high and bright, the air hazy with dust and exhaust and heat shimmer. Trees were losing their leaves. The only real color was on the slopes of Timp, where the scrub oak burned bright red.

At Lehi, I exited the highway and followed the directions I'd scribbled on a piece of paper, heading away from the residential part of the city and toward the new development, where other tech companies had built headquarters and satellite offices. When I spotted the Zodiac sign—a huge, stainless-steel monstrosity—I turned, and the building came into view. My first thought was that it looked like something out of the future. Future-industrial—maybe that's what Ms. Prinze would have called it. It was a sprawling, multi-story building with glass walls, like someone had dissected it for an exhibit. Massive steel supports slanted dramatically, and everywhere I looked, wire mesh panels and concrete slabs seemed to be serving as decorations. The sun raked it with white-hot tines; I had to blink and lower the visor.

As I drove toward the building, I started running through the next part in my head. There would be people at Zodiac on a Sunday afternoon—I'd been on enough dates-slash-hookups (my favorite app was Prowler) with tech bros to know that they kept all sorts of weird hours. Getting to Moriarty wouldn't be easy—I wasn't stupid enough to believe that—but I didn't think it would be complicated. All I had to do was get to a receptionist, heck, even a security guard, and tell them I needed to talk to Margaret Moriarty. They'd probably look at me like I was crazy, but I'd just stay cool and keep asking. Eventually, they'd call her because they'd realize they couldn't shake me, and I figured she'd tell them she didn't know who I was. She'd probably tell them to kick me off campus. But then I'd say, *Tell her it's about Sarah Watson*, and it'd be like in the movies—she'd have to talk to me.

I was still fleshing out this plan, considering contingencies, wondering if maybe I should say *Watson* instead of *Sarah Watson*, when I saw the next sign: WELCOME TO ZODIAC'S CAMPUS. And then there were arrows and words like LEO and CANCER and ARIES. I slowed. Some jagweed in a Tesla behind me laid on the horn. Then he hit the accelerator and whipped around me. I stared at the campus that was opening up in front of me. It wasn't just one building. It wasn't just one place where I could walk in and ask for Margaret Moriarty. I could see ten buildings climbing the foothills, and to judge by the sign, there were even more that I couldn't see yet. My foot hovered over the gas. I could still try it. I could go into the first building, find somebody, and tell them I wanted to talk to Margaret Moriarty. But what if they just looked at me? What if they had no idea what I was talking about?

In the seat behind me, the tarp rustled, and I shouted. I hit the gas, and then, almost as quickly, I slammed my foot on the brakes. Heart pounding, I twisted around in my seat.

Holloway Holmes sat up from where he'd been hiding under the tarp. He pushed the plastic off him, cramming it down into the footwell, and straightened his hair. I realized he was looking at himself in the rearview mirror.

"What the hell?" I asked, and my voice might have been squeakier than usual. He was still fixing his hair, so I gave it another go. "Jesus Christ, what the hell are you doing back there?"

"Following you." He glanced at me, and then a horn blatted, and he looked over his shoulder to study the BMW behind us. When he turned forward, he pointed to the left. "Maggie's office is in Scorpio—that way."

"What do you mean, following me?"

The Beamer honked again—longer this time.

"Is there more than one meaning?" Holmes cocked his head. His eyes were the same color as all that steel and concrete. A series of staccato honks came from the outraged tech bro still waiting for us, and he said, "I think he wants us to move."

"Oh my God," I whispered. "What is going on?"

But I took my foot off the brake, and the truck rolled forward. I turned in the direction Holmes had pointed, following signs toward Scorpio.

Holmes settled back against the seat. He was fixing his hair again. Then he stopped, frowning at me in the rearview mirror. "Did you really think my password was cutebutt?"

"Oh my actual God," I said under my breath, sinking down into my seat as I died a little.

Chapter 12

The Scenic Route

I parked where Holmes indicated, a large asphalt lot that looked almost as new as the cars and SUVS parked there—all of them shiny, all of them with luxury trims, all of them probably with fewer than twenty thousand miles on them. Even on a Sunday, the place looked busy. If I knew how to boost a car, and if a chop shop only gave me a fraction of what they were worth, I still could have made enough from that one lot to pay for college. And, hell, maybe med school.

By the time I shifted into park and killed the engine, I felt like my brain had caught up with this brand-new nightmare. I turned around in my seat to face Holmes. He was reading something on his phone.

"You broke into my truck."

He looked up.

"And you stowed away."

He blinked.

"And you—you hid under a tarp and were silent for the entire ride." I was having a hard time coming up with complete sentences. "In my truck."

"I think that's the definition of stowing away," Holmes said. "Although it's possible you can only stow away on a ship. I'd need to check the dictionary."

"You need to check the dictionary," I said. Then I laughed. "Because, what? I guess it's not installed on your mainframe."

"Mainframe computers aren't like personal computers, and I don't think anyone has needed to install a dictionary program or application since high-speed internet made it possible to—"

I was making a high-pitched noise in the back of my throat that I couldn't seem to stop.

Holmes cocked his head again. The corner of his mouth twitched—not a smile, and not intentional. "You seem on edge."

I laughed again. "Do I?"

He nodded. Aside from that tic at the corner of his mouth, his features were smooth, his face expressionless. It was oddly calming. I mean, it made me feel like I was hysterical in comparison, but it helped me take a step back from everything and breathe. I rubbed my forehead. I looked him over again.

"How?" I said.

"Your father was asleep, and you leave the keys by the carport door."

"Great. You were in my house. Did you go through my underwear drawer while you were at it?"

To my surprise, Holmes turned red. "Of course not."

"Why?"

"Underwear drawers are private—"

"No, Jesus." Pinching the bridge of my nose, I gestured with my free hand to the truck.

"Oh. Because you had information and you weren't willing to give it to me."

"Oh my God."

"I did try to ask." He seemed to think I needed clarification because he said in a questioning tone, like I might have forgotten, "In the maintenance garage?"

"I should leave you here. I should make you get out of the truck, and I'll leave you here, and fuck, I don't know, maybe I'll go bowling."

"You don't like bowling," Holmes said. "You like baseball, but you also played football your freshman year of high school, and you've been to at least one basketball game and planned on going to more, although I don't think you did."

I stared at him.

His blush deepened. "There are bowling coupons in your trash. And pictures of you in your football uniform in the kitchen. And a refillable cup from a Jazz game, but you've got pencils in it."

I pinched the bridge of my nose again. "There are so many things to say right now. Did you wake up my dad?"

Holmes looked offended.

"No," I said, "I guess you didn't. Because you're too good a snoop."

"I am not a snoop."

"I bet you did go through my underwear drawer. So help me God, H, if you took my good trunks, I am going to lose my shit."

Those bright spots in his cheeks looked like embers. "You're being crass."

I studied him, and I got another surprise. Holmes wasn't just embarrassed. He was...mortified. He shifted in his seat, his head turned away. His eyes were wet, and he was staring at something and blinking rapidly.

"Hey," I said. "It was a joke. Well, mostly. You are a snoop."

He gave a stiff nod. He still wasn't looking at me.

"Look, forget it. I was just saying dumb stuff because you spooked me."

All he did was nod, but some of the stiffness eased in his body.

I watched him for another moment, trying to figure out what had happened and how hard it would be to stay mad at him. Then I gave up and said, "So, I'm going out on a limb here, but I figure I'm not going to get an apology."

"For what?"

"Yeah, that's what I thought. Ok, we'll move past that. Why did you think Margaret was involved in Watson's death? And yes, cute butt, I read your journal or notebook or whatever you call that thing where you write all your crazy."

Holmes opened his mouth at *cute butt*, but then he paused and said, "She's a Moriarty. If someone kills a Watson, it makes sense to look at the Moriartys first."

"Uh huh..."

"Do you know who James Moriarty was?"

"Is that Professor Moriarty? Like, Sherlock Holmes's nemesis?"

Holmes nodded. "He was the spider in the web—the master criminal, managing an empire of pain and suffering. But he stayed at the center of the web, pulling strings, while everyone else did his dirty work. Among other things, he employed assassins to attempt to kill Sherlock Holmes. And, of course, John Watson."

"But that was, I don't know, a hundred years ago. You're not seriously telling me that your families are still, what? Rivals?"

Holmes frowned. "The Moriartys are what they are. The Holmeses are too. And the Watsons."

"That's nuts."

Holmes scowled. He was way too good-looking for a serious scowl, and besides, this was like remedial-level Scowling for Robots, but I have to admit he gave it a solid try.

"I'm serious," I said. "Families change. People change. Sure, I've got a lot of stuff in common with my dad, but I'm not my dad. I'm different in a lot of ways." I offered a lopsided grin. "I hate bowling, for example. And I'm sure you're not like your dad in some ways."

Holmes stiffened again. He set his jaw. When he spoke, the words were stilted. "You're welcome to think whatever you like, but I'm telling you, our families are...entangled." Then he fixed me with those hard gray eyes and said, "And don't talk about my father."

The wind pushed against the truck, howling against the steel. Where the asphalt ended and the scrub began, a tumbleweed rocked back and forth, not quite able to get free from the Russian thistle it had gotten tangled in.

"Ok," I said. "That's not really the point, I guess. You think Margaret Moriarty had something to do with Watson's death. So do I."

"Why?"

"Because I told you: I've got information."

"What information?"

"Well, for starters, I know that Margaret Moriarty called Watson the night she was killed."

I hadn't actually seen Holmes reboot before, but I realized now, watching his jaw hang, his eyes soften and lose their focus, that it needed to happen more frequently. When he wasn't looking so ferociously intense all the time, like he meant to chew his way through a brick wall, he looked, well, human. Maybe Holmes bots came with a reset switch.

"What do you mean?"

"Is there more than one meaning?" I tried to copy his voice.

He scowled again, and this time, he did better. "The details, Jack. Now."

"Yowza. So bossy. I told you: Margaret called Watson. It was right after I found her; I was standing there when the phone rang." In a defensive tone I couldn't quite shake, I added, "The screen only showed the initials MM, but who else could it be?"

Holmes's eyes had regained their closed-off intensity. For almost a full minute, he was silent. Then he said, to himself, his voice so low I could barely hear him, "Maggie called her?"

"Looks like it. So, now we've got to get in there and talk to her. Find out why she called Watson."

"She might have been—"

"Establishing an alibi," I said with a grin and tapped my head. "Light years ahead of you."

The corner of his mouth was twitching again. "There could, of course, be other explanations."

"Totes."

He stared at me. "The call could have been completely unrelated to Watson's death."

"Yeppers."

It was obvious he was trying not to say more, but the words slipped out of him: "It's unwise to reach conclusions without all the data."

"Insufficient data," I said with a smirk. "Does not compute."

"Are you always this annoying?"

"It depends."

His eyes narrowed to slits of storm.

"You're supposed to ask me, 'On what?'" I prompted.

It seemed impossible, but those eyes narrowed further.

"On how much fun it is," I told him. "In case you're wondering. Come on. We'll go in there, and we'll ask for Margaret and say it's about Watson—"

"Are you out of your mind? We'll be lucky if all they do is throw us off campus."

"But she called Watson," I said. "And we need to talk to her."

"You've never met a Moriarty, have you? They don't do anything except what they want, and what they want—what they always want—is to make life harder for any Holmes they can find. If Margaret's thinking quickly, she'll probably try to have us framed for corporate espionage or sabotage or—"

"Streaking," I suggested.

"No, that's not nearly serious enough."

"It's not a victimless crime."

Holmes went for the hat trick of scowls and withdrew inside himself. The wind battered the truck. The sun blazed on the glass of the Zodiac building. The curve where Holmes's shoulder joined his neck was slender and smooth. I'd thought of oil painting when I saw him, but now I was thinking about statues. Ms. Prinze had taught us about form and negative space. Good old Ms. Prinze. The form of the sculpture. And the space around it that activates it. And I thought, looking at the wren's wing of his shoulder, what is the negative space that activates Holloway Holmes? It would be another body. The head slotting into his shoulder. One thigh fitted between his legs. A hand at the small of his back.

Then Holmes shook himself. "Are you dehydrated?"

I had to work moisture into my mouth. Then I quirked a smile. "The kids just say thirsty these days."

"Dehydration is serious, Jack."

"Oh yeah. I'm starting to think I am seriously thirsty."

After a moment of silent consideration, Holmes said, "You are completely unintelligible sometimes."

"Hey, I resemble that remark." I offered another smile. "That's a dad joke, which I think is like poison to robot systems."

"Robots can't be poisoned because they're not organic—" He stopped himself, his hand tight on the door handle, and got out of the truck.

I wondered if it was supposed to be this much fun. Or, for that matter, this easy.

When I got out, I saw that Holmes had brought a backpack with him. He had it on the ground between his feet, and he was drawing out a gray blazer that looked close enough to match the chinos. He shrugged into the jacket. Then he reached into the backpack and produced a red power tie.

As he worked it under his collar, I said, "I know suit porn is a thing—"

He made a choking noise, yanked on his collar, and turned to spit onto the asphalt. Then he glared at me.

"—but," I continued with eyebrows raised, "I'm not sure that's going to get us past security."

"I don't know what suit porn is—"

I opened my mouth.

"—and don't tell me," he said in a rush. For a moment, he worked on the tie some more. Then, in a more normal voice, he said, "The Holmeses are masters of disguise. I'm going to infiltrate the building as a federal agent."

The laugh burst out of me before I could stop it.

Holmes stopped. He became very still. Then he looked at me, and in a surprisingly rumbly voice for such a skinny-assed white boy, he said, "What?"

I shook my head.

"I have a badge," he said.

I covered my mouth.

"This is going to work." He yanked on the tie. "I've done it before."

Gesturing him over, I nodded. I took the tie away from him and began to fix it. I had to try twice before I could say it without breaking down laughing, but I finally managed to ask, "Can I see the badge?"

He must have suspected something because his brows drew together and the corner of his mouth was twitching like crazy, but he reached into the blazer's pocket and took out a badge holder. I flipped it open.

Do not laugh, I told myself. But my jaw was trembling.

The top half of the badge holder contained an ID card. It had a picture of Holmes, although the name said Juni Cortez, and it identified him as a special agent for the Department of Investigation. In his suit and tie and Ivy League haircut, he looked all of twelve years old. The bottom half of the badge holder held the badge itself and an affidavit—or whatever you called it—signed by the US Attorney General. It looked legit. For all I knew, it was legit.

"What?" Holmes asked again.

"Nothing," I said. "I'm sure it's going to be great."

He huffed a breath.

"Plus, it'll come in super handy when you film *Spy Kids 3: The Boy Who Boinked*."

Holmes snatched the badge out of my hand.

"Come on," I said, laughing. I still had a hold of his tie, so he couldn't get far. "I'm just teasing."

"Do you have any idea how much this cost?"

"Ok, calm down."

"This is a real badge. Even the badge number is real; it would hold up to light investigation."

"Hey," I said, knotting the tie. "I'm sorry. I didn't mean to hurt your feelings."

"You did not hurt my feelings!"

The shout echoed through the parking lot. I was pretty sure it was the first time I'd heard him raise his voice. I smoothed the tie down, and I stepped back. The Vans' old soles squeaked on the asphalt.

"You think this is a bad idea," Holmes said. His voice was quiet again, but it was taut. "Explain."

I shook my head and held up my hands.

"Don't do that," Holmes said in that same voice. "I don't need to be coddled."

"Ok," I said slowly. "I think that you look way too young to pass for a federal agent. I don't think it's a bad idea, but I don't think you can pull it off yet. Maybe in five years. Actually, maybe in ten. You've got really good skin, and you're always going to look younger than you are."

"It's worked before."

"At a multinational tech conglomerate?"

His face twisted. He slid two fingers behind the knot of the tie like he was about to yank it off.

"Don't mess that up," I said. "I worked hard on that. Besides, you look good."

"If my idea is so stupid—"

"Hey, hey, hey. I didn't say it was stupid. I said I didn't think it was going to work. And I'm sorry I laughed; whoever made that badge for you, they put a joke in there. That's what the *Spy Kids* crack was about."

Some of the tension in his face slackened. "I didn't bring any other disguises—"

"Thank God," I muttered under my breath. When his head snapped toward me, I held up my hands and smiled again. "Because I don't think you need a different one. We just need to tweak this one."

"Tweak it how?"

I studied him for a minute. Then I slid the tie loose and dropped it back into the backpack. I took hold of his oxford, my hands riding the ridge of his hips, and he twisted away.

"Hold still," I said, trying to grab his shirt again.

"Don't." He put a hand between us, his body still angled away from me like I might rush him. He was breathing too fast. When I didn't say anything, his gaze dropped to the asphalt, and he said, "I need you not to stand so close."

"Oh. Yeah." I pulled the collar of my polo up over my nose, breathed in, and made a face. "Sorry—I missed laundry day."

He was still staring at the asphalt.

After almost another ten seconds of him frozen like that, I said, "Untuck your shirt."

He yanked the tail of the shirt out from the waistband of the chinos.

"Can you smooth it down? It can look wrinkly, but maybe not quite so—no, right here, run your hand over it—"

When I moved, he retreated a full yard.

"Bro," I said, "I don't smell that bad."

He focused on the shirt, flattening it with the heels of his hands. Finally, he looked up, his eyes not quite meeting mine.

"Looks good," I said. "Can you cuff your trousers? Tight cuffs, just above the chukkas."

He did it exactly right, which made sense, since I thought he did most things exactly right—well, except disguises, apparently.

I gave him another once-over, grinned, and offered a thumbs-up. "Nailed it."

Looking down at himself, he shook his head. "What am I? A homeless person?"

I burst out laughing. "You haven't seen a lot of homeless people, have you? You are now Spencer Cole. No, wait. Spencer Dynamite. No, never mind, Spencer Cole. Nobody really has the last name Dynamite, do they?"

Holmes stared at me.

"You're a tech bro," I said. "Now you just have to act super awkward and talk about, um, some feminist coding project that you think has its heart in the right place but is fundamentally misguided, and...oh you've got to talk about your fitness tracker. Do you have a fitness tracker?"

"No."

"Then you've got to talk about getting one. And how you've been doing a lot of research. You can say something about algorithms, right? Of course you can. Ok, give me five seconds."

As I turned to the truck and rummaged around in the back seat, Holmes said, "I am not a tech bro."

"That's a good line," I said as I came up with an old Utes tee that I used as a work shirt. "Use that one."

"This disguise won't work, I—"

I stripped out of the Walker polo, tossed it into the truck, and turned around as I dragged the Utes tee over my head. Holmes was staring at me.

"It won't work," I prompted as I got one arm through a sleeve. I got the other arm in, and I straightened the tee. "H?"

He made a questioning noise, but he didn't seem to have really heard me.

Checking my hair in the mirror, I tried to fix it and gave up. I grabbed a toolbox from the cab—miscellaneous stuff, sockets and ratchets and screwdrivers and pliers—and shut the door. I gave my hair one last check, shook my head in disgust, and said, "Ok, ready."

It sounded like it cost Holmes a lot of effort to say, "Hm?"

I glanced at him. Those gray eyes were softly focused again. Color stained his cheeks. "What's wrong with you?"

He blinked. If anything, he got redder. "Nothing."

"It's a good plan. It's going to work."

"I don't even know what the plan is."

"We go in there. You tell them you're tech bro extraordinaire Samuel Cole—"

"Spencer."

"I'm pretty sure it's Samuel."

"I think I know my own name," Holmes snapped. When my grin slipped out, he started blushing all over again and said, "You did that on purpose."

"Come on." I started toward the Scorpio building, sockets jingling as they slid in the toolbox. "Tell them I'm a plumber, and you're supposed to take me upstairs. They probably won't ask, but if they do, tell them you left your ID in the office when you came down to get me."

"But why would I come down to get you?"

"I don't know. You're a control freak? Is that too on the nose?"

"I came down to get you because you're bothersome and untrustworthy and…and mischievous." He kind of limped to an end, and he refused to look at me.

I yanked the door open, and climate-controlled air, cool against the September day, rushed out to us. "You have some seriously strong feelings about your plumber."

He stalked past me.

"Mischievous?" I asked him to his back.

He walked faster.

I let him get a head start. The lobby matched the exterior of the buildings: more concrete, tilted walls of glass, huge columns that broke up the open space, and conversation areas made up of minimalist leather-upholstered seating. I doubted anyone had ever sat on the furniture, let alone had an actual conversation there. The open space and the concrete made for a lot of echoes, even though only a handful of people were in the lobby. In case you forgot this was a tech company, they'd hung huge transparent displays on the walls, where digital patterns flowed and reassembled. Looking up at all that empty space made me dizzy, so I kept my gaze fixed on the security gates and the guard—a beefy white guy who probably looked great with his shirt off.

Holmes glanced back at me, and I gave him a thumbs-up. For a moment, doubt filled his face. Then it was gone, and the Holmes bot was back. He turned forward and continued toward the security gates and the guard.

Following him slowly, I took out my phone, checked the paper where I'd copied down information from the computer, and placed a call to the Zodiac main number. I kept pressing zero to get through a string of automated menus until a woman said brightly, "This is Sally with Zodiac. How may I help you?"

"Yeah, Alex here. I'm in Scorpio, and I cannot get a hold of the guy at the security desk. Am I calling the wrong number?"

"This isn't the right number for internal support—"

"I can't get the right number. We're a fucking tech company, and we can't even get our own phones to work. At this point, I might as well walk down there myself."

Silence dragged out one beat, then two. Then Sally said, "Hold, please, while I transfer you."

I got a burst of hold music—something with a lot of drums—and then, twenty yards ahead of me, where Holmes was talking to the guard, the phone rang. The guard picked up, and I turned my back to him.

"Scorpio front desk," he said.

"Yeah, this is Alex." I went for a tech bro voice. "I've been trying to reach you for twenty minutes. Look, is my plumber here?"

"I'm sorry, sir. Your last name?"

"I've got shit coming out the walls here, and that is not a fucking exaggeration. It's coming out of the light fixtures. I sent that wiener Cole down there to bring him up. Oh my God, Jill, use the fucking flowerpot to catch some of it. If that plumber isn't up here in the next five minutes, I'm going to have you clean it up. What's your name? Who am I talking to?"

"Great news, sir: it looks like the plumber just arrived. I'll send him up with Mr. Cole right now."

"Jill, for the love of cocks—hey, buddy, I'm not going to ask you again: what's your name?"

I turned around in time to see the guard disconnect. He did it so fast that the phone slipped out of the cradle, and he had to do it again. He stood halfway up from his seat, waving at me like I was supposed to hurry, but I took my time. I was pocketing my phone as I reached him.

"Sorry," I said, directing the comment somewhere between the two men. "If I don't pick up, she loses her shit."

"Yeah, well, Mr. Alex is waiting for you," the guard said. He pressed something, and the security gates opened. Glancing at Holmes, he said, "You're taking him up there, right? Mr. Alex wants him ASAP."

Holmes gave me a hard look. "We're going right now."

He stepped through the gate. No alarms blared. Steel shutters didn't come down, sealing off the doors and windows. I figured maybe Margaret Moriarty was watching us on the security cameras, petting an albino cat or something, but if she was, she hadn't decided to activate whatever trap Holmes was expecting. Not yet, anyway. I followed him as he crossed toward the bank of elevators.

Instead of stopping to take one of the cars, Holmes continued past the elevators. That made sense; in a place like this, you might need an ID badge to use the elevators, and while I thought we could badger the security guard into helping us get upstairs, I also realized that might entail some additional risk—he'd want to know what floor "Mr. Alex" worked on, and the wrong answer might make him start asking more questions that we couldn't answer.

Holmes had clearly reached the same conclusion. He led me down a short hallway and then stopped at a door marked STAIRS along with several of those emergency warning placards—place of refuge, that kind of thing. A keycard reader showed the door was secure. Holmes glanced both ways as he took out his wallet. His movements had suddenly become confident, almost relaxed, and he pulled out a card without even looking at it. In one quick movement, he slid it between the door and the frame, sliced down, and yanked the door open.

For the second time that day, I breathed out in relief. No alarms. Again.

"Up," Holmes whispered as he stepped into the stairwell.

I followed him, letting the door fall shut behind me, and we took the stairs. Fluorescents provided dim light, and unlike the rest of the building, no attempt had been made to give this place a techno-future vibe. It seemed perfectly serviceable, and I realized that's probably what it was meant for—service access. Or emergencies. But not day-to-day use. The sound of our footsteps and the rattle of the toolbox were the only noises as we hurried.

"I thought that only worked on cheap doors," I said as I trotted at Holmes's side.

"It works on all spring latches."

"Did you know it was a spring latch?"

He looked over at me. He had that little line between his eyebrows again. "How would I have known that?"

I tried to process that for the next flight of stairs. Then I asked the most important question: "Was that a Café Rio loyalty card?"

It was hard to tell in the stairwell's gloom, but it looked like Holmes was blushing again.

"It's ok if it was," I said. "But I need to know if you get the burritos enchilada style."

"Of course I get them enchilada style," he snapped, still not looking at me. He started taking the steps two at a time. "I'm not insane."

Ok, I thought, and I was surprised to realize I was grinning as I went after him. Item number three-hundred-and-whatever-the-hell: apparently

Holmes bots have a food port. I thought about repeating that sentence out loud, just to see his face, and my grin got even bigger.

It was a ten-story building, and when we got to the tenth-floor landing, Holmes studied the door and frowned. It was a fire door like the others we had passed on our way up, although this door didn't have a half-lite of safety glass. It had a keycard reader. It didn't have a handle or a knob or anything to grab on to.

"Are you going to try your magic burrito card?" I asked.

"Silence," Holmes said. "I'm thinking."

"Did you really say 'silence'? Like a cartoon villain?"

But he didn't respond. After a moment, he turned and started down the steps again. His voice floated back to me.

"The weakest point of any security system is the human element," he said. "The human element is the easiest to compromise—"

"Unless you forget to lock the door. Then the door is the easiest element to compromise."

He shot me a look over his shoulder. "—and the human element," he said as though I hadn't spoken, "is the surest way to bypass high-tech security features."

"Yeah, I know. I called the guard, remember?"

On the ninth-floor landing, which had a normal door, Holmes repeated his trick with the Café Rio card.

"What's so special about the tenth floor?" I asked.

"Maggie has always preferred her privacy." He didn't pull the door open all the way this time; instead, he looked at me.

"Steal a keycard," I said. "I figured it out too, me and my big janitor brain."

Something strange flickered in his expression. Then it went out, and I was staring into the raw concrete of those gray eyes. "We'll need to find someone likely to have access to the tenth floor. A security guard, possibly. Perhaps a mid-level executive. Ideally, we'll obtain the card by subterfuge or stealth. If necessary, though, I'm not opposed to physically incapacitating a target."

"Aww." I offered him my biggest smile. "I bet you say that to all the boys."

His cheeks caught fire again, and he yanked the door open. He started down the hall first, and I followed him. It was about what I expected the inside of one of these places to look like: this end of the hallway had standard interior doors that probably led to supply rooms, utility closets, that kind of thing, but after twenty yards, the hallway ended, and we passed through a large, open work area. There were all kinds of seating: high and low, soft and hard, chairs and couches and enormous bean bags. There were these giant floating things that I guessed were nap pods but that looked like maybe they'd clone you while you were asleep. One area had a sink and microwave, as well as snacks(the expensive ones), and coffee, and a cooler case stocked with soda and juice that you could see through the glass door. Another area just had toys—lots of Legos, but also stress balls, tiny foam basketballs and a tiny hoop, that kind of thing. The art on the walls was all abstract and probably all expensive, and the air smelled almost like nothing—like an HVAC system with expensive air filters. Probably for all those tech bros who were sensitive to smells.

People were working here, but they didn't pay us any attention. One guy was in a polo and cargo shorts, his Tevas abandoned next to the couch where he lay with his feet planted against the wall. A girl in an enormous polka-dot hoop skirt and antique eyeglasses was channeling her inner *Good Will Hunting* on a whiteboard. A couple of fresh-out-of-the-packaging tech bros passed us. Even if they'd tried, they couldn't have been more cliched—for hell's sake, they were both wearing Patagonia quarter-zips.

"No, bro, I'm serious, you've got to try it. Intermittent fasting is the shit."

"No way, man, I'm going keto. It's the ultimate biohack."

This grade-A conversation was interrupted by a third tech bro (also in a Patagonia quarter-zip), who shouted, "Holy shit, Abrams," and then, in what was clearly meant to be a complimentary way, "This guy fucks!" The voices faded as they moved into a conference room, and the last thing I heard before the door swung shut was, "So, tell me what's getting you wet about this media portal?"

"Jesus," I said under my breath.

Holmes glanced at me, his face blank.

"Those guys," I prompted, tipping my head toward the conference room.

His face remained blank, and after a moment, I sighed and shook my head.

As we made a loop of the floor, we passed a few more workspaces before we reached another hallway, this one with offices that had, you know, actual walls and doors. A lot of the doors stood open, and many of the offices were empty. Holmes made a curt gesture before turning in to one of the rooms. I kept walking. The door to the next office was open, and the lights were off. I swung around the doorway. Then I stopped.

An older guy, probably in his thirties, sat behind the desk, studying the screen of his laptop. He was cute in a *Mad Men* kind of way. Lots of daddy vibes under the blazer and the crisp white shirt. He definitely focused on arms and chest days. When he looked up, he frowned.

"Sorry," I said and hoisted the toolbox with a jangle. A hint of steel and oil wafted up to me as I smiled. "You don't literally have shit coming out of your walls, so I think I got the wrong office."

The guy laughed, and it was a nice, low chuckle. He leaned back from his desk. He looked me up and down. His smile shifted. He set the Daddy Ray to a hundred and gave me a blast. "No problem," he said in a voice that was almost as low as the chuckle. "Shit coming out of the walls would be a relief, actually. At least you can do something about that. There's nothing I can do about last month's numbers." Then genuine amusement whetted the grin. "And I meant you, specifically, by the way. I'm totally incompetent when it comes to anything handy."

And there it was: the opening. It was like riding a bike. It didn't matter if they were sixteen or thirty-six or sixty. I slouched against the doorway, found the right smile, and adjusted my hold on the toolbox so my biceps was on display. At the back of my head, I imagined telling Holmes about tickets to the gun show, and that made my smile even bigger. "You don't look like you're doing too bad," I said. Then I shrugged, and I looked at him, and I held the look. "You look pretty good to me."

He pushed back from the desk, rocked back in his chair, and touched two fingers to his chest. "Anthony."

I pointed to his nameplate. "Mr. Vice-President."

He gave me that same low chuckle again, and this time, I felt it at the base of my spine. His fingers were still touching his chest, and his eyes stayed on my face. Maybe he only went for the young ones, I thought. There were guys like that—chicken-hawks. They only went for the under-twenties. They were one of the reasons I mostly stuck with girls.

Shifting my weight, I repositioned myself so I could look out of the corner of my eye and see down the hall. Holmes was standing there, arms folded across his chest, his mouth like a razor cut. I turned my attention back to Anthony. "So," I said slowly, "I need to find the bathroom. Maybe you have a minute to show me?"

"A minute?" He grinned, and he made me think of this boy from my old school. Jerzey—I shit you not, that was his name—had a grin like that when he told everyone Brilee Winger had jerked him off after seminary. "I think we can do better than that."

When he stood, he was taller than I expected, and he came around the desk with the casual grace of an athlete. He didn't touch me, but he got close enough to me in the doorway that I could feel the heat off his body, and I realized how much bigger he was than me—and I wasn't a skinny-assed Holmes bot to begin with. Anthony smirked, not making any effort to hide how he was staring at me, and when I retreated, he stepped out into the hall and began to pull the door shut. Then he stopped.

"Actually," he said, cupping himself, that jerkoff-boy smile getting wider, "why don't I have you take a look at something in my office first?"

That was when Holmes crashed into him from behind. Anthony staggered forward, colliding with me, sending the ratchets and sockets clattering. Coffee arched up behind him, spattering the wall and the door; some of it rained back down on the shoulders of what had to be an expensive blazer. His head cracked against the door jamb, and he swore. Then he spun around.

"What the fuck is wrong with you?"

Holmes was clutching an eco-friendly disposable cup, which was now completely empty. More coffee stained Holmes's oxford and blazer, although significantly less than what I could see on Anthony's back. "I'm sorry. Here, let me—"

For a few moments, the two of them did an awkward dance, Holmes trying to wipe coffee off of Anthony's jacket—and, I noticed, in the process getting his hands in Anthony's pockets—and Anthony trying to fend him off.

Finally he shoved Holmes back and wiped one hand down his shirt. "You're sorry! Hey, fucktard, this jacket cost me two thousand dollars! You'd better be more than sorry!"

"I was looking at my phone. You really shouldn't be standing in the middle of the hallway."

I could only see the back of Anthony's expensive-looking haircut, but his silence spoke for itself. When he finally managed to talk again, he sounded strangled, "I shouldn't beat the shit out of you, that's what I shouldn't do."

"No," Holmes said in what he probably honestly believed was a helpful tone. "You shouldn't."

"You little fuck. Do you think you're funny?"

"God," I said, sliding out from behind Anthony. "He bumped into you. Chill."

"Hold on." Anthony was clearly trying to reload the daddy vibes. "I'm handling this, and then I want to talk to you."

For a moment, white-hot fury glowed in Holmes's face.

"Uh," I said, "I'd better get back to work."

"You don't even know where the bathroom is," Anthony said, and it sounded like he was still fighting the edge in his voice. "I'll show you."

"Yeah, no, I'm good." I inched backward. He turned to look at me, but he didn't follow. I shot him a half-wave, turned, and hurried down the hall. I glanced back to see him round on Holmes just before he started shouting again.

I navigated the maze of offices until I found the stairwell again. This one wasn't secured from the inside—presumably, if you were up here and needed to get out, say, in a fire, they didn't want you to worry about a keycard. I stepped out onto the landing, propped the door open with the toolbox, and waited.

Holmes arrived two minutes later. He was trying to blot coffee from his shirt with a paper towel. It was getting easier to read the microexpressions on his face—the tiny lines around his mouth and eyes as he tried to lift the coffee with the paper towel. When he stepped onto the landing, though, he looked up at me, and the lines around his mouth and eyes deepened.

"What?" I asked. "You didn't get it?"

He fished in his pocket and came up a moment later with the keycard.

"Will it work? He's a VP, so I figure there's at least a shot."

Holmes shrugged. I'd never seen anybody so interested in a coffee stain before.

"Ok…" I said. When he didn't rise to the bait, I asked, "What's going on?"

"Nothing." He bit the word into two syllables. "I'm trying to clean my shirt."

"Why are you mad at me about that? You're the one who decided to spill coffee on him."

"I'm not mad."

"Oh, great, I'm so relieved."

Holmes made a disgusted noise, wadded up the paper towel, and shoved it into his pocket. He started up the stairs, and I had to yank the toolbox free from the door and hurry after him.

"Because, you know," I said, and his shoulders tightened at the sound of my voice, "this is how normal people act when they're mad."

He started taking the stairs two at a time. So did I.

"And you're all out of stairs, dumbass," I said when we reached the tenth-floor landing, "so unless you want me shouting at your back while we walk through the halls, you'd better tell me what kind of bug got in your coding."

He whirled around, and this time, they weren't microexpressions: his cheeks were red, his eyes wide, his pupils constricted—the color of old iron in concrete.

I had the brief but distinct thought: Oh shit.

"We were supposed to find an acceptable target together. You weren't supposed to—to take an unacceptable risk."

"I walked in on him," I said, fighting the rising volume of my voice. "He was right there. What was I supposed to say? 'Oops, you're not the guy I wanted to rob?'"

"You didn't have to—to make a spectacle of yourself." Holmes sounded choked with his anger. "Drawing attention to yourself. Pandering to his interest."

It took me a couple of blinks for that to land. "You're mad because I was flirting with him? He thought I was cute, and at first, I was just trying to cover my ass, and then I saw he was VP, and I thought—"

"Trust me," Holmes said, his lip curling. "I know exactly what you thought."

"What the fuck did you just say?"

Holmes stared at me. He was breathing hard, but then, so was I. I couldn't seem to get enough air. The stairwell had contracted around us.

"We got the card, didn't we?" I said, trying to level out my voice. "It worked, didn't it? So I don't understand why you care—"

"I don't care!" The shout echoed up and down the stairwell. The sound of it shocked me back to myself, and I realized I was standing there arguing with Holmes like he was a jealous boyfriend instead of—what? A cybernetic killing machine who I temporarily needed? He was biting his lip now, biting it so hard that his lip turned white under his teeth, about to draw blood. Then it was like somebody flipped all the breakers. The light went out of his face. His expression smooth. When he spoke, his voice was cool and flat. "I do not care."

I honestly had no idea what to say to that, so I let out a disbelieving breath and looked away.

A moment later, Holmes's steps moved toward the door, and then the keycard reader beeped. When I looked over, Holmes was holding the door open with his hip. He wasn't looking at me, but he was waiting, and I guess for robots that's some kind of peace offering. I followed him into the hall.

At first, the décor looked like what I'd seen on the floor below: the neutral paint tones, the abstract art on the walls, the doors that suggested utilitarian spaces located near the stairwell. But after a few minutes, I realized this space was different. There was no open floorplan, no nap pods, no Legos, no kitchen stocked with snacks. There weren't even that many doors. We passed a set of steel fire doors with a lot of complicated security—not only a keypad, but two different things that I thought were biometric readers. And then nothing. A long empty wall that ended with a door at the corner of the hall. The plaque next to it read: *Margaret Moriarty—Chief AI Scientist*.

Holmes glanced at me, and I nodded stiffly. He opened the door.

A woman sat in a wingback chair upholstered in what looked like black velvet, and my first impression of her was that she apparently liked a very specific style of outfit because Margaret Moriarty looked exactly as she had in her pictures: the ripped jeans, the studded leather jacket, the massive boots. The only difference was that her long hair was held up in a bun with two pencils sticking out of it. I put her at about ten years older than us.

She looked at her phone. "Seventeen minutes, Holloway. Did you take the scenic route?"

Chapter 13

Boys and Their Toys

I shifted my weight and glanced over my shoulder, waiting for the stormtroopers. But the hallway behind us remained empty. When I looked back, Margaret Moriarty was still staring at Holmes.

"Well," she finally said. "If you're just going to stand there, you might as well come in."

Holmes didn't move.

A moment limped past. Then another. I touched the small of his back and whispered, "H?"

He startled like I'd poked him. Then he took a step, and I followed him into the room.

The black velvet chairs, I realized, were only the beginning. The Goth-Punk intersection had clearly been the guiding principle behind Moriarty's interior design. With a touch of—what? I studied the enormous chandelier; the glass desk with chrome legs, where someone had added the delightful detail of fake blood running down the metal; a massive painting of a woman's hand wearing a slave bracelet and giving the room the middle finger; a vase made out of a skull—God, please let it be from a Halloween store—holding an arrangement of dead roses; a blood-colored leopard-print chaise pushed up under the massive corner window. The Queen Mother goes dark, I decided. Although even that didn't really capture it. A frame on one wall held a piece of digital artwork. Age progression, I realized. It started with a teenage Moriarty and accelerated through the aging process, then decomposition, until nothing but a skeleton stared back at us.

Great, I thought. There is someone even creepier than Supercreep.

"Sit down," Moriarty said. I could hear the English accent in her voice. It sounded—like they said on Netflix shows sometimes—posh. She was curled up, her legs tucked under her, and she gestured at the empty chairs. "Holloway, Holloway, Holloway. Biting your lip is really too much. It's a tell, darling; I thought Blackfriar would have trained you out of it by now."

I glanced over in time to see Holmes stop biting his lip, but then the corner of his mouth twitched. It explained a lot. More than I wanted to know, actually.

We sat, and the toolbox clanked as I set it on the floor next to me. Moriarty leaned forward. On the coffee table, a silver dish that looked like a human shoulder blade held an array of drugs. I recognized 'shrooms and joints and what I thought were tabs of acid. The paper backing had a stylized MM on it. I guessed she had a couple thousand dollars laid out in front of us. And that, I guessed, was just for guests.

Following my gaze, Moriarty nudged the silver dish toward us and took one of the tabs. She swallowed, her head tilted back. She had high cheekbones, a long neck, perfect skin. It was hard to call someone beautiful, though, when the digital art on the wall showed you what she looked like with maggots crawling around her eye sockets.

"LSD," she said in what she must have thought was an encouraging tone. "Please, help yourself."

"Uh, no," I said. "Thanks."

"Not to trip," she said with a laugh. "It's called microdosing. It's not enough to experience the hallucinogenic properties of the drug. It helps with focus. And it's a mood boost. The 'shrooms are for play, and the cannabis is to relax. Would you like to try?"

"No, thank you. The only microdosing I do is clean living and good old American sunshine."

She burst out laughing. "I like this one, Holloway. But you have to tell me: where do you keep finding them?"

"Why did you call Watson, Maggie?"

It was shocking, hearing Holmes after listening to Moriarty talk, how American he sounded. We were in America, and he sounded like an American, but he was a Holmes...God, even thinking through it, I sounded stupid to myself.

Moriarty was still for a moment.

"She died," I said. "Someone killed her. Did you know that?"

"Yes," Moriarty said softly. "I did."

"You called her the night she was killed," Holmes said. "Why?"

Moriarty straightened in her chair, her legs coming down, the boots clunking against the floor. "Why do you want to know?"

Holmes stared at her. The corner of his mouth was twitching.

"Do you know what happened to her?" I asked. "We're trying to—"

Something clicked in Holmes's throat, and he said, "Don't tell her."

"Let me guess," she said, studying me. "Jack Sixsmith Moreno. Six feet tall. A hundred and sixty-two pounds. You like the Dodgers. You watch a variety of Twitch streams, including several of the so-called Stream Queens. The last book you checked out from your school library was *The Catcher in the Rye*, which is so depressingly predictable that I want to encourage you not to be such a stereotype. And now an unpaid janitor. Tragic car accident, father disabled, so on and so forth. The good little boy trying to put his world back together with Sellotape. And, currently, the Utah County Sheriff's Department's primary person of interest in the death of Sarah Elizabeth Watson."

My throat was so tight it ached. I managed to smile. "A hundred and sixty-seven, now," I said. "I found a place that does buy-one get-one taco night."

A tiny curve touched her lips. "Oh, yes, Holloway, you've outdone yourself with this one."

He inched forward on his seat. "Answer the question, Maggie."

"We were supposed to meet."

"What? Why?"

For a moment, I could see her considering whether to tell us. Then she shrugged. "We were seeing each other."

Holmes's silence had a white-noise hiss behind it. When he spoke again, it was only one word: "Romantically?"

"Oh my God, you sound like you're twelve. We enjoyed each other's company. We helped each other. Did each other favors."

"What kind of favors?" I asked.

"Is this about Zodiac?" Holmes asked over me.

Clicking her tongue, Moriarty shook her head. "Holloway Harrowgate Holmes, this whole thing would be much cuter if you weren't wasting my time. I have a meeting in an hour with a Stanford professor I'm trying to poach."

"Is this about the IPO? What are your mother and father planning?"

That same tiny smile traced her mouth again. "It's like watching a puppy stumble around and bang his nose on things."

Holmes must have reached his limit because he bit his lip savagely at that, breathing hard through his nose. Before he could open his mouth, I sat forward and asked, "You said you did each other favors. What kind of favors?"

"How to explain..." She trailed off, eyebrows shooting up. "Jack, I happen to know you are not quite as innocent as your face might make one believe. Holloway, on the other hand, well, I'm not sure he's even learned about it in Health class yet. Despite the best efforts of that boy at Hewdenhouse—what was his name, darling? The one that had that terrible accident?"

Holmes was still breathing hard, blood staining his lip now, his fingers curled around the arms of the chair.

"Well, I suppose I can try to explain," Moriarty said with a smirk, "but it's different for boys, I imagine."

"Quit fucking around," I said. Moriarty raised her head, her eyes narrowing, and I felt like she was really looking at me for the first time. "Do you know who did this to Watson?"

Moriarty shifted, brushing the velvet's nap, and it was the only sound aside from Holmes's ragged breathing. "No," she finally said. "I don't."

"What kind of favors did you trade?"

"Information. That's always been the Watsons' stock in trade, didn't you know? Hawking their little stories, shilling rumors and half-truths to the highest bidder. Of course, Sarah took it to another level. She was quite clever, actually, unlike most Watsons. She figured out rather quickly that most people would pay more for discretion than they would for a good story."

I had to turn that one around in my head; Holmes spoke first: "She was blackmailing people?"

"Of course, darling. And, of course, selling stories about you."

The color drained from Holmes's face until the blood on his lip was the only bright spot left.

"You didn't know?" Moriarty laughed. "She sold dozens of them. Got quite a good price, too. Oh Holloway, darling, don't tell me you never suspected."

Holmes looked like she'd slapped him.

"Your face," she said. "I'm sorry, I am. Of course, I did think you'd have figured it out by now."

"Don't talk to him like that," I said. The rawness of my voice surprised me. "In fact, don't talk to him at all."

Moriarty raised an eyebrow as she turned to face me fully. "It's the truth. He ought to know, don't you think?"

"I think you want to hurt him, and it's just convenient that it happens to be true. Where were you Friday night?"

For the first time since we'd entered, the playfulness, the smug superiority, the twist-your-balls attitude—it all dropped away. "Now, Jack, what exactly are you asking me?"

"I'm asking where you were Friday night because I think you might have killed Watson."

Emotions flitted across her face like in Dad's old hacker movies, the lines of code streaming across a computer screen in glowing green text, too fast and too complicated for me to understand what I was seeing. And then her expression went blank.

"I was at a charity dinner. I sat at a table with the mayor of Salt Lake, the governor, and a senator. I imagine that for Holloway, three witnesses with unimpeachable credentials still won't be enough, so you can check the cameras. The event was held in the Joseph Smith Building—I'm sure they'll be happy to help a Holmes."

I stared at her, but her face didn't change. I glanced at Holmes.

"You have to believe I'll verify that," he said, his voice a rough approximation of its usual cold detachment.

"God, it's not even fun when I'm playing two steps ahead. You do realize you sound like one of those awful TV adaptations, don't you?" Moriarty sat up straighter, considered us for a moment, and then stood. She made her way around the desk. "I'll do you a favor, shall I? Because I…cared for Watson, and because watching you chase your tail is losing its fun. She was excited the last few weeks. More excited than I'd ever seen her. And nervous, too. I think she knew she was doing something dangerous." Moriarty's mouth quirked. "More dangerous than usual. She said she had something big. A story. A secret. She said someone would pay a fortune to keep this secret."

"If you cared about her," I said, "why aren't you trying to find whoever did this to her?"

"I said I cared about her; I didn't say I was suicidal."

She didn't do anything that I could see—she didn't press a red button dramatically, she didn't shout, "Guards"—but the next moment, the door flew open, and four stormtroopers rushed in. These guys didn't look like the bozo in the lobby. These guys wore body armor and tactical gear, with rifles hanging from straps across their shoulders and pistols holstered at their sides. Two of them had me out of my chair before I could finish turning around, and they slammed me into the wall. The other two went for Holmes, but he slipped out of the chair like he was boneless. He kicked it into their path, and the closest one stumbled into it. The second one kept going toward Holmes, but Moriarty lifted a finger, and he stopped.

"Let him go," Holmes said in a dead voice.

"My, my," Moriarty murmured.

"Tell them to get their fucking hands off Jack." He didn't sound American right then. He sounded upper-crust and hella pissed off.

"Holloway, darling, I'm going to make you a deal: I want to play a game, and if you're perfectly quiet and well behaved, I will let you have your toy back when we're finished. I might not even break him. But if you throw a fit, I'll have to call your father. How does that sound?"

With my cheek pressed against the wall, I could only see Holmes's face out of the corner of my eye. He was biting his lip, the blood freshly bright again, his gray eyes cutting between me and Moriarty.

"I'm fine," I said, although the words were a little smushed. "Not that anybody asked."

"Now, the game is called, 'Stop,'" Moriarty said. I could hear the smile in her voice even if I couldn't see her. "All you have to do is convince me to stop."

"Stop," Holmes said.

"Darling, that's not even close."

There was no signal that I could see, but one of the guards gripped my wrist and bent my finger back. The pain was sudden and intense, and I let out a shout. He applied more pressure, and I twisted—more out of instinct, the need to get away from the pain, than from any real hope that I'd be able to get away. It was useless; the second guard had me by the back of the neck, and between the two of them, there was no way for me to get loose. The one working on my finger applied a little more pressure, and this time, I shouted and couldn't stop. I could feel something straining in my hand, a bone or tendon or ligament forced beyond where it should have been, and the pain lit up the inside of my skull. In the background, I could hear Holmes shouting, "Stop!" over and over again.

Then, suddenly, the pressure was gone, and the pain ebbed. My throat hurt. My head hurt, and I vaguely remembered thumping it against the wall when I tried to get free. There was a noise in my throat, and I was fighting to keep it from slipping out. It was the second time in two days that someone had done this to me—first Holmes, and now Moriarty's thug. I was getting pretty fucking sick of it.

"Really, Holloway, if that's the best you can do, I'm afraid we might send you home with a broken toy after all. And put that knife away; my men will shoot your toy if you try anything so stupid."

I couldn't see Holmes now, or the knife, or Moriarty. I kept blinking my eyes, trying to get them clear, but they filled again immediately. I'd been helpless like this before. I remembered the feeling, the incredible weakness, the unreality of it all. I remembered being in the car, the pain, the knowledge that I needed to do something, only I couldn't do anything. I could make out the shape of Mom and Dad in the front seats, and they weren't moving.

The guard adjusted his grip on my hand, and he yanked it behind my back, forcing it up until it was somewhere between my shoulder blades. It felt like someone had run a hot wire from my shoulder down to my elbow and then looped it back up from elbow to wrist. I went up on tiptoes.

"I'd like to hear him scream," Moriarty said.

When the guard yanked on my hand, I screamed. I tried to go up higher, my body fighting to ease the strain on my shoulder and elbow and wrist, but I was already on tiptoes. I screamed, and I thrashed, and I screamed some more until my throat was raw. Something in my shoulder felt like it was separating. I hit my head against the wall again, and that pain, which was so much smaller, was a kind of relief.

"Maggie, please!" Holmes was shouting. "Please stop! Please stop! Please!"

And then they released me, and I dropped like someone had cut my strings. I landed on my knees, my face still pressed against the wall. I managed to stop screaming, but I was still making noises—choked, uneven breaths that I couldn't get under control. I managed to bring my arm around in front of me and cradle it. My shoulder and elbow felt like they had been spun out of glass.

"Say, 'I'm sorry for bothering you, Maggie.'"

"I'm sorry," Holmes said. His voice had none of its usual control; the words were choppy, his voice pitchy. "I'm sorry for bothering you."

"Say, 'Thank you for letting me have my toy back.'"

"Thank you for letting me—" He stopped. His voice was thick when he managed to finish: "—for letting me have my toy back."

"Yes, well, boys and their toys." Moriarty made a soft, disappointed noise that sounded weirdly parental. "I really thought you'd have learned by now. Go on, Holloway. Go solve your crime."

I heard the toolbox rattle when he picked it up, but I didn't hear his steps, so when his arm went around my waist, I flinched. He helped me to my feet. I'd managed to start breathing like a normal person again, but I was still blinking, trying to get my eyes to work. I glanced at the guards, the two that had held me, and they looked back with thousand-yard stares.

"And darling," Moriarty called as Holmes helped me to the door. "Do take the elevator this time. With his arm and shoulder, those stairs would be murder."

Chapter 14

Interstate Love Song

When we got to the truck, the mountains to the west already clipped the bottom of the sun, and clouds had moved in. Holmes patted me down.

"I can drive," I said. When Holmes tried to get the keys out of my pocket, I pushed him away. "I said I'm fine."

We got in the truck, and I took a moment to breathe. My arm and shoulder and finger all ached, but the pain wasn't too bad. I'd take a couple of ibuprofen and sleep it off; I'd had worse after a bad tackle in football. I took a few more breaths. I tried to feel like I was here, really here.

Clouds weren't common in summer, and they changed the light, the air, the valley, everything cooling to blue, the mountains dissolving in the dusk until I couldn't tell where they ended and the sky began. Holmes's face was blue too—darker shadows around the eyes, on the planes of his cheeks, in the hollow of his throat. I could fit two fingers there, I thought. They would fit just about perfectly in those blue bruised shadows.

Then he looked over, and he looked very much not like a Holmes bot. His hair was colorless in the blue light, the Ivy League cut mussed, a lick of it sticking up on one side. His eyes were wider, his pupils dilated, his lips slightly parted. They were raw, scabbed in places from biting them. Someone had tried to train that out of him, I thought. Someone had tried to make him someone else. To break someone, I thought. That was the phrase. Like you broke a horse or a dog. My eyes stung, and I had to close them.

"Jack—"

"Hey." I kept my eyes closed a moment longer, blinked a few times, and opened them. "Sorry. I can't believe I did that." Around us, the parking lot had shifted, some cars gone, others arrived while we'd been inside. Fewer cars overall, though. Which made sense. It was Sunday evening. And then I sat up straighter, ignoring the flash in my arm, and fumbled for the keys. "Oh shit, my dad is going to kill me."

"Jack, I don't think you're in any condition to drive—"

"I'm fine."

The engine grumbled to life—it started right up this time, thank God—and I eased out of the parking stall. I started back toward the highway. I used my injured arm as little as I could, which made the turns a little more difficult, but I managed. Once we got onto I-15, it was smooth sailing. The valley opened up ahead of us: the miles of dirt and concrete, the pinched band of the sky between the clouds and the mountains. Driving I-15 at night was like driving a neon alley: the sparkling brand-new shopping centers—DICK'S, Cinemark, Costco, Walmart—the fast food signs—Buffalo Wild Wings, Chick-fil-A, Little Caesar's, McDonald's. And then, all of a sudden, there'd be a dark patch—an old industrial park, or a weed-choked lot surrounded by a chain-link fence, or a post-frame building, the skin of its galvanized steel panels streaked with headlights. Utah was like that, the old and the new, the rural and the suburban, all of it elbowing for the same space. Traffic on I-15 was steady—it was always either steady, or it was a butt-hair snarl—and I kept the truck in the righthand lane, going exactly the speed limit, while cars zipped past me.

Lots of people were out tonight, I thought. And then I thought some of them were my age. And they were going home from church, from visiting grandparents, from dinner with a friend. They were going to eat dinner with their parents and their siblings, and they were going to sit at a table, and it wouldn't be pasta and red sauce. They were going to do their homework, or they were going to fight about doing their homework, or they were going to lie about doing their homework and try to catch up in first period the next day. They'd message their friends. They'd go to sleep. They wouldn't have collection letters shoved in their pillowcase where they figured their dads wouldn't find them. They wouldn't be worrying about the police showing up on their doorstep, or about what would happen if their dad was driving when he seized the next time, or what they were supposed to do with a Holmes bot that seemed to have imprinted on them. They'd worry about girls and boys and clothes and hair and whether they were jacking off too much. I remembered that life, kind of. It was like I'd read it all in a book.

"I understand that this is my fault," Holmes said, the words jarring me back to the present. "And I understand that I erred in taking you to see Maggie, and I understand that I failed to keep you safe—"

"First of all," I said, "nobody says err. So, don't say it again. Ok?"

The tires thrummed. Something under the hood was making a whining noise that I didn't like.

"H?" I asked.

"I'm explaining that it's my fault—"

"Don't say it again, ok?"

"It's a perfectly valid word." His tone had bristles. "It's more economical than other phrasing—"

"Did you hear me or didn't you?"

"Yes, fine," he snapped, and he sounded a little more like himself. "Will you let me finish—"

"No. Because it's not your fault. I drove the truck. I went to see Maggie on my own. You were hiding in the back like a—like a stowaway, but in a truck instead of a boat—"

"You can just say stowaway," Holmes said. "I looked it up. It applies to any vehicle."

"Oh my God, you looked it up?"

"There was some uncertainty—"

"And it's not your fault that she's a psychopath and wanted to torture you—"

"She didn't hurt me. She hurt you."

"H," I said, and for a moment, I was honestly at a loss because he genuinely didn't seem to get it. All I could come up with was, "Come on."

He didn't respond, and for the next half mile, the tires hummed to keep us company. He reached out, his touch feather light, and took my arm. He scooted closer on the bench until our knees bumped. Then he laid my arm over his knee. He touched my fingers, testing them until I grunted when he moved the injured one. Then he probed around that one. I made some noises to let him know how I felt about it.

"Stop being a baby," he said. And then he attacked my elbow.

Maybe, in some alternate medical universe, Holmes's poking and jabbing and prodding might have constituted a legitimate examination. I endured it as best I could, but the third time he stuck his finger into my shoulder and made me yelp, I tried to twist away and growled, "Knock it off."

He stopped prodding, but he didn't let go of my arm. "Nothing appears to be permanently damaged."

"I thought Watson was supposed to be the doctor."

"I can have outside interests." That made me laugh, and for some reason, he blushed. "When you learn Krav Maga, especially those kinds of holds and locks, you learn to check for damage after."

"Krav Maga, huh."

He nodded.

"That's how you keep kicking my ass?"

He nodded again. "Although, to be fair, you're genuinely incompetent in a fight, so I probably could do it without the training."

That made me burst out laughing again.

Holmes frowned, blond eyebrows arched in a question. I wasn't ready to answer it. A hint of color had come into his cheeks—not a blush, just enough warmth to break his usual cold perfection and make him look vibrantly alive. I had to look at the road, but every time my eyes came back, he was still staring at me. One of his fingers moved, tracing the crook of my elbow, and goose bumps tightened my skin.

Then my stomach rumbled.

Flinching, Holmes dropped my arm. He stared at me for a moment. His face was full of wordless outrage, like I had tricked him somehow, and then he scooted along the bench toward the passenger door.

"H—"

His reflection rode in the glass of the passenger window, and Holmes directed his words toward it: "If you'd like to see a doctor, I can pay for it."

It was the way he said it—like it wouldn't be an inconvenience for him, like he knew I would need it.

"I'm fine, thanks."

He looked over. The color in his cheeks had died.

"Are you ok?" I asked.

He took out his phone.

"Hey H, I asked you a question."

Attention locked on the screen, he scrolled and tapped. That little furrow was back between his eyebrows. I had this thought of smoothing it away with my thumb, and that made me angry. I sat forward and hit the volume dial on the stereo. The CD player whirred, and a moment later, music pounded into the truck. Holmes's head came up, and he looked at me. I gave him a paper grin and turned the volume up until it hurt my ears. He reached for the dial, and I caught his hand and shoved it away. It was such a petty, bitchy thing to do, but it was worth it to see the shock in his eyes.

I started to sing along. It was a mix CD, one of Dad's, and this song was Stone Temple Pilots—"Interstate Love Song." I screamed the words until my throat was raw. Since the accident, I'd played this song a lot. A lot, a lot. They weren't wrong about breathing, I thought. I'd thought it a lot, driving into town to get Dad's medicine, waiting in the truck while he did PT, the nights coming home from Joslyn's place after seeing Ariana, when I shouldn't have been behind the wheel and I was full of a sick dislike of myself. Sometimes, breathing was the hardest thing to do.

"I don't like this," Holmes shouted, reaching for the dial again.

I grabbed his hand and kept him from the dial. If he wanted to do his Krav Maga bullshit, I wouldn't be able to stop him, but he let me pull him away from the stereo. "This is how I drive," I shouted back. "I either listen to my music, or I talk to someone."

For a moment, his features whited out, and I thought maybe he hadn't heard me. Then he twisted his wrist, freed his hand, and slapped the volume dial before I could stop him. The music died, my ears still ringing from how loud I'd had it.

"I'm fine." Holmes spoke toward the windshield. The light from the dash traced his profile. "Can I please have some silence—"

"Good," I said over him. "Because that's exactly how normal people sound when they're fine."

He risked a glance and then looked forward again. As my ears adjusted, the sound of the tires came back, along with that faint whining from under the hood. When he spoke, his voice was so low I could barely hear him. "I don't know what you want from me."

"Well, you could start by telling me you're not fine."

He was biting his lip again. When he opened his mouth to speak, blood stained his teeth. He enunciated each word clearly. "I am fine."

"It's ok if you're not. Fine, I mean. You learned some seriously awful stuff about your best friend, and Moriarty treated you like shit, and she threatened you, and she played that awful fucking mind game with you and me, and no normal person would be ok."

We drove another mile in silence, the bowl of the mountains darkening until the only light was a blue rim beneath the clouds and the long lanes of electric signs. They gave everything a dozen shadows, even inside the cab of the car. Like there were a dozen other of me and a dozen other of Holmes. I'd read the Wikipedia article on string theory about twenty times. The stuff about quantum gravity and nuclear physics and branes all went over my head, no matter how many links I followed and how many rabbit holes I went down. I couldn't even scratch the surface of the subsection about monstrous moonshine; it was like the Wikipedia equivalent of Holloway Holmes. But I remembered something about a landscape of possible universes, and I hoped one of those shadow Jacks and one of those shadow Holmeses were getting it right somewhere.

"Earlier, you said you were fine," Holmes said. "You are a liar."

"Of course. I lie all the time."

"I mean right now. Tonight. You're not fine." I opened my mouth, but he said, "When was the last time you ate?"

My stomach was a treacherous bastard and chose that moment to grumble again.

Holmes's eyes were bright. "That's what I thought. Take this next exit; we'll get In-N-Out, since you're craving it."

He was right: ahead, the crooked red arrow for In-N-Out beckoned, and in the back of my head, I'd been thinking that it had been almost a year since I'd had a 4x4, animal style. Right after the accident, maybe. When it seemed like things could still be normal one day. I signaled. I got over. I tried to watch him out of the corner of my eye.

"Ok," I finally said. "How?"

He blinked and looked up from his phone. "A half mile back, you looked at the sign that showed food options at the next exit. And then, when we got close to this exit, you looked again."

"But there's, I don't know, Sonic and a taco place and Zupas."

"Yes, but they're all on the north side of the street. You were looking south."

As we took the exit, I frowned. "Zupas is on the south side."

He bent over the phone again, his voice distracted as he said, "You are a straight adolescent male with TikTok hair. I know boys like you; you were not thinking about a soup-and-salad place."

I laughed. And then, chest prickling, face hot, I said, "Ok, you're right about In-N-Out. But you didn't get all your facts straight."

I chose the word on purpose. But Holmes didn't react: he didn't make a noise, he didn't lift his head, he didn't even shift in his seat. We pulled into the parking lot in silence, and I rolled up behind the car in the drive-thru line. Foot on the brake, I raised my hips so I could get my wallet out— it was an old Superman wallet, held together mostly with duct tape at this point. I'd gotten it when I was twelve, and now I was too stubborn to let it go. I looked inside, made a face, and said, "How do you feel about splitting a burger? It'll have to be a kid's one."

Without looking up, Holmes withdrew his wallet and tossed it over. It was leather, so soft and thin I thought I might be able to tear it with my bare hands, and inside it was stuffed with cash.

"No credit card made out of solid platinum," I said as I tossed the wallet back. "I'm disappointed."

"Father canceled my credit cards. It was one of the conditions when I came here." He looked up. "What's going on? Do you need more?"

"Do I need more than that wad of fifties you've got crammed in there? Uh, no. Look, I changed my mind—"

"Don't be ridiculous. I proposed stopping for a meal; I'm paying for it."

"Like it's a date, huh?"

"No, not at all like a date." He yanked cash out of the wallet and tossed it at me—a hundred and fifty dollars landed in my lap just like that. "Now stop interrupting me."

I guess I could have tried to make a point out of it. I could have thrown the money back. I could have told him I didn't want it or need it. But it had taken all my resolve to hand the wallet back the first time, and who the hell was I kidding? I definitely wanted it. I absolutely needed it.

When we got to the drive-thru's intercom, I ordered a 4x4, animal style, and a large fry, also animal style, and a large Coke, light ice.

"H?"

"I'm not hungry," he said without looking up.

I wasn't sure what fuel Holmes bots were capable of processing, so I got him a Double-Double, fries, and a Coke. When we got to the window, I paid with one of the fifties. It was almost physically painful to bundle the change with the other two fifties.

"Ok, H, here's—"

"Keep it," he said and kept scrolling. "For gas."

"You don't know how much stuff costs, do you?"

He made an annoyed noise and bent closer to read something.

Before I could do something stupid like try to be a gentleman again, I shoved the cash into my Superman wallet. I took the food and drinks, and I eased the truck into a stall at the back of the lot. One of the security lights was overhead, and it gave plenty of light in the cab—a dry, fluttering gray that made me think of snow spinning off the back of Timp.

Between bites of my 4x4, I took out my phone. I had several texts from Shivers and from Ariana, but I ignored those. I didn't have any messages from my dad. That was strange, so I shot him a quick text: *Went into town to see some friends and lost track of time. Headed home now.*

I waited for a reply, but nothing came.

I looked at Holmes, still bent over his phone. The spindrift light picked out the texture of his hair, highlighted the knobs of vertebrae at the base of his neck, gave the swoop of his shoulder a cool shadow. I still had my phone out, and so I didn't even let myself think about it. I opened my message history with Mom and typed out another text.

I could really use your advice right now.

It's about a boy.

This is officially the most embarrassing text chain of my life.

When the screen was about to time out, I sent one last message: *BTW, he might actually be a robot.*

Then I locked the phone and put it away.

I reached for a fry—with extra cheese, sauce, and grilled onions—and was outraged to find that I'd somehow already finished them.

Holmes's food sat on the bench between us, untouched.

"H."

He made a disgruntled noise.

"H!"

"What?"

"You need to eat."

"I told you, I'm not hungry."

"Is it your fuel cells? Did they get damaged by a blaster?"

"I have no idea what that means, and I'm far too busy to engage with it."

"Is it the charging pins? They got bent the last time you docked, is that it?"

He raised his head to stare blankly at me before returning to the phone.

"If you don't eat something," I said, "I'm going to get bored and decide you need some musical accompaniment."

Without looking up, Holmes snatched a fry and shoved it savagely into his mouth.

"And the burger," I said.

He pretended to ignore me.

"All right." I reached for the stereo. "I think Pearl Jam is up next."

"Good God Almighty, fine!" He dropped the phone onto his lap, grabbed the burger, and tore it neatly in half. He polished off one half in two bites. He ate two more fries. Then he frowned.

"What?" I asked.

"It's good."

"Uh, yeah. It's In-N-Out."

He frowned, obviously still grappling with this revelation. Then he found a paper napkin, wiped his hands, and returned to the phone. "You can dispose of the rest," he said. "I can't eat anymore."

"Even though I've seen you hit the gym," I said, picking up the other half of the burger. Between bites, I continued, "And you've got to burn a million calories a day working out like that. And even though you weigh about as much as a doormat."

"A doormat who, how did you put it? Handed you your ass?"

I grinned as I reached for some fries. "I didn't say you weren't tough as balls. What are you reading?"

For a moment, he stared out the windshield into the chain-link privacy fencing that closed off the back of the lot. The cone of light caught a few motes of dust that spun.

I ate a few more fries. "H?"

"What? Oh, I was verifying Maggie's alibi; there are several publicity stills of her at the dinner. Then I was trying to figure out what stories Watson sold—" He stopped. When he started again, his voice was as smooth as ever, but I thought I detected the current running beneath the words. "She sold stories about me to a woman named Lissa Keahi. I'll have to speak to my father about having them pulled down. Eventually."

"I'm sorry, H. That's super shitty."

Holmes's jaw was tight. "We don't know that Maggie was telling the truth about Watson. About anything, actually. As you…experienced—" If anything, his jaw got tighter; it looked like he could have chewed a hole in the truck door. "—Maggie enjoys games, and she enjoys making people look—" He stopped. His throat moved.

"She enjoys torturing people," I said. "You in particular, I'd guess, although I'm not sure why. Yeah, she's psycho. I already knew that. But she genuinely seemed to care about Watson. She wasn't lying about Watson selling stories about you, and it didn't feel like she was lying when she told us Watson was blackmailing people. As far as I could tell, she really believes that's what got Watson killed."

"But she's an excellent liar," Holmes said. He stared past me. "Is this a bluff? Or is it the truth? Or is it both? Her alibi is irrelevant; Maggie didn't need to be at Walker. That's the Moriarty way, after all. She would have stayed at the center of her web and let someone else do the dirty work. She could have been at the charity dinner and still be the one behind Watson's death."

"I've got a decent bullshit meter, and I'm telling you, I don't think she was lying. But ok, let's say you're right. Why? Why would she want to kill Watson?"

"The Moriartys—and various other parties—have always wanted to keep the Holmeses and the Watsons separate. My father does not agree, but it's clear from the historical trajectory of our family that we're more effective when we work together." He frowned. "When a Holmes and a Watson work together, I mean."

"Ok," I said. "So, she wants to keep you and Watson from working together...why? That just begs the question. Because Watson was blabbing about you to the press?"

If Holmes heard me, he gave no sign of it. His hand tightened around the phone. When Holmes spoke, it sounded like he was talking to himself: "I don't know why she would do that."

"Moriarty? Or Watson?"

He shook his head. "Maggie's not wrong. The Watsons have always loved learning other people's stories and finding a way to profit from them. John Watson sold the commercialized versions of Sherlock Holmes's adventures. Other Watsons have done what Sarah did — cannibalized their relationship with the Holmeses by selling stories to the gossip rags."

"Maybe she didn't want to hurt you, but she felt like she didn't have any other choice. Maybe she needed money —"

"Did Dr. Watson need money? I'm surprised Sherlock didn't kill him for stealing his life like that."

His last few words were surprisingly un-Holmes bot, hotly poisonous.

I let the moment lose some of its tension, and then I said, "H, I'm sorry."

He waved a hand, but his eyes looked like liquid silver in the glow from the security light.

"She did something awful to you," I said. "You trusted her, and she let you down. I'm really sorry."

"I'm fine," he said, but his voice was raspy, and he shook his head and looked away to stare out the passenger window. "It was to be expected. And, as my father will undoubtedly point out, it was yet another of my massive lapses in judgment."

"She did something awful to you," I said. "She was the one who did something wrong. Not you."

"Of course I did." When he turned to look at me, his eyes were dry again, hard as concrete. "I trusted her. I was trained better than that."

That was so bizarro that I didn't know how to respond. What came out was, "But, I mean, it's not a big deal, right? I get it — it's your life, and so of course it's a big deal. But what kind of stuff could she tell that would, you know..." I trailed off because there wasn't a good way to say, *Yes, everything about your life is incredibly important, but in the big picture, it's just celebrity gossip and nobody will remember it in two weeks?*

Some of it must have come through in my voice, though, because Holmes offered a tight, bitter grimace. "Yes, well, there are some things that would have repercussions. For me and for my family. And right now, with Zodiac's IPO around the corner, the last thing my family needs is bad press."

Traffic whooshed by us on I-15, the lights steady in both directions. The sun had set, and the valley had dropped into the dark. A girl in an In-N-Out uniform rolled a cart full of garbage bags toward the dumpsters, and one of the casters squealed along the asphalt. I wanted to tell her she needed a can of WD-40. I could fix that for her in ten seconds.

Holmes had fallen back into that brooding silence, so I asked, "Is an IPO an internet thing?"

"No, it stands for initial public offering—when a privately owned company is first traded publicly. Typically, it's when the stock is highest, at least for a while."

"So, lots of money."

"Yes."

"Wait. Your family is involved with Zodiac?"

"Of course." Holmes frowned at me. "My father founded it."

"And he hired that bitch?"

"Of course," Holmes said again. "Maggie is fantastic at what she does."

"But she's a Moriarty."

"Father has always believed in keeping his enemies close. And—" He took a breath. "And people always assume, Jack. I know they can't help it. There are the books and the movies. And the story has been stolen and adapted in so many ways. Yes, Maggie is horrible. But the Holmeses aren't...well, they aren't exactly good either. My family isn't what people believe. We're...strange and unpleasant. We have our interests, our fixations. One might as well call them obsessions. We all have our blind spots. The first Sherlock wasn't the hero people like to imagine, the one Dr. Watson created in his stories."

"He solved crimes, though, right? He brought people to justice?"

"He liked puzzles, and the strangeness of humans, especially their crimes, offered an interesting opportunity. When that became dull, he enjoyed matching wits with Professor Moriarty. He wasn't a hero. And none of us is good."

"I think you're a good person," I said.

"I'm not," Holmes said. "I'd like you to remember that."

For a moment, I struggled to find the next thing to say. "Can't you just, you know, use deduction or whatever to figure out who killed Watson? Like you did when you figured out I wanted In-N-Out? I mean, I gave you all the clues—the call from Moriarty, the broken flash drive, the note in her wallet? Isn't that what Sherlock Holmes did?"

"I am not Sherlock Holmes." The words hit like a slap, and I blinked. "Do you understand?"

"I didn't—"

"Do you understand me?"

"Yes, God, sorry."

Holmes took a breath. Embers burned in his cheeks. After a moment, in what was clearly a forced attempt at being calm, he said, "Sherlock Holmes did not use deduction."

"Ok, but in the movies—"

"Yes, I know. Everyone thinks he used deduction. He didn't, except possibly in one case, and Dr. Watson didn't even write about that one. Deduction is what's called top-down reasoning, using general principles and then specific pieces of evidence to draw conclusions. It always produces logically true statements."

"Uh huh. Just an FYI, I have not read this Wikipedia page yet." Although God knew I was going to as soon as I got a chance.

"It's fairly straightforward. You start with the general principle: all men will die."

"Cheery."

"Then you take another piece of data, something local. Holmes is a man. By applying the general principle to the specific piece of data, you have a logically true conclusion: Holmes will die."

"Better example," I said. "All guys named Jack are hot. General principle."

"That is not a general principle," Holmes said.

"I am a guy named Jack. Therefore…"

When I let the sentence hang, Holmes rolled his eyes.

"Therefore, you, Jack Moreno, are hot," I finished for him. "Aww, gee, H, thank you. I'm blushing."

Holmes rolled his eyes again. "What Sherlock Holmes used was not deduction but abduction. It's also called abductive reasoning. Abductive reasoning is not, by its nature, logically true. It yields a plausible conclusion, but it does not positively verify it—a degree of uncertainty remains."

"Uh huh," I said.

"In contrast to our earlier example —"

"The one where you deduced I was hot."

" — abduction might sound more like this: You drive a truck. That is my observation — notice that, instead of beginning with a general principle, as we did in deduction, we begin with an observation. Then, I must suggest a possible premise: People who drive legally hold a state-issued driver's license. Therefore, it is reasonable to assume that you hold a valid driver's license — that is the most likely conclusion."

"I don't, actually."

"Yes, I know. The point of the example is to demonstrate that abduction yields probable conclusions. For a genius like Sherlock, it allowed him to make phenomenally incisive conclusions based on limited data. This is also an example, by the way, of your..." His mouth twisted like he was trying not to bite his lip again. "Lawlessness."

That made me smile for a moment. "But in the movies, Holmes, like, smells the cork from a bottle and he immediately knows where the wine is from and what time the bottle was opened and the fact that the man who brought it to dinner was left-handed and that kind of stuff. He never says, 'Um, Watson, I think maybe he was left-handed. It's, like, the best possible conclusion.'"

"That's because he wasn't a teenager who spends most of his free time watching drag queens play video games."

My jaw dropped. "How do you —" I managed to stop myself because I refused to give him the satisfaction.

Holmes's face didn't change, but for a Holmes bot, he was giving off some seriously smug vibes. "The stories — and the movies — do not highlight the remainder of doubt because, in the first place, Sherlock Holmes truly was a genius, and in the second place, because Watson was devoted to him and left out most of the times Sherlock got it wrong. Not all of them, incidentally. Watson must have realized he was stretching the limits of credibility."

I thought about that for a moment. I looked at Holmes. The dust-light from the overhead lamp hit his jaw at the right angle to show the faintest hint of stubble on his cheeks — not everywhere, and not much. It probably wouldn't really start to show for another day or two, but of course, Holmes would shave before then. I thought about what a stubbly Holmes might look like, especially when he scowled and snarled and snapped. Then, because my mind was starting to wander, I said, "Do another."

"What?"

"Do it again, but a real one this time. Don't do one you know is wrong."

"What did you call it? My party trick?"

"Come on. You're good at it; I know you are."

"You have no evidence that I am good at abduction."

"But you didn't deny that you're good at it," I said with a grin. "Which means you know you're good at it, and you really, really want to show off for me." When Holmes didn't respond, I asked, "Or should I test my vocal chords again?"

"No," Holmes said a little too quickly, and when I smiled, his brows drew together again. "Fine. You are a competent mechanic and handyman, but you learned those skills because you are poor, not because you wanted to learn them or because you enjoy them. You are also too proud to ask for or receive help; in fact, you derive a degree of satisfaction from being able to take care of yourself, and part of that has to do with knowing that you're much smarter than the people around you. Of course, that's a source of frustration to you as well."

"I'm poor, so I have to fix things," I said. "You've got to do better than that, H. You literally see me being poor and fixing things every day at school."

"This truck is old. It is well cared for, but it hasn't been restored, which means you're not driving it because it's a classic. You might drive it for sentimental reasons, but, of course, it's filled with tools and equipment, and it lacks any sort of personalization except for those godawful CDs, all of which suggest that the choice is practical rather than emotional. You didn't want to take the money for the hamburgers, even though you couldn't pay for them yourself. You have a system on campus to separate people who are not as smart as you from their money."

"I'm not robbing them," I said. "I sell them stuff."

"Two hundred dollars for that Korean soda?"

"Ok, I sell them stuff with a padded profit margin. Only the dumb ones. Some of those kids drive a hard bargain, though—Watson was always tough. She wouldn't buy if I jacked up the price too high."

"Yes, Sarah was...savvy."

Holmes fell silent after that, his eyes the dark of dead stars.

"Do another one," I said. "Come on, it's no fair to call me out for being poor when you literally have seen the holes in my underwear."

For a moment, I thought it wouldn't work. Then Holmes rolled his eyes, and he cocked his head, and it was like a magician's trick or a hypnotist: the whole world dropped away, and it was just me and those dead-star eyes. No one—no one—had ever seen me the way Holloway Holmes was seeing me; in that moment, I was absolutely certain of it. It made my skin tighten. It turned my breath to a lump of ice in my chest, and at the same time, I felt like I was on fire.

"You have patterns of antisocial behavior," he said, and the words were his usual voice reduced to a murmur—low and smooth and even, lulling me. "Many of the students on campus are afraid of you. But you are also a natural caregiver, and guilt has intensified that trait. You left school to take care of your father, and most days, you cover his job for him. You were kind to me when I became...agitated in Watson's room. And, of course, you care that something terrible happened to Watson, even though I don't think you really knew her."

The intimacy of the moment was so intense that I cleared my throat, trying to break it—I needed him to look away for a moment, just for a moment. "I knew she liked zannies," I said.

But Holmes's eyes didn't change, and in spite of my best efforts, I kept falling into that lusterless gray. It was dizzying. It was exhilarating. The ice in my chest was gone; now it was just the simple matter of not being able to breathe at all.

"You are resilient, of course," Holmes said, and now it sounded like he was speaking to himself. "Few adults would be able to do what you've done, rebuilding your life after such a tragedy, finding themselves without resources, without a support system, without any preparation for how to move forward. And yet you have not only found a way to keep yourself and your father safe, but you seem well adjusted, healthy, and happy."

Maybe it wouldn't have happened if I hadn't already been disoriented from the way he was looking at me. Maybe I could have brushed it off, packed it away. But he was saying what no one had said to me, not once in the last year. My eyes filled with tears that I couldn't blink away fast enough. Part of me was back there, back in the car, watching Mom and Dad so still in the seats in front of me, smelling hot metal and burned rubber.

"Stop," I said.

"You are very brave." Holmes's voice was barely more than a breath. The words were warm on my face. "You don't back down from confrontations. You drove to Zodiac, thinking you would take on Maggie by yourself. And when she hurt you, you didn't beg or plead. I'm not sure I've ever met anyone as brave—"

I was back then, back there, with the stink of torn-up tires in my throat, with the smell of gasoline chasing me, my steps slapping the asphalt as I ran. As I ran. As I fucking ran away from my parents, who were still in the car. And I remember looking back, seeing the shadow man, seeing him coming closer to the driver's side window, seeing the glint of metal—something he held low against his leg. And I had kept running.

"Stop," I said. The word was ragged, the sound chopped off. I gulped air, wiped my face, and turned away from Holmes. For a moment, I propped myself on the steering wheel, hands over my eyes. Then, when I thought I could do it, I said again, "Stop."

"Jack, what—"

I shook my head, and he broke off. I held myself together, duct tape and sheer will, until I wasn't back then, a year ago, running. Running like a fucking coward. Then I took a deep breath. I forced myself to lower my hands and then—this was even harder—to look over at Holmes.

"Let's not do that again, ok?" My voice caught. "That's my bad. I shouldn't have—" I shook my head because I didn't know what else to do.

Holmes stared at me. His face, usually so hard to read, suddenly became transparent: he set his jaw, his eyes tightened, that little line appeared between his brows. Holloway Holmes, about to tame a lion. He reached out and put his hand on my shoulder.

It racked a wet noise out of me, something between a sob and a laugh. I put my hand on top of his, squeezed once, and moved it back to the seat. "I'm fine, H. Just—you're nice, but I'm not any of those things. Not really. I guess you were right about that abduction stuff, probable conclusions and all that. You're really good at it, but that's not me."

He didn't put his hand on my shoulder again, but he did keep looking at me.

"Don't be a creeper," I told him.

"Am I supposed to look out the window?"

"You're supposed to look at me and then look away and then look out the window and then look back, and neither of us knows where to look."

"That sounds time-consuming. And you're supposed to look people in the eyes."

"Yes, well, this is what humans do when we're in a very fucking awkward situation." I cleared my throat. "Let's talk about something else. Let's talk about the case. Your dad is here, Moriarty is here, you're here. And Watson. I mean, did you plan it that way? Is that why you came here?"

"My father certainly sent me to Walker for a reason," Holmes said slowly. He was still watching me. "But as far as I know, finding Watson here was simply—well, it happens. Holmeses and Watsons find each other. They have for over a hundred years. I had an uncle who was on a krill fishing boat doing the most amazing research, and when they returned to Punta Arenas, one of the Watson cousins was standing on the dock." Holmes rolled his eyes. "He'd dropped his hotel key and was trying to find it."

I shook my head. "You know that sounds crazy, right?"

"I suppose. That doesn't make it any less true."

I thought about the likelihood of all that, of Holmeses and Watsons stumbling into each other in cafes and archaeology sites and in Siberia and, apparently, at a private school for kids who were too much trouble for their rich parents. "Quantum entanglement," I said. "Maybe that's what it is. You know, when their quantum state, like their spin, is linked no matter how far apart they are." When Holmes raised his eyebrows, I said, "Wikipedia. Again."

Holmes nodded. "Something like that, perhaps. It can be extremely irritating. I was in line for a concert once when Watson's aunt just happened to be getting out of a taxi—" He stopped, horror filling his face.

For a moment, I forgot how genuinely awful I felt, and a ghost of a grin found my face. "Holy shit."

Holmes's mouth was still open. He shook his head in denial.

"Holy shit," I whispered. Then, in a louder voice, "You went to a concert."

"You misheard me."

"Bullshit. You, Holloway Herringbone Holmes—"

"Harrowgate," he snapped.

"—you went to a concert. Who'd you see?"

"I was investigating—"

"Nope. Who did you see?"

If anything, his eyes got wider.

"Taylor Swift? Justin Bieber? Oh my God."

"Jack."

"Oh my God!"

"You don't know what—"

It was a stab in the dark, but my gut told me I was right: "You saw One Direction in concert?"

"You're—when you say it like that—"

"Oh my God, so many questions. What's your favorite song? Do you have posters? Which one do you think is the hottest? For me, it's, like, basically any of them except Niall, but if I had to choose, maybe Harry—oh, or Louis—"

"This is not amusing," Holmes said, the words cracking. "Stop acting stupid."

I sat back in my seat. A car rolled past in the drive-thru lane, bass thumping, girls screaming along with a song I didn't recognize.

"I want to go home," Holmes said.

"I was joking. Well, I mean not about Harry. Or Louis, for that matter—"

"I told you this is not funny. You're making a fool of yourself." He settled himself and looked out the window. "Drive me home. Now."

I stared at him. Then I said, "No."

He whirled around, and Holloway Holmes angry was something to look at. His eyes, I thought. The Wikipedia article on epithets in Homer—that was back when I was still trying to keep up with the curriculum—talked about Athena's bright gray eyes. "I told you to drive me home."

"I'm trying to apologize—"

"I don't care about your apologies. I'm done talking for tonight, and I would like to—"

"Horseshit. I'm sorry for saying something that made you feel weird. Now you have to say that you're sorry too, and then we can go back to normal."

His lips parted, but no sound came out. Finally he managed, "I do not feel weird, and I am not interested in discussing this further—"

"I don't care. We're discussing it. Right now." My volume kept rising. "I was joking around, and I didn't mean anything by it, and yeah, I should have kept my mouth shut, but I'm in a weird place and it felt good to joke about something—about anything. And I don't like you making me feel bad about myself because I think a couple of guys are cute! Because it's twenty-fucking-twenty, and I should be able to talk about that stuff whether you like it or not! And this is technically still an apology even though I'm yelling!"

When I finished, the sound of my voice filled the truck. Holmes's eyes were huge, and he had his arms folded across his chest, which was rising and falling rapidly. As the anger leached out of me, I had to look away. My face got hot, and I fumbled for the keys in the ignition.

"I thought—" Holmes stopped. It was that same Holmes bot voice, so unemotional that it was almost uninflected, but with a fresh hesitancy. "I should not have reacted the way I did. I haven't slept in several days." He made a weird noise that I couldn't quite break down into anything I understood. "Although that's not an excuse; I don't sleep much even at the best of times."

My hand was so tight around the keys that their teeth bit into my palm. I stared out the windshield at the chain-link fence shivering in the night breeze off the mountain. After a moment, when my throat unlocked, I said, "Nobody says 'even at the best of times' anymore. You sound like a book."

"I will update my conversation matrix."

I raised my eyebrows and looked over at him. "Was that a joke?"

"Humor algorithms were included for all Holmes bots in the latest software patch."

A grin slipped out, and I beat it down into a frown. "Don't think I didn't notice that you never actually apologized."

He bit his lip, apparently without even realizing it. His teeth left fresh white crescents. "I am sorry, Jack."

"Yeah, well, me too."

"For what?"

"I don't know, H." I started the truck and backed out of the stall. "That's just what people say at the end of a fight."

Holmes opened his mouth to say something else, but then something crossed his face, and he picked up his phone. Blackfriar flashed on the screen again, and he answered in a low voice, "Yes, Father?"

So, Blackfriar was his father, and whatever he said it made Holmes flinch and draw down in his seat. He closed his eyes and leaned his head against the passenger window. I stopped the truck at the edge of the In-N-Out parking lot, but without opening his eyes, Holmes gestured for me to keep driving, and so I did and came to a stop at the light for the on-ramp.

"Yes, Father," he said again. And then, several minutes later, "No, Father." And then, "I understand." Holmes's final words were spoken with a kind of constrained insistence—I'd heard a much louder, much more abrasive version of it out of my own mouth that morning, when I'd gotten into it with Dad—as he said, "This is not the same thing at all. This is not Hewdenhouse." He listened for another moment, his knuckles white around the phone, and then the hand with the phone dropped to the seat.

The light changed, and I merged onto the highway.

"Everything ok?" I asked after a few more minutes of silence.

Holmes shook his head. And then, his voice thick with emotion, he said, "Maggie called him. He's furious, of course."

"H, what—"

He shook his head again, rocking it against the glass. "Leave me alone." Even though it must have cost him, he managed to add, "Please."

We drove south along that neon funnel of signs and shopping and security lights, the mountains rendered down to fuzzy black humps to the east. I couldn't see Utah Lake to the west except as a black spot where the city lights ended. We passed a kid who had to be our age, his sixty-thousand-dollar Jeep dead on the shoulder of I-15. He was pacing, phone to his ear, and when our headlights flashed across his face, I saw that he was laughing.

When we exited at 800 North in Orem, Holmes's head bounced against the glass, and he made a strange noise. I glanced over at him to ask if he was ok, but then he made another of those noises. This time, my brain decoded it as sleepy discontent, and I remembered what he'd said about never sleeping well. We drove toward the mountains—past the old stuff, like the Macey's, and newer stuff, like the Grinders, past Harmons, which Mom insisted had the best peaches in the summer. Holmes's head bounced, and he stirred, his arm drifting across the seat, kicking the footwell, moving every few minutes.

Finally I let out a disgusted breath, hooked a belt loop of his chinos, and tugged.

His head came up, his eyes bleary with sleep, and he made a noise that was something like, "Mwua?"

"Come here."

Sleep-mode apparently left Holmes bots highly susceptible to suggestion—plus, I was already hauling his skinny ass across the bench. A moment later, he was tucked under my arm, his head resting on my shoulder.

He said something like, "Not gonna slirp."

"It's fine," I said. "You can slirp all you want. If you don't slirp, I'm probably going to kill you."

He mumbled something that sounded faintly outraged, and then a moment later, he let out a prodigious snore. When we started down the hill from Orem into Provo, I was smiling. He didn't kick or bounce or jerk himself awake after that.

We coasted down the hill toward the bridge across the Provo River. We turned left and followed the road into the canyon. Tonight, the granite walls glimmered like they had frosted over—which maybe they had, although it didn't feel cold enough. The weak light of the moon and stars gave everything a shimmering haze that softened the ridges. A bird made a paper kite against the stars—an owl, I thought—and then it dove, and I realized something had probably just died. The smell of his soap or his deodorant came up to me—warm, woodsy, and a kind of heat that when I breathed it in, kindled something in my chest. His shoulder didn't feel nearly as sharp as I had expected. His head fit between my shoulder and my neck. I told myself it was stupid to think something like that. I told myself I couldn't help noticing.

When we got to Walker, the aspens were quivering, and when the headlights ran over the scrub oak, it looked like they were on fire. We drove on empty streets between the darkened buildings. The security lights created unreal islands: the practice fields; a bench; a stretch of sidewalk; a statue of Morris Bedell, the first head of the Walker School, who held a book in one hand and had his finger pointed out in front of him. I had decided, the first time I'd seen him, that he must have been a colossal prick when he'd been alive.

When I stopped in front of Baker House, Holmes was still asleep.

"H," I whispered.

He was still snoring—small, raspy snores.

When I rubbed his arm, his head shot up from my shoulder. He blinked. Then he stared at me. Then something seemed to seize him, and he jerked backward along the bench, putting space between us. The side of my body where he'd been felt cold.

"You dozed off—"

"I need to go." He yanked on the door handle. The door swung open, and the chill mountain air popped me on the cheek. "Thank you for—" He cut off. Then he started to slide out of the truck.

"Hold on."

He was halfway out of the truck, but he stopped.

I hadn't figured out what to say. The first thing that came out of my mouth was, "Can I get your number?" A flash fire went through me, my face and chest and belly itching with the heat, and I stumbled through, "I mean—you know—we've got to keep looking—"

Maybe Holmes bots had a pity module. Maybe he was simply being practical. Maybe he felt it too, whatever was moving underneath everything between us, an ocean current tossing an ice floe along its path. He nodded and held out his hand, and I passed over my brick of a dumb phone.

If it surprised him, he gave no sign of it. He tapped in a number, pressed call, and a moment later, his phone lit up. He handed mine back, and then he slid the rest of the way out of the truck. He stood for a moment, hand on the door, his face a sentence still being written. And then something scrubbed everything out, and he shut the door.

I waited until he got inside the residence hall. Then I eased the truck forward. My brain kept replaying the last few minutes—his reaction when he'd woken, his face when I'd asked for his number, those long fingers with that one knobby knuckle, moving across my phone. I went through it again. And again. And again. I was looking for something; I just didn't know what.

My phone buzzed, and it was a number I didn't know. My brain made two leaps: first, that Holmes hadn't bothered programming in his name; and second, that he was already calling me. Maybe he wanted to tell me something about the case. Maybe he wanted to talk about—

I put the brakes on that.

When I answered the phone, though, it wasn't Holmes's voice that came back to me.

"Hello, Jack," Detective Rivera said. "Glad I caught you. Yazzie and I were wondering if you could talk to your dad about coming into the station tomorrow. We've got a few questions we wanted to ask you. Routine follow-up, Jack. No big deal. What do you say?"

I said something, although I had no idea what—the words came out on autopilot because my brain was frozen.

It must have been the right thing—or close to the right thing—because Rivera said, "Good, good. How about ten?"

This time, I managed to say, "Yes."

Rivera said something else, but my brain couldn't keep track of it, and then the call disconnected. I idled along for the next hundred yards. I couldn't get a signal from my brain to the rest of my body. All I could do was think, Trap. This was a trap. The questions weren't routine. And they didn't just want to follow up with me. This was something else. I couldn't decide if it was about me or about dad, but I knew I had to get home, and I had to talk to him about getting a lawyer.

It was like flipping a breaker; all of a sudden, my body worked again, and I dropped my foot on the gas. I drove down the empty streets of Walker. Most of my attention was turned inward. I knew these streets like the back of my hand, and I could drive home without even thinking about it. My thoughts were all about money: how much would it cost to get a lawyer just to talk to us? And how much then to get him to go to the station? And how much if they arrested me? And if I went to jail, would Dad be able to keep up with the work around Walker? How much would Taylor put up with before he decided to throw Dad out on his butt?

I was so caught up in all that worrying that I almost missed the second trap: at the turnoff for the staff housing, in an opening in the windbreak of haw and pine and scrub oak, a deputy's cruiser waited with its lights off. It was like someone had laid the whole thing out in front of me, every step of what was going to happen: I'd turn, and the deputy would pull in behind me, and I'd be trapped. Rivera wasn't at home or working late at the station. Rivera was here. He was at my house. And he had called me, had wanted to scare me, so that I'd come running home. Because he couldn't find me, and he needed me to help him out.

The panic that froze me turned out, in this instance, to be a good thing. Instead of turning, I kept rolling forward. In the darkened cruiser, the deputy was a dark outline. I couldn't tell if he was watching me or not, so I kept a consistent speed and faced forward. Please, I thought. Please let him not be worried about a random truck on Walker's main road. Please let him be focused on the staff housing. Sweat built on my nape as I headed for the road that led back down the canyon.

When I couldn't see the cruiser behind me, I killed the headlights. Then I turned at the next street, and I parked the truck on a patch of gravel near the maintenance shed where we stored the lawnmowers. When I got out of the truck, I could smell the old clippings, a hint of motor oil, the chalkiness of the gravel crunching under my Vans. I jogged back toward the main road.

Campus still looked deserted, so I slipped through the windbreak, wincing when a pine branch caught my cheek and the smell of resin exploded in my nose. I stayed in the thickest shadows as I moved from cottage to cottage.

And then I could see my house. All the lights were on. The curtains were drawn back. In the kitchen, Yazzie was talking to a deputy who was holding what looked like the bag of zannies I'd bought for Watson; in the background behind her, another deputy was opening the cabinet where we kept Dad's medicine. I squatted, my heart so loud that it sounded like it was filling up the canyon. I should go up there, I told myself. I should walk right up to them and ask to see a warrant, and if they didn't have one, I'd tell them to get the fuck out of our home. I told myself that again and again.

Then Dad shuffled into view. He stood on the porch, and it took me a moment to understand why he was standing so strangely—he looked like an old man, I thought, his head bent in thought, hands clasped at the small of his back. But then I realized he was cuffed, and he was probably still dealing with that migraine from this morning.

Rivera appeared behind him, one hand holding Dad's arm to guide him down the steps. He was talking, and although he probably thought he was being quiet, voices carried in the canyon, and the night was completely still.

"—if you can't explain how your prints got all over that girl and all over the garbage that was covering her, you're not giving me any other choice." Rivera shook Dad by the arm to emphasize the point. "How about that, Juan? What do you think about that?"

Dad said something, but I couldn't hear him. Rivera gave a hard laugh, and then he put Dad into a cruiser. He turned back to the house, and as he stepped up onto the porch, a woman appeared in a jean jacket, her hair tucked up under a beanie. She said something to him.

Rivera's voice came back clearly. "He'll show up; I lit a fire under his ass. I'm telling you, you'd better take that kid to a locked facility tonight. You try any of that group home or foster care shit, and he's going to be back on the street in less than a day. He's smart. He's an asswipe, but he's definitely smart."

The woman said something to him, but I didn't care; I knew who she was, and I knew what she wanted. I inched backward. My legs felt like they weren't even there, like they'd been cut off, but somehow, when I got into the pines, I managed to turn around. I moved from tree to tree, my hand sticky with sap, scraped raw by the bark. The thick clumps of haw scratched my arms and neck as I stumbled through them. And then I was clear. I sped up into a shuffling trot. I had dealt with the Division of Child and Family Services before; after the accident, when nobody knew how bad it was going to be, they had wanted to take me away from Dad.

When I got to the truck, I sat with my hands over my mouth, trying to remember how to breathe.

Snap out of it, I told myself. You've got to snap out of it.

They had arrested Dad. That was a fact.

They thought he had killed Watson. Something about his prints, which didn't make any sense. But that was another fact.

They wanted to take me. That was another.

My hands were still shaking when I started the truck, and it whined and groaned and chugged before the engine finally turned over. I drove with the lights off until I was a half mile down the canyon, and then I flicked them on and hammered the gas, the granite floating like great shears of ice, everything the color of moonlight as I fled.

Chapter 15

Haven't Seen Shit

I drove into Provo slowly. When the canyon opened up and the valley spread out in a blanket of electric lights, I let out a shuddering breath and had to squeeze my eyes shut, just for a moment, so I didn't start to cry.

I ended up in front of Joslyn's apartment. The street was practically empty, and I parked two spots down from her building. I turned off the truck, and then I sat there, the engine ticking as it cooled, the night breeze picking up until it howled around the seams of the door and then faded again. I took out my phone and went to my messages.

Ignoring the ones from Shivers, I opened Ariana's thread: *heyy* and *what's up* and *are you ok?*

I texted back: *Sorry, crazy day. Are you at J's? Parked outside.*

A moment later, light unfolded like a fan across the landing outside Joslyn's apartment. Ariana's silhouette moved to the railing. I couldn't see her face because of the shadows, but she held up a hand, and then a text came through on my phone: *Coming up?*

My hands were still trembling when I reached to undo the seat belt. I clutched the old metal buckle until they steadied. Then I released the latch, opened the door, and got out.

I heard her and smelled her before I saw her: the brush of bare feet on the carpet, the smell of a watermelon body spray I'd told her I liked. When I got to the landing, that fan of light from inside the apartment was enough to see by: she'd put her long, curly hair up, and she wore a t-shirt with a heart made out of gold sequins, along with sweat shorts that made all her curves easy to see. Her nails were painted the same turquoise as the shirt. She smiled, ducked toward me, and at the same time, I went to kiss her. We were both moving too fast, and our front teeth clicked together.

She made a dismayed noise, pulled back, and started laughing.

I rubbed my mouth. "Sorry."

She was still laughing. She shook her head, took my hand, and led me inside.

It seemed like Joslyn always had someone over, and tonight wasn't an exception. She was on the couch with a big white guy with a crazy bushy beard and a t-shirt that said NO FUCKS GIVEN; you could tell she and Ariana were sisters, and you could also tell she should have been out of this guy's league. He had his hand on Joslyn's leg, and he looked ten years older than her, minimum. Alma was there too, Shivers's round-faced henchman, his hair in that stupid Beatles cut. He was talking to another girl, Ruby—one of Joslyn and Ariana's friends. She was tiny, her hair shaved on the sides and in a quiff almost as big as her head, and wearing chunky black glasses. She had a colored pencil in her hand, and one of those adult coloring books lay on the coffee table in front of her. Her body was angled away from Alma, and she kept sneaking glances at Joslyn. I figured Alma was too dumb to realize he was barking up the wrong tree.

"This is Pete," Ariana said over the music from the Bluetooth speaker—Drake was playing.

Pete gave me a tough-guy nod and moved his hand along Joslyn's knee, just enough to let me know, in case I hadn't gotten a clue already.

"You want a drink?" Ariana asked, already moving to the cooler where they'd set up an impromptu bar.

I followed her. The need for a drink—for maybe more than a drink—hit me out of nowhere. I hadn't been thinking about it, I hadn't been thinking about anything except how Dad looked, his shoulders slumped, his wrists restrained awkwardly behind his back, as he shuffled toward Rivera's car. But now all I could think about was a drink.

It was the apartment, I told myself. It was hot, even with only a handful of people there—it seemed like Joslyn's place was always hot. And it stank. Some of that came from the kitchen, where chemically bright mac and cheese was crusting over in a pot, the Western Family box on the counter next to it, the ripped-off top laid across the back of the box like a bookmark. You know, in case you forgot which step you were on—add butter. But some of the foulness in the air came from the vape that Pete kept hitting and passing to Joslyn. I could smell the marijuana in the vape juice, but it had some sort of flavor that was doing a poor job of covering it up. I was pretty sure it was supposed to be creamsicle, and it was so bad it made my stomach turn. Sweat started under my arms and between my shoulder blades.

"Um, rum and Coke?" Ariana asked, half guess, half statement.

"Sure."

"Who paid for that?" Pete said between hits. "That shit ain't free."

"It's ok," Joslyn said. "Jack's like family."

"Family still pays," Pete said.

"Don't listen to him," Ariana said in a low voice as she got ice from the cooler. Joslyn and Pete were arguing now; that was how it usually went, and that was why Joslyn went through them so fast. She added rum, looked at me, and added more.

"That bad, huh?"

She smiled and shrugged. "You look good to me."

"—because I brought the bottle!" Pete shouted over Joslyn.

"You are such an asshole!" Joslyn shouted back.

"Jesus," I muttered as I took out the Superman wallet. I found a twenty—maybe it was technically Holmes's, although he'd told me to keep the change—and held it out to Pete between two fingers. Alma watched me, his big head with that Beatles haircut turning to follow the money. "Ok?"

Pete snatched it and sat back heavily on the sofa. His face was red under the bushy beard, and he waved the folded-up twenty under Joslyn's nose. "See? He gets it. Was that so fucking hard?"

"You don't have to be so cheap," Joslyn began.

I tuned them out, put my head back, and pounded the rum and Coke. It went down all right; when it got to my stomach, it was hot, and that warmth worked its way through me. I mixed myself another, ignoring Ariana's look. I was sweating more now, but I didn't mind as much. My shoulder and elbow and finger weren't bothering me as much. When I put back the second drink, I had to close my eyes.

When I opened them, Ariana was watching me. "I need a lawyer," I said, and just saying it made something tear loose inside me, and I had to breathe faster and blink my eyes. "Joslyn knows a guy, right? I think I met him once."

"Jos?" Ariana asked.

Joslyn was still shouting at Pete.

"Jos?"

"God damn it, what?" Joslyn asked, turning to face us.

"Jack wants to talk to that lawyer."

"It's two-fifty for driving without a license," she said without missing a beat. "But it's only, like, forty-five for speeding."

I laughed. My fingers slipped along the glass I was holding. "He does traffic tickets?"

"Uh, yeah. And he makes a shit-ton of money doing it. And he was never cheap—"

"I'm not cheap!" Pete roared back at her.

I mixed up a third and drank that one too, and when Ariana touched my arm, I pretended I didn't notice. He did traffic tickets. I'd been thinking—

"Jack?" Ariana asked.

"I drove down here," I said, but it was more to myself. "And he does speeding tickets."

Ariana said something, but it sank under the music. My whole body felt like a heat shimmer, rippling, floating. I saw Dad, Rivera's hand on the back of his head, forcing him to duck to fit into the back seat. Had they taken his medicine with them? Did they know how much to give him? Sometimes Dad didn't know—he got confused, or he couldn't read the labels. Did they know he needed ice packs when the migraines got really bad? Did they know sometimes he didn't want any noise, not even a fan? Did they know he needed all the lights off? Who was going to tell them? I guessed I was supposed to, but instead, I'd run away like a coward. For a moment, the night of the accident swam up at me out of the rum. I'd run. Again.

When I opened my eyes, the room tilted, and I had to steady myself against the wall so I could reach for the Bacardi.

Ariana caught my hand. "Let's smoke, instead. How about that?"

I opened my mouth to tell her no; I wanted another drink, fuel to keep the fire going. It wasn't that hot in here. Not really. Or maybe it was, but I was hot too, just a ripple of hot air, almost nothing. One more drink, and maybe I'd be nothing at all.

High-risk behavior, the therapist had told me. Fuck, I wanted to say. You haven't seen shit.

But when I went to find the words, they were all jumbled, and before I could straighten them out, she took my hand and dragged me over to sit on the floor next to the couch. Ruby was staring at me, a curled-up smile on her mouth.

"What?" I asked her.

She covered her mouth when she laughed. Alma laughed too, his eyes sliding from Ruby to me and back to Ruby.

Joslyn and Pete weren't arguing anymore. Pete's hand had slid up between Joslyn's legs. She was wearing tiny jersey shorts, and two of his fingers had disappeared behind the cotton. Ruby noticed too, and then she wasn't laughing anymore. Ariana left. When she came back, she had a vape pen, and she took a hit and passed it to me. I wasn't sure I could do it—the creamsicle smell was still turning my stomach—but when I pulled the vapor into my lungs, it was just weed. My eyes watered, and I squeezed them shut. It went through me like a wind, swinging open all the doors in my head and then slamming them shut, all those doors clapping back and forth in that wind. Then they all clapped shut at the same time, and for a while, it was dark, and it was nice, because nobody could get in. And, even more importantly, I couldn't get out.

Drake was still singing about being all alone. When you're all alone. I saw gray eyes and hair the color of aspen leaves ready to fall. When you're all alone. When you're all alone, I hope you know. The weight of his head against my shoulder, the way he fit under my arm. Drake singing, I want to be there.

At some point that night, some of the doors opened again. I remembered hitting Ariana's vape some more, her mouth turned down, her eyes tight. I remembered Ruby's sneer, and then shouting at her, and then Alma shouting at me. I remember taking a swing, only instead of landing the punch, I stumbled into the coffee table. It hit me at the shins, and I ended up falling face first into Joslyn's lap. Someone hauled me off her, and then I was on the floor, the oatmeal-colored carpet like a rash against my cheek.

"This is ridiculous," Joslyn said. "Make him go home."

"He can't go home," Ariana said. "Not like this."

They fought, and then nobody was fighting anymore, and then a door (a real one, this time) slammed. Joslyn's door, I realized. She and Pete had gone to her room. Alma and Ruby were gone. My chest felt bruised, and I thought maybe I remembered Alma kicking me while I was down. Ariana was moving around the apartment, her steps heavy, her movements brusque and tightly controlled: snatching a pillow off the sofa, snapping out a flat sheet to lay over me, the slap of her hand against the Bluetooth speaker. The silence that followed was like a slap as well. Then the lights went off.

"Don't you dare puke on the carpet," she said. She was sitting next to me, carding my hair. Her hand felt cool against my forehead, and I was hot again, struggling to get out from under the sheet. She pulled it back into place. "Do you hear me?"

I mumbled something.

For a moment, she was silent, her hand moving steadily. Her fingers felt good when they scratched lightly at my scalp. "I like you, Jack. You're sweet—most of the time—and you don't let yourself get pushed around, and God knows you're cute. But you are a hot mess, boy. You know that?"

The room insisted on being spinny, so I closed my eyes and offered a noise that I hoped made sense to her.

She laughed, but then her voice was serious. "I'm not doing this forever, having you show up so we can mess around and you can get trashed. You don't answer my texts. You disappear. And then you show up, and I like you, but—it's got to be more, Jack."

I made that noise again, but it sounded suspiciously sleepier this time.

"God, I'm going to have to do this all over again," she said, and then she laughed, but it didn't sound happy. "I'm serious, Jack. Don't you dare puke."

For a while, I was aware of her moving around again. Then she lay on the couch, and her breathing evened out into sleep. I drifted. All those doors inside me were swinging open and shut like a breeze was moving them. For a while, grunts and the sound of bodies slapping together came from Joslyn's room. And then, later, Pete staggered out, hooked a shoe from next to the sofa, and let himself out of the apartment. Then all the doors were closed, and when a few of them opened again, I was hot all over, waves of nausea cresting and then dropping. I tried to breathe through them. Then I gave it up, crawled into the bathroom, and heaved for a while. I lay on the floor, the tile cool against my cheek, my eyes filling up. I got out my phone. I couldn't see the screen clearly, but by that point I didn't care.

I need you.

That was what it was supposed to be, anyway, but at some point, I passed out.

Shouts woke me. It took me a moment to process the sounds and filter them out from sleep. My body was stiff and sore from a night spent on the bathroom tile. My head pounded, and my stomach and throat clenched. A little light made its way from under the door, which meant it was morning. The shouts moved toward me. When I checked my phone, my vision was too blurry for me to actually read the display, but it looked like I'd missed a lot of calls. I tried to get my head up, but the wave of pain and nausea made me squeeze my eyes shut and drop down to the tile again.

"Oh, yeah, no problem!" It was Shivers's voice, and he was shouting, but his tone had a false friendliness and—even worse—a manic energy that I recognized. It was the way guys sounded when they'd been up all night, getting cranked on meth or coke or speed and trying to tamp it down with booze or bennies or weed, then amping up again. "Hey, hey,

hey, I'm not going to bother him." The door flew open, missing my head by inches, and cracked against the wall. "I'm just going to square things up."

"Shivers—" I tried to say.

But he was flying on some strong shit, and he swooped down toward me before I could finish. I had an impression of the acne scars, his uneven jaw, the twitchiness of his eyes, his greasy mullet. Then he grabbed me by the hair and hauled me toward the door.

I screamed and scrambled after him, trying to get to my feet before he could rip my scalp off. I had enough sense to try to grab his wrist and break his hold, but Shivers slowed down long enough to club me on the side of the head with his free hand a few times. The world came apart at the seams, and I let go of him. He kept dragging me, and by some miracle I stayed upright.

"Stop!" Ariana was screaming from where she sat on the floor. "Leave him alone!"

"What the hell is going on?" Joslyn demanded from her bedroom doorway.

Shivers hauled me toward the door.

When we got to the stairs, I couldn't keep up with him and manage the steps, and I fell. Either Shivers lost his grip or—less likely—he decided to be merciful, because instead of letting me rip the hair out of my head when I fell, he released me. I rolled down the concrete steps to the landing and came up hard against the railing; the steel bit into my back. Shivers came down the steps slowly, giving me enough time to get to my hands and knees. I crawled toward the next flight of stairs going down, but before I reached them, Shivers caught up with me.

"Jacky tough shit," he said in a singsong voice, and then he kicked me in the gut. All the breath whooshed out of my lungs. The pain in my head went nuclear. My stomach heaved, and I tried to throw up, but my body wasn't doing anything right anymore, and for a moment, all I could do was spasm—trying to get air and, at the same time, trying to empty my guts. Shivers caught me by the collar this time and dragged me down the stairs. "Not so tough now, though, are you?"

Somehow, I managed to get a breath, and then another. Shivers dumped me next to the truck. He kicked me a few more times until I stopped trying to get up—until I stopped trying to move at all, actually—and then he patted me down. When he found the keys, he shook them out and started testing them on the door.

"See, Jacky, it's pretty fucking stupid to go around flashing money when you owe me. And you owe me big, Jacky. And it's really fucking stupid to go flashing money in front of Alma. And it's mega fucking stupid to take a swing at my boy that same night. So, here's what we're going to do. You're going to pay me. And then I'm going to fuck you up. And that's me being nice to you, Jacky, because I was having such a good fucking night until you fucked it up."

I stared up at the gray pre-dawn sky, trying to breathe, aftershocks running through me.

Shivers got the truck door open. He fumbled around inside for a minute or two. Then he swore and dropped into a crouch next to me. He dug the tip of a key into the skin at the corner of my eye, and the pain and pressure and panic made tears well up. I couldn't blink them away because I was afraid my next movement would make him drive the key home. The smell of him filled my nose, choking me: BO and the burned-plastic stink of meth.

"Where's my money?"

"I'll get it. I've got it, I just need to get it."

"That's what you keep telling me. Where's my money?"

"I swear to God, I've got it. I just need a day to put it together."

"Jacky tough shit." Shivers shook his head, and the key pressed in harder. I could feel the strain in my eye. In my head, I had the vivid vision of a balloon popping. "How pretty do you think you're going to be when I'm done with you?"

And then the pressure left my eye, and Shivers disappeared. There was a metallic thump, like sheet metal flexing. I stared up at the sky. The gray had lightened until, combined with the texture of the clouds, it looked like aluminum foil.

Metal shivered and protested again. Someone cried out, and it took me a moment to realize it was Shivers. I managed to sit up, and I stared at the scene in front of me. I told myself that was it, no more weed, no more green outs, because I was pretty sure this was a schizoid break.

Holloway Holmes held Shivers by his greasy mullet and, as I watched, slammed his head into the truck's side panel again. The metal gave slightly, warping under the impact and giving off that sound again. Shivers whoofed. His eyes were unfocused, and he'd dropped the keys to try to get free of Holmes, fumbling at his wrist to pull his hand away. He didn't have the strength to break his grip—or maybe he was too out of it from having his head put halfway through the side of the Ram. Holmes gave him another considering look, smashed his head into the truck one last time, and released him. Shivers toppled sideways, and Holmes caught his jacket and dragged him into the street. Shivers moaned, his head bouncing over the asphalt.

All of that was the part of the vision that made sense. The part that made me question my sanity was Holmes's appearance: his hair stuck up in back, dirt and scratches covered his face, and his lip was raw where he'd clearly been chewing it. He wore a fleece jacket, unzipped, over a tank printed with hibiscus flowers. Instead of chinos, he had on teal-and-pink striped jersey shorts that barely came to the middle of his thighs. I was vaguely aware of approximately a mile of long, pale, muscled calves and thighs, with more straight blond hair on them than I'd seen anywhere else on Holmes's body. His skin was pebbled with the cold. And, of course, he was wearing the chukkas, although they were scraped to hell now.

"Are those your pajamas?" I asked. And then, "What are you—what's—" I couldn't finish the question. Another wave of nausea rolled in, and cold sweat broke out all over me.

"Your message sounded urgent." Holmes considered Shivers and then stooped to pick up my keys. "I would have gotten here sooner, but I had to hike almost to the mouth of the canyon before I could hitch a ride."

I vaguely remembered sending a text at some point in the night, although I realized now I'd clicked the wrong number and gotten Holmes instead of Mom's, and I had a million questions—one of them was, *You hiked and hitched almost twenty miles in the middle of the night because I said I needed you?* Another was, *How the hell did you find me?*—but my stomach roiled, and my guts made a weird squeaking noise that did not sound good.

Color infused Holmes's face, and I realized I was still staring at him. He yanked the fleece together and ran the zipper up. He crossed his arms. He looked so uncertain, so uncomfortable, so un-Holmes bot, that I knew I needed to say something.

"Holloway Holmes—" I began.

He immediately began to scowl. He was getting pretty good at it.

"—you are righteously badass, and you are my savior, and in those booty shorts, you are complete and total dongbait—"

His face caught fire.

"—and I've got more stuff I'm going to tell you about how fucking fire you are, but right now, I need to throw up."

I crawled over to the gutter, the asphalt scraping my knees and the heels of my hands, and puked up half my internal organs. The cold sweats were worse, and I was shaking all over by the time I finished and seriously worried I was about to shit myself. When I finished, I crawled a few feet away and rested my forehead on the street. I could smell old mulch, cold concrete, a hint of smoke that I guessed was from a hibachi on an apartment balcony. Holmes's hand came to rest feather light on my nape. Then it slid down, following the bumps of my spine, and then back up. I had a vision of a Holmes bot learning to pet a cat, and I wanted to laugh. And then, instead, I was on the brink of crying.

Holmes stepped closer, his hand scruffing the hair on the side of my head, pressing me against his bare thigh. I squeezed my eyes shut. He was warm—unbelievably warm on such a cold, bleached morning. After a few moments, I wasn't going to cry anymore, but I wasn't ready to pull away either. Then, after another minute, I moved back, the cold twice as bad now on my face where I'd been pressed against him.

"How do you feel?"

I croaked a sound that was supposed to be a laugh. "I feel like I just got off *Chicago's Little Lady*."

The tiny line appeared between those fine blond brows. "Is that a sex worker?"

The laugh came from somewhere real inside me this time, and I wiped my eyes, which were stinging again, but in a good way this time. I shook my head. "A tour bus emptied its septic tank onto the boat *Chicago's Little Lady*. 2004. Eight hundred pounds of shit raining down on all these tourists who just wanted a ride on the river. Found it on Wikipedia when I was trying to write a paper on Dave Matthews Band."

That line between his eyebrows deepened. "A paper for whom?"

"For me, so I'm not so stupid. Help me up."

Holmes took my arm and pulled me to my feet. The ease with which he lifted me reminded me again that he was much stronger than he looked. He held out the keys, and I took them. Then he looked away. His shoulders drew up, and when he spoke, his voice was so quiet that even in the morning stillness, I could barely hear him. "You are not stupid. You're quite intelligent, actually."

"Yeah, well," I said because I couldn't come up with anything else. And then, after a beat, I added, "This morning kind of proves otherwise, right?"

"You owe him money for drugs," Holmes said as a statement, not a question.

I nodded. Shivers was still moaning softly in the center of the street. His face was a bloody mess, his nose smashed, his eyes half closed.

Holmes had done that, I thought, and I shivered. He'd done it without even trying, and it didn't look like it had bothered him at all.

"H—"

"It was a mistake to attempt a conclusion with insufficient data," Holmes said, and maybe he was reading my mind again because his words were neat and precise and detached, closing me off from whatever we'd shared a moment ago. "I should never have assumed it was Maggie. We need more data, Jack. And that means we need to go back to where we should have begun: with the footage from the security cameras."

Chapter 16

Holloway Holmes Throws Shade

Holmes insisted no one would be watching the cottage, and he was right. I parked under the carport and got out of the truck. Holmes caught up with me on the porch. He was shivering as I unlocked the front door, and a part of my brain wondered how it had been to hike thirteen or fourteen miles in shorts and a tank top and a fleece jacket, in the middle of the night, without a compass or a map, just hoping someone would pick you up and take you the rest of the way. Because a guy you'd met a few days before sent you one text.

When the door swung open, I said, "I'm sorry."

Holmes furrowed his brow. "For what?"

"For being an asshole. Never mind, it'll take too long to explain. Come on, you've got to be freezing."

He trailed me into the house, looking around. I focused on the disaster zone that had previously been my home. The deputies had torn it apart—in some cases, literally. Drawers and cabinets hung open. Furniture had been moved away from the wall. Fingerprint powder covered everything, a fine black dust that I could already tell was going to be impossible to clean up completely. Muddy footprints tracked across the linoleum and carpet. In the kitchen, they'd dumped out the silverware, the Krusteaz, Mom's cookbooks, spatulas and turners and those weird silicone brushes we never used for anything—all of it piled in the middle of the floor. In the living room, they'd turned Dad's recliner on its side and cut away the dust cover. In case he'd been hiding something, I guessed. And the bitter part of it was that they hadn't been wrong; they'd found the zannies after all.

Maybe a half a minute went by before I trusted my voice enough to say, "Sorry it's a bit of a mess; I wasn't expecting visitors."

"You can file a complaint," Holmes said. "Possibly a lawsuit. This is not how an appropriate search is conducted, and it suggests a degree of personal animosity that might be actionable."

I nodded along with his words, my head on a string. I wasn't really hearing anything. Moving deeper into the house, I continued to inspect the damage. The bathroom was actually ok—they'd tossed everything from the sink and medicine cabinet into the tub, but at least they hadn't taken the toilet as evidence. Dad's room looked like a tornado had gone through it. I stared at the chaos from where I stood in the hall, and then I shut the door. I'd deal with it later.

My room was almost as bad. My desk was upside down, and they'd staved in the bottoms of two of the drawers and broken one of the legs. Most of my clothes had already been on the floor, but now they were everywhere. My mattress and box spring were standing against the wall, both of them cut open—the box spring's dust cover gone, and the mattress slit open on one side. I tried to get the box spring back onto the bed frame, but no matter what I did, it wouldn't fit. It was too big—or it seemed like it anyway. So I'd pull it off and try again. The third time, I stood, kicked it, and shouted, "You motherfucking piece of shit, go on!" and kept kicking it.

I finally got it into place, or good enough. I wiped my face. I checked my phone. I had a bunch of missed calls and texts from Ariana, all of them asking versions of the same thing: *Are you ok?*

I texted back: *I'm fine. Sorry about that, emergency. Text you later.*

Then I realized what I should have said and texted: *Are you ok?*

Holmes appeared in the doorway. He stood there, watching me.

I stepped back from the mattress, ran a hand through my hair, and then pressed both hands against my eyes. When I spoke, I could hear the high-wire thinness of my own voice. "Do you need a ride back to your residence?"

"I straightened the bathroom."

I laughed, and it sounded like it was coming out of a tin can. "Thanks."

"Maybe you'd like to take a shower."

"I've got a lot to do here, in case you hadn't noticed. And I've got to convince Taylor to let me cover Dad's shift—if they haven't fired him already." I squatted and began to pick through the clothes, trying to find something with the Walker logo, because the reality was that I had to handle work first, and then I could come home and deal with this shit. "If you need a ride, I'll take you now. Otherwise—"

Holmes had crossed the room without my noticing, and he crouched next to me now. He reached out like he might touch my shoulder or arm. Then he dropped his hand. It was classic Holmes bot programming— prime directive, be awkward as hell.

"Jack," he said quietly. "I think you should take a shower. And brush your teeth." When I opened my mouth to argue, he said, "Mr. Taylor is looking for reasons to terminate your employment."

I stared at him. And then I stood. I kicked off the Vans, and as I stripped out of the jeans and tee, Holmes fled. I went into the bathroom. I ditched my boxers and started the water. Holmes had told the truth; he'd straightened the bathroom. I stood in front of the mirror, looking at myself, and somebody seriously messed up looked back at me. I chafed my arms as goose bumps ran across my chest, down my belly, along my thighs. I opened the medicine cabinet, just for the hell of it. He'd started with A for aloe on the top, and everything went alphabetically through toothpaste at the bottom. I smiled and let my head fall against the door. The sound of the running water covered up everything else. That was good, because when I got in the shower, I cried for a long time.

When I got out, the house was silent, and noticeably warmer. Holmes must have turned up the heat. I dried off, wrapped the towel around my waist, and stepped out into the hall.

"H?"

No answer. I padded toward the living room and kitchen, but they were empty. I went back down the hall, gave Dad's room a quick check, and went into mine. No Holmes. Maybe he'd gotten tired of dealing with my particular brand of fuck-up, I thought as I hung the towel on the back of my chair. Maybe he figured it had been a mistake, getting involved with me at all. I picked through the clothes, trying to find what was clean and what wasn't, but it was all jumbled together now. I did the sniff test. I did spot checks. I just wanted a clean pair of underwear, and I realized even that might be asking for too much.

I had just pulled on a pair of heart-print boxers when Holmes squeaked, "Oh my God."

I looked up, and three things made themselves immediately clear to me:

First, Holmes was standing in my doorway holding improvised takeout containers: paper plates covered with paper plates.

Second, he was staring at me, and his eyes were huge.

Third, I was four inches of cotton away from naked.

Before I could say anything, Holmes sprinted back down the hallway. A moment later, his voice compressed like a spring, he said, "Jack, I am very sorry."

"Uh, it's ok?" I said, although it came out like a question.

The silence limped past. "I didn't see anything."

Which was exactly what someone said when they did see something. For some reason, that made me grin. It was like the alphabetical medicine cabinet.

"Jack?"

I found a Walker polo that smelled all right and walked out to the kitchen. Holmes stood near the door, his back to me—he practically had his nose in the corner. He was still carrying the make-shift takeout containers. Whatever they held, it smelled delicious—I could pick out the scent of sausage.

Holmes threw a glance over his shoulder, and his eyes went to my face. Then, even though he was obviously trying to resist, they ran down me, like he was trying to match what he'd seen to the outline of my body under the clothes. And then he turned even redder and looked back at a tiny wallet-sized photo of my great-grandma Doris that we kept on the fridge.

"That's Grandma Doris," I said, righting a stool to sit at the counter. "She was a stone-cold bitch, and she's dead."

He whipped around.

"Kidding," I said. "She was super sweet. She is dead, though." He looked so indignant that my grin got even bigger. "What'd you bring me?"

He moved over to the counter, his body tense, his head down, and he slid one of the plates in front of me. I watched him as I flipped off the improvised lid. He was staring at his own doubled-up plates, his shoulders curled in, his face closed off. I checked my plate: scrambled eggs, two biscuits the size of hubcaps, and a lake of gravy. I forked some of all of it, including the eggs, and popped it in my mouth. I made a noise, and when Holmes turned even redder, I started to laugh.

"You should put on pants," he said, lifting his head long enough to throw a scowl at me.

"Look who's talking."

"These are shorts. They're clothing."

"They're booty shorts. Of course, if I had legs and an ass like yours, I might wear booty shorts too."

"I do not wear them—" Holmes stopped. His throat moved. "They are not for public—" And then, with an un-Holmes bot whine: "Can't you at least put on socks?"

I ducked my head, curling my toes around the stool's lowest rung, and started to laugh again.

"It's really good," I managed to say through the fit of laughter—and the remaining biscuit, sausage gravy, and eggs. "Thank you."

He shrugged. "It's dining hall food."

It didn't taste like it; I'd eaten my share of cafeteria breakfasts and lunches at my old school, and it definitely hadn't been anything like this. Sure, every once in a while, I snuck a pastry or a coffee from the kitchen at Walker, but I now realized that I had been missing out on some seriously good chow.

"That isn't too much gravy?" Holmes asked. He still hadn't uncovered his food, and he was toying with the edge of the foam plate, worrying it back and forth.

"Actually—no." My eyebrows went up. "I like a ton of gravy, and usually I don't get enough."

He nodded. Something smoothed out in his face.

"Which," I said slowly, "you already knew."

"You used up all the animal sauce when you ate your fries."

My smile was softer this time. "Holloway Holmes."

His eyes came up to mine and then cut away.

"You had better eat some food," I said, "or I'm going to go for it."

He shrugged. "I brought it for you."

He didn't say anymore, but he also wasn't hiding his face anymore. He was studying the house—the wreckage of it—those cold gray eyes taking in everything. Not cold, I realized. He really wasn't cold at all. He was awkward as hell, sure. And he had a trick of...detaching himself, I guess. Putting the real Holmes away so the Holmes bot could play. But not cold. In fact, remembering how he'd looked at me when he'd stumbled into the bedroom, remembering the way his eyes moved, trying to find me again through the clothes, I thought maybe there was a lot of fire in Holloway Holmes. You just had to figure out how to get to it.

"Hey H?"

He glanced over.

"I'm sorry." When he didn't say anything, more words spilled out of me. "For, uh, texting you. Last night. It was an accident, and I didn't mean to drag you into my personal crap. And—" Now my face was hot. I tried to spear another bite of biscuit, and the fork went all the way through the foam plate. Holmes's eyes widened because, of course, he hadn't missed that. "—I really appreciate it."

He nodded. Then he said, "Why would you be sorry?"

From outside came voices—older voices, a man and a woman, doubtless Walker faculty—growing closer and then moving away again. The man started to laugh. And then they were too far away to hear anymore.

"Well," I said, "you, like, hiked twenty miles or something. In a canyon. In the dark. And then you hitched a ride and—" I frowned. "Wait, how did you find me?"

"The Hundred Hour Board." When I shook my head, Holmes said, "You haven't heard of it? It's something designed for BYU students. They can post a question, and in a hundred hours or fewer, they're supposed to get an answer. Crowdsourced information, which as we both know can be problematic—"

"Uh huh," I said. "So you asked a bunch of strangers on the internet where I was, and someone knew? Are they hackers? Did they hack my phone?"

"I don't think anyone could hack your phone," Holmes said. "It would be like trying to hack a rock."

I stared at him. "Holy shit, is Holloway Holmes throwing shade?"

"I told them my roommate borrowed my truck, he wasn't answering his phone, and I needed to find him to tell him his pet cat, Pollyanna, needed to go to the vet."

"Pollyanna? And, what, someone happened to see me?"

"No, several people went out looking for you." Holmes snapped off the piece of foam plate he'd been bending. "They're relentless do-gooders; it's quite useful."

I shook my head.

"You could use it too," Holmes said, "if you had any questions. For example, if you were curious about how far cellphone technology has advanced since 1994."

"Holy shit."

He rolled his eyes.

"No, this is some next-level holy shit."

"Are you going to eat these biscuits too?" He uncovered the second plate and pushed them toward me.

"Holloway Holmes is standing in my kitchen, giving me shit about my phone."

"Fine. If you're not hungry, I'll dispose of them."

"No, no, no!" I caught his arm. "I'll eat them!"

I drew the plate over to my side of the counter. Then I stopped. "You have to at least eat half."

"I don't need to eat half."

His pupils were tiny black dots. He was flexing the piece of foam that he'd torn off from the plate, his fingers restless. Since we'd gotten back, he'd been moving constantly—he certainly hadn't sat down. And he'd been fiddling with things in the truck on the drive back. And that was after a night hike, a fight, and a full day before that. *I don't sleep much.*

"How much are you taking?"

He was a second too slow. "What?"

"Oh no. I sell you that shit, so I know you use it. How many addies did you take last night?"

After a moment of hesitation, he said. "One."

"Bullshit."

"Two."

"H, I will beat your ass if you lie to me again."

He set his jaw. "Two."

I thought about it. Then I said. "How many since midnight?"

That line deepened between his eyebrows again.

"Yeah, you thought I'd be too dumb to think of that," I said. "How many?"

"I do not think you're dumb."

"You think I'm stupid enough to fall for that. You took two last night. How many since midnight, since that's technically the start of a new day?"

The corner of his mouth trembled; he was trying so hard not to bite his lip, and I wondered what it had taken to try to train that out of him, and I wondered why they had done it. Moriarty had said it was a tell, and maybe that was the truth, but I thought of him biting his lip in the truck, I thought of him biting his lip with the light coming in silver on the side of his face, I thought of what he'd look like with his knees pulled up to his chest, reading a book that rested there, biting his lip, his whole face locked into that pure Holmes focus.

He wavered. Then he snapped, "Two."

"You took four last night? Jesus, H, I sell you the thirty-milligram ones. You're supposed to take—"

"I do not need you telling me what I'm supposed to do."

The words weren't exactly a shout, but they were loud, and they came out too fast.

For a moment, there was nothing between us. Then something moved outside—a squirrel, maybe a fox. The sound seemed to set everything moving again, and Holmes angled his body away from me, his chest rising and falling rapidly.

"I will eat half," he said quietly.

"Why fucking bother?" I said and slid the plate into the trash. "You said you wanted my help. That's why you came and dragged Shivers off me, right?"

Without waiting for a response, I stood and made my way toward my room.

Holmes trailed after me. "That's not why I—" He stopped. When he started again, his voice sounded like he was threading a needle. "Is he going to bother you again? If he wants money—"

"I'll handle it," I said, kicking aside clothes until I came up with a pair of work jeans. I pulled them on. Sure, I told myself. You've got no cash, you've got no zannies, you've got nothing else you can sell, and oh yeah, Dad's in jail. Jacky tough shit definitely has it all handled. "What do you need?"

He didn't say anything. He was like this black hole behind me; I could feel him, his gravity dragging on me. Sure, I thought as I kicked aside more clothes, trying to find a pair of socks. Sure, a black hole sounded about right. Stars that got too close to black holes got shredded by the gravity. Thank you, Wikipedia and the two weeks I spent reading about astrophysics.

"Do you need help?" H asked.

"Nope."

"I think I see—"

"I'm fine."

He shifted his weight; I could hear the rustle of his clothing. In the part of my brain that didn't feel like I was on fire, I was pretty sure not being allowed to make observations was killing him. I found a black running sock. And then I found a white crew sock that had been washed so many times it was gray.

"If you want a matching pair—" Holmes tried again.

"I don't," I said. "In fact, I don't have any matching pairs because every time I do laundry, I lose socks. Stephen Hawking and Roger Penrose said spontaneous black holes are responsible for lost socks, so maybe that's why."

"I don't think so. A spontaneous black hole, even a tiny one, would cause tremendous damage."

"It's on Wikipedia." I turned the crew sock right side out and snapped it straight. "Look it up."

When I shot him a glance, the corner of his mouth was trembling, and he was rubbing his arm. "Jack, you're upset—"

"I need to go. There's this weird thing I have to do every day. It's called a job. If you want help, fine. I need to get my dad out of jail. But if this is a game to you, or if you're not really serious, then I should probably work on my own. Being locked up like this might kill my dad, so, you know, I can't just jerk off about this anymore."

Those fevered patches appeared in his cheeks again, but when he spoke, his voice was soft. "It is not a game."

I grunted and fished my Vans out of the chaos.

"I need your help because I can't do this alone," Holmes said. "There will be several stages, but the first is reconnaissance, and unfortunately, people tend to pay attention to me, so I can't do it—not all of it."

"Yeah, don't worry. Nobody pays attention to me."

He was still rubbing his arm, and his gray eyes were big, following me as I moved around the room, collecting my wallet, the Walker keys, my phone. "The first thing we need to know is what kind of surveillance surrounds the security office. The second thing we need to know is what kind of locks secure the door."

Shoving my wallet into my pocket, I snorted and met his eyes. He broke first, looking away. I held up my hand, and with my other hand, I traced an L on my palm. H followed my movements without meeting my gaze again. "The security office is here." I touched the short leg of the L. "The only camera is here." I touched the corner where the two legs met. "You can't get to the security office without passing the camera."

Holmes nodded. "If you can examine the camera closely today and identify the make and model, I can look up the schematics—"

"Unless you go through the tunnels." I tapped the short leg of the L again. "There's an access stairway here, from back when they used to worry about getting everyone to a fallout shelter."

Holmes's eyes studied my hand again. Then he looked at me. "You're sure?"

I snorted again and started toward the door. He moved out of my path at the last moment; I thought maybe I could feel the warmth of his body, the phantom heat of him, that's how close we came to a collision. "And I installed the new lock two weeks ago. It's one of those RFID and fingerprint models. I think the manual is in the maintenance office, in one of the filing cabinets. I can get it for you on my lunch break."

"No," Holmes said. "I can retrieve it myself, if it is where you said it is. Are you sure—"

"No, God, you're right. I'm so fucking stupid that I don't actually remember if I installed the lock or not. Thanks, H. I was too embarrassed to tell you that I can't remember what I did two fucking weeks ago."

"Jack, I was simply asking—"

"I don't know what you think we're going to see. The camera by the maintenance building was disabled on the night of the murder, and the detectives will have already checked the other cameras."

"Perhaps. But we need data, and I believe we'll be able to assemble a pattern based on the footage from the cameras that were functional that night."

"Everybody is out of Walker Hall by seven," I said as I let myself out of the cottage. "But to be safe, let's meet at the maintenance building at nine tonight. If you try to go without me, I'll call the detectives working this case and tell them everything. Do you understand?"

Cheeks bright, Holmes gave a savage nod.

I don't know why I had to twist the knife. I didn't know why it embarrassed him so much, and I didn't know why I wanted to hurt him so bad. But I knew it would work, so I smirked and shot back at him as I pulled the door shut, "And H? Try not to sniff my dirty undies."

Chapter 17

Obviously

That night, my alarm woke me at ten minutes to nine, and I fumbled for it in the gloom until it stopped beeping. I lay there for a moment, blinking my gummed-up eyes, trying to orient myself. I was on the sofa, contorted so that my legs weren't hanging off the end, under a blanket I'd taken from my room. When I'd gotten home from work—not at four, when my shift was supposed to end, but at seven, after busting my ass to finish the extra projects Taylor had given me—I'd been too wiped to try to put the bed to rights. So I lay on the sofa, and the only light came from the blink and flicker of the TV, a pallid glow that, in my half sleep, made me think of corpses.

It had been a bad day—the technical term is fucking awful, I believe. It had been terrible starting with the not-fight with Holmes, and then it had gotten worse when I'd had to beg Taylor—I'd literally used the words "I'm begging you" three times before he relented—to let me work Dad's shift. It meant lying through my teeth, telling Taylor how kind he was, how grateful I was, that yes, I'd already done the intake for DCFS, that yes, they were perfectly happy to let me live independently until things with my dad were resolved. Taylor must have known it was bullshit, but he also knew he could squeeze free labor out of me. I'd spent the day doing the shit work that Taylor always farmed out to me because nobody else wanted to do it—the last two hours of my extended shift, instead of eating dinner, I'd dug up a broken sprinkler line. When I'd finally gotten home, I'd collapsed.

I had to pee, so I stumbled to the bathroom, my arm and elbow and finger zinging as they were forced to move again, on top of the dull ache in my back and shoulders and ribs from the trench work. And getting pummeled by Shivers. And all that puking. I washed my hands. I washed my face. I tried to fix my hair and then I gave up, because I didn't care what Holloway Holmes thought about me or my hair or anything, and then I hit my head against the door a few times and gave up and tried to fix it again.

It was a minute after nine when I got to the maintenance building, and I was swallowing the last of the peanut butter sandwich I'd slapped together before rushing out of the cottage. The night was alive with the canyon breeze—a stiff, rushing force tonight, whipping the pine and scrub oak, filling the air with the dusty, desert scent of resin and sage and the cold bones of granite. The security lights around the maintenance building broke the darkness, and they made it look like an island—the last outpost in a world that had gone dark. I was licking peanut butter from my thumb, trying to get the keys off my belt loop, when a shadow detached itself from the wall and came toward me. I swore, took a step back, and then waved the keys I was clutching at Holmes.

"What the hell? Are you trying to scare me to death?"

Nothing crossed Holmes's face. He was dressed all in black: jacket and oxford, jeans, and sneakers. Even his soles were black. And while I knew one explanation, the surface explanation, was that we were sneaking around campus, and black was a great color for sneaking around at night, I couldn't help thinking about how he'd dressed earlier that day—the splashes of pink and teal, the hibiscus flowers. And all the dumb jokes I'd made. And the fight. And now he was here, in black. Another coat of armor for Holloway Holmes.

"We agreed to meet at nine," was all he said.

"Yeah, but maybe don't jump out from the shadows when I'm already freaked out." I pulled up the hood on my hoodie, glanced around, and let out a breath. We were still alone. "This way."

I led him to the door to the tunnels, the one set into the side of the maintenance building that Rivera had used. I found the key, put it into the lock, and turned. For a moment, nothing happened, and I thought maybe Rivera had ordered them to change the lock. The vague thought came to me that somehow Rivera had planned this, that it was a trap. But then the key turned, and the door creaked open. I winced and eased it back as quietly as I could.

Air washed over me, weirdly warmer than the gale ripping down the canyon. It smelled like old smoke, like pot, and what I thought of as an underground smell—stone and concrete that never saw the sun. I slipped through the opening, and Holmes came after me.

Emergency lights were always on in the tunnels, although they were spaced out twenty or thirty yards, and they were dim and yellow with age.

In between them, shadows pooled. It was enough light to see the stairs charred from an old fire, the concrete blackened, the ancient paint bubbled up and curling away in strips. When we got to the bottom of the steps, the smell of pot was stronger. I held up a hand to stop Holmes and listened; kids came down here sometimes, through other access points that were less secure. But no noise came back to me, and after a moment, I beckoned for him to follow. The shadows striped his face. They covered his eyes. I wanted to see them, to see if I could figure out what the hell was going on in there, but instead, I kept going.

The tunnels were…well, the best way to describe it might be a trip. They were unreal, and at the same time, they were totally real. In most places, the walls were cinderblock that in places had been painted and in other places not, the floor and ceiling were poured concrete, and the walkable space was made cramped by pipes that ran on one side of the tunnel and overhead. Some of them were hot to the touch—hot enough to burn, as I'd learned the first time I'd come down here, and I'd had a bandage on my arm for a week.

We passed riveted steel doors marked with old tin signs painted yellow and black—three triangles point-down inside a circle, and the words FALLOUT SHELTER. I'd gone in one of them once before I got the willies so bad I ran and didn't come back down here for a month. I remembered the metal shelving, the cans of food, a rectangular box that said CHEMICAL TOILET, the steel-frame bunk beds with moldering blankets of undyed wool. Something—a rat, I think—had moved under one of the beds, and I'd jumped back so fast I'd hit my head on the bunk behind me, and that was when I'd decided to get the hell out of there.

As we continued along the tunnels, we passed through some of the buildings that dotted campus. In some of these, steel grilles looked in on darkened basement classrooms: rows of desks, the gleam of the white board. In other places, side passages opened up, some of them at strange heights or angles, providing access to crawlspaces. Taylor had never sent me into any of those—I wasn't even sure he knew about them—but I had no intention of ever squeezing my ass into one of those tiny, dark holes. In some places, the tunnel floor was lower, the difference bridged by a few steps, and the rails were gritty and left orange streaks on my hands. In other places, the tunnels opened up—at intersections, or in the basements of school buildings. Girders ran above us, and dead fluorescents hung in wire cages, and chain-link fences protected old boilers and furnaces that were no longer in use. One of these cages had been ripped down halfway, and a sheet of plywood had been tacked into place, the wood spongy after years in the relatively high humidity down here. Some of the side passages were closed off, grates welded into place across the openings, although even those weren't foolproof—in places, generations of Walker kids had loosened some of the supports, or cut through them completely, so you could never tell if a passage was truly sealed without a close inspection.

Two things remained constant about the tunnels under Walker. The first was the graffiti. It covered everything—the cinderblock, the chain-link fencing, the doors, the registers, the girders, even the pipes. A lot of it was what you'd expect: names, tags, Jojo sucks dick, Vanessa puts out, and then a phone number, smiley faces. But then there were the unique ones: a giant penis with a Prince Albert piercing and the words, *Hi, my name is Doug*; stapled to a sheet of plywood, the centerfold from the 1997 January edition of *Playboy*, the boobs circled with red spray paint; and in one of the largest rooms, taking up an entire wall in bright orange spray paint: *Mr. Humps got you*. At intersections and forks in the path, Sharpied arrows and labels indicated routes to various spots on campus, and I checked these occasionally; I knew the way to Walker Hall, but the last thing I needed was to get lost and make myself look like an ass all over again in front of Holmes.

The other thing that never ended in the tunnels was the noises. Pipes clanked. Steam hissed as it escaped. Our steps came back at us in the closed spaces, and when the tunnels were at their narrowest, our breathing sounded like an animal at our backs. More than once, I looked back over my shoulder, checking Holmes's face in the yellow glow from the security lights. Every time, his face was unreadable. There was something weirdly reassuring about going into the tunnels with a Holmes bot. All the creep vibes bounced off his titanium exoskeleton. And I was pretty sure that, even if he hated me now, he wouldn't leave me if shit went down. His decency chip wouldn't allow it.

Hearing that thought, I spent the next several minutes trying to decide if I was as much of an asshole as I sometimes sounded in my head. Holmes was more than decent. And he definitely wasn't a robot. Sure, he'd pissed me off, yelling at me when I was trying to—well, I'd almost said *take care of him*, but obviously he didn't need that. So what, exactly, had I been trying to do? I was attempting to figure that out when I heard the voices ahead of us.

The sound came from the next intersection. I glanced back, caught the flicker of worry on Holmes's face, and considered our options. We were halfway down one of the longest stretches of tunnel—it ran at least a hundred yards behind us, and then it opened up into a larger room without any decent hiding spots before continuing on again. In other words, absolutely no chance of running and hiding. The voices were coming toward us, which meant we couldn't wait and hope they'd pass us by. That left only one option: try to bluff our way out of this.

"Do you trust me?" I asked Holmes over my shoulder.

His brows drew together, but he nodded.

"Play along." And then, because I definitely was as much of an asshole as I thought I was, I added, "Engage acting protocol."

He scowled, and then the voices reached the intersection, and his face went blank.

I turned around to see Aston and Dawson, two-fifths of the Boy Band. For an instant, I was able to see them before they'd seen us. They were both smiling, their heads close together, their bodies bumping as they filled each other's space. They were whispering, and I couldn't make out the exact words, but the sound of whispers still carried a long way in the tunnels. They were both dressed like they'd snuck out of bed: slides, crew socks, shorts, tanks, hoodies. Aston's blond hair was mussed worse than usual, and a hickey glowed on the side of his neck. Dawson's lips looked puffy, and unless he was carrying a banana around, he was happy to see Aston, or however that joke was supposed to go. Aston hit a vape hard, exhaling the scent of marijuana. Then Aston's head came up, and his eyes went wide with shock when he saw us. Dawson furrowed his Neanderthal forehead, and his jaw tightened. For a moment, all four of us were silent.

Dawson opened his mouth, the furrows on his forehead getting deeper.

I smirked, held a finger to my lips, and reached back to take Holmes's hand. The coolness of his skin felt like sparks under my palm, which didn't make any sense, and a flush started in my chest and moved up to my face. Then I started forward, toward Aston and Dawson, tugging Holmes behind me. He stumbled along. Judging by how stiff his hand felt in mine, he probably looked as freaked out and awkward as a Holmes bot could get, which was perfect for what I wanted.

Aston was still staring at us, his eyes wide with incomprehension. But Dawson was starting to grin back at me, his eyes appraising me again before moving to Holmes. Holmes stumbled, but I kept a firm grip of his hand and pulled him along. They were still blocking the intersection, but I stayed on course, and when I got close enough, Dawson hooked a finger under the elastic of Aston's shorts and tugged him back a step, clearing the way for us. Dawson's hand lingered there, curling around Aston's hip with a kind of suggestive possessiveness, but his eyes were still on me, half question, half challenge. And maybe, if I was reading him right, part invitation. Maybe later, I thought, the smirk getting hotter on my face. I didn't usually like them rough, but Dawson definitely had a vibe. Then I thought of Ariana, about those half-remembered conversations, and I thought maybe not. Not if she was serious about locking this down.

And then, without anyone saying a word, we were past them. I looked back once in time to notice Dawson checking us out—checking me out, I was pretty sure—and Aston noticing him noticing. Aston's face screwed up, and he twisted out from under Dawson's hand. Then I turned forward again, grateful for the intersection ahead. As we rounded the corner and lost Aston and Dawson behind us, I heard Aston say, "Are you fucking kidding me, Daw?"

We'd gone another hundred paces when Holmes tried to get his hand free.

"Better not," I whispered. "In case they come back this way."

He hesitated.

"In fact," I said, "maybe I should suck on your neck for a few minutes. Just to be convincing."

Holmes wrenched his hand free. When I glanced back, those red spots glowed in his cheeks, his eyebrows drawing a vee, his jaw tight.

"Or if you want to be the one doing the sucking—"

"I understand that I was wrong," he said. The words were brittle, but they were too breathy, and under that crackling cold, they were full of hurt. "I tried to apologize. And you're still being cruel."

I took a better look at his face. "H, I wasn't—"

He pushed past me, and when I tried to catch his arm, he broke my grip without even trying. Which, come to think of it, was pretty much our thing at this point. I decided I should feel lucky he didn't tear my arm off and shove it up my ass.

By that point, we were close to Walker, and Holmes seemed to have no trouble following the directions scribbled on the walls. I trailed after him until we reached a reinforced steel door. An EXIT sign glowed overhead, and the light threw a red glow over everything. Shadows filled the hollows under Holmes's eyes, ran across his mouth like spider silk, pooled in the shell of his ear. Even the shadows were tinged red.

I held up both hands. "I'm sorry."

He stood there like a Holmes bot.

"It goes both ways," I said. "If we're going to get better at apologizing, which obviously, um, we have to, then we both have to accept the apology. Understand?"

The EXIT sign buzzed overhead. A pipe rattled like it meant to come loose from its brackets.

"Why obviously?" Holmes asked.

"What?"

"You said obviously we have to get better at apologizing. Why?"

"Because we're friends. And because we have this way of seriously pissing each other off sometimes. Why do you think?"

Maybe it was the shadows. Maybe it was the fact that I was exhausted from digging trenches and cleaning up shit and mopping linoleum and having my ass handed to me multiple times in the last few days, all without any sleep. Maybe it was simply the fact that Holloway Holmes was the most confusing, frustrating, and maddening human being I had ever met. But whatever it was, I couldn't understand what I saw in his face in that moment: the softening around his eyes, the tremor at the corner of his mouth, the flex of his throat as he swallowed.

"Yes," he said, his voice scratchy. "Of course. Obviously."

I waited; it sounded like there was more, a thread hanging at the end of his sentence. When nothing came, I said, "So, I'm sorry."

He nodded. "I'm sorry too."

"I do need you to know, though, that if it were, like, a genuine emergency, I would suck on your neck. I would throw myself on that grenade, H."

"You are a moron," he said, but without any heat behind it. If anything, he sounded amused.

"It would be a noble sacrifice."

"You are not stupid, but you are a tremendous moron sometimes."

"And if I'm being honest, I think you would suck on my neck too. Because that's what friends do."

"Will you please stop talking and open this door?"

"It is open, boner," I said, grinning as I hip-checked the door. "It's an emergency exit."

The chagrin in Holmes's face was priceless. Then he shoved me out of the way and headed through the door.

"Maybe we should have a secret handshake," I said, scrambling after him. The stairwell on the other side was dark, but faint light came from overhead. This part of the building was still cinderblock and concrete, but it was clearly maintained: the steps swept, the railings solid and freshly painted, the emergency lights bright behind their wire mesh. "Because we're friends, and because, you know, that's probably something we should bring back. I was reading the Wikipedia article because

BoyfriendCam was down for like six hours and I was super bored—I mean, because I was doing research for a school project."

Holmes hesitated for a moment on the stairs, but he didn't bite.

"Anyway, the article talks about giving dap, and it also talks about fist bumping, maybe pound hugging. We could start high-low-high-low, and then we could spin around and—um, how do you feel about bumping butts?"

"That doesn't sound very secret."

"Well, it's more like a cool handshake, but we call it a secret because, you know, that sounds cool."

"No."

"Is that a no to the handshake in general or to the butt-bumping—"

That was when Holloway Holmes pushed my face into the wall. He took the steps two at a time.

I managed not to laugh as I went after him, but I did call up the stairs, "You just get back to me about the butt stuff anytime."

I wasn't sure, but I thought I heard him mutter, "Butt stuff," and then, in an even more horrified tone, "Oh my God," as he started to walk faster.

When we got to the first-floor landing, I took the lead again. I eased my hand down on the crash bar, and then I slowly opened the fire door. More darkness met us, broken only by the dim glow of another EXIT sign. I could make out the shape of the hallway, and I'd cleaned Walker enough times to know where I was. I pointed to a door on the right.

"That's the security office," I whispered.

Holmes nodded. He reached to his back pocket and withdrew a neoprene case, and then he slipped past me. I followed him into the hall.

Unlike the stairwell, the public areas of Walker had been built to impress: wood paneling, thick rugs, little tables with little trinkets, massive oil paintings of past heads of the school, chandeliers strung with crystals. One of the old radiators clanged. The air smelled like Murphy oil soap; a building like this took a lot of it, and some nights, I came home and smelled it on myself until I went to bed, no matter how much I washed up.

Holmes was crouching next to the security office door when I heard the steps. They came from inside the office, and at first, all I did was tense, waiting for Holmes to move. He stayed where he was, studying the lock, and I realized he hadn't heard. I sprinted over to him, staying on the heavy carpets so they would absorb the sound of my steps, and grabbed his arm. He looked up and started to open his mouth.

I shook my head and dragged him to his feet and then, without giving him time to get settled, across the hallway. The stairwell was farther away, and the steps sounded close now. I didn't think we could make it back to the stairs, so instead, I opened the maintenance closet and shoved him inside. I followed him, pulling the door shut behind me, and Holmes and I got tangled in the darkness—the closet was smaller than I remembered, and we had to wriggle around, arms and legs and bodies slotting together as we pressed in against each other to fit. At the same moment, the door to the security office flew open. I stopped, the closet door still open an inch, and tried to slow my breathing. If I pulled the door closed now, the sound of the latch hitting the strike plate would be unmistakable. All I could do was hope that whoever had emerged from the security office wouldn't notice that the door across the hall was slightly ajar.

Straining to listen, I waited for the sound of more steps, the confirmation that whoever had emerged from the office was moving away from us. Nothing came. The skin on the back of my neck prickled. Whoever it was, they were just standing there. Why? Waiting for someone. Or—had they heard us?

I was suddenly more aware of everything: the perfume of the all-purpose cleaner that we stocked in here, the mop handle jabbing me in the back, the tightly muscled firmness of Holmes's thighs around mine, his hand on my hip, half steadying me and half bracing himself, like he was trying to push as far away from me as he could. My shirt had ridden up, and his thumb, rough with a callus, touched my bare skin. Sweat started to dampen the hair at my nape. It gathered under my arms. I knew I had more important things to focus on, but here was all of Holloway Holmes, all those lean, coiled muscles, all that cold reserve like an obsidian crust over an active volcano. I tried to shift so that the vee of my legs wasn't making contact with him. My face was on fire. Whether I liked it or not, I was having a bit of a volcano situation myself. But when I tried to ease back so I wasn't, uh, poking him, Holmes's hand tightened on my waist, that callused thumb digging into my flesh, pinning me in place. All I could do was breathe, and even that sounded raspy in the darkness that we were both breathing.

The steps broke the silence with crisp determination. They moved away from us, and a moment later, I heard the sound change when whoever it was turned at the end of the L and began to move toward the front of the building. The sound continued to fade, and Holmes's reaction was immediate: he released me, pulled away from me, his movements silent and controlled. He erased every point of contact between us, and it was like he was slipping into dark water. Gone. Then he pushed open the maintenance door and left.

I let my head fall back and got a mop handle in the neck as my reward. I took a few more breaths, trying to slow them down. Then I squeezed my eyes shut and called myself fifteen types of idiot. I don't even like him, I told myself. Not like that. I mean, yes, ok, he has that cute butt, and yes, sure, when the sunlight hits his hair exactly right, there are approximately a hundred different shades of gold, and fine, that one knobby finger weirdly does something for me, and he's smart and he's brave and someone has obviously put him through hell, and in spite of that—and in spite of being a major weirdo—he tries really hard to be kind. And the lip biting thing, God, it made me want to wrap him up in one of those hooded blankets and plunk him down in the cottage and not let him leave until he realized it was ok to be human sometimes.

But he wasn't my type. I liked guys who had more muscle, and I liked guys who made me laugh, and I liked guys who had their shit together, because I so clearly did not. And anyway, he wasn't interested; he'd made that perfectly clear. Many times. Again. Literally fifteen seconds ago, in fact.

So.

Yes, I reminded myself, squirming slightly so that I didn't develop a case of permanent mop-neck. I don't even like him.

And then I remembered what he looked like doing squats and hurried out of the closet before I could spend any more time remembering things.

Holmes knelt next to the security office door. He was removing a screw from the front of the electronic lock, and when I crouched next to him, I saw that it was the only thing securing the faceplate to the front of the lock. When the screw came loose, he passed it to me.

"That seems like a design flaw," I whispered.

"It has an anti-tamper switch." He reached into a pocket of his black jeans and produced a paper clip, which he straightened. Then, as I watched, he eased the faceplate open slightly, lifting the bottom just enough to slide the paper clip inside.

"What are you doing?"

"Neutralizing the anti-tamper mechanism."

"Uh, yeah, der. Details."

That little crease appeared between his eyebrows. "When the faceplate is correctly positioned, a spring is compressed. If someone tries to remove the faceplate—"

"Like you're doing."

"—the spring relaxes, which triggers the anti-tamper switch, and the lock is disabled."

"But instead, you're going to—and now you fill in the blank."

"I'm keeping the spring compressed with the paperclip while I remove the faceplate." And without any expression on his face at all, as though this were the Holmes bot equivalent of riding a bike, he slid the faceplate back, keeping the paperclip in place as he did so, and turned to show it to me. "If you could hold this and apply pressure to the spring?"

I took the faceplate from him, wincing as I pressed down on the spring and he pulled the paperclip away. But no alarms sounded, and stormtroopers didn't come rushing out of nearby doorways. Holmes didn't smile, but he did look suspiciously amused as he watched me.

"You're enjoying this," I muttered.

"You are very expressive. It's...pleasant."

And what the hell was that supposed to mean? I had no idea, so I settled for glaring at him, but since he was a Holmes bot, it ricocheted right off his casing.

Meanwhile, Holmes turned his attention back to the lock. There were four wires connected to some kind of circuit board. He leaned closer, examining each in turn.

"Do you know what they do?"

"I should hope so."

"Oh my God."

"The red and the black are the power and the ground. The yellow and the orange are an open circuit. And to answer your implied question, no, I did not ask you to compress the spring simply to enjoy your expression of panic."

"Simply?"

He shrugged. "An added bonus. I needed the paperclip."

"Paperclips cost, like, two dollars for a hundred. I would have gotten you another paperclip."

Holmes definitely wasn't smiling this time, but he was definitely— definitely—amused. "Close the circuit—" He laid the paperclip across the exposed copper, and the lock made a thunking noise. "—and the lock opens." He nudged the door, and it swung inwards.

It only took Holmes a few minutes to wipe down each part of the lock that we'd touched and reassemble it. When he'd finished, he stood and headed into the office, and I followed. The security office wasn't just one room; it was a warren of small, interconnected rooms that had been cobbled together because Walker hadn't been designed to have a security office. All the rooms had the same wood paneling as the rest of Walker, the same old wooden floors covered by thick rugs, the same high ceilings with dark exposed timber and ancient light fixtures that, even when they were all on, didn't give enough light. Maps and blueprints of campus covered the walls, hung next to a corkboard tacked with faded flyers—HR policies and security regulations and the 2015 softball team sign-up. Jackknifed filing cabinets lined the walls, and dusty desks took up the rest of the space.

Holmes hesitated, scanning the office. I tapped his arm. Occasionally, under Mr. Campbell's supervision, I cleaned in here; custodial crew wasn't allowed inside unaccompanied. I knew that the bank of computer monitors connected to the campus security cameras was in a room at the back, and I pointed in that direction. Holmes nodded and padded across the room.

To my relief, the door was unlocked, and inside, we found the system on—at least a dozen monitors, along with a computer that controlled the display. It was a tiny room, and it smelled like farts and the peanut shells that filled a paper lunch bag on the desk. Holmes sat at the computer and began to click and type. I watched as he navigated through the backups toward Friday, the night Watson had been killed.

Then he stopped. He clicked something, closed the window, and opened a fresh one. He did it all over again.

When he went still again, I asked, "What?"

"They're gone."

"What's gone? The recordings?"

"All of them. Everything from Friday is gone."

"Maybe the police took them," I said. "Maybe they erased them after they took copies."

Holmes's face had a bluish cast in the light from the screens.

"H?"

After a moment, he shook his head.

"Then what? Somebody else erased it?"

"I'm going to try to recover the files. It might take me some time."

"Ok."

I waited for more, but Holmes didn't say anything. After a minute of watching him click and type and frown, I got bored. After five minutes, it was mind-numbing. I tried to pace in the tiny office. I tried to keep myself busy: I pulled on the rubberized banding on the side of the desk, seeing if I could get it free, and then I kicked the casters so they were all pointing in the same direction, which I thought Holmes would appreciate, and then I picked up the bag of empty peanut shells and realized it made a decent maraca.

"Jack, for the love of God!" Holmes snapped.

"Oh. Right. Sorry."

He pointed at the door.

"I'll be quiet."

"You are constitutionally incapable of being anything less than distracting. It's like you're trying to draw my attention. Get out!"

My anger had faded over the course of the day; I'd spent a long time telling myself I should have known better than to get between him and those stupid pills. So, I made my voice light as I said, "I'm not trying to get your attention. If I wanted to get your attention, I'd do one of these numbers." I hitched up the collar of my shirt so I could bite on it absentmindedly, and then I scratched the inches of bare belly that were now exposed, and then I stretched, both arms behind my head, because I had a lot of shit in my life, but I'd worked hard on my biceps and shoulders.

I grunted when something hit me in the stomach, and I looked down to see the stapler on the floor.

"Out," Holmes whispered ferociously, stabbing a finger at the door. "And get your polo out of your mouth; it's got to be filthy."

"Oh," I said with a smirk. "Yeah, uh huh, tell me I'm dirty—"

I dodged the tape dispenser, but the pencil got me in the neck, and I staggered out of the tiny room, clasping my carotid like I was trying to staunch a fountain of blood.

Holmes did not laugh. But I figured he appreciated it; he was just going to tell me later.

I passed through the front office again and tried a door that I was pretty sure connected to a storage room—full of pepper spray and walkies and all that good stuff. This door, unfortunately, was locked; I figured Holmes could probably sneeze on it and get it open, but that could wait. I crossed the room and tried the door on the opposite side, which led to Campbell's office.

Like the other rooms, it was small, with a desk and a computer and an executive's chair. I caught a whiff of something foul, a little like sewage, and I wondered if I'd be back tomorrow when someone reported a broken pipe. Campbell had mounted a TV on a swing arm, and it was pulled out from the wall. Maybe he liked to catch up on the news while he was working. Maybe he wanted to watch a game—I didn't know what Campbell liked, but I was guessing it wasn't the Dodgers. Maybe sometimes he got a hankering for *Looney Tunes*. I walked around the desk, jiggled the mouse, and frowned at the locked screen that came on. I wasn't willing to risk the secret password I'd tried on Holmes's laptop, so instead, I opened drawers. Pens and pencils. Rubber bands. Stamps and red ink pads. The lower drawers held files, but they didn't look like anything interesting—invoices from supply companies, a form letter from the Department of Education, a copy of a memo from Burrows—OFFICE OF THE HEADMASTER was printed at the top in black-letter font.

I turned in place, considering the closet door on the wall opposite me, the pictures of a dachshund—one of the photos clearly taken by a professional, one of the photos featuring the dachshund in a top hat and monocle, one of the photos with Campbell and the dachshund on a boat—and then moving on to the stacked in-and-out trays (more bills) and then the filing cabinets. I stopped, frowned, and hunkered down. On one of the cabinets, the corner of the bottom drawer was bent, as though someone had applied a lot of force to it—to judge by the indentations in the steel, somebody who owned a framing hammer. It took me a few tries to get the drawer open—someone had forced the drawer free from the cabinet's locking mechanism, but in doing so, they'd warped the drawer so that it was difficult to open. I finally sat on the ground, planted both feet on the cabinet, and hauled on the handle. The drawer squealed and then, all of a sudden, flew open. I scrambled onto my knees to look inside.

At the bottom of the drawer lay a box full of flash drives. They ran in two neat rows. And one was clearly missing—it had been taken from the row on the right, near the front. I thought about that. I tried, for a minute, to be Holmes. I figured the odds were likely that most people would fill a box from left to right, back to front. If that were correct, then the missing flash drive would have been one of the newer ones. I took the drive at the front, on the right—in theory, the most recent one—and examined it. A number in tight ballpoint was the only marking, but I recognized Campbell's writing. I thought about the broken drive that I'd found on the ground near Watson's body—the damn thing that had gotten me into this mess. After a moment of consideration, I pocketed the drive. Then I did my best Holmes bot impersonation and wiped down everything I'd touched.

I was on my knees, using my shirt to scrub out any prints I'd left on the drawer handle, when I saw the remote control for the TV. It lay under the desk, on its side, like it had fallen there. And that seemed strange because Olin Campbell wasn't the kind of guy who made messes—or, for that matter, who left them. I considered the remote. I thought about how that might have happened, the remote falling under the desk like that. Maybe if Campbell had been in his chair, pushed back from the desk, leaning back as he watched TV. And then he heard something — something he hadn't expected, something that startled him. He sat up. He dropped the remote because he was focused on — what? An intruder?

My heart was pounding in my chest. I felt sick, hot pins and needles running all over me. I reached for the remote and pressed the power button.

The TV came on silently, and I was surprised to see that the picture was grainy, even though the TV looked new. It took me a moment to understand what I was looking at: an aerial view of buildings that I recognized as the Walker School, the banner at the top that said KUTV and the banner at the bottom that said STUDENT SLAYING — KILLER ON THE LOOSE. It was news footage, I realized. Old news footage. I found play on the remote, and a woman's voice came on as the video rolled forward: "Police are baffled by the murder; since finding Seward's body on Wednesday, there have been no developments."

"What are you doing?" Holmes asked from the doorway.

I jammed buttons on the remote until the video stopped. Then I gestured at the screen. "He was watching this, I think. Campbell, I mean. He had it queued up, something about the old murder here."

Holmes studied the screen. A flurry of expressions snowed across his face, and then it was blank again. He took two steps and yanked on the closet door. It was locked, but it opened when he did his trick with the Café Rio reward card.

Olin Campbell had been wedged into the cramped space, his head lolling at an unnatural angle, his knees forced up against his chest. His throat had been cut, and gore covered the white shirt of his uniform, the closet walls, the back of the door.

The thunder of heavy steps came from the hallway. Running steps. A woman saying, "The light's on in that office, and I know it's not supposed to be on, so I called —"

"The window," Holmes said, his voice a whip crack.

I fumbled with the clasps while he sprinted out of the room. By the time I had the window open, he was back, and he crouched and made a saddle of his hands before I could protest. He boosted me to the window, steadied me as I pivoted to stick my legs out and begin lowering myself, and then took my hands, leaning out the window to help lower me as close to the ground as possible. When he released me, I fell a few feet, and my heels hit with a jolt that went straight up my spine.

Holmes, head and shoulders sticking out of the window, stared down at me.

"What are you doing?" I whispered. "Hurry!"

Deeper in the building, a man shouted, "Police!"

Holmes shook his head. "Run, Jack. And don't go home. Someone is covering their tracks."

Then he turned, raising his hands in surrender.

I hesitated. Then I ran.

Chapter 18

Rivers

At first, I ran blindly. The night breeze ripped down the canyon, slashing leaves from the aspens and maples, tumbling them through the air so fast that when the edge of one struck the side of my face, I felt like it had cut me. When I stumbled clear of a clump of scraggly cedars and found myself under a security light, the leaves made a spindrift of red and orange and gold. The smell of broken cedar needles rose on the clouds of my breath. For a moment, I blinked, trying to adjust to the light. And then sirens started in the distance, and I ran again.

When the cottage came into sight, I picked up the pace. This year's leaves crunched underfoot as I made my way from shadow to shadow, heading for the blur of white siding ahead, and every step seemed to make too much noise: the Vans' soles squeaking when I hit a patch of asphalt; a branch creaking when it snagged my shirt; my breathing. I kept my eyes on the cottage. I just had to get home, and then I could —

On the other side of the glass, in the deeper darkness of the living room, something moved.

I stopped. I was under one of the canyon maples, a good-sized one that still had plenty of leaves and threw a thick shadow. I leaned up against the trunk, trying to minimize my outline, the bark rough even through my clothing. I kept trying to get more air, and a part of me realized I might be hyperventilating.

Don't go home. Those had been his last words. Almost his last words. *Someone is trying to cover their tracks.*

The rush of adrenaline was burning off, and in the exhaustion that followed, the whole thing seemed unreal. Mr. Campbell was dead. And that was—awful. There had been so much blood. But Holmes would explain, in his cold, robotic way, and the police would let him go, and in the meantime, I could go home and get my first real sleep in half a week.

There wasn't anybody inside the house. There wasn't anyone waiting for me. There wasn't; that was crazy.

Only I'd seen something move.

I watched the windows. The security lights folded white wrinkles into the glass, and the glare made it hard to see. With the inside of the house completely dark, the glass acted as a mirror, although the reflections were faint. That's what I'd seen, I decided. The light moving on the glass. Hell, maybe my own reflection. It had been nothing, and here I was, scaring myself silly, which was a nice way of saying I felt like I was simultaneously about to shit myself and pee my pants. Yep, very silly. So, I could go home now, walk up on the porch, let myself inside the way I always did, and go to sleep.

Except, again, for the fact that I'd seen something. I knew I'd seen something. And more importantly, Holmes had told me not to go home. Yes, Holmes had sent some seriously mixed signals over the last few days. Yes, he was confusing as hell. Yes, half the time I felt a moral obligation to tease him because he was world-class annoying. But I trusted him, and he had warned me.

The truck was nosed up under the carport. It was approximately three feet from the back door of the house to the truck. Plenty of time for someone to run out and cut my throat while I was trying to unlock the driver's door. A memory of Campbell surged up: the raw edges of his throat; the blood, rust-colored and clotted black. I decided to take the long way.

Sticking to the screen of haws and pines as best I could, I moved counterclockwise around the cottage so I could approach it from the other side. The mulch of old needles whispered like sandpaper as I crept through the shadows. Down the street, a light was on in one of the staff cottages—I thought it was Mr. Sanderson's, but I didn't trust my judgment. I kept glancing over, checking the bright square of that window. I wasn't sure that it mattered. Then again, everything was starting to feel unreal, like maybe they were all in on it, like it was a conspiracy. Then, from behind me, voices burst out.

"That's bullshit! Let me see that again!"

The next sound was muffled. A video, a detached part of my brain suggested. On a phone.

"What a fucking piece of shit! I'm going to kick his ass..."

By then the voices were already fading. Boys' voices. Probably third or fourth years, because they didn't have the pipsqueak quality that a lot of the first and second years did. I crouched, fresh sweat soaking me again, the breeze wicking heat from my body as it tore away toward the mouth of the canyon. When I finally got myself up, my legs were shaking.

I had to cross the street. It was a narrow band of pavement, barely wide enough for two cars, and I chose the spot farthest from the security lights. It would be only a matter of seconds—just a blip. It still took me three tries to work up the nerve, and as I sprinted across the black asphalt, I was screaming inside my head. Then I stumbled into the shadow of another pine, smacked into it, and bounced off. I looked around to check if a crazy killer had come running at the noise, struggling to hear over the pounding of my pulse. Nothing. After another moment, a dazed relief started to drag me under. I was so tired. And I had the giggles, although I couldn't explain why. I was still choking them down as I crept toward the passenger side of the truck.

I got the key in on the first try. The thud as the latch drew back sounded like a thunderclap, but nobody came running. I slid onto the seat, wormed forward, and hooked the door with my toe to drag it shut.

Too late, I realized that I had used too much force.

The door slammed shut, and the thunk ran down the silent street.

I sat up and scooted into the driver's seat, and I jammed the key into the ignition. The truck grumbled. The dash lights came on. Then they flickered. The grumble shrank down to a whine.

"Come on," I whispered, pumping the gas and turning the key. "Come on, you son of a bitch. Come on, you fucking son of a bitch!"

This time, there was no way to tell myself I was imagining it. Something—someone—was moving on the other side of the door; I could see them through the half-lite, nothing more than a shadow coming across the living room.

"Come the fuck on!" I shouted.

The engine roared to life. I slammed the truck into reverse, arced out onto the street, and hammered the shifter into drive. Someone came out of the cottage, but they stayed under the carport, and in the deeper darkness there, I couldn't make out anything. Then I hauled ass.

I drove toward the mouth of the canyon; getting to a city, with lights and people and police, seemed like the logical choice. But after a couple of miles, I slowed and eased onto the shoulder. The road was empty. Behind a line of cottonwoods that looked like charcoal rubbings, the Provo River was black. Where the current caught the ambient light, the edges of the water tumbled like broken glass. The granite looked white in the moonlight, porous. In ninth-grade Language Arts, *ossify* had been in the last vocab unit.

I couldn't go to the police—or, in this case, the deputies—because they already had Holmes, and anything I did would get me involved and probably make things worse for him in the process. I couldn't go back to Walker because Holmes had been right: someone was clearly trying to tie up loose ends. I couldn't go to Joslyn's place because Shivers was looking for me. I stared out the windshield. Where the weak light caught my breath, it looked like stardust.

They would expect me to go to Provo, I decided. I hit the gas and pulled out in a U-turn, heading back up the canyon. This time, though, I passed the fork that led up to Walker, and I kept following 189. When I got to Deer Creek Reservoir, the canyon opened up into blunt hills dressed in sage and scrub. I found one of the two-lanes that crisscrossed the mountains, and I followed it for another mile until I found a dirt road that turned off and went south. It didn't have a gate, and I didn't plan on staying long. I eased the truck onto the shoulder—which was practically nonexistent—under some big brush that was brown and skeletal. Then I killed the engine and the lights.

Cold rushed in almost immediately. I crawled into the back seat, found the emergency blanket, and wrapped myself in that. Then I grabbed the tarp Holmes had used and laid that on top of me as well. I squirmed around until I was semi-comfortable on the back bench, and then I closed my eyes. It was just my imagination, but I thought I could smell him—that woodsy heat I associated with him, a burn without the fire. I thought of him riding all the way to Lehi under this damn tarp. And then I thought of him above me, head and shoulders sticking out the window of Campbell's office, the severe perfection of his face. He'd known. As soon as he'd heard those steps, he'd known what he was going to do, and he hadn't asked me, hadn't even bothered to let me know. There had been this moment, when he was holding my hands to help me get down, when I'd felt—what? Safe? Weirdly reassured by the combination of that ferocious intensity in his face; the knowledge that Holmes wouldn't let anything bad happen to me, which was crazy, in hindsight, because plenty of bad things had happened that he couldn't stop. But you can't argue with feelings, and that's what I'd felt, looking up at him. And then he'd been gone.

I lived those last few minutes again and again: discovering Campbell's body; the stampede of heavy steps toward us; Holmes's graceful fingers and that one knobby knuckle as he knelt and made a stirrup for me, the whole thing strangely formal and antiquated and kind, which was a good set of words for this particular Holmes bot; the cold air against my back as I slid out the window; his hands; the light from behind picking out his ears, the clean part of his Ivy League hair, the line of his jaw. I went over his face again and again. And then I started over, dissecting it all layer by layer, looking for the moment when I should have done something different—been smarter, faster, better.

Go to sleep, I told myself.

But the memories kept coming. They were like a river that wouldn't stop flowing over me. I thought of the Provo, the black-glass riffles.

In India, a long time ago, they'd dissected human bodies. Only they didn't want to cut the body open; that was taboo. (This is according to Wikipedia, and I thought of Holmes not-so-discreetly rolling his eyes at that.) So, what they did instead was run water over the corpse until the skin came loose and softened enough to slough off. All that water, over and over again. They liked to use rivers.

At some point, I started to cry because my shoulder and my arm were throbbing and because I was cold and because I had no idea what to do and because I couldn't stop seeing Holmes's face. And then I slept.

Chapter 19

Ellis Seward

When I woke, the light coming in had the quality of dawn, and I was stiff and cramped from lying contorted on the bench all night. Waking arrived all at once, a distinct clarity that told me I wasn't going back to sleep. I gave it a solid try, and then I surrendered. I crawled out from under the tarp and blanket, and I groaned and bitched and stretched as I let myself down from the truck. I figured this was what people felt like when they were forty. Dad said forty had kicked his ass; the first time he'd said that, he'd laughed and told me not to tell Mom.

The cold raked my cheeks and stung my eyes, and my breath bloomed before being torn to ribbons. I stumbled up toward the brush, and at the last moment, I had enough of a brain not to pee uphill and into the wind—which, even though I wasn't a camper, I'd heard enough jokes about. I was half surprised that the pee didn't freeze in midair, even though, all things considered, it actually would have been kind of awesome.

Back in the truck, I started the engine—the stupid thing started right up this time, of course—cranked up the heat, and did a three-point turn to get back on the two-lane road and head down the canyon. Deer Creek looked like hammered steel in the morning light. A few guys were parked around the reservoir—fishermen, I guessed, although I had no idea what people came up here to catch. I pointed the truck south and headed into Provo.

As I drove, I thought. If I were lucky, Holmes would be out of custody already—or, at the longest, in a few hours. But the last year had taught me not to rely on luck. The worst-case scenario was that Holmes would be held and charged with Campbell's murder. And Dad was still in jail for Watson's death. It felt unreal that his arrest had happened less than forty-eight hours before. I thought about trying to contact him. And then I thought, again, that any interaction I had with law enforcement at this point would only make things worse for everyone. What I could do—the only thing I could do until I had more information—was try to figure out who was behind all of this and get both my dad and Holmes off the hook.

Ok, great, I thought. I have a plan. Solve two murders that had completely baffled trained detectives and a fully licensed and functioning Holmes bot. And do it by myself. With no help, no resources, and no clues. Perfect. Jack Moreno, I told myself, you are a fucking genius.

That was approximately when my stomach started to rumble.

I made it into Provo, stopped at the McDonald's on Freedom, and, because my wallet was still in the cottage, found enough change in the cupholder to get myself one (yep, one) Egg McMuffin. It was gone in three bites. The girl behind the counter was cute in a Provo kind of way—hair dyed blond, too skinny, gel nails. I drank a lot of water, and I did some Jack Moreno-special moping, with lots of eye contact, hoping she'd get the message. She just smiled a lot, and eventually I gave up and left.

My next stop was the Provo Library. They had public access computers, and I'd gotten a library card with a little creative finagling that involved a gas bill for Joslyn's place. Oh, bonus feature about the Provo Library's public computers: they were set in privacy carrells that kinda-sorta made it possible to ignore what the creepy guys on either side of me were looking at. And trust me, I'd had open access to the internet since I was thirteen, and I still didn't want to see what they were looking at.

I opened up a browser. And then I paused. I took out my phone, saw a dozen missed calls from a number I suspected belonged to either Rivera or Yazzie, and several voicemails. I ignored those. I also saw several texts from Ariana that had come in over the last night. I sent her a quick message telling her I was ok but that things were complicated. I let her know I might not be able to talk for a few days. I was feeling very responsible and, ok, pseudo-boyfriendly by the time I finished. Look at me—master of the bare minimum of communicating with the girl I hooked up with.

There was nothing from Holmes, so I sent him a quick message, asking him what kind of burger he'd gotten the last time we'd gone to Burgers Supreme. If Holmes had his phone, I was sure he'd be pleased to correct me and remind me we'd gone to In-N-Out. If somebody was trying to pull a fast one and trick me into thinking they were Holmes, well, maybe they'd do something stupid.

Then I called Mr. Taylor and told him I was sick and wouldn't be in to work; I didn't want to give him any excuse to fire me or dad. From the way

Taylor responded, with an abundance of concern and well-wishing and questions about what I needed and if he could drop off some soup, I figured Rivera and Yazzie had enlisted him in their efforts to track me down. I mean, I suppose there was the possibility he'd had a genuine change of heart, but I figured the odds were better that he was a sneaky rat and a police informant. Finding new ways to get me into trouble was definitely his vibe.

Next, I took out the flash drive and inserted it into the computer. I waited for some kind of prompt demanding a password, but instead, the computer made a soft noise, and a little bubble appeared letting me know that the drive was ready. I opened it. It contained a single video file. I double-clicked it and hunkered down. I didn't know what to expect: Watson's murder seemed like the best possibility.

Instead, though, I saw a screen that was almost entirely dark with the exception of a security light. The light picked out a sidewalk, a stretch of lawn and, at the edge of the frame, trees. It took me a moment to recognize the path that ran alongside the Toqueah Creek.

Two figures jogged into view, one in the lead, the other following. The one in the lead kept looking back. The one following kept to a steady pace. I sat forward, my hands wrapping around the arms of the chair. Was this how it had started? Was this where the killer had gone after Watson? In a moment, would the one in front begin to sprint, trying to get away?

But instead, they moved into the light, and Aston glanced at the camera. It was only for a moment, but it was long enough to erase any doubt about his identity. And he was smiling. Grinning, actually, and looking back over his shoulder with a mixture of anticipation and excitement. The one following passed under the security light a moment later, and I recognized Dawson. It only took a moment, seeing Aston lope and look back, seeing Dawson follow with a smile that only touched his eyes, and I remembered them in the tunnels, Dawson asking me to hook him up with some lube, the way Dawson looked at me sometimes. As though in confirmation, Dawson caught up with Aston at the edge of the camera's line of sight, and the two boys tussled together as they went to the ground. Dawson was on top of Aston, and unless Aston suddenly needed such life-saving operations as having his shirt rucked up and his nipples licked and intense mouth-to-mouth, there was really only one possibility for what they were doing.

I tried to think through the significance of what I'd seen. My first thought was that it had been a risk—yes, they'd been out on campus after curfew, and yes, the darkness was deep enough to make things safer. But it had been a risk all the same. Not that risks had ever stopped anyone; Mr. Taylor had sent me to clean up, uh, a misfire in the library one time. A boy had been jacking it while he FaceTimed with his long-distance girlfriend. Fine, ok, long distance has got to be hard. But he was just sitting between two bookshelves in the library. In the part with all the Bibles.

My second thought was that whatever else the video and the flash drive implied, one thing was clear: Olin Campbell, head of security, had been a pervert and, pretty much definitely, a blackmailer.

"If you like that, I can show you some other ones." The voice startled me; the breath reeked, onions and something like rot, and when I glanced over, one of my fellow computer buddies was leaning around the carrell divider. He had black teeth, a stringy gray beard, and a noticeable erection under his filthy trench coat. Or is that a bookmark in your pocket—that was the only coherent thought I could form in the first moment. "I've got one where he chokes the other boy until you can't hear him squeal anymore."

On the screen, Dawson was still straddling Aston, and if it was still CPR, they were definitely doing things differently than we'd learned in Lifetime Health. I clicked a button to close the video. "Thanks," I said. "I'm gonna pass."

The old man's eyes, jittery and black, followed me as I turned back to the screen and opened a browser. I opened some random news sites and scrolled until he huffed another breath of onions and tooth decay and left. Then I opened a new tab and went to Instagram.

I didn't have a smartphone. But that didn't mean I was totally out of the loop. The web platforms weren't the same as having them on your phone, but I could at least follow my old friends, see what kind of lives they were living—parents and school and sports and girls and boys. I searched until I found Aston's profile, which was private, and then I sent him a DM. I kept it short—my name, my number, and a single sentence: *Text me—I need to talk to you about Campbell.* I left the tab open in case he decided to ignore my instructions (he was, after all, one of the Boy Band) and replied on Instagram.

Then I sat back in the chair and tried to think. Holmes would have seen it all right away, of course. He would have known what it meant. But Holmes wasn't here to help me. I tried to lay out the pieces of what I knew. Olin Campbell had kept video recordings of people in compromising situations. Someone had killed Campbell. And someone had forced open his filing cabinet and taken one of the flash drives. Ok, that chain suggested pretty clearly that Campbell had been blackmailing people and gotten killed for it.

What was interesting was that, according to Moriarty, Watson had been doing some blackmailing of her own. I guess I should have been surprised that there were two of them operating on campus, and for a moment I toyed with the idea that they'd been working together, but I couldn't make that story work. It seemed possible that more than one person might try to take advantage of people's secrets. Walker was, after all, basically built for that purpose—a dumping ground for kids who embarrassed their parents. And Holmes had said that the Watsons had always found ways to profit from other people's stories. Nothing except the flash drive suggested an overlap between Campbell and Watson, and even that could have boiled down to necessity—if you were going to physically deliver blackmail material, you probably weren't going to burn a DVD.

Moriarty had told us that Watson was onto something. Something big. And it seemed logical that she had gotten herself killed by going after it. Now Campbell, also a blackmailer, was dead too, and on his TV, I'd seen news footage about a twenty-year-old murder. What were the odds of that? What were the odds of any of it? It all felt unreal. I was just supposed to be a part-time janitor who spent too much time on Twitch and read Wikipedia articles instead of actually studying for the GED. None of this was supposed to be happening.

Aston still hadn't responded, so I closed the Instagram tab and searched for *murder Walker school*. Stories about Watson's murder flooded my results. I grimaced, tried to remember what, exactly, I'd seen in Campbell's office, and went back to the search box. I added *KUTV*. More stories about Watson, but now they were all from the CBS affiliate. I thought for another moment, went to the search filters, and changed the dates so that it would only give me results from before 2020.

Bingo.

The first five results were from 2009, all of them fitting into that weird news genre of 'where are they now,' only for horrifying deaths. TEN YEARS AND STILL NO ANSWERS AT WALKER and IT COST ONE SHERIFF HIS JOB AND A DEPARTMENT ITS REPUTATION: THE WALKER SLAYING TODAY. Stuff like that, when a slow news cycle and a significant anniversary had prompted a spate of articles about the killing. I read through the top results carefully.

The facts were straightforward because there weren't many of them. A boy named Ellis Seward had been found dead by a Walker School groundskeeper on May 5, 1999. The body had been stuffed into the incinerator— apparently, back in the good old days of 1999, you could just burn your trash on the mountain—but the groundskeeper found him before that day's garbage had been burned. The varying reports described Seward's injuries in similar terms: *beaten to death, physical trauma, blunt object*. They'd run a photo of Seward from the Walker yearbook (1998-1999): a frail-looking white boy with long blond hair and soft, nervous features. And, if I had to make a guess, a grade-A twink. Sure, that was based on one photo from over twenty years ago, but sometimes you can tell, and God, I think a nun could have looked at that boy and figured it out.

The groundskeeper had, of course, been investigated thoroughly and been cleared. His name—Gene Fife—didn't mean anything to me. And the Utah County Sheriff's Department had done their best to discover other clues. But according to the articles, who phrased it with different degrees of tact, they'd come up with jack shit. No suspects. No leads. Not even a person of interest. Campbell's name appeared a few times in the stories, always identified as the new head of security after the previous one had resigned in disgrace. He'd been promoted, several of the stories said, although it wasn't clear what he'd been doing at Walker before. In these retrospective articles, the writers apparently felt a degree of liberty in offering their opinions, and more than one suggested that Seward's troubled home life hadn't helped anything. One reporter came out and stated that Seward's parents had been so self-involved, even in their grief, that there had been no one to put pressure on the sheriff's department when the case went cold. Others suggested some sort of payoff. Ellis Seward had been killed, was the subtext, and no one had cared enough to keep trying to find his killer.

But that wasn't entirely true. Someone had figured it out. Maybe two people. And when they'd tried to blackmail the killer, they'd ended up dead.

The logic seemed straightforward. Maybe, if Holmes had been there, he could have pointed out all the things I was overlooking. But I felt like I had enough coordinates to start mapping this out: Ellis Seward's death in 1999; Watson's death after she told Moriarty she had uncovered something big; and Campbell's death as he was reviewing news footage about a murder from more than two decades before. I felt like I could draw a line from A to B to C. And I felt like I could tell what point D was, where the line went next.

Point D was obvious. Necessary. It was—what was Holmes's word? It was an abduction. But it was a strong one.

Point D was that the killer had been at Walker twenty years ago and was still at Walker today.

Based on the news articles, my first guess would have been Campbell. He was named in the reports, and he was in the perfect position to have committed the crime and covered it up. The obvious obstacle to that, though, was the slightly inconvenient fact that somebody had butchered Campbell in his office.

With the information I had now, I did another search and read through as many of the original reports and articles—the ones from May 1999, when the murder had dominated the news—as I could find. I read for two hours, and then I made myself get up, and something in my back popped, and all the morning's stiffness had locked my joints again. I hobbled around and peed and drank some water. And then I went back and read more articles about a boy named Ellis Seward who had been killed, and no one knew why, and no one knew who had done it, and no one had even really cared once that first, vicious thrill had subsided.

When I finished, I looked at the clock and was surprised to see that it was after three. I got up and did my I'm-not-old-I-just-slept-in-a-truck-and-yes-stop-looking-at-me-like-that-I'm-still-using-that-computer. I peed. I drank more water. My stomach was doing some serious grumbling, although once it was full of water, it was some serious sloshing instead. I went back to the computer.

Nothing I'd read had added any real facts, although it had been helpful to see how information about the case had developed, some of the initial details incorrect, some becoming clearer as the investigation continued, none of the early efforts panning out. I was still where I had started, with the same facts that had led the police to the dead end.

Only now I knew something they hadn't known back then. I knew that the killer was still at Walker after all these years, and that narrowed my search considerably.

I pulled up Walker's staff directory. Each staff member had a brief bio and their years of service listed next to their name. I read through them slowly; I wanted to go fast and only look at the number, but I made myself read every word.

There was one.

There was only one staff member—besides Campbell—who had been working at Walker High School in 1999.

My phone buzzed, and I was so startled that my knee thumped the side of the carrell. When I checked the screen, the message was from Holmes.

I've never been to Burgers Supreme with you. It was In-N-Out, and you called it a Double-Double.

The next message came through almost immediately: *And we need a better verification system. Someone could have figured that one out.*

And then another message: *Where are you?*

I was grinning so hard my face hurt. I texted: *Library.*

I sent that one, and then I sent another: *Don't look so shocked. They let me check out all the Pete the Cat books I want.*

Thirty seconds must have passed before a message came through: *I have no idea what you're talking about.*

A laugh escaped me. From the direction of the circulation desk came a scandalized shush. Ignoring it, I bent over the phone and tapped out another message: *Where are you? We need to talk. Laura Soares, the biology teacher? The resident master of Butters, where Watson lived? She did it. She killed both of them.*

Chapter 20

Extremely Satisfying

I left the truck behind one of the athletic supply sheds, hiked across the baseball diamonds, and entered Baker House through the basement. I took the stairs up to the second floor. A kid with a towel and a serious case of backne was padding toward the showers, and someone down the hall was blasting Elton John's "Goodbye, Yellow Brick Road." I could feel my underwear turning rainbow with every step I took.

The door opened before I could knock, and there he was: in a white oxford, blue chinos, gold-toe socks, his hair back in its perfect Ivy League part. I stepped into the room, pretending I didn't notice how wide his eyes got, and I pulled him into a hug. He stood stiffly, arms at his sides. He was warm, his body harder than I expected—everything sheared down to bone and muscle—and he smelled like a well-oiled Holmes bot: that woodsy heat I remembered, catching like kindling in my lungs.

The tears came so suddenly that I had to fight to blink them back, my whole face hot and prickling, because he'd been gone, and my dad had been gone, and because of that night in the truck, the river of memories scouring me away, his face like the moon before he'd given himself up.

"What's wrong?" he asked. "Are you hurt? What happened?"

"No, I'm not hurt." He was wriggling, so I let him go, and I wiped my face. "I'm crying, H, because I'm happy to see you and because today, last night—hell, the last week—because it's been awful, and I thought—" And then I cuffed him on the head—not hard, but not soft, either, and fully aware that he was letting it happen because he probably could have snapped my hand off at the wrist. "And because I've been scared to death for you, dumbass. What the hell were you thinking?"

Holmes frowned and rubbed the side of his head—not like it hurt, but like he was checking to see if his hair was mussed. "I was—"

"And don't tell me you were trying to keep me safe because that shit is not going to fly. We keep each other safe, H."

"They would have arrested both of us," he said, his tone wary and, at the same time, clearly confused. "It was—"

"If you say logical, H, I am going to tan your ass."

For the first time in my memory, I saw a Holmes bot reboot its audio track. "It was, uh, calculated." He raised his eyebrows, and I snorted. "It was preferable that one of us remain free to continue investigating, and it was—" He stopped again, looked at my face, and swallowed. "—reasonable, considering all the factors in play, that of the two of us, I would be more likely to be released. Besides, I thought you would be even more upset if you were unable to continue trying to help your father." The next part seemed to slip out before he could stop it. "And sometimes you are...belligerent."

I stared at him. Then I said, "You are the one who literally hiked out of the mountains like the Terminator, found me on a random street, and slammed a stranger's head into a car until he stopped moving."

"It wasn't a random street, and it was a truck, not a car—" He stopped. He was trying not to bite his lip again. "I did not want you to do something unadvised. Like resist arrest."

Letting out a breath, I rubbed my forehead. Between the bad night's sleep, the strain from the last few days, and almost twelve hours without eating anything, I had a headache roaring in. I nodded. "You couldn't have told me?"

"You exhibit a maladaptive degree of protective behavior—"

I held up my free hand.

When Holmes spoke, his voice was that of a man testing ice. "Jack, are you ok?"

It took me a moment to say, "Fine."

Elton John changed to The Weather Girls. "It's Raining Men."

"I'm sorry," Holmes said, although it sounded more like a hypothesis.

I snorted again. "You don't even know what you should be sorry for. I'm just—it's just been a lot. I'm the one who should be sorry, I guess. I knew you had good reasons. And I'm sorry I got emotional."

"Boys can cry too," Holmes said. When I looked at him, color brightened his cheeks, and his eyes slid away. "That's the title of a book. And I think it displays a healthy attachment type and degree of emotional maturity that you are...expressive."

"Please," I said, "stop. No more compliments." Then I sniffed. Now that the storm of emotions was fading, I could pick out the unmistakable aroma of something fried. "What's that?"

"Chicken strips. And fries." He waited a moment and then added, as though he sensed the need for clarification: "You're always hungry."

When he stepped aside, I saw what I'd missed. Until now, we'd stood near the doorway, with Holmes blocking my view of the room. Now, as he moved out of the way, my breath faltered, and then I swore. His room had been torn apart. The bed was flipped upside down, the dresser lay on its side, the drawers had been ripped apart, the desk had one side panel staved in. Anything soft had been slashed: the seat cushions, the mattress, the pillows. The plate of chicken fingers and a mountain of French fries was perched on top of a chair spilling out batting, and it looked like something I would have seen when Ms. Prinze, in seventh grade, took the entire class to the museum of Contemporary Art.

"H, what happened? Did the police—" But I stopped myself. There was no fingerprint powder. And the degree of destruction was more than what could be passed off as incidental to a search. "Who did this?"

"I suspect the killer." He frowned. "Aren't you hungry? The chairs are ruined, so if you don't mind sitting on the floor…"

I was hungry. I was starving, in fact, so when Holmes pressed the plate into my hands, I sat, and he sat too, his knees pulled to his chest. I was two chicken fingers in before I realized he was watching me. He did it openly—not the kind of quick, stolen looks of people who know it's rude to stare.

"What did you eat?" I asked through approximately eighteen fries.

"I didn't understand that."

I swallowed, pointed at him with another fry, and said, "Bullshit, you understood me perfectly. What did you eat?"

"Dinner. Did you want dipping sauces? I think you like dipping sauces, but they didn't have animal sauce like you ordered at In-N-Out—"

"Don't change the subject. I'm the master of changing the subject. What did you eat for dinner?"

"I don't think anyone can be the master of—"

"Holloway Hogwater Holmes!"

He wrapped his arms around his knees, pulling them tighter against his chest, and glared at me. He made it two words: "Harrow. Gate."

With a sigh, I set the plate on the ground and pushed it to a middle spot between us. "Eat."

"I'm not—"

"So help me God, H."

He snatched a chicken finger, bit into it savagely, and managed to maintain his glare as he chewed. His pupils were hard and contracted.

"How much did you take when you got home?"

I thought, for a moment, he wouldn't answer. Then he bit out: "Sixty milligrams."

"Jesus."

"I do not need your feedback on this matter."

"Yeah, sure, because you're making such good life choices."

"This from a boy who was so intoxicated that when his drug dealer dragged him out into the street and attempted to put his eye out—"

"Ok, ok, ok. Truce. My God." I chewed for a moment. "Did they take your computer?"

"Yes. I'm sure they'll have no trouble cracking the master password of 'cutebutt.'"

"You're eating more than one chicken finger, and you're eating some fries too. And sarcastic is actually kind of cute on you, so keep it up. What about your journal? Oh, shit. What about Watson's laptop?"

"Hidden," he said. "Where no one will find them."

"You're sure they didn't get them?"

"I'm sure."

"You checked?"

"Of course not. If I were the killer, I would assume that the victim of a search might sooner rather than later go check on his hidden property, so I would wait and let them lead me to it. But I'm confident no one has found them. I wasn't gone long, Jack—not even a full day."

"It felt long." I ate another chicken finger. They were good—a little soft because they'd absorbed some of the steam they'd been giving off, and the breading had gotten mushy, but still delicious. I ate some fries. I pushed the plate against H's foot until he took another chicken finger.

He took a bite, and after he'd swallowed, he said quietly, "They could have kept me three days, Jack. Without charging me, I mean. That's the longest they can hold you without actually turning it into a legal proceeding. But they didn't have any evidence besides finding me in the security office. I explained that I had wanted to talk to Mr. Campbell about the security footage from the night Watson was killed, and I told them that when I arrived the door was open. I told them that his private office door was open as well, as was the closet, and that when I saw the body, I shut the closet because it was so upsetting."

I wondered what Rivera had thought, hearing that explanation in Holmes's cool, clipped tones.

"They couldn't prove that I wasn't telling the truth. In fact, they may very well have believed me. Their assumption was that I will play the amateur sleuth, and I gave them an explanation that lined up with their expectations."

"Which, to be fair, we kind of are doing—the amateur sleuth thing."

"Don't be ridiculous; I'm not an amateur." Apparently, the thought was so ridiculous that he had to eat a handful of fries to get over it. When he'd finished, he said, "Of course, my father got wind of it, and that's why they didn't hold me the full three days. It does help, occasionally, to be a Holmes. No one ever believes you might be the bad guy." It was such a strange comment that I opened my mouth to ask him about it, but H spoke again—he had forgotten he was glaring at me, and his expression was unreadable now. "I knew you would follow up on it, the murder report on Campbell's TV. That was the worst part about being detained: I knew we'd uncovered something critical, and I couldn't do anything about it. When you texted me and told me that you'd already figured it out, it was extremely satisfying."

"Ok, thank you, but don't say 'extremely satisfying' ever again. Not out loud, anyway. And also, because I'm a glutton for compliments, I am now going to tell you in excruciating detail what I did over the last twenty-four hours, and you're going to shower me with praise."

"Don't say 'shower me' ever again," Holmes said, his voice smooth as lake water. "Not out loud, anyway."

I choked on a French fry.

After successfully not dying—while Holmes did nothing but watch—I told him. And because he was a Holmes bot, programmed to find fault and poke holes and in general, be a pain in my ass, instead of showering me—yes, I hear it now—with praise, he said things like "Why didn't you simply withdraw to the tunnels, where you could have stolen bedding and food from other buildings on campus and remained safe and warm for the night?" and "Why didn't you have any money?" and "Why did you choose an Egg McMuffin?"

"Because they're delicious," I snapped. "And stop interrupting me!"

When I'd finished, Holmes frowned. "It still doesn't make sense."

"I know. I mean, it's 2020. Why would Aston care if anyone knew he was gay? He could be a preppy gay. That's definitely a thing. Although—" I frowned. "I saw Aston the night I found Watson. He was down by the creek, trying to wash something off him. At the time—well, I don't know, I didn't really think about it. Do you think Watson was blackmailing him too? And he killed her and was trying to clean himself up?"

"In a creek? Near the murder scene?" Holmes shook his head. "And clean up what? There was minimal blood; she was strangled. It's more likely that he had some sort of sexual encounter, although it's still not clear to me why he wouldn't wait to clean up when he got home."

"Well, walking through a boy's dorm smelling like cum might have been a bit of a giveaway."

For some reason, that made Holmes blush, and the corner of his mouth went crazy as he tried not to bite his lip. "To your other point, while you are correct that most people would not care enough about their sexual identity being exposed for it to be an effective piece of blackmail, Aston is in a unique situation: his grandfather is an apostle in the Mormon church—one of their topmost leaders. He and his family have a tremendous incentive to keep his orientation secret."

And what about you, I thought, studying the pale, chiseled perfection of his face. Why would a Holmes bot get so worked up when I made dumb comments about guys? Why would a Holmes bot—to use the vernacular— get so freaked the fuck out when I even joked about being gay? Moriarty had said something about a boy.

Holmes shifted and looked away as he said, "Regardless, our focus is Soares, not Aston Young. If your hypothesis is correct, and the same killer is acting again to cover their secret, then Soares is our primary suspect."

"My hypothesis? H, the coincidences are freaky. Both victims were blond. Both victims were small enough to be overpowered. Both victims were Walker students. Both victims were beaten to death. Both victims were thrown in the trash. Both victims were found by janitors."

"I thought he was a groundskeeper."

"That's not the point. The point is that the similarities are too much. It's got to be Soares; she's the only one besides Campbell who was even here in 1999. And she was acting super weird the night of the murder. I saw her in the stairwell of Butters, and she had this bag that she said was trash, and she wouldn't give it to me, and I could tell she wanted to get rid of me."

Holmes frowned. "That behavior is strange," he said slowly. "But there are other explanations for it, and other possibilities for the similarities. We could be dealing with a killer who adopted the details of that previous killing intentionally."

"What, a copycat?"

"Not exactly. Copycats are often motivated by a desire to be linked with the notoriety and attention that another killer has received. In this case, it might be a strategic decision—the killer wants us to believe that the same person is killing again. That's something a Moriarty would do. Or, alternatively, it may be as you said, that we're dealing with the same killer, but that the killer is no longer associated with the Walker School. They may be living regionally and, when Watson tried to blackmail them, they may have returned to Walker solely to eliminate a problem."

"Can't you just—" I waved a hand.

"I already told you no. I am not Sherlock Holmes. I do not want to repeat myself on this matter again."

He hadn't shouted, not exactly, but the words had been delivered with a brutal force—the verbal equivalent of being slapped down. For a moment, face hot, I stared at the splintered panel of the desk. Then I stared at the closet door. Then because the universe is a small place sometimes and probably because of something to do with gravity, I stared at him. In seventh-grade science, we'd had to memorize the definition: a force that causes any two bodies to be attracted toward each other. The Newtonian model, I had learned last year, on a Wikipedia dive. Attracted, I thought, staring at him, him staring back, his face unyielding. And then I wanted to laugh, and I thought of Einstein, and the curvature of spacetime, the event horizons of black holes, and I thought, fuck you, Newton.

"You did very well, making these connections," Holmes said.

"Oh my God."

Holmes blinked.

"I don't need you to patronize me. And I don't like you yelling at me because I messed up and forgot what you'd already told me."

"I was not being patronizing—"

"Look," I said, folding the now-empty plate and standing, "are we taking this to the police or not?"

Holmes unfolded himself, all that long, lean muscle coming up to stand. I forgot sometimes that we were the same height, and then moments like this would surprise me again and again. "No. I still need to conduct certain elements of this investigation. When I have finished, I will let you know—"

"You have got to be shitting me!" Ok, this time, I shouted. I reined in my voice, but all I could manage was a variation: "Are you shitting me right now?"

"I don't know what you—"

"We literally had an argument about this, like, five minutes ago. You don't get to cut me out of things. You don't get to make decisions for me. Even when you think you're doing it to keep me safe—and I feel like that's a stretch right now—you don't get to decide that stuff, not on your own. I would sure as hell hate to think that you learned absolutely nothing from that conversation."

Holmes bit his lip, silent. My pulse beat out the seconds inside my skull. When he spoke, his voice sounded like a Holmes bot who needed a tune-up. "I have reconsidered the situation, and I believe it would be in everyone's best interest if you accompanied me."

I creased the folded plate between my finger and thumb. "Accompanied?"

With a kind of strained optimism that was also a question, Holmes said, "Because you are my friend?"

I snorted and tossed the plate in the trash. "Yes, dumbass. We're friends. Now let's go talk to Soares."

Chapter 21

Mr. Octopods

We went to Butters first—the residence hall where Watson had lived and where Soares was resident master—but she wasn't there.

"Anderson," I suggested. "That's where she has her office."

Holmes nodded, and we headed east, crossing the quad as we backtracked. The evening breeze down the canyon wasn't as strong as it had been the night before, but it was colder, and wearing nothing but a (day-old) Walker polo, I was shivering. The aspens were shivering too, and in the last light of day—barely more than a glow that filtered around Timp to reach us—they looked like stamped gold.

"Thank you," Holmes said, and I could barely hear him over the whisper of the leaves.

"I should be thanking you." The darkness was falling deeper, and even though he was only a few feet away, it felt like he was gone. "Moriarty probably would have killed me if I'd gone in there alone, and even if she hadn't, I'd never have gotten this far."

Our soles against the asphalt spoke for both of us for a while. And then he said, "I thought she was my friend."

He didn't need to say who. Watson was who. Watson, who had taken his trust and turned it against him—and, if my guess was right, she hadn't been the first.

I shivered. I blew out a breath. I couldn't see the vapor, but goose bumps ran up and down my arms. I couldn't hear my heartbeat because of the wind, but I could feel it. We'd gone to Strawberry Days when I'd been, I don't know, ten, maybe. And they always had a carnival—the midway, the smell of cotton candy and roasted nuts and sizzling hot dogs. And I remembered, when I got on Mr. Octopods, the guy who ran the machine pushed this lever all the way forward, and I got spun around faster than ever in my life, and when I got off, I immediately threw up all over Mom's shoes.

Yeah, I thought as the darkness put out the gold of the leaves. Something like that.

I reached out and took his hand.

He didn't pull away, but his fingers stiffened for a moment, and if he made a noise, the wind carried it away. I squeezed once. After a moment, he squeezed back. We walked like that, and at first I felt like someone was watching me, like we were center stage with the spotlight on us, but then it got better. When we got to Anderson, he turned his hand and pulled it free.

On the outside, Anderson looked like so many of the original campus buildings: a sprawling, redbrick manor with a steeply gabled roof of slate. At this hour, all the classroom buildings were locked, so I used one of my keys to let us inside. Anderson Science Center, as it was officially called, did not look like a Victorian manor on the inside. Inside, it was a cross between a hospital and a spaceship: white vinyl tiles, white walls, chrome handrails, and lots of glass—walls of it, gathering up the blaze of the fluorescents in sheets that rippled as we walked past.

We checked the directory, took the stairs up two floors, and stopped in front of the door with the plaque that said SOARES. I looked at Holmes. Instead of knocking, he tested the handle. Then he opened the door and walked inside.

The office had the same sterile techno-nightmare aesthetic as the rest of the building, although accented here with Soares's personal touch: a sit-stand desk with a motor, the surface covered in folders and pens and stacks of student lab books and two enormous, curved monitors; an ergonomic desk chair, the kind with casters and a mesh back and unyielding lumbar support; the faint smell of rubber and what might have been ammonia. One of the monitors displayed some sort of spreadsheet, and the other showed a complicated graph. The tubular chairs in front of the desk had orange upholstery pilled from decades of the wear and tear of sweaty student asses.

Soares stood at a filing cabinet. She had frozen with one hand inside a drawer, and she was staring at us. She looked like she always did: a tall woman with brown skin, her hair in pink and purple and red spikes, a hint of a neck tattoo visible under the collar of her button-up.

"May I help you?" she asked coolly.

I shut the door behind me as Holmes said, "Yes. We need to talk. Where were you Friday night?"

Ah, I thought. He must have engaged his subtlety protocols.

Soares examined us. The diplomas on the wall behind her said she was smart, but I didn't need them—I could tell from her eyes. "You're the Holmes boy," she said after a moment. And then, looking at me, "And you're the janitor." Then nothing again. The cat clock on the wall ticked to fill the silence. "Whatever you think you're doing, I'm not interested in being part of it. Please leave my office."

"Where were you Friday night? Specifically, where were you between eight o'clock and midnight?"

She touched the hint of the tattoo on her neck, the gesture light and seemingly unconscious. Then she said, "If you're suggesting what I think you're suggesting, then you're not as smart as everyone believes. I'm going to say it one more time, and then I'm going to call campus security. I'll call them anyway, I think, but if you don't make a scene, it will be better. Get out of my office. Now."

"We know Olin Campbell was blackmailing you," Holmes said. "We know you broke into his office, retrieved the blackmail material, and murdered him. We know you were involved in Ellis Seward's murder twenty years ago. And we know you killed Sarah Watson on Friday night. You can either confess now, or you can let the police tear your life apart. I'm giving you this opportunity because—how did you put it? It will be better if you confess."

Soares's face grew blotchy, and when she reached for the phone on her desk, she knocked it out of its cradle. She swept it up again almost immediately and started to dial.

"Show her," Holmes said.

The big word in the first sentence of the Wikipedia entry on telepathy is *purported*. The *purported* transmission of information through psychic means, etc. I didn't believe in telepathy, but if you read the whole article (which I did, thank you, the week in January when we were snowed in), then you'd eventually get to the cross-linked article on *ishin-denshin*, the Japanese term for an East Asian concept of like minds and silent understanding. I must have been getting really good at the silent understanding of Holmes bots because I knew, without him saying another word, what he meant.

I pulled the flash drive that held the recording of Aston and Dawson from my pocket and held it up, covering the number scrawled on it with my thumb. Soares stopped dialing.

"Didn't you consider that Campbell would have backups?" Holmes asked. "Hang up the phone."

After a moment, Soares returned the phone to its cradle. She didn't lick her lips, but her tongue did poke out briefly, and she was supporting her weight with one hand on the desk.

"What would Headmaster Burrows say," Holmes asked, "if I gave him this?"

"It's just the data." The words sounded ripped from Soares's throat. She clamped her mouth shut, but then she spoke again: " The hypothesis was valid, I know it was, but the data—that stupid Barnes girl destroyed half my samples before I could finish analyzing them, so my sample size was too small. I didn't have the time to do it all over again."

I kept my gaze on Soares, but I could feel Holmes's mind racing.

"I wouldn't kill someone for a job." Soares shook her head and looked up at the ceiling, but a moment later her eyes came back to the flash drive. "What you said about Campbell, I wouldn't have done that. It's a fucking community college. I wouldn't risk everything for that kind of job. I just wanted out of here. I've got a master's degree in Biology, and the kids here, the kind of kids that get sent to Walker, they don't care about that. To them, I'm just another adult who's supposed to eat their shit. So, yeah, I faked it. Because the hypothesis really is sound. But the rest of it—" She stopped. Outrage tinged her voice. "I liked Sarah Watson. And I was here when the Seward boy was killed, and it was one of the worst days of my life, but the police looked at me then. They looked at all of us. I had nothing to do with that."

"Where were you Friday night?" I asked.

"I was running an orientation for the first-years in Butters. An orientation isn't exactly the right word. We have pizza, play games. It's supposed to help them get through the transition. I had a dozen girls with me that night."

"What time?"

"Midnight," Soares said. Then she frowned. "I saw you. I was still taking out the trash when I saw you."

"Jack says you behaved atypically." Holmes cocked his head as he looked at her. "He says you refused his offer of help."

Soares croaked a laugh. "Because I wanted a smoke. Oh my God, is that what this is about?"

"You were at Campbell's office last night."

That extinguished any hint of amusement in her face. "I called him to tell him I wasn't going to pay. I don't know how he found out; that man was here before I was, and I heard whispers that he was...well, doing something like this, I suppose. But he never did or said anything unusual until I started submitting my paper for publication. Then he showed up here, out of the blue." A smile twisted her lips. "Like you two. And he said he knew I'd faked the results, and he had proof, and if I didn't want my reputation ruined, I'd pay him a thousand dollars. Reputation." She wiped her eyes. "I don't have a reputation—not one that matters, anyway. That was the whole point of the paper. They won't even look at your application if you don't have recent publications, not even the community colleges. I paid him. And then, a few weeks later, he was back. And then he came back again, and the paper was still under review, and I didn't care anymore. That's what I went to tell him. I was going to tell him to fuck off, in not so many words. He could do whatever he wanted with whatever proof he had; I didn't care."

"And?" Holmes asked.

"I got there, and the door was open. I went inside. Nobody was there." She swallowed and lost some of her color. "I mean, he was there. I know that now. But at the time—God, he was inside the closet." Her voice was high pitched, like wire twisted to the point of snapping. "I went through his office, looking for the flash drive. He'd shown it to me. I finally had to beat the hell out of that filing cabinet to get it open, and that's where I found the drives. I went through them until I saw the one he'd shown me, the same number, I mean. And then I left. That's all. I swear to God."

Holmes's expression was distant, so I asked, "You knew Ellis Seward?"

She nodded.

"You said it was one of the worst days of your life."

"It was." When I kept silent, she continued, "I was a new teacher. Young, fresh out of grad school. And I was—Walker was different. The students were different. It was before we had been...repurposed as a holding pen. And, like every new teacher, I was close with my students, probably too close. Ellis was one of them. He was shy, very bright, and quite clearly gay, although he wasn't out. No one was back then, not here, I mean. Not even me. But you could see it, the way he was always on the periphery with the other boys, the ones he got attached to. When he was killed—" She stopped. "I'll never have children, but I can imagine what it feels like to lose one."

When the words had died inside her cramped office, nothing came to fill their void, and I was surprised to hear myself say, "I'm sorry."

She nodded, her eyes roving the room, looking for something that wasn't there.

"Do you know who killed Ellis?" Holmes asked.

"If I knew who killed Ellis, I would tell the police. If I'd known back then, I might have killed the bastard myself."

"Are you the only staff member at Walker who was employed here at that time?"

The question caught her off guard; I could see her trying to puzzle out its significance, but she nodded and said, "Yes. Olin was the only other person here from that time."

"What about support staff?" I asked.

"Oh God, no. The turnover is terrible." She frowned. "Why are you asking about Ellis and the staff? Do you believe there's some sort of connection between Ellis's death and Sarah's?"

"We've taken enough of your time, Ms. Soares," Holmes said. "If you think of anything else we should know, please contact me."

She watched as Holmes turned to open the door. Then she said, "And the flash drive?"

"It's not yours, I'm afraid." Holmes stepped out into the hallway. "You'll have to excuse the bluff. But you would be wise to assume that other copies of that information exist, perhaps even a contingency plan in the event of his death; Campbell seemed like a man to take precautions."

The last thing I saw as I pulled the door shut was fear spreading across Soares's face: the tightness of her skin, her pallor, the empty eyes.

As we walked through the halls of Anderson, I asked, "Well?"

"I don't know," Holmes said. "It will be easy enough to verify her story about the first-year orientation Friday night. If she's telling the truth, then she didn't kill Watson. At least, not personally."

"What about Campbell?"

The only answer at first was the sound of Holmes's chukkas, the crepe soles soft against the vinyl tiles. "Unlikely," he finally said. "It would have been a massive error in judgment to kill Campbell, hide his body, and then remove only the flash drive containing blackmail material about herself. It would have signaled her as the killer. Her story is more believable—that she found the office seemingly empty and took advantage of the opportunity."

"Unless she's smart enough to assume that we'd believe she's telling the truth because the alternative would be a huge mistake."

Holmes glanced over at me. "That's particularly devious. Jack, I didn't realize you had such a sinister mind."

"Try watching eight seasons of RuPaul and see how sinister your mind is. Drag queens make the Moriartys look like church mice."

As we pushed out into the night and the cold scrape of the wind, Holmes said, "If Soares is not involved in any of the deaths—"

I saw it too late: the baseball bat whistled out of the darkness and connected with the side of Holmes's head, and he fell.

Chapter 22

Jacky Tough Shit

"H!" I shouted. Before I could reach him, the bat whistled through the air again, and I retreated.

In the distant illumination from the security light, I could make out their features: Shivers, with his greasy mullet and his skewed jawline; Alma, with his round face and his Beatles haircut; and Vearl, with his high forehead, one hand in his pocket. Now the hand came out, his wrist flicked, and the blade of a knife glimmered.

"Jacky tough shit," Shivers said, swinging the bat one-handed—big, dramatic loops, like he was warming up for a grand slam. Bruises marked one side of his face from when Holmes had introduced him to the side of the Dodge. "You are one stupid motherfucker."

I didn't bother replying. I was still moving backward, and the sound of my Vans changed as I reached one of the gravel walks that crisscrossed campus. Shivers and Alma stalked after me. Alma held something too—long, but not thick enough to be a bat. Maybe a tire iron. Vearl, however, didn't follow; he stopped to crouch next to Holmes, who still wasn't moving. The blade of the knife spun as Vearl drilled the tip into Holmes's shirt, light knitting its way up the steel.

You're running, my brain said. This is just like the accident. You're running again.

I stopped retreating and shouted, "Get away from him!"

Still swinging the bat, Shivers glanced over his shoulder. Then he grinned at me. "Ah, don't worry about your boyfriend. Vearl's just going to have some fun. Hey, tell you what? Since you're a big faggot now, Jacky tough shit, how about Vearl does you a solid? How about he gives your boyfriend a nice, new cunny for you to play with?"

"Leave him alone," I said, directing the words past Shivers towards Vearl. "You hurt him, and you have no fucking idea what I'll do to you."

"There he is," Shivers said, but it sounded like he was talking to himself. "There's Jacky tough shit. I've been waiting for this for a long time."

Ishin-denshin. Silent communication. No more running. I felt it, the moment before Shivers and Alma started to move.

I dipped, scooping up gravel, and chucked it at Shivers's face. He howled and stumbled back, clawing at his eyes. I charged forward, closing the distance between me and Alma; Alma was bigger, and I knew if I gave him room to work me over with that tire iron, he'd beat the hell out of me—maybe, if he really got going, beat me to death. He was quiet, and you never knew with the quiet ones.

My charge caught Alma off guard. He'd been expecting me to retreat or dodge, and he was still winding up, bringing the tire iron back over his shoulder. He tried to react, swinging the iron around to strike me as I came toward him, but he was too slow, and he lost the momentum he'd generated. The iron clipped my arm. It didn't feel like anything, really— impact, but no pain, a sensation of shock that my brain interpreted as cool.

Then I reached him, and I drove my shoulder into him the way we'd learned at two-a-days. He weighed more than I did, and I hadn't had time to build up much speed. I didn't pick him up and send him flying, but I did knock him flat on his back. I stumbled forward, going after him, and dropped down on top of him. Distantly, the iron rang out where it struck stone. I punched him as hard as I could in the face.

The impact rippled up my arm, throbbing in my elbow and shoulder, and Alma's head made a crunching noise as I drove it into the gravel. His eyes came open, and he didn't seem to see anything. I hit him again, and his eyes shut and didn't open again.

Everything narrowed to this tiny tunnel in front of me, and I was aware of sounds and sensation washing over me and being rejected by my brain. I scrambled off Alma. I needed to find Holmes. I had to get to him before Vearl hurt him, but black holes ringed my vision, and I was having a hard time orienting myself. I stumbled over an uneven patch of ground. It saved my life.

The bat clipped the back of my head and bounced up, whiffing over me, instead of breaking my neck or slamming into the back of my skull. It didn't hurt, not really, but it did seem to lift me up. For a moment, I had this sensation like I was stretched out—there was my body, stumbling, falling, my feet slipping on the gravel, and there was me, being pulled out of my body like Laffy Taffy. I hit the ground, rolled, tasted gravel dust and grass and dirt. Then I was on my back. Overhead, the stars glinted in the sky, and I thought of the Provo, the river crests of broken glass.

A shadow blocked out the stars, and then something settled on my chest, and something else pressed down on my throat, cutting off my air. The baseball bat, I realized. Shivers looked awful—the stones had cut up the tender skin around his eyes and across the bridge of his nose, and one eye was red and kept blinking automatically, like maybe he wasn't seeing anything out of that one anymore. I clawed at his hands, trying to rip them free from the bat, but Shivers had all the leverage, and he used it, bearing down on me with his full weight. I couldn't get any air, and the trapped blood in my head made it feel like a balloon. Black spots danced in front of me.

I bucked, trying to throw Shivers, but the best I did was shift him sideways, and a moment later, he pressed down again. I brought my knee up between his legs, but the angle was wrong. He yelped, so maybe I'd clipped him, but he didn't ease up. The pressure in my head was like a scream now, and static washed out my vision. And then, all of a sudden, it felt better. Maybe this was dying.

Only I wasn't dying, I decided, as air rushed into my lungs and my brain began to function again. My vision cleared, and I was staring up at the stars again. I managed to get upright, my head pounding. I gasped for breath as I turned, trying to figure out where Shivers was, and Vearl, and—

Blood covered half of Holmes's face, a mask of gore that made him look inhuman. He stood behind Shivers, and in his hand, a blade glinted. Vearl's blade. It was pressed against the soft skin behind Shivers's chin, with enough pressure that Shivers had raised up on tiptoe to keep the steel from going in. I was still having a hard time understanding what I was seeing, so I glanced around. Alma was on the ground where I'd left him, and a few yards away, Vearl knelt, clutching his arm. The blood running between his fingers looked black in the starlight.

"Go," Holmes said.

He lowered the knife, and Shivers ran. Vearl crawled over to Alma, and somehow he got the bigger guy on his feet. A moment later, they had disappeared between the trees, stumbling in the direction Shivers had gone. Then even the sound of their steps faded.

Holmes swayed on his feet. The hand with the knife hung at his side, so loose around the handle that the blade tilted when the breeze picked up.

"H," I said, and somehow I managed to stand. "Holloway, are you ok?"

He looked at me, but he wasn't seeing me. Then his eyes rolled up into his head, and he collapsed.

Chapter 23

Hewdenhouse

The Dodge's suspension creaked, and wind howled against the glass as we rocketed down the canyon. Holmes lay on the seat, the belt looped awkwardly around him, his head pillowed on my polo because in my haste, I hadn't been able to find anything else. When we took each turn down the snakey bends of the road, he rocked back and forth; only the belt kept him from falling off the bench. There was so much blood.

I remembered fragments of getting him to the truck: the surprising weight of his body, my panicked efforts at first to carry him in my arms like we were on the cover of one of Mom's ancient romance novels, not being able to catch my breath, the heat in my skin, the pain in my throat.

The headlights picked out the gleam of granite, the gnarled arms of scrub oak, leaves leeched of their color, movement at the edge of the cone of light—a blurred grayness, and I remembered seventh-grade art, Ms. Prinze teaching us to blend charcoal with our fingers. Then light flashed off gold eyes. Coyote, the tiny, remaining rational part of my brain told me. Hunting.

Holmes made a noise and tried to sit up.

"Don't move," I told him. "Everything's going to be ok. You're going to be fine. Just lie there, and we'll be at the hospital—"

"No hospital." He clawed at the seat belt. He mumbled the words. "No hospital."

"Yes hospital." I pushed his hands away from the belt. "Lie your ass back down, H. Right now!"

Instead, he made a weird, groaning noise and flopped onto his side. His whole body convulsed, and I waited for the ocean of vomit. Nothing came up, and a few moments later, he was bracing one hand on the dash, trying to get himself upright. I had to check the road as we came around another curve in the canyon. The blackness of the Provo, the skeletons of the old maples, the wedge of sky between the peaks so dark and so deep that the stars had to be drowning—it all imprinted itself in that moment as I guided us onto a straight stretch. Then something clicked.

When I looked over, Holmes had the seat belt unlatched, and he was trying to crawl out between the lap belt and the one that was supposed to run diagonally. It would have been funny if, you know, he hadn't been covered in blood and acting like a zombie.

"Stop it." I reached over to secure the buckle, but I was trying to do it one-handed, and Holmes fought me off. "H, cut it out! You got hurt bad—"

"No hospital." The words had a cut-glass sharpness like the riffles on the Provo. And then, with a note of uncertainty that I barely caught, he added, "Jack."

"Yes," I said. "Jack. And yes, hospital. And quit trying to climb through your seat belt, God damn it. You look like a cat in a pillowcase."

That must have puzzled him because his eyebrows knitted together, and he stopped trying to get his knee up and over the lap belt.

"You got hit in the head, H, and you might have a concussion, which would be bad enough, but it might be a hell of a lot worse." My throat tightened, and it was a moment before I could say, "So, we've got to get you checked out, even though I know you don't like the idea."

Holmes and the seat belt seemed to reach some sort of standoff, and he slumped back against the seat. For an instant, his eyes closed, and his breathing became slower and deeper. Then, without opening his eyes, he said, "I cannot go to the hospital, and certainly not for brawling with a drug dealer. This is a precarious time for my father; any bad publicity before the Zodiac IPO could jeopardize all his hard work."

"Yeah, ok, he might only make a hundred billion dollars instead of two hundred," I said. "Big loss. H, if you've got bleeding on your brain, you could die. I'm taking you to the hospital. Fuck your dad's IPO." The tires thrummed, and I said in a quieter voice, "And sorry for saying that, because I know it's important, but you know what I mean."

When he spoke again, he sounded more like the Holmes bot I knew—every word measured, weighed, and precisely inflected: "If you do not turn this truck around, I will throw myself out of it and return to Walker on foot."

We flew down another hundred yards of pavement. I felt like I'd left my brain behind. He'd do it. I knew he would. Because Holmes bots were programmed to do whatever they said they were going to do. And because he'd already hiked through the mountains like the Terminator in booty shorts. It was what Mr. Scholz, in eighth-grade Language Arts, would have called a classic dilemma: Holmes needed a hospital, but he refused to go. And I had no idea what to do next.

"As you like," Holmes said and yanked on the door handle. The truck door opened, although the resistance of the air pressing against the vehicle kept it mostly closed. More air shrilled through the crack in the seal, whipping through the cab. He was still tangled in the seat belt—his ancient enemy—but he leaned into the door, forcing it open. The sound grew to a roar, and the cold was like a lash, raising goose bumps across my bare chest and shoulder.

I grabbed his shirt and hauled him toward me. Or, I tried to. As I had learned earlier that evening, Holmes bots weren't as lightweight as they looked. He twisted, trying to escape my hold. One of his hands found my fingers, and I had the strange thought that now, of all times, Holloway Holmes was trying not to hurt me. Maybe it was because he was so focused on committing suicide-by-diving-out-of-a-truck.

"Fine!" I had to shout for my voice to carry over the air rushing into the cab. I slowed the truck onto the shoulder, and we rolled to a stop.

There was a picnic area to our right, a playground, security lights buzzing and flickering. A couple was walking hand in hand, stopping now and then to shine a light on a piece of paper and then look up. Probably a cute little Mormon couple, barely older than Holmes and me, from BYU. Some sort of endearing little date. And they'd talk and hold hands and maybe he'd get bold enough to kiss her when they got back to her door. What would that be like, I wondered. What would it be like not to have to deal with a boy who hid under tarps and talked like he was in an operating theater and picked locks and smelled like moss and animal heat and did squats like a fucking beast and, apparently, threw himself out of moving vehicles because he was so fucking determined that it made you want to put your head through the engine block? Probably nice, I thought. Probably great. They'd probably get married before they were twenty and have nice little bunny sex until they were forty.

Holmes shifted as though he might try to slide out the door.

I yanked on his shirt and growled, "I said fine, you goddamn maniac. Will you cut it out?"

He looked over at me. He was squinting, probably because of a colossal headache. His eyes were the color of the stars, with the same soft luminance.

"I'm scared to death, in case your emotional radar got jammed. I'm freaked the fuck out if you want to get technical. And here I am, worried blood is going to accumulate in your brain until you die, and you can't give two fucks because you're too busy trying to throw yourself out of a truck going fifty miles an hour."

"I'm fine—"

"You don't know that you're fine! People die, H. They die all the time. They die because their heart gives out, because they slip and hit their head wrong, because a car swerves into their lane—" Now why, I thought, why had I said that? The headlights sliding like ice across the double yellow line. Just a memory, but I couldn't breathe, which took a lot of the punch out of my next line: "Did nobody put that little fact in your coding?"

He said something, but I couldn't hear him because I was back there, back then: in the rear seat of the Lexus, some sort of warning sound dinging on and off again, everything askew like the world had tilted without taking me with it, Mom and Dad not moving in the front seats. And the man. I saw him again, coming toward us, something held low against his thigh. When he passed through the lights, metal gleamed.

Holmes's hand on my shoulder made me start. The cool weight was real, present, insistent on this moment and the reality of his body against mine.

"Jack, you need to breathe in slowly. Like you showed me. Do you remember that?"

I sagged back against the seat. Exhaustion dragged me down against the ancient upholstery, and I could barely keep my eyes open. He moved his hand higher. It rested on the ridge of my collarbone. His thumb settled on my chest. I didn't have a shirt on because I'd been a sucker and given it to him as a pillow, and now it felt like I had miles and miles of bare skin, and Holmes kept moving his hand, like he meant to explore every inch of it. The goose bumps on my chest had nothing to do with the cold now.

If we ever did, I thought. If it ever happened. He'd be gentle, probably because he knew how to hurt so easily. He'd be careful because he did everything with so much cautious attention. He'd be kind because there was a great well of kindness in him that everyone else in his life had tried to cap and bury. I could imagine how he would look, that familiar ferocious intensity in his expression, but with me as its sole focus. Oh my God, I thought, with an edge of humor so sharp that it felt like hysteria. He'd probably be a gentleman.

"Why are you smiling?" Holmes asked.

It took me a moment to find words. "Because you're groping me like a first-year after Homecoming."

Holmes scowled, and his hand lightened, but he didn't pull it away. "You were having a panic attack."

"And now I'm not," I said. I sat forward, the movement enough to dislodge Holmes's hand, and it fell from my shoulder. "You're not going to let me take you to a hospital?"

"I'm fine, Jack. I appreciate the concern. I need to rest; that's all."

"If anything changes—if your headache gets worse, if you start getting mumbly, if you can't answer questions, anything—I'm taking you to the hospital. Do you understand? And don't even think about getting out of this truck because right now I am so goddamn pissed off that I will run you down, and I don't care if you are the Terminator in booty shorts, I will beat your ass like a red-headed stepchild and drag you to the hospital by the hair if I have to."

Holmes was silent for a long minute. Then he cocked his head. "If I get mumbly?"

"Great," I said, shifting into drive. "He rebooted in smartass mode."

When we got back to Walker, the campus was dark and empty. I parked under the carport, killed the engine, and studied the cottage. No lights were on, and I watched, waiting for movement.

"No one will bother us tonight," Holmes said.

"I'm in charge. I'm going to decide whether it's safe or not." I waited, the seconds itching at me, and then I threw open the door. "Stay here. And wipe that look off your face by the time I get back."

"I have no idea what you're talking about."

I slammed the door and went inside.

The cottage was dark and empty, just like campus, so I went back to the carport and waved Holmes inside. I locked the doors and turned on the lights. I went to the medicine cabinet first and found the Tylenol, and I brought back two for Holmes with a cup of water. He swallowed them and drank the rest of the water. I wet a washcloth and used it to work on the blood covering his face. When I touched the side of his head, he shied away, and I cupped a hand against the side of his neck to steady him.

"It'll just take a second," I murmured.

He flinched again when I parted his blood-crusted hair. "It's not bad," I said. "Probably doesn't even need stitches, but it's going to hurt like hell when you shower."

I finished cleaning up his face as best I could, and then I lowered the washcloth. He was looking at me so intensely that I looked away first, hitching a thumb under the waistband of my jeans because I had no idea what to do. The moment got longer and longer, so I walked away to turn up the thermostat. Then I went down the hall and pulled on my favorite Dodgers tee, the blue starting to gray and the cotton super soft because it had been washed a million times. I grabbed the blanket and pillow from my bed. When I got back, Holmes was studying the picture of Dad and me. Dad kept it in the living room. You couldn't see it because of the frame, but he'd folded Mom out of it.

"Why is it folded?" Holmes asked.

Ok, I thought. Most people couldn't see it

"You noticed that, of course. Lie down." I passed him the pillow, and he sat on the couch. I studied him for a moment. Then I took the pillow back and fluffed it. "I said lie. Not sit. We're going to have to work on that. Do you want a t-shirt and a pair of shorts?"

"Why would I want a pair of shorts?"

"To sleep in, H. I don't know. Do you sleep in your pants? Do they just roll you into the closet at the end of the day and store you upright?"

"Why are you upset?"

I shook my head and knelt. Yanking on the laces of his chukkas, I set to work removing them.

"I can do that," Holmes said.

"I said lie down. What don't you understand about that?"

When the boots came off, Holmes stretched out on the sofa, and I tucked the blanket in around him. "Don't move," I said. "If I have to re-tuck you in, there's going to be hell to pay."

He didn't say anything this time. He just watched me with those gray eyes, brilliant like they'd soaked up enough starlight to keep them charged for a long, long time. I looked away first again. Then, even standing there was too much, and I crossed to the kitchen. I took out a pot, filled it with water, and then went through the cabinets until I found noodles. I considered a jar of red sauce. Then I checked the fridge. We still had some sticks of butter, so I took one out along with the container of ground parmesan cheese. While the water came to a boil, I cut the butter into squares. I found the kosher salt and the pepper. And then I stood there, staring at the counter, my heart beating faster and faster.

"What are you doing?" Holmes asked, raising his head to look across the room at me.

"What the hell did I say about making me tuck you back in?"

His eyes widened, and he dropped his head back onto the pillow.

For the ten minutes that the fettucine cooked, I had blessed silence — well, the silence of a gurgling pot, a refrigerator motor whining and smelling like it was about to burst into flames, a furnace chugging as it struggled to heat the tiny house, and somehow louder than all of it, Holmes's breathing. When the pasta was ready, I drained the water, tossed the cubed butter in with the noodles, and seasoned it with salt and pepper and the parm. I put it on two plates and carried it over to the living room.

"You can sit up," I said.

He sat up. His eyes were still wider than usual, but he took the plate when I passed it to him.

"You eat this, and then you're going straight to sleep. Understand?"

"You can't possibly be hungry again. I saw how many chicken tenders you ate."

"I ate a reasonable human amount of chicken tenders," I said, my face heating. "I don't operate on lithium fuel cells. And don't think you fooled me, all the time you spent nibbling on that second tender. You need food. Not too much, but a little. And then you need sleep."

Maybe it was a fault in his wiring, something that had been knocked loose in the scuffle. Maybe the latest update was missing a line of code. Whatever the reason, he took the fork and began to eat—no arguing, no making faces, not even the familiar tension at the corner of his mouth, when he was trying not to bite his lip. And for the first time in my life, I saw a Holmes bot go whole hog on a meal. That boy ate like he was starving, which, to be fair, he probably was.

He'd devoured half the plate when he looked up, his lips shiny, and asked, "What is this?"

"Butter noodles."

"They're...quite good."

"Understatement works better when you aren't slurping a noodle *Lady and the Tramp* style."

He finished pulling the noodle into his mouth and frowned. "I don't know what that means."

"Oh my God. We've got a lot of catching up to do."

We ate in silence for a few minutes. Then, without looking up, Holmes asked, "Jack, where is your mother?"

I stirred the noodles with my fork. "Can we—how about we talk about my parents another night? I'm not up for it tonight. What about your parents?"

He must not have known he was doing it because the movement was so transparent: he reached down and touched his pocket through the blanket. Then he said, "Are there more noodles?"

"How's your head?"

"Much better."

"Liar."

"I would like some more noodles. I can get them myself."

"Oh God, not a chance." I took his plate. I made sure I didn't look back at first. I was the master of high-risk behavior; Holmes was strictly amateur night.

When I thought he'd had enough time, I set the plates on the counter and turned. He had one hand loose at his side, fingers curled. I dropped onto the couch next to him.

"Are you going to give it to me?" I asked. "Or do I have to take it away?"

He stared back at me. His face was as smooth as ice.

"Fine—" I reached for him.

He drew his hand back reflexively.

"Your head is messed up enough right now." I beckoned for the pill he was hiding. "Hand them over, all of them."

"It is not your concern—"

"It is my concern."

"—what I do—"

"Pills, H."

"—or what I choose—"

I spoke over him, my voice clear and light. Almost chipper. "It sure as hell is. Pills, H. Now."

"You do not get to tell me—"

"Yes, I do!"

Those chips of color floated in his cheeks, and he raised his voice back at me. "What makes you think—"

"Because I care about you, dickcheese! Now give me the goddamn pills!"

For a moment, his lips quirked soundlessly, like he might say something. Then, his eyes still locked on my face, he stretched out his hand and pressed the pill into mine.

"The rest," I said.

That furrow appeared between his eyebrows, but he brought out the brown prescription vial and handed it over.

"And don't ever use pasta for evil, H. I'm very disappointed in you."

He studied me for a moment. "I can't tell if you're joking."

"Of course I'm not joking."

There was no point hiding the pills—he'd have found them in five seconds—so I replaced the loose pill in the vial and then put the vial in my pocket. I brought him back more food, and to my surprise, he ate everything on his plate. I ate too, and between us, we emptied the pot. Then I carried everything over to the sink. I knew the responsible thing was to wash up, but Dad was in prison and might not ever come home, Holloway Holmes was stretched out on my couch, someone wanted to kill us, and the dirty dishes didn't seem like such a big deal. I sprayed some water over them and went back to Dad's armchair.

Holmes was lying down again, his eyes moving restlessly behind closed lids.

"Do you want to watch something?" I asked.

He shook his head.

We sat there, the silence growing thicker between us, with its own texture — comfortable, strangely warm. In the last year, I'd spent a lot of time alone. I knew a lot about silence, and I'd never had silence like this.

"How's your head?" I asked after a while.

He gave me a thumbs-up, and I laughed and covered my mouth. When he opened one eye to stare at me suspiciously, I laughed harder.

"What?"

"Nothing."

He gave me that one-eyed glare for another moment. Then he closed his eye again. The wind tapped at the glass. The old cottage creaked as it shifted and settled.

"Why do you do that stuff anyway? You're the smartest person I know."

The corner of his mouth trembled. "Not smart enough."

"We're going to figure it out, H. We'll find whoever did this. My dad will get to come home. I know it won't change everything; I'm sorry about Watson, I really am. But at least she'll get justice."

Holmes's eyes flicked open. Their gray was deeper in the cottage's low light, almost the color of smoke. "I wasn't friends with Watson."

I frowned. "I thought—"

"I believed we were friends. It was a conclusion based on data — we spent time together, and she was patient with me, and she laughed at some of the things I said. I didn't have anything else to compare it to." He was looking at me again with that tremendous force behind his gaze. "Before I met you."

"Yeah, H," I said, grinning, my face hot. "I read between the lines."

He was still studying me, his face blank, almost as white as paper, ready for a thousand stories to be written on it. And somebody was going to get to write those stories with him, I realized. And, the second realization coming hard on the heels of the first, was that it wasn't going to be me. When this investigation ended, we'd try to stay friends; I was sure of that. But it wouldn't be the same. He'd have classes. He'd have responsibilities. He'd be a student. And I'd go back to cobbling together hours and shifts, odd jobs to keep Dad and me afloat. We might limp through a couple more years, seeing each other every once in a while. But when he left Walker, it would be over for good. He had his family, and I'm sure the Holmeses, with their legacy and their secrets and their multi-billion-dollar IPO, didn't want a drop-out janitor hanging around their son. He'd have college. He'd have a life. He'd have someone he woke up next to in the middle of the night. A lot of someones, probably. Some of them because of his cold-forged perfection. Some of them because of his family. And the lucky ones, the ones who got to see the real Holloway Holmes under all of that, who would tell him when he needed to eat and wouldn't let him do dumb stuff like chem up until he crashed and who would remind him, whenever he needed it, that it was ok to bite your lip.

"What's wrong?" he asked.

I shook my head and tried to swallow.

"Jack—"

"I'm tired," I said, my voice raggedy. "I'm going to turn off the lights."

His eyes followed me to the switch, and then darkness came down like a curtain. I stumbled back to the chair. A weak glow made it through the blinds. It was the color of the mountains, and it gave a hardscape gleam to whatever it touched—the TV's black plastic, the glass in the framed photos on the wall, one lean, pale arm curled on top of the blanket—that made me close my eyes.

"I do not want to…to change schools again."

Holmes's voice was tentative, as though the words were feeling their way through the darkness to me. I opened my eyes; they had started to adjust, and I could pick out the shape of him, the glitter of his eyes. He was staring up at the ceiling.

"That's why you do addies?"

"My father expects a great deal. I do not want to disappoint him again."

"H, you're a fucking genius, pardon my language. You don't need addies to pass sophomore chem."

"I have had problems before. The medication helps me stay focused."

Outside, the aspens and pine stirred, and the sound of leaves and needles was like the sound of the ocean, like a vast tide was rushing in, darkness to swallow us.

"Do you want to talk about it?"

He made a croaking noise, and it took me a moment to realize it was laughter—mangled, splintered laughter. "I do not."

"Ok. You don't have to if you don't want to. But sometimes it helps. Talking, I mean."

The silence knitted itself together again. In the dark, with the sound of that black flood rushing towards us, my eyes began to sag. I was so far gone that I barely heard him when he started speaking again, and I had to haul myself back.

"You heard Maggie." It was half statement, half question. "What she said, about a toy. A...a boy."

"Yeah. She was being a bitch."

Something in the refrigerator clicked off.

"His name was Nick. Nicholas Desmond Cathrow."

"God," I said. My tongue felt too big for my mouth. Prickles ran up and down my skin. "He already sounds like a twat."

Holmes's laughter sounded less broken this time. "No, he was...he was sweet. Or I thought he was, although now, when I remember, I can see that many of the things I took for endearments were actually his little cruelties. His favorite thing was to laugh and tell me I didn't know how to smile. 'Haven't you ever seen a smile, Holloway?' That's what he'd ask. 'Haven't you ever seen a human smile?'"

"Are you kidding me?" But part of me was also trying to remember if I'd ever seen Holmes smile, and I wasn't sure I had. "Where is this little shit?"

I was asking because I was planning a quick, easy international murder, but Holmes, of course, took it seriously. "At Hewdenhouse still. It's a public school in England. It is a rigorous place. Demanding. I suppose to many people, it would seem cruel. Nick and I became friends."

It was the way he said it that told me everything, and something hot and feral, crouching low in my belly, started kneading its claws. I tried to keep it out of my voice when I said, "Oh yeah?"

Holmes laughed again, the sound fuller this time. "Jack."

"What?"

He laughed some more. When he spoke again, the tension had eased. "He knew what he was doing, and I...did not. My education had been extensive in many ways. My—" His voice got hung up on something. "—training had covered a great deal. But in many ways, I was—am— sheltered. I understand that now, but I didn't then. So, I believed him when he told me that this was what friends did. I didn't understand what I felt for him. It was so much more than friends, but when I tried to explain, he said that no, this was purely what friends did." Something disconnected, and Holmes's words became detached. "I was in love with him until I found the photos and videos of our time together. He had already composed the email. He was selling them to the *Daily Mail*."

"H—" I stopped myself. "Holloway, God, I'm so sorry. That's awful."

"It is reality, I believe. Watson reminded me of that; I shouldn't have forgotten so easily."

"What happened?"

"My father handled things, as he always does. But I—I did something precipitous." The silence had its own breath between us now. "He was an excellent footballer. He was very proud of it. So, I broke his knee."

I let out the air in my lungs slowly.

Holmes made that croaking noise again. "Didn't you wonder why I was at Walker?"

"H, I'm so sorry someone did that to you—"

"My father was furious, of course. All that training. All those years of lessons, of tasks, of tutors, tests and games and challenges, all his—his conditioning." In my mind, I saw the corner of his mouth, the frantic, half-repressed need that his father had tried to beat out of him. In that moment, I wanted to kill Blackfriar Holmes—and kill Nicholas Desmond Cathrow, licensed twat and scum of the earth, too. Holmes kept speaking, words laced with bitterness. "I don't know what he expected. I've always been a disappointment. My temper, my...attachments, the night terrors—"

Nothing came after, just a drop into the dark. I waited. Then I moved over onto the couch. Holmes retreated, pulling his body away from mine. I kicked off the Vans and put my feet up, lying on the blanket, both of us crammed onto the couch—our shoulders and hips touching, and Holmes curving his body away from me everywhere else.

"I'm sorry," Holmes said, his voice thick, "but I would like to be alone—"

"So, that's why you're in Utah? Because that's the weirdest part of all this. You're supposed to be in London. And you're supposed to be, I don't know, solving crimes with Scotland Yard. And instead, you're here. And your father is here. And Moriarty is here. And you don't even sound English—your accent, I mean. Moriarty does, but you don't."

I threw out the questions as a lifeline; I'd wanted to ask, but until now, things had been too busy, too crazy, and now I knew that if I didn't keep talking, Holmes would shut down, and if he shut down now, he might shut down for good.

"Partially," Holmes said after a long moment. "Utah has a whole industry of this type of facility for troubled teens, and the Walker School is one of the best. It is remote, and it puts me at a disadvantage: I'm without the resources I would have in England or, for that matter, on the East Coast—I spent half my time growing up in New York, which is why I'm bidialectal." His voice shifted, becoming slightly more resonant with what I was now officially thinking of as a posh English accent. "I can sound like a—what did you say?—a twat when I want to."

"English boys and their accents. Now say something about bangers and mash—"

He shoved me, and I almost rolled off the couch.

Grinning, I righted myself. Either I was taking up more room—very probable—or Holmes had relaxed and wasn't trying to twist away from me; I could feel the hard lines of his body against my side. "You said that's partially why you're here; what's the rest of it?"

He hesitated. "Have you read the Sherlock Holmes stories? I'm not talking about the movies, but the original stories, the ones John Watson wrote and sold?"

"No."

"Sherlock Holmes and Professor Moriarty both had a...a fascination with the American West. With Utah, in particular. It appears again and again—a place of wealth and opportunity, but also violence, greed, secrets, conspiracy, corruption."

"Somewhere perfect for the Moriartys."

"And for the Holmeses. Not much has changed in the last hundred years, except now the riches of the West aren't in mineral rights but in technology. Why do you think my father chose to run Zodiac from here? He could kill two birds with one stone: take advantage of the abundance of tech talent and, at the same time, keep a close eye on his wayward son." Holmes let out a breath. "Of course, all of that is immaterial at this point. When Father learns about this disaster, he will move me again. This time, I suspect it will be an even more stringent environment. For my own good, of course." Something savage twisted in his next words: "Did you know Holloway is the name of a prison? For much of its existence, a prison for women—insult to injury, don't you think?"

I hadn't known any of that, but I'd read about places like that, wilderness camps, places in the middle of nowhere so that you couldn't run away, where they worked you like a dog and beat the hell out of you if you tried to say no. Some places were worse. There was almost no regulation, no one for the kids to complain to. Just a few adults with all the power and some very vulnerable teens, and no one would believe you if you told them one of the "teachers" came into your cabin night after night to take one more thing away from you.

"That's not going to happen," I said.

Holmes managed a lying-down shrug.

"And even if it does, you'll be ok. You're strong and smart and tough. And I'd come find you, and we can Thelma and Louise the hell out of there."

"Thank you, but I'm afraid I'm not terribly smart or tough or strong."

"Well, that's kind of disheartening for me considering you've handed me my ass a couple of times without even trying."

"Because you don't know how to escape a wrist lock," Holmes said with another of those lying-down shrugs. "Roll your arm toward the thumb, where the hold is weakest. Keep moving—roll or fall forward. And remember that when they're close enough to grab you, they're also close enough to hurt. Go for the knee or groin. Headbutt them. There, Jack. Now you have nothing to fear from me."

"I'm not afraid of you," I said.

"That's strange," Holmes said. "Because sometimes, Jack, I'm terrified of you, of what you could do to me."

I opened my mouth to speak into that brokenness, but then I stopped myself. Words weren't going to help anything; Holmes had heard enough words in his life. What he needed was someone to show him, again and again, day after day. But, of course, it wouldn't be me. I'd already figured that out.

"Let's get some sleep." I flopped around until I got under the blanket. "No hogging the pillow."

We squirmed around for a while.

"Jesus Christ," I said. "How many elbows do you have?"

"This couch isn't big enough for two people."

"Tough shit. How long are your legs?"

"We're the same height."

"I know. And I've seen you in your booty shorts, and you look like you have normal, human-length legs."

"My legs are perfectly proportionate."

"H, for the love of God, how the hell can you take up so much room? I swear I could put both hands around your waist, but now it's like sharing a bed with King Kong—"

Holmes elbowed me—on purpose that time, I was pretty sure—and breath whooshed out of my lungs. I groaned and rolled and rubbed my side.

"Stop being so dramatic."

Somehow, after that, we fit together on the couch.

"I do not sleep well," Holmes said. His head rested on my shoulder. His breath tickled the underside of my jaw.

Night terrors, he had said. Which his father had tried to beat out of him. Or which might have come because of the beatings. I smoothed his hair. It was the first time I'd touched it, as far as I could remember, and it felt like silk.

"That's what you keep telling me," I said, "but I remember somebody who snored the whole way home in the truck."

He didn't answer, and I heard his breath even out in sleep. I touched his hair again. My fingers trembled at the shell of his ear. The aspens sang their flood song. And dark waters buoyed me up and carried me away.

Chapter 24

Just Following Up

I woke to a morning like the gleam of a blade, the song of a chickadee, and the warmth and weight of Holmes on top of me. My arm wrapped around him had fallen asleep. The smell of his hair product, crisp and clean and so light I only noticed it up close like this, came in on every breath. Then, as my brain kicked into gear, two more facts came to light. I tried to ignore them. I tried to shove them away. But as soon as I'd recognized them, the reality of my situation grew clearer and clearer, my brain going into hyperdrive. Fact one: I was sporting some serious morning wood. Fact two: pressed against me, so was Holmes.

Before I could do anything—although God knew what I could do; think about batting averages, I guess—Holmes stirred and made a sleepy, un-Holmes bot noise. I knew the exact instant he realized the situation: he froze. Then his breathing changed, becoming faster and shallower. Even with my arm asleep, I could feel the muscles in his back tightening. The idea was starting to come to me that the best thing would be to pretend I was still asleep—Jack Moreno, Boy Genius—when all of a sudden, Holmes scrambled over me to climb off the couch. His knee drove into my gut, and his elbow barely missed my windpipe, and for a guy who had trained in Krav Maga and who was usually quite graceful, he stumbled and wobbled like a newborn colt on the linoleum.

I sat up, grunting from having his kneecap press all the way to my spine, and rubbed my stomach. Holmes stood in the middle of the living room, staring at me. He was wild eyed, panting. He didn't look embarrassed—his face wasn't red. He was chalk white. I thought, through the last haze of sleep, that he was terrified. His breathing quickened, so shrill and short it sounded like a whistle. I opened my mouth, and he turned and ran. The bathroom door slammed shut, and the crash echoed through the cottage.

Counting to ten, I rubbed my eyes. I got to my feet, winced at how cold the floor was, and shuffled after him. When I got to the bathroom door, I stood there, chafing my arms and listening.

"Hey, H?" I tried again. "Holloway?"

From the other side of the door came those panting breaths.

"It's ok. It's not a big deal." I tried to channel my inner *Your Changing Body* teacher; my face felt like it was about to melt off. "That happens to everybody sometimes."

It was hard to tell, but I thought, under the ragged breathing, he was crying.

I tried the handle—locked. "H, you're kind of scaring me. Can I come in? Just to check on you. And then I'll leave you alone for as long as you want."

"Go away!"

The words were a shriek, torn from his throat. He didn't sound like a Holmes bot, so cool and controlled. He didn't even sound like a human being. He sounded like a cocktail shaken up out of pure raw hatred and grief. I took a step back. I was still chafing my arms, but now my hands had frozen in place. I opened my mouth, and nothing came out.

After another moment of staring at the door's thin paneling, the thick layers of off-white paint, I padded back to the living room. I could still hear those frantic breaths, and I knew—the way I was starting to understand a lot of things about Holmes—that he wouldn't want me to hear him like this, every stop and stay undone. And he wouldn't let me help him, so the best thing I could do was give him some space. I pulled on my Vans. I got my jacket. I stepped out onto the porch, making sure my steps rang out on the boards, and I shut the door hard.

The morning was the steel of a flensing knife, bright and so thin that it seemed like it would flex if you pressed on it. The air smelled like cedar and the cold. I started west, toward the main campus, my steps clipping along the concrete walk. A few people were out and about—I saw a couple of the instructors ahead of me, making their way to their classrooms to set up labs or catch up on grading. I had the half-formed idea of begging some breakfast from the dining hall and taking it back to him, the way he'd done for me.

With every step, my mind went back to the cottage. Was it a mistake, leaving him alone? What if he did something stupid? But that wasn't like Holmes, was it? He was so calculating. So relentlessly resolved. A kind of helpless amusement infused my thoughts: he was a Holmes bot. But I knew he wasn't a robot, not at all. I just didn't understand what had happened. Sure, it had been embarrassing—it would have been embarrassing for any guy. But also, kind of…not, right? I mean, whatever this was, whatever kept zinging back and forth between Holmes and me, we both felt it. And I'd popped a bone cuddling with girls from school or with tech bros that I'd met on Prowler. And yeah, I mean, there's something awkward about your body betraying your intentions in a way that nobody could miss, but also, it's kind of flattering. I'd felt guys get hard against me, and it was something to laugh about, just a little, before the next part.

Or not, I thought, the sound of my steps coming back from the aspens.

I turned around and headed back to the cottage before I realized I'd decided to check on Holmes. He wouldn't like it, but I could come up with a cover. I'd left my phone in the living room. That was the truth, so even if he suspected me of just wanting to make sure he was all right, at least I wouldn't be lying. Maybe he'd already be out of the bathroom. Maybe, after that initial surge of emotion, he was ready to laugh about it or—ok, since this was Holmes we were talking about—at least be coldly indifferent about it. Maybe he'd even tell me why this was such a big deal. I mean, I knew he was gay, or at least bi. He'd told me about Nick, and he'd held my hand, and there'd been no mixed messages about that stiffy this morning. But every time I'd made comments about guys, or joked, or come anywhere close to talking about, well, anything along those lines, Holmes had gone into fight mode. It wasn't like he was closeted. So, I wondered as I took the steps up to the porch two at a time, what was it?

The front door was still unlocked, and I stepped into the narrow space between the living room and the kitchen. Holmes stood next to the couch, and I thought with a kind of dizzying relief, Everything's ok. Then more details came in: his face was still the color of bone, and he had one hand at the level of his chest, his fingers clutching my old brick of a phone.

I took a step. "H, oh my God, I'm so glad—"

"Do you want to explain this?"

His tone stopped me. My blood rushed in my ears. "What—"

Holding up the phone, he read from the screen. "This is Lissa Keahi, just following up on your email. You said you had information you were interested in selling about HH. Give me a call day or night."

The chickadee was still singing. Down the street, a car rumbled to life. A storm door clattered shut, the next cottage over. It felt like it was inside me, something swinging shut, so that I was a few inches away from everything.

He tossed the phone onto the couch. He looked at me, his face blank. Then he turned toward the back door.

I lunged after him. "H, hold on—"

I don't know what he did. He turned back toward me, the movement a blur, and the next thing I knew, I was lying on the floor. My cheek was pressed against the linoleum, which felt slightly sticky against bare skin. Everything was moving except me: the TV, Dad's recliner, the door, Holmes. The pain came a moment later, starting in my head, and then, more distantly, all along my body where I had hit the floor.

"It was bad enough that it was Watson, but I should have expected it from her. But I told you—" He stopped. The pain yawned in that silence, and when he continued, his voice trembled. "I told you everything, Jack." He made a weird noise that must have been a laugh. Then he said, "Maybe you've got a bit of Watson in you after all."

"H, I wasn't going to—"

"If you wanted money so badly," Holmes said, the words brittle like ice about to break, "you only needed to tell me, Jack. I'm sure I could have found more interesting ways for you to whore yourself out."

He was doing something with his hands, but my eyes wouldn't focus. Then, a moment later, something hit me in the face—not hard enough to hurt, but startling me. I managed to get up on one elbow. My vision swam, and then I saw the wad of bills Holmes had tossed.

I looked up at him. His face doubled, split, came back together again. For a moment, I saw him, his whole body like a blade. Then my vision went wonky again. "H." I tried to push myself up, but everything went loose and juddery again, and it was all I could do to keep from falling. "Holloway."

He doubled and split and came apart. And then the door crashed shut behind him, and he was gone.

It took me longer than I liked to get to my feet, and even then, I didn't feel steady. He must have hit me on the side of the head, and he must have done it just right to screw up my balance. Somehow I got out the door. I stumbled on the steps, half fell, and hip-checked the truck. It was the only thing that saved me from face-planting. I couldn't find Holmes. All I could see were the aspens and the pines and the scrub oak, lines of them moving back and forth like in one of those magic eye pictures. I dragged myself along the truck, keeping one hand on it for support. When I got to the end of the carport, I looked down the street in each direction. Nothing. Then I bent at the waist and puked.

Somehow, I crawled back inside. I got on the couch. Something hard was under me, digging into my ribs, and I realized it was my phone — my stupid phone with that stupid, fucking message that had ruined everything. And then I squeezed my eyes shut, my face going pins and needles, because it wasn't Lissa's fault or my phone's fault. It wasn't anybody's fault except mine. I had done this. I had taken the one good thing in my life and broken it beyond repair. A sob hitched my chest, and I burrowed into the cushion.

A sharp knock at the door brought me upright. Maybe it was Holmes. The thought was delirious, and part of me recognized it as stupid, but I ignored that part. Maybe he'd come back to beat the shit out of me. That was all right. If it meant at some point he'd forgive me, then he could whale on me for a while. When I got up from the couch, my vision was steady, and the world had stopped spinning.

I opened the door, and Headmaster Burrows stared back at me. He was in jeans and a gingham shirt and a fleece vest with the Walker crest over the heart. It was hard, seeing him like that, to place him, to understand why he was there. Part of it was that he had that face like I'd seen him somewhere else, although I'd never been able to figure out where. And part of it was that he was young and good looking, and if I hadn't known him, I would have pegged him as a zipper-sex tech bro instead of the head of a prestigious private school. And part of the disorientation was that he wasn't Holmes, and right then, I only had room in my brain for him.

"Jack," Burrows said. "Could I — what's wrong?"

I shook my head and wiped my face with the heel of one hand.

"Are you sure? You look very upset."

"How can I help you, Headmaster?"

"Well, Ms. Soares was waiting to speak to me first thing this morning. I understand that you entered her office last night and had a confrontation."

You, he said. Not *You and Holmes*. Which made sense. Whatever shit was coming, it was only going to roll downhill.

My silence was long enough that Burrows spoke again, a worry line creasing his forehead. He put a hand on the door and applied gentle pressure. "Jack, to be honest, this conversation would be easier in private. I'd like to sit down and talk about — "

I shook my head again and braced the door with one shoulder. It wasn't something I thought about; it was something instinctive, something animal — this was my territory.

Burrows pursed his lips and let out a breath. "All right." But he pushed on the door again, lightly, as though testing my resolve. "Maybe you'd like to go for a walk. We can talk about whatever's got you like this. If it's your father, I hope you know that we all believe he'll be vindicated — he's not the kind of man who would do something like this."

For the third time, I shook my head. Then, my voice barely more than a croak, I managed to say, "Mr. Burrows, I need to get to work."

The worry line was back. "Well, Jack, that's the problem. You see, you're not actually an employee at Walker. And while I understand that Mr. Taylor has made allowances so that you could help your father, we've reached a point where that's no longer an option." He offered a sad smile. "I can't have people accosting my staff, threatening them in their offices, and turn a blind eye, Jack."

"Ok," I said. The word sounded wooden. "I won't work —"

"I also can't have a minor living unattended on campus. There are legal issues, Jack. Liability issues. I'd like to sit down with you while we wait for Ms. Meehan, and then we can pack your bags —"

I slammed the door and threw the bolt. Burrows made an annoyed noise and began to knock, but I ignored him. I didn't have time to pack. I didn't have time to plan. He'd already called her. Someone had seen the truck, someone had known I was back, and Burrows had called the woman from DCFS, and she was going to take me to a residential treatment center.

I grabbed my phone, the keys, and my wallet. I moved so fast I barked my shin on the coffee table, and I swore as I hopped toward the back door. Then, hating myself, I hesitated. I looked at the money Holmes had thrown at me. I saw the look on his face, the unyielding hardness of it. And I scooped up the cash and hobbled toward the truck.

Burrows's voice sounded like he was coming around the side of the cottage. "Jack! Jack! Stop for a second and think —"

But by then, I'd hauled myself up behind the steering wheel. I turned the key. The dome light flickered. The engine groaned. The starter clicked.

Burrows appeared ahead of me as he came into the carport. His face was red, and his hands were balled at his sides. "Jack!"

The engine gave a throaty cough, and then something sparked, and the engine grumbled to life. I hit the shifter and backed out of the carport. Burrows slapped the hood of the truck, and a metallic clang rang out, but he didn't chase after me. He was saying something, but I couldn't hear him anymore, and then I was gone, the canyon swallowing me up.

Chapter 25

You Have to Say It

I didn't stop until I got to Provo. Every time I passed a car going the opposite direction, my brain told me that it was Ms. Meehan from DCFS, so I kept my foot on the gas until I reached the valley. It was still early morning, the dome of the sky blue white and the streets starting to fill with Provo's version of rush hour. I bumped along until all of a sudden, my adrenaline burned itself out, and I slumped in the seat. I turned into the tiny parking lot of Day's Market. A shack that sold shaved ice in the summer was boarded up, a skirt of plastic grocery bags trapped along one side and rustling whenever someone drove past. A few trees lined the lot, and their leaves still hadn't fallen—a hint of red-brown, old yellow wax.

For a moment, I sat there. I still felt like that storm door hung shut inside my head, like everything was inches away. I'd felt like this before. I closed my eyes, and I saw the back seat of the Lexus, saw Mom and Dad not moving. I opened my eyes. I was glad for a little bit of distance, for something in my brain that kept everything far away. I knew it wouldn't last forever. My brain played me snippets: the sound of Holmes's panicked breathing on the other side of the bathroom door; the worry twisting my gut as I hoofed it across campus with the dumb idea I was going to bring us back a stack of hotcakes; Holmes's face when I walked into the cottage. Maybe it was my brain filling in details. Maybe I'd seen it and only now was able to process what I'd seen. But I thought, now, in my memory, I could see the hurt in his face. The pain of a blow that cleaves sinew and bone. And then, because my brain was a treacherous fuck, I remembered the weight of him, his warmth, that half-awake dream that this could go on forever.

It was either stop thinking about him or start bawling, so I made myself stop thinking. Instead, I tried to take stock. I was homeless. I was a fugitive—maybe not from the law, but definitely from DCFS. The only money I had was the wad of cash that Holmes had thrown at me.

At some point, I could go get clothes and pictures from the cottage; Burrows couldn't prevent me from taking stuff that was legally mine. But I had to wait until the DCFS woman left. So, those two points became my full plan: wait, and then go crawling back to Walker to get my stuff. After that, I was a free man. The world, I thought, looking at the plastic bags pinned against the shaved ice shack, is my goddamn oyster.

So, I waited. I went to the library. I joined my fellow people who were homeless. From the glimpses I caught of their computer screens, I was grateful for the minimal privacy of the carrells and, even more so, for the fact that none of the computers had speakers. For a while, I stared at the screen, telling myself this was an opportunity. I knew that someone connected to Ellis Seward's death had killed Watson. And I knew that Soares was the only person on campus who had been staff or faculty all those years ago. But she had a solid alibi, and I had no idea how to discover if she was lying.

The real problem was that I had no ideas at all. I'd started off this investigation independently, but more and more, I'd come to rely on Holmes. Not like in the old stories from Dr. Watson, where Watson bumbled along and Holmes solved everything by examining cigar ash. But like a partner. He knew things I didn't know. And I knew things he didn't know. And we made a good team. He was annoying as hell sometimes. And he had zero sense of humor. And when he went full Holmes bot, I sometimes wished I had somebody else around—you know, like a real human. But he was also strong and kind and...and strangely vulnerable. And he'd proven more than once that I could trust him with—well, with pretty much everything. In return, of course, I'd stabbed him in the back.

After a while, I stopped even pretending, and my hand lay still on the mouse, and eventually, the screen timed out.

"You done?"

I thought maybe he was the same guy from—had it been the day before? Two days? A Tweedledee cap, the kind with the little propeller on top. A white beard. A trench coat. He wasn't wearing socks, and where I could see his ankles, they looked bony and thin. He stood behind me, peering over my shoulder.

"Because if you're done, there are people waiting."

I wasn't sure about *people*—as far as I could tell, there was one person waiting, and he was in a Tweedledee cap. But I gave up the computer and wandered around for a while. It was a beautiful library. The floors were the color of honey. The ceilings were high, and windows spilled light into the large, bright rooms. I passed the circulation desk, where a woman in a pencil skirt and pearls was eating something made out of shredded carrots and cucumber that smelled like a vat of vinegar. She had a Sunday School teacher vibe, which in Utah Valley, was like seventy percent of the adult population. I realized, with a detached kind of interest, that I wasn't hungry. What would Holmes have said about that?

I tried to read. I tried to sleep in the comfy chairs. The Sunday School lady asked me if I was supposed to be in school, and I told her my mom homeschooled me. At some point, I forgot and took out my phone. The text from Lissa was waiting there. I sent her a message: *Don't contact me again.* Then I deleted the conversation history. I only had a few texts from Holmes—the ones about the cheeseburgers—and I deleted those too. And I had probably a dozen messages from Ariana that I'd missed. I looked at them. Scrolled through them. Thought about what level of assclown I was.

In the other room, someone was reading a book about a cat with red shoes, and it sounded like the little kids were loving it.

Hey. I sent it before I could back out. Then another: *Could we talk? In person?*

A minute passed. Then another. The clock said it was almost two, which was hard to believe. The odds were good that Ariana was in school—she was serious about graduating, which meant she had to stay on track junior year, and she had plans for college after high school. She was going to be a dental hygienist. She'd probably get a place of her own. No more dealing with her parents and their crazy crap. No more Joslyn. No more Joslyn's douche of the week. Ariana was smart, and she had her life together in spite of all the odds, and once she got clear of her nutso family, she'd find other people like her. She'd probably end up working for a dentist, a young one. God, in a few years she'd probably have kids.

Please, I sent her. *It's serious.*

And then, for good form's sake: *I haven't been ignoring you. Things have been bad.*

I got nothing, and that wasn't a good sign. Sure, she was probably in school. But before, even when Ariana had been in school, she'd texted me back right away. The reality was that she was pissed. She'd been worried about me, and she'd messaged, and I hadn't replied because I'd been too busy playing *Treehouse Detectives* with Holmes. I sat there for a while, my head resting on the back of the chair so I could stare up at the ceiling. The quality of the light changed. It was gold now, thick, staining everything to beeswax. I didn't sleep. I didn't think about Holmes. But I did wonder if he'd gone back to the cottage—if not for me, then for the addies.

When the clock said four, I got in the truck and drove to the Kneaders next to the hospital. It looked like all the other Kneaders in the valley: the tan stucco, the fieldstone accents, the glass. I got out of the truck, and the smell of unlimited French toast and maple syrup rolled over me. I don't know how they made money on unlimited French toast in a college town. I'd tried a few times to put them out of business all by myself.

Inside, I waited in line behind a woman who was classic Utah Valley: bottle blond, in a Wrangler t-shirt and mom jeans up to her belly button. The shirt said SADDLE UP AND RIDE FAST with a silhouette of a cowboy. Next to her, a little boy was picking his nose and staring off into space, while a little girl left handprints on the glass as she tried to lick her way through the display case. I wondered if Holmes had sisters or nieces or if he liked kids or if they drove him crazy. I tried to picture him with a toddler hanging around his neck. When they got to the register, they took forever, and the little girl started kicking and screaming, and the nose-picker made a break for it—the mom barely caught him before he got to the parking lot. Something was going on in my stomach, something like a bird spreading its wings—all of a sudden, it would be huge, taking up all the space in my stomach so I couldn't even breathe, fluttering and moving like it was trying to take off. And then it would fold its wings in and shrink back down. And then it would be at it again, and I'd feel like I was about to pass out because I couldn't get any air.

I didn't look at her until the mom dragged the kids toward the fountain drinks. Then I did. Ariana stood behind the register, her hair in a ponytail, the coppery highlights glimmering under the fluorescents. Her dark eyes watched me, unreadable. She wore a white vee-neck under the green Kneaders apron, and my eyes tried to follow that vee all the way down before I dragged them back up. She rolled her eyes and tapped long, red nails on the side of the register.

"I'm at work."

"I know." I took out the duct-taped Superman wallet. I hadn't even counted the cash Holmes had thrown at me, and now I saw it was all fifties. Of course it was. Because Holloway Holmes wouldn't have used ones and fives to make a dramatic exit. "I'll buy something."

"What do you want, Jack?"

"Can I do the unlimited French toast?"

"We don't do that after eleven."

"I don't know. I need a minute to think."

"Jack." She opened her mouth and then shut it again and shook her head. "What do you want?"

I opened my mouth to tell her, but nothing came out. The bell jingled, and I looked over my shoulder as five old ladies trooped in. They all looked like the apple dolls we'd carved in sixth-grade Language Arts, when Mrs. Smith made us read story after story about the Mormon pioneers. The lady in front, who seemed to be the leader, wore some sort of robe over pink biker shorts. She came at me like a bulldozer, and I figured it was either get out of the way or get on board.

"If you're not going to order something, you need to leave," Ariana said.

"I just want to talk. I know I messed up."

"I don't have time to talk. I've got to work." She waited, and when I didn't move, she made a disgusted noise and said, "Jack!"

So, I went out to the truck. It might have been an accident, but the old lady in the pink shorts grabbed my butt as I passed, and then all the hens burst out cackling, so I figured it probably wasn't. It did, weirdly, make me feel better. Maybe I should have turned around and planted one on her. Maybe it would have made Ariana crazy jealous.

I was sitting behind the steering wheel, staring up at the ancient headliner, thinking about my big plans to marry that old lady and become a kept man, and then thinking about how she'd probably figure out I was a genuine piece of shit pretty fast just like Holmes and Ariana had, and then thinking about driving into Utah Lake to save the world some trouble, and then thinking about how I'd float, because I was a turd, and I'd be this one big floater that they couldn't flush—in other words, I was doing some grade-A spiraling—when the passenger door opened, and Ariana got into the truck.

She set something wrapped in brown paper on my lap, and the unmistakable scent of bacon wafted up to me. "I'm on my break, so you've got fifteen minutes."

"Good because I have a date with that lady who molested me in fifteen minutes."

Ariana rolled her eyes again, but a hint of a smile appeared. "She told her friends that if she were ten years younger, she'd have dragged you into the bathroom."

I choked on my spit, wiped my mouth with the back of my hand, and glanced at Ariana. The smile was a little bigger now. "Thanks." I touched the brown paper, felt the shape of the sandwich underneath. "Is it ok if I don't—I mean, I haven't been hungry today. I'm in kind of a weird place."

"It's a sandwich, Jack. I don't care if you don't eat the sandwich. I care that you don't answer my texts unless you want something. Is that what you'd want someone to do to you? Did you even think about how that makes me feel?"

"No," I said, which was true, albeit shitty. "I'm sorry." My hands were doing their own thing, unwrapping the sandwich. Just to check. Because I definitely smelled bacon. "I—I don't even know where to start. It all started when I found this girl." And then I told her—not all of it, not everything, but enough to explain the last few days. "It doesn't matter, I guess. The point is, I screwed up everything. Including—" I focused on the brown paper, on the wrinkles where it had folded and taken a crease. "—well, you, I guess. I really screwed up with you."

Ariana shifted in her seat. She looked at me. And then she looked ahead. We were facing the hospital, pale stone and glass, and it looked like it was glowing. "Do you even like me?"

"What? Yes, God. I like you a lot. I wouldn't be here if I didn't like you."

"Sure, you would. Because you need something, right? You're going to ask me for a favor. That's why you're here."

"I don't know. I hadn't thought that far ahead." I toyed with the corner of the paper, bending it back and forth. "Dad's in jail, you know. And they kicked us out of the cottage. But that's not why I came here. I can sleep in the truck. I felt bad about all the messages I missed. I knew you were worried, and I know what it's like when you're worried about someone and they won't tell you how they're doing, won't tell you anything at all—" I had to stop because my throat was tight. "I wanted to apologize, I guess. And see if I screwed things up too badly to try to fix."

She folded her hands in her lap. She'd already chipped one of her nails; she hated that. She was still looking out the windshield when she said, "You can always try."

My hands were taking care of their own business again, picking open the wrapper. "So, how would I do that? Fix things, I mean."

"Well, you start by apologizing."

"I'm sorry. I'm really, really sorry."

"And then we have to decide what's going on." She turned to face me now. Her dark eyes fixed on me, searching my face. "I like you, Jack. I already told you that. But I'm not going to keep hooking up with you whenever you feel bad or want to get high or need a place to crash. I deserve better than that."

"You do."

"I think you've got a lot of potential, but half the time, you make me think of Joslyn—she's so smart, and she's a total train wreck. I don't need another train wreck in my life."

"I'm going to get my life together. Honest. It's this thing with my dad—"

I saw it then, the shadow moving under the surface of her expression. Ariana was smart; that was one of the reasons I liked her. And she was smart enough to have thought ahead, to already be planning, to be asking the questions that kept me up at night: how long was I going to take care of my dad like this, how long was I going to be scrambling for the cash to buy his meds, to put a roof overhead, to keep food on the table? I probably should have told her right then: forever. I'm going to do it forever because it was my fault. And because when he needed me the first time, I ran away.

But she asked something different instead: "Is there someone else?"

Traffic had backed up at the light. A woman in a green Volvo was laying on the horn, waving her middle finger. The bumper sticker on the back of the car said JESUS WANTS ME FOR A SUNBEAM.

"No," I said. In my mind, I saw him: the curve of his spine when he leaned over, the slight swell of his biceps, the hard lines of his body hidden under oxfords and chinos, that one finger with the knobby knuckle. I shook my head. "There's nobody."

She relaxed—a tiny, barely visible release of tension in her shoulders and spine that, until now, I hadn't realized was there. The light changed. Traffic streamed north and south on State. She was still looking at me.

"Oh," I said, and I leaned forward and kissed her.

We kept it light. Then someone hooted, and when Ariana pulled away, I looked over my shoulder. My future sugar momma in the biker shorts was pumping her fist and cheering as her friends stood around her and laughed.

"Oh my God," I breathed.

Ariana laughed as she opened the door and slid out of the truck. "I'll talk to Joslyn. You can crash on the couch for a few nights if you need to, but I've got to be at my parents' place. My dad lost his shit last night, and I can't go out until he cools down."

"You don't need to do that."

"You have to say it, you know. You have to ask me to be your girlfriend."

"Do you want to be my girlfriend?"

"I'll think about it." She started to swing the door shut. Then she stopped. "And Jack? Buy a toothbrush."

Chapter 26

Your Heart as an Arrow

That night, I slept on Joslyn's couch. I'd gone to Walmart and bought a toothbrush, deodorant, soap, and a change of underwear. So, I was about as prepared as I could be except for the earplugs, and I had to settle for pillows over my ears as Joslyn and this creep with a neck beard smushed in the other room.

Ariana and I had gone to dinner at Carrabba's, and the waiter had laughed when I'd tried to order a bottle of wine. When I asked her again if she'd be my girlfriend, Ariana laughed too. I grinned and ate my steak and thought my friends at my old school didn't have to put up with this bullshit. Everybody just hooked up. Nobody actually had girlfriends and boyfriends anymore. Then I looked at Ariana, who had changed into a blue top with sequins on the shoulders and jean shorts that showed off all her curves, and I watched as she pulled her hair back from her neck, and I watched as she looked at me and smiled and shook her head, and I thought the guys at my old school had been pretty stupid.

But now it was just me, alone with the grunts and slap of flesh from the room at the end of the hall. The air smelled like mango vape and carpet spray; Joslyn had the kind for pets for some reason, and when Ariana and I had shown up, she had started spraying it around the couch, blushing and giggling as she threw glances at her latest guy.

In the bedroom, Joslyn said something I couldn't make out. Then she moaned. The pillows definitely weren't enough of a distraction, so I opened the slider and slipped out onto the balcony. The air cut through my t-shirt and trunks, so I went back and got the blanket from the couch and bundled up in it. That was better, and I stood for a while, leaning on the railing, the night spread out. In a lot of Dad's old movies, when they showed you a high-tech command center—maybe NASA, maybe a bad guy's lair, maybe the deck of the starship *Enterprise*—they had banks and banks of consoles, only instead of screens, they had lights. Hundreds of amber lights. And I guess they meant something because a light would blink on or off and somebody would say something like, "Sir, there's a meltdown in sector nine."

When my breath stopped pluming, I grabbed my phone and opened up the messages. I opened up the chain with Mom. I tapped out a message, erased it, and composed a different one. *Do you remember when we went to Disney?* I sent it before I could stop myself. Then I sent another. *I really miss you.*

The phone vibrated in my hand, and a text came back: *Wrong number.*

I stared at it for a moment. Then, shaking, I punched buttons to make my way through the settings and blocked her number. I went back inside and slid the door shut. I collapsed on the couch. I pulled my knees up so I'd fit. A part of my brain said, At least they're done fucking.

After the accident—not right away, because at first, I thought things would eventually be normal again, I thought this was a blip and life would go back to the way it had been, but later, when I'd still been serious about the homeschool thing, when I'd made myself pick something every day and learn as much as I could about it—I'd read about grief. It's one of the messier Wikipedia pages. Not because it has bad editors or contributors, but because it's such a complicated topic and because the bottom line, over and over again, is that nobody really understands it, and nobody knows what to do about it. Why do we grieve when, in terms of evolution, it's costly but without any apparent benefit? Why do we grieve when it seems maladaptive? Why didn't something come along after us, something that was fitter for survival because it didn't hurt like this?

Over the last year, I'd forgotten most of the mush-mouthed answers that researchers had tried to give. I remembered, though, the term *disenfranchised grief*, the kind of grief that isn't acknowledged by society. I hadn't understood it then, but I understood it now because even if I could tell someone about Holmes, even if I explained it as best I could, how would they ever understand? It wasn't even a week, they'd say. You barely knew him. No, I said back. But I didn't know how else to explain it.

The other thing I remembered was the phrase *trajectory of grief*. I didn't remember what it meant, but I remembered what it meant to me, sixteen and alone and hurting so much I wanted to die rather than keep feeling so much pain. Picture your soul bent like a bow and your heart as an arrow, I told myself. The tremendous strain of being drawn back. The release. I had gotten through the worst nights like that, picturing it over and over again, the bow and the arrow vivid in my mind, all the pain flying away from me. And then, the next night, I had done it again. And then again. Until somehow, one day, I was a little better. I liked it because it was a kind of promise; if you could picture it clearly enough, you could make yourself believe that at some point, the arrow stopped falling.

I fell into a sleep of muddled dreams and half-waking thoughts. I woke once, the microwave clock blinking a blue 2:19 at me, when Joslyn's guy snuck out of the apartment. And I woke again when Joslyn slammed her bedroom door and the microwave clock was a blue eye that said 6:52.

"Get up," Joslyn said. She smelled like peach body spray, an invisible cloud of it spreading out from her as she came into the living room, and she was fussing with her hair. "I've got to go to work."

I folded the blanket, dragged on my jeans and socks and Vans. So much for a shower and clean underwear. I arranged everything as neatly as I could next to the side of the couch because I was a guest and because Mom would have told me to make my bed. By the time I'd finished, Joslyn was tapping her foot and checking her phone. She moved aside, and when I stepped out of the apartment, she made an annoyed noise. Then she pulled the door shut, locked it, and started for the stairs.

"Thanks," I said, hanging back to let her get a head start.

"You can stay two more nights," Joslyn said without looking back, her voice echoing up the concrete stairwell. "Don't fuck over my sister."

"I won't," I said, but it sounded small compared to those concrete echoes, and I wasn't sure she heard me. I went down the stairs slowly, and by the time I reached the bottom, Joslyn was gone.

I drove around for a while, while the streets were still clear. Then, when Provo's morning traffic began to back up, I turned off Center Street and dicked around in the two hundreds for a while, cruising. Men and women were leaving for work and school—this part of Provo still had a lot of student housing for the university. Kids got on buses. Other kids walked in clumps. The day had the clean-cut clarity of a fall morning. I cracked my window, and I could hear the kids scuffing the dry, fresh-fallen leaves.

Then the city emptied out again, and I felt like I was waking up. I'd been wasting gas, I realized, tooling around like that. Gas that would cost money to replace. I parked in a lot for one of the Mormon churches that were all over around here, and I killed the Dodge's engine. I thought about going to the library again, but why? I thought about finding a job—I'd need to do it sooner rather than later, but I already knew I wouldn't be able to find anything as good as what we'd had at Walker. Nobody was going to hire a sixteen-year-old to work full-time doing maintenance. It was a problem I shoved to the bottom of the stack. I thought about trying to visit Dad. I wanted to see him. More than anything, I wanted to talk to him. He'd tell me everything was going to be all right, and I'd believe him. For a little while, anyway. He'd tell me what to do. He'd help me figure things out. But I knew that was a fantasy. Visiting Dad was only going to make things worse; as soon as a deputy saw my name, they'd detain me until Ms. Meehan, or whatever her name was, got there from DCFS, and then Rivera would talk her into putting me in one of those residential treatment centers, and I'd be there until I turned eighteen or Rivera figured out a way to charge me with murder and they put me in prison. I knew it was different for kids than for adults, and I knew they'd call it something different, but prison was prison.

For a while, I sat there, feeling restless and sorry for myself and generally miserable. It was like the second day of being sick — the novelty had worn off, and that made the situation even worse somehow. Then I realized I could take advantage of the free time. I could drive up to Walker, pack up some of our stuff, and bring a load down to the valley. I didn't think Joslyn would be thrilled with me lugging it up to her place, but I'd keep it on the balcony. Just for a day or two. Until I figured the next part.

I started toward Provo Canyon. The sun perched above the mountains, the shadows tipping down the foothills. I passed the canals, which looked like they'd been drawn with lead, and the bristling steel and aluminum and carbon of the electrical substation. Barely visible up to my left was the red-ribbed roof of Will's Canyon Stop. A few cars passed me in the opposite direction, but traffic was light; it was Friday morning, and unless you were playing hooky to do some fishing or hiking, you were already at work or wherever you were supposed to be.

I was halfway to Walker when my phone buzzed. I didn't recognize the number. Part of my brain suggested that it was a trap — Rivera still trying to track me down. Part of my brain suggested it was Holmes, that he needed to contact me without using his personal phone. Yes, it was willful self-delusion. It still won out. I answered, the phone cradled against my shoulder as I took the next turn.

"Jack?" my dad said.

"Oh my God," I said and started to cry. They weren't huge tears, but they stung my eyes and blurred my vision, and I had to white-knuckle the steering wheel to stay on my side of the two-lane. "Dad?"

"Hey." He sounded worn out, the way he did after a three-day migraine, or when he'd been seizing bad. "Are you ok? Talk to me. God, it's good to hear your voice."

"I'm ok." I wiped my eyes. "Are you ok? Did they hurt you? Do you have your meds? Are you in your own room? They don't call it a room, I guess. Did you tell them about your balance? They shouldn't make you wear those handcuffs if you have to do stairs. We can sue the shit out of them if they do."

Dad laughed softly. "I'm fine, Jack. When I told them what medications I was on, they took some time checking with the doctors, but they got everything for me. This place is fine. Well, I could go for a Jack Moreno signature burger, but other than that, it's fine." He was quiet a moment. "I'm sorry I couldn't get in touch before this. They sat me in an interview room almost a full day. Then they bounced me around — first up to Salt Lake before they realized it was a mistake, and then I had to stay the night up there because it was too late to bring me back down, and then it took them almost a full day to process me. The lawyer says they do that sometimes. It's a delaying tactic. Anyway, this is the first chance I've had to call. The lawyer put twenty bucks on your phone, but he says you're going to have to add more money so I can call you."

"On my phone? What do you mean?"

"That's how they do it, I guess. Your phone number. Listen, Jack, we don't have a lot of time. I want to know about you. Are you ok? What's been going on?"

Ahead, the shoulder widened into a narrow gravel patch for twenty yards — the kind of pull-off that people used if they wanted to stop to take a picture or stretch their legs or pee or fish this stretch of the Provo. I pulled off. And then I told him. Not all of it — I couldn't stand telling him about Holmes, not yet. But I told him about how I'd tried to figure out what was going on, and how it had backfired, and how Burrows had kicked me out.

By then I was crying too hard to mask it. I ran my free hand back and forth, trying to dry my eyes, and said, "I really fucked up, Dad."

"Jack, you didn't do anything wrong."

"I did. I got us fired, and now we don't have anywhere to live, and you're still in jail, and I can't prove who did this, and — "

"Jack, Jack, Jack." Dad waited for my silence, and then he spoke into it: "Son, I need you to do something for me, ok? We're almost out of time, so I need you to listen really carefully."

I sniffled and made a noise that I was listening.

"What you did the last few days — what you've done for me over the last year — it's more than anybody your age should have to deal with. I think about myself at your age, Jack. Twenty years ago, I wouldn't have had any idea what to do in your situation. But you keep your head up, and you keep going, and you don't let anything stop you. I am so proud of you. But I need you to stop now. I need you to come to the sheriff's office, and I need you to let them call someone from DCFS. You're an amazing young man, Jack. I couldn't ask for a better son. But you're not an adult yet, and I can't take care of you right now, and you have no idea how scared I've been the last few days. For you. Worrying about you. So, I need you to do the smart thing for both of us and come in."

I was silent. My eyes itched. I could feel my pulse in my whole face, throbbing.

"Jack, tell me you'll—"

His words cut off, and a recorded message came on informing me that the prepaid time had run out and that I would need to add more funds. I listened to the message repeat itself twice. I laid the phone in my lap, and I closed my eyes. The whine of a struggling engine made me open them again, and an ancient Chevy puttered past, more rust than steel at this point, a tiny woman with a beehive hairdo behind the wheel. I closed my eyes again. Maybe if I went to sleep, I thought. Maybe nobody would wake me up.

He wanted me to give up. He wanted me to hand myself over. It sounded…great, actually. Not the residential facility, which still scared the shit out of me. But not having to do this anymore. Not having to run. Not having to hide. Not having to be afraid that whoever had killed Watson would get me next. Not having to wonder how I was going to eat, or where I was going to sleep. Picture your soul as a bow.

I figured Dad was right. I couldn't do this, not on my own. It was nice of him to say that kind of stuff, talking about how twenty years ago, when he'd been my age, he wouldn't have—

It went through me like electricity. The hairs on my arms stood up.

Twenty years ago. When he'd been my age.

"Oh my fucking God," I said, the words bouncing around the cab.

Then I shifted into drive and raced toward Walker.

Chapter 27

That Night

I found him in the weight room—spotted him through the window, the way I had the first time, which felt like forever ago. I still had my keys, so I let myself in through the service door, passed through the utility room, and stalled for a moment in front of the display cases full of trophies and photos. Then I entered the weight room. The air smelled like rubber tiles, iron, sweat, and all-purpose cleaner. His back was to me, the muscles tight as he performed another squat. Where the t-shirt clung to his back, I could see the definition of his body: the architecture of tendon and sinew, the column of his spine. He racked the weights, toweling his face as he turned, and when he saw me, he stopped. For a moment, he stared at me. His knuckles were almost as white as the towel in his hand. Then he lowered the towel to his side, his gaze sliding past me as he moved toward a weight bench.

I was so focused on Holmes that I didn't see Aston until he caught my arm. A couple of other boys—not the Boy Band, thank God—were standing by the free weights, watching us.

"What are you doing here, Abercrombie?" Aston said. The words were the nasty-nice of a bully still wearing his mask. "Burrows said your ass got fired."

I looked at his hand on my arm. I looked at his face. Salon nails. Salon tan. The perfectly messy blond hair. I kept looking.

Aston's grin shrank, but then his features hardened, and he tightened his grip around my arm. "Burrows said we were supposed to report you if we saw you on campus."

I knew what he wanted. He wanted me to pull away. He wanted me to start something so, in his mind, he could finish it. He was embarrassed because I'd seen him with Dawson, and he wanted to reclaim some of that power, wanted to make sure I knew who was in charge. His face was like a page in a book, and I wondered if this was how Holmes saw everyone, if he could read them the way I could read Aston right then.

"Take your hand off me," I said.

Aston's fingers spasmed. Then they loosened, but he didn't pull his hand away.

"Now." I leaned closer. My voice dropped. "Or what do you think Grandpa will say when he finds out what I know about you and Dawson? Campbell's not the only one who saw that video."

He blanched, and his hand dropped from my arm. His mouth twisted. I'd seen hatred before, but never directed at me, not this kind of insane fury, and for a moment, the intensity of it threw me off balance. But Aston hurried toward the door, and over his shoulder, he called, "It's getting too freaky in here for me," and the other boys followed him, trading looks. And then Holmes and I were alone.

I took a deep breath. The afterimage of that incandescent hatred hung in my vision. Then I shook it off.

Iron clinked as Holmes loaded more weight onto the bar. He already had a pump going, a sheen of sweat glistening on the veins, mapping the swell of biceps and triceps and forearms. I wondered how long he'd been going at this, how many classes he'd skipped. I wondered if he knew he was punishing himself or if he still thought he was punishing me.

"H," I said. "Can I talk to you?"

He turned and stepped around me to pick up another thirty. When he hoisted it, I got in his path, and when he tried to step around me, I moved with him.

"Please."

His eyes focused on something over my shoulder.

"H—"

"Do not call me that." He took a breath. "Move."

A smile slipped out. I didn't feel like smiling, but there it was, hurting my face as I asked, "How bad do you want to put me in a wrist lock right now?"

"I wouldn't use a wrist lock. There are a variety of alternate pain compliance holds—" His jaw snapped shut, and his eyes found mine for a heartbeat, long enough to show his fury, the outraged disbelief as though I'd tricked him somehow.

"How bad do you want to use one of those?"

"If you don't move, you'll find out."

"I know you hate me, and I don't blame you, but—"

"You have no idea what I feel. You know nothing about me. You are nothing to me. I don't care for your assessments or your evaluations. Feel free to peddle them, if anyone will still buy them. You may find that it's more difficult to make money off the Holmes family than you expect."

"H—"

"I said don't call me that!"

The shout bounced back from the glass. Holmes's chest hitched unevenly, the illusion of control shattered. For a moment, he stood there, staring at me. Then he dropped the weight to the side; it hit the rubber tiles with a muffled clang.

"You're right," I said. "I don't know what you're feeling. And maybe you're right that I don't know anything about you, but I think maybe I do know some things, maybe a few." You make this little whistling noise when you're sleeping deeply, I thought. Your eyes look like silver in the morning. You're gentle when you think you're hard, and you're stronger than anyone I've met. "But I want to tell you something about me. I want you to know something about me, something nobody else in the whole world knows."

"I don't care." His lip curled. "It's too bad no one will pay for stories about nobodies."

"Even if you don't care, I'd like for you to know something about me. I don't even know why; that's not why I came here. Maybe it's because you're important to me." I took a breath. "You asked about my parents. I don't like talking about them. It's...hard. A little over a year ago, we were in a car accident. A bad one. Someone swerved out of their lane and hit us. Mom was driving, and she went off the road. It was a stretch of I-80, going up the canyon, so we went down this steep hill. I don't really remember it, but the report said we flipped a couple of times." What I remembered was waking up. The belt biting into my neck. The stillness of their bodies. The angle of Mom's head. "My dad got hurt. A traumatic brain injury. He's got what they call long-term symptoms. He forgets things sometimes, and his balance isn't great. But the bad ones are the migraines and the seizures. He can't work, not really. We faked it well enough to get the job at Walker, but that's why I'm always covering his shifts for him, and that's why I dropped out of school, and that's why I have no idea what we're going to do now." I shook my head. "That's not what I was trying to tell you."

Holmes shifted his weight. He wrapped his arms around himself, but he didn't say anything. His eyes were the color of steel.

"My mom," I said, my voice shakier now, "died. She hit her head hard enough to kill her. They said it was the bleeding inside her brain. The pressure, I mean."

"Jack—"

I shook my head again and wiped my eyes. "I know you already know all that. You're smart, and you have the internet, and you're Holloway Holmes, which means you know everything already, and anything you don't know you can figure out in five seconds. But I wanted to tell you what nobody knows. I want someone to know. And I want it to be you. I was...I was pretty messed up after the accident. Not hurt. I had a few scratches, that's all. But because it was my fault she died. We got in this huge fight—" I remembered her turning around. I remembered the headlights swinging toward us. "She was always a safe driver, but she wasn't watching the road."

"That is not your fault."

"Maybe. It feels like it is, which is the same thing, I think. But that's not all of it. Someone came to check on us. This guy, like a Good Samaritan type. He got down the slope somehow, and he was coming toward the car. I saw something in his hand, something metal." A tiny, tired smile worked its way to the surface. "I thought it was a gun, so I opened the door and ran. I left them. I left my parents in that fucking car. I didn't know if they were alive or dead. I didn't even think about that. I saw the gun, and I ran."

Holmes's face was a study of dark consideration.

I laughed. "It wasn't a gun, H. It was one of those emergency tools they use to break auto glass. But you want to know the real kicker? He came after me. I could hear him, and I kept running and hiding and running and hiding, and he kept coming. See, he was worried about this injured kid who'd run off down the canyon. And I thought he was hunting me. And the whole time, blood was pooling in my mom's brain. If I'd stayed where I was, if I'd told him we needed an ambulance, if he'd called first thing—" I took a deep breath. "I asked the doctors how much time she had, and they didn't want to tell me. But that's kind of its own answer, right? If she'd gotten help right away, she'd still be alive. That really puts me in a special class of fuckups, doesn't it?"

"Jack," Holmes said.

I shrugged. "This part isn't as bad, even though it's still embarrassing. I still text her. Used to text her. My mom, I mean. Even though she's dead. I know it's messed up. But it feels real sometimes. Anyway, that's over now, but nobody else in the world knows that except you, and you're right, nobody's going to pay for a story about Jack Moreno, but I wanted to give that to you, so you can write it on the bathroom stall or you can tell Riker or you can laugh at me inside your head if you ever see me again. 'There's that kid who killed his mom and still texts her—'"

Holmes moved forward while I was still talking. I had a single instant where I thought some scrambled version of *Oh God, wrist lock,* and then he slipped his arms around me, pulling me into a hug. He smelled like warm skin and clean sweat and a hint of laundry detergent. Kind of a nice smell, actually. And then I squeezed my eyes shut and started to cry.

He didn't rub my back. He didn't make any soothing noises. He stood there, his arms locked around me, while I shook apart from tears I hadn't permitted myself, not since the first few weeks after the accident. His cheek was soft against the side of my face. When the worst of the storm had passed and I was trying to breathe through a face full of snot, when I was suddenly, intensely aware of the hard lines of his arms and chest, I felt the rasp of his invisible blond stubble.

Somehow, Holmes got both of us seated on the weight bench. He kept an arm around my waist, kept me close enough that our knees and hips and sides touched. The poor guy sat so stiffly that anybody walking by must have thought they were about to call him up for the firing squad, and I wanted to laugh, but instead I started crying harder than ever and had to endure the total humiliation and surprising comfort of having Holmes pull my head to his shoulder. We sat there for a long time while I cried myself through the second round of weeping. And then it ended, and I wiped my face with my shirt. We were facing one of the walls of windows, and outside, the day was bright and clear and blue. Someone had planted a line of tamaracks, and their golden needles stirred and lifted in a breeze I couldn't feel or hear. I understood that. Something was moving in me, too.

"I'm ok," I said, lifting my head from his shoulder. I wasn't ready for eye contact yet. "Please don't get the defibrillator or use the Heimlich or try mouth to mouth."

Holmes's silence continued. His arm was still around me. I could feel his knee, his hip. He was skin and bone. I wondered what it would feel like if he turned his hand, if his fingertips slid down to the inside of my thigh. I wondered how I could even think about that kind of thing right then, but then, I'd been thinking it in one way or another since I'd met him.

"Jack," Holmes said quietly, "you know you're not to blame for your mother's death, right?"

"That's what everybody tells me."

"The coincidence of your mother becoming distracted at that exact moment is independent of anything you did. And your choice to respond appropriately to a perceived threat—"

"H," I said, and he stopped. "Thank you. Seriously. But not right now."

We sat in silence for a few minutes. He still felt stiff as a board next to me, so I offered a wet laugh, wiped my burning eyes, and said, "You can have your arm back. Sorry, I'm sure this is terrible."

The silence ticked out again, and then Holmes said, "I've never done this before."

I had to think my way through that. *This* probably didn't mean listen to a nut job explain how he'd single-handedly destroyed his family, oh, and also, had a kind of *Psycho*-level attachment to his mom that manifested in continuing to text her after she'd died. I'd barely known Holmes for a week, but I had the feeling that *this* referred to the point I had made: sitting like this with me.

"In that case," I said, "you're doing really well. Maybe you could try to turn a little bit, though? Yeah, so we overlap a bit, and I kind of fit in here. And do you ever relax? Pretend you're in disguise as a teenager who slouches a little and doesn't pick up his room and occasionally sneaks a beer when he thinks his parents won't notice. Yeah, like that, but a little more—here, take a breath, let it out, and loosen up your shoulders. Yeah." I squirmed around to settle against him again. His breath was warm on the side of my ear. For a moment, he felt so good, the right combination of strength and softness, that I forgot—let myself forget—that all too soon, he'd be out of my life.

"I reacted poorly yesterday because of several factors. Firstly—"

"H, you don't have to explain. You don't like me that way. That's fine; I mean, it sucks, but it's fine. You're still my friend. I'm sorry I made you feel weird. I'm probably making you feel weird right now, which is why I said you can have your arm back if you want it."

Classes must have dismissed because outside, students streamed across the campus. In a few minutes, the athletic center would fill with a rush of students, some of them intending to use the weight room.

"No," Holmes said. His voice was off, the tenor strained and unfamiliar. "No, you're upset, and I want to—" And then, in a strangely defensive tone, "We're friends."

"Yes, weirdo, I just said that." I rubbed my eyes. Then I turned to straddle the bench, and Holmes's arm fell away. I made myself look him in the face. "H, I did what you said. I emailed that woman. I told her I'd sell her stories about you. I found her contact info in Watson's desk with some cash. I'm sorry I did it; I knew it was a shitty thing to do when I was doing it, and I knew it was wrong, and I never should have done it. I know this doesn't matter, but I think you should know that I did that stuff before I really knew you. I was angry because you wouldn't help me, and I—I did something stupid. And, to be honest, I needed the money. I know those aren't good reasons, and I understand if you still hate me, but I wanted you to know that I wasn't going to do it. Not after I—" What was the word for it? When you felt like you were falling, but someone was going to catch you. When you felt like your eyes were closed, but you were looking at the sun. When a wind moved through you and moved everything within you. "Not after I got to know you."

Holmes looked down. He was digging his fingers into the weight bench's pad. "Abduction is about most probable conclusions."

That hurt, but I nodded.

"I allowed my experience with Watson and Nick to color my expectations," Holmes said and looked up. "I should not have done that. I am sorry for how I reacted and for not giving you a chance to explain."

"Look at that," I said. "We both managed semi-decent apologies."

"I've been practicing."

I groaned.

"What?" Holmes asked. "You said we needed to know how to apologize if we were going to be friends."

"Yeah, but that was more of a—I mean, is there a book or something? No, oh my God, don't answer that." I grinned. It had a kind of ache to it, but in a pleasant way, like after a workout. "Hey, maybe I'm a Watson, right? Shitty person, helps you solve crimes. How about that?"

"You are quite a good person, I think," Holmes said quietly. "And I checked your mother's maiden name. You are not a Watson."

That was so strange that it took me a moment; I gave up on trying to find a segue and went with: "H, I know who killed Watson. We were right; the same person who killed Ellis Seward twenty years ago killed her to keep her silent."

"I thought we had already checked the staff biographies. The only staff member who was present at the time of Seward's death—"

Grabbing his shirt, I stood. I dragged him up from the bench and after me as I went toward the hall.

"That's because it wasn't a staff member," I said. When I reached the display cases, I stopped, and I pointed at one of the photos, where I had seen him before, seen him so many times that, even as an adult, he looked familiar. "He was a student."

His name was in the caption: Bohen Burrows, Utah State Wrestling Champion 1999, Class 1A.

Chapter 28

Guilty Knowledge

That night, we hid in the library stacks and waited.

It had been a busy day. Holmes had skipped classes so that we could work, and I'd taken us to one of the storage sheds that nobody used. First, we had rehashed everything about both murders: Holmes had acquired (although he wouldn't say how) the police records of the investigation into Ellis Seward's death, and we were both experts at this point on everything that had happened with Watson.

The facts were few, but they seemed to hold together. Burrows—now Headmaster Burrows—had been a student at Walker in 1999. Neither of us knew what Burrows's connection to Ellis Seward had been, but we could draw some conclusions based on data points (abduction, my dear Holmes). Burrows was a good-looking guy who was in his mid-thirties and still single; when he'd been a student, he'd been the definition of what my mom would have called "hunky." Ellis Seward, based on the photographs, had been a teenage twink. Both Seward and Watson had died from physical trauma. And Burrows was definitely strong enough—and trained—to do that kind of damage. He'd won the state wrestling championship, after all.

After that, though, we didn't have anything solid to pin Burrows to either murder. Watson must have had something, or Burrows wouldn't have killed her, but Holmes still hadn't been able to decrypt anything on her laptop that could help us. When I asked about the laptop, in fact, he became surprisingly cagey and refused to retrieve it, insisting that it was in a safe space where no one would look. Well, he became as cagey as Holmes could be, which meant a lot of silence and pretending he hadn't heard me.

Without evidence to take to the police, the excitement had drained out of me. We were back where we'd started—Rivera and Yazzie weren't going to believe a wild story about the respected headmaster of the school being responsible for three murders. Exhaustion had dragged me down to the dusty concrete floor, where the chill had soaked through my jacket and shirt, and I'd stared up at the cobwebbed corrugated steel above.

And then Holmes had told me his plan. It had taken a single email, sent from his phone. And, just to be little shits, we'd used the anonymous email address that Burrows had used to lure Watson to her death — the one that I'd found written on the paper in her wallet. *Vonkramm.* Like a lot of anonymous email servers, it didn't require a password — which meant we could use it as easily as Burrows.

So, now we waited. An emergency light near the front door of the library softened the shadows. Tall, skinny windows opened two sides of the building, and weak light spilled over chairs and carrels and shelves like salt. Holmes and I crouched in the darkness, listening to the silence of an empty building: the rattling breath of the HVAC system, the wind scratching at the glass, the whir of computer fans. The air smelled like binding glue, paper, the musty carpet that was worn with the tracks of generations of students. In the stripes of salt-light, old posters stared back at me: a boy at an old-fashioned school desk, his nose buried in a book, the words printed above his head, *Johnny's Not Dull, He Needs His Eyes Checked*. Another: an older man sunk in a recliner, a stack of books next to him, a cane propped against his leg, and the words, *Me Travel? The Mobile Library Comes to Me!*

It was less a sound and more a sensation — the air pressure changing slightly. Next to me, Holmes buzzed with trapped energy, and I reached down and squeezed his arm. Movement drew my eyes, and I squinted, trying to see farther in the darkness. The movement took on shape and form. And then a figure dressed in black slipped behind the circulation desk. For a moment, their silhouette blocked out the gleam of the brass tufting buttons on the back of the librarian's chair. Then the buttons glittered again, and the dark shape was gone — vanished between two rows of shelves.

Holmes rose, the movement so graceful it looked almost boneless, and padded after him. I brought up the rear. At the back of the library, a sign above a steel fire door read ARCHIVE. Holmes tested the door, and the handle turned. He pushed it open. Stairs led down, and at the bottom, the faint yellow glow of incandescent bulbs outlined another doorway.

When we stepped into the archive, it was empty. I'd never been here before — Ms. Carver, the librarian, insisted on cleaning this room herself. It consisted of several rectangular tables, raw concrete walls lined with cabinets, and nylon carpet dyed almost the same color as the concrete. There was another fire door opposite us, and this one was marked STAFF ONLY. To the right, steel shelving held long, flat boxes. One of the shelves was marked *Deseret News*. Another said, *Tribune*.

Headmaster Burrows stepped out from between the shelves. Now that I knew what to look for, I could see the boy from the photograph in the man's face: the short, dark hair; the Super Bowl smile; the slightly crooked nose. Broken in a wrestling match, I decided. He wore a black jacket, a black shirt, dark jeans, black Doc Martens. He was smiling now — a little puzzled, a little confused.

"Holloway," he said. "Jack. What are you boys doing here?"

"What are you doing here?" Holloway asked.

"Well, doing Mr. Campbell's job, I'm afraid. Someone set off the security alarm, and since Mr. Campbell has...passed, it's my job to check that out. I suppose the two of you are responsible. Holloway, you know the rules about curfew. And Jack, your position was terminated. You should have returned your keys; using them like this is illegal. You understand that you're trespassing, don't you?"

"I believe we're breaking and entering," Holmes said. "Not trespassing."

"Let's go, boys. Holloway, we'll walk you back to your residence. Then, Jack, I'll walk you back to your truck. And I will have to ask for the Walker keys."

Holloway stared at him. His pulse fluttered in his throat. His jaw was tight.

Burrows took a step.

"Stay where you are, Headmaster, or I will be forced to disable you," Holmes said quietly.

"Disable me?" Burrows stopped next to one of the tables. "Holloway, I don't think you understand how serious this situation is. We'll have to call your father—"

"Jack," Holmes said. "Why is he doing this?"

"Because he's bluffing," I said. "He thinks he can separate us. And then I imagine he's going to bash my head in as soon as he's got me alone. Well, he's going to try, anyway."

"He might succeed. You're terrible in a fight."

"Ok, well, first, thank you for that—"

"Boys," Burrows said, in a teacher's whip-crack voice. "This is not a game. I don't understand what you think you're doing—"

"We're luring you into a trap," Holmes said. "We sent you that email, as you certainly know by now. We asked you to meet us where you killed Ellis Seward. And here you are, Headmaster."

Some of the pretense sloughed off. Burrows's gaze sharpened. He was still giving us that all-American smile, but it had a fresh edge to it. "I don't know what you mean. I came here because an alarm was triggered."

"Of course you didn't. There are no alarms in the library, which the sheriff's detectives will be able to confirm."

If anything, Burrows's smile got bigger. "I was on a late walk, and I thought I saw something."

"Headmaster, in a short while, representatives from the Utah County Sheriff's Department will arrive. I recommend that by the time they get here, you have prepared your full confession and contacted an attorney to represent you."

"Because of this email," Burrows said. "This alleged email."

"Yes. You killed Ellis Seward right here, in the library archive. That information wasn't released to the public; the sheriff's department didn't know at first, not until they discovered trace evidence here that confirmed the location of the assault. They held that information back to weed out false confessions, and the press was only told that his body had been found in the incinerator. The only way for you to have known where he was killed was for you to be the one who killed him."

"You knew," Burrows sounded like we were in class, like he was pressing us to make a better argument. "But you didn't kill him."

"Of course not. I acquired a copy of the sheriff's department's investigation."

"Well, there you go. Anybody could have done that."

Holmes shook his head. "The investigation is not public record."

"It's a small school, Holloway. There have always been rumors. I was here when Ellis died; did you know that? It was a tragedy. And people talked about it. Everybody knew what happened."

"No," Holmes said quietly. "They didn't. You killed him. And you killed Watson because she was threatening to expose you. Please sit down, Headmaster. We will wait here for the authorities."

Burrows laughed. "That's your proof? I walked into the library archives? Nobody's going to buy that. And what in the world does that have to do with Sarah?"

"She was blackmailing you. Or she attempted to. You had to remove her."

"This is crazy." He jerked his thumb. "Get out of the way; Holloway, I'm going to call your father right now. You're not well—"

"Sit down," Holmes said.

Burrows tried for the smile again, but it didn't have the same shine. "No one is going to believe—"

"Stop saying that," I said. "You knew where Ellis was killed. That will make Rivera and Yazzie suspicious. Then they'll start looking at you, putting your life under a microscope. They'll start asking questions. Who could have disabled the camera by the maintenance building? Who would Mr. Campbell trust enough to let into the security office? Who would have been authorized to access the security camera recordings so he could delete them? They'll track the IP you used for that anonymous email you sent to Watson. They'll go back, and they'll find people who remember things about you and Ellis, things you thought everybody had forgotten. They'll put the case together piece by piece. Rivera is like a dog with a bone; trust me, I know. Once he starts, he won't stop until he gets you."

It was like watching sand and wind scour away stone: the Super Bowl smile crumbled away. Burrows's face was hard, his mouth tight. He looked older. "Is that all?"

Holmes nodded. "We'll wait for the detectives now."

"No, Holloway, I don't think we will." Burrows pulled a pistol from the pocket of his jacket. The gun was matte black, and it soaked up the light. He pointed it at us. "I think we'll go for a walk."

"This is a mistake," Holmes said.

"I asked you to go for a walk with me, Jack. Do you remember? Things would have been easier if you'd said yes. You wouldn't have felt anything, and we could have avoided this mess. I didn't have to worry about Holloway; a phone call to his father would have made sure he wasn't a problem anymore. But you, well, you just wouldn't fucking stop."

The swear, spoken so clearly and coolly, was more shocking than if he had yelled it. This was the guy who played pickup games with kids. This was the guy who told dad jokes on the quad. This was the guy who girls and boys watched when he jogged in shorts and a tank top.

"Upstairs," Burrows said. "Now. I'm sorry it came to this, if that makes any difference. I liked you, Jack. You remind me of me. Just stupider, I guess. Here we go—up."

I glanced sidelong at Holmes, and he gave a tiny nod. I turned and went first. My legs felt soft, like they might fold under me at any moment, and my hand skated on the rail, the layers of paint rough against my palm. I had the weird sense that I was walking backward, with everything in me attuned to the gun behind me. It was almost like being blind. More than once, I didn't bring my foot up high enough, and the toes of my Vans struck the concrete riser instead of finding the step. Holmes was a void behind me—I couldn't even hear him, and it was like he'd disappeared. I wanted to turn around, and at the same time, I didn't want to, because what if he was gone?

When I opened the fire door and stepped out into the main library, the air felt cooler, and I tried to force myself to take deeper breaths. I glanced over my shoulder. Holmes looked like he'd been carved out of ice: the gold glitter of his hair, the hardness of his eyes. He came through the fire door without catching it. Burrows made an annoyed noise and lunged forward to stop it before it closed.

Holmes whirled around, grabbed Burrows by the jacket, and hauled him off balance. The gun went off. The muzzle flash blinded me for a moment, and the sound clapped against my ear. I stumbled toward them, but I was too slow. Holmes brought his elbow up, and the blow caught Burrows on the side of the head. The older man sagged, and Holmes slammed his hand twice against the wall before he released the gun. It hit the musty carpet, bounced twice, and disappeared under the closest row of shelves.

Burrows started to fall, and Holmes released him. The headmaster slid down to a half-reclining position at the base of the wall. His eyes were open but had a blank, unseeing look. Blood marked the corner of his mouth, and more blood trickled from his nose.

Holmes turned around, and blood soaked his sleeve and was starting to stain the front of his oxford. I opened my mouth. I had the weird urge to laugh. The words in my head were jokey—*Burrows barely got a split lip; how did he possibly get that much blood on you?* And then my brain caught up, and I realized Holmes had been shot.

"H, oh my God—"

But as I took my first step toward Holmes, something moved behind him. A figure lunged out of the shadows. I had a single moment where the spilled salt-light from the windows showed me Aston, his face blank under his perfectly messy side-part. Then he clubbed Holmes across the back of the head with a lacrosse stick, and Holmes went down.

Chapter 29

Close Enough to Hurt

I tried to reach Holmes, but something caught my ankle, and I stumbled. For a moment, I wobbled, trying to regain my balance. Then Burrows yanked, and my foot flew out from under me. I fell and hit the floor hard. My chin bounced off the carpet, and stars exploded in my vision.

Playing football in middle school and high school had paid off. My body was already responding, trying to get up from the floor, before my vision had cleared. I blinked. I tried to pull in air. As my eyes focused, I could make out Holmes and Aston struggling—the fact that Holmes wasn't dead or unconscious seemed both impossibly unreal and, at the same time, perfectly normal. Then the two boys stumbled backward, their struggle carrying them between a pair of bookshelves.

I started to go after Holmes, and at the last moment, my foggy brain reminded me of Burrows. I turned, trying to find him. A flicker in my peripheral vision told me that the headmaster was right behind me. The hammer blow meant to catch me on the back of the head or neck hit me on the shoulder instead. The pain was dull, but the force of the blow drove me down and to the side. I stumbled, trying to stay upright while also putting distance between us. I backed into a chair and scrambled around it. My ass clipped a shelf, and I jinked right.

Burrows stalked after me, his movements slow and sure. I gave one last glance, trying to find Holmes, and got nothing. The sounds of his struggle with Aston were muffled—the occasional shout or thump, but mostly silence. My world narrowed to Burrows. He hadn't recovered the gun, but that didn't matter. His stance was loose, almost relaxed. He had won a championship. He had killed Ellis Seward and Sarah Watson with his bare hands.

"You're not going to get away with this," I said.

With a laugh, Burrows shook his head. "Come on, Jack. You've been spending too much time with Holloway; you sound like you're in one of Dr. Watson's books. You and I both know that the world isn't a story. The world is a hard, brutal place, where hard, brutal people win. I'm going to kill you, and I'm going to turn Holloway over to his father, and then I'm going to go back to my life. The life I deserve."

My mouth was salty, and it wasn't until I spat that I realized it was blood.

"Aston won't say anything if that's what you're thinking," Burrows said. "He's too terrified of being outed. The poor boy would do just about anything to keep his secret. Most people will; that's something I learned the hard way, unfortunately."

"That's why you killed Watson. Is that why you killed Ellis?"

"I killed Sarah because she was a meddling bitch. All of that was in the past; why did she have to go digging it up?" Burrows shook his head. "Ellis, though. Ellis wouldn't talk to me. He wouldn't even let me explain. I wanted what was best for him, and he refused to hear me out. He would have ruined everything—for me, for him. It was an accident. It was a terrible accident, and I've regretted it every day of my life. But I shouldn't have to give up my life because of one accident."

It had the sound of a tired song, of words that had been rehearsed so many times that they'd lost all their meaning.

"Do you know, Jack, things would have been fine if you'd left well enough alone? We wouldn't be here if you hadn't been so obstinate. You could have had a good life. That's what I wanted for you; I told you, I see a lot of myself in you."

"You're sick." I bumped a small table, and it fell over with a crash. I tried to get around it, but I misjudged its size, and my heel caught. I started to fall, and Burrows lunged. I scrambled back, and Burrows let me get away. He was laughing quietly. "You're full of shit. You like this. You enjoy it."

"If you hadn't stuck your nose into my business, things would have been fine. Sarah was dead. And your father was a godsend. Do you know, I watched him? I'd barely disposed of Sarah when I heard him coming, and I hid. I watched him as he started to throw some trash in the dumpster. I watched as he found her. I was already making plans—I thought maybe I should take care of him right then, before he could alert anyone. But he handled the situation for me. He had a seizure, and then he passed out. I got his prints all over everything, and I made sure some of Sarah's blood got on his clothes, and then I left. I had hoped that whoever found the body would find him there too, but no—things are never that easy."

No, I thought. Dad had woken up from the seizure, and he hadn't remembered finding Sarah. He'd gone home. He hadn't even remembered going to the maintenance building.

"That would have solved everything," Burrows said. "You could have stayed at Walker; I would have found a way to let you stay. And Sarah would have been gone. And everything would have been fine."

Two more rows of bookshelves separated me from the main area of the library. The salt-colored light fell in thicker bands, making it easier to see. As soon as the path was clear, I could sprint to the exit. I'd get somewhere safe and—

Holmes screamed, and the sound was full of so much pain that, for a moment, my heart stopped, and I turned toward the noise.

And I realized I was about to run. Again. Like I'd run the night of the accident. Like I'd run when Shivers had caught up with us. Like a coward, abandoning Holmes so I could save my own sorry ass. I was doing it all over again.

I stopped backing up.

Burrows took a step, and I retreated a pace before I stopped myself. My eyes felt gummy. My bladder screamed at me, and I was pretty sure I was about to pee myself.

Burrows took another step.

Holmes needed me.

Somehow, I managed to hold my ground. "I won't let you—"

Before I could finish, Burrows launched himself forward.

I tried to dodge, but I was too slow. Burrows hit me with his shoulder, and we both went down. I landed hard, my head bouncing again, and stars exploded across my vision. Burrows landed on top of me, his weight making it hard for me to draw breath. I bucked, and Burrows slid halfway off me. I got to my knees. He still had his arms around me as I tried to crawl forward, and he dragged me back toward him. I kicked. He shouted and let go.

I crawled a few more feet, got to one knee, and tried to push myself up. Instead, arms wrapped around me, one tightening around my neck, the other coming up under my arm. I thrashed, and Burrows tightened his hold. He had all the leverage, and when he tightened his grip, all I could do was writhe and twist, trying to wriggle free. It wasn't going to work. I couldn't get any air, and already my vision was blackening. Not from the lack of air, I realized. Because he was cutting off the blood flow to my brain. In a few seconds, I was going to pass out, and that would be the end.

For another heartbeat, I tried to throw him off me, bucking in the hold, but Burrows just tightened his grip. Black spots flurried in front of me. The pressure in my head was tremendous. And then it was like I'd come detached from my body. I felt like I'd slipped an inch or two outside my skin. Burrows's breath was hot on my ear, and I remembered like a series of flash bulbs going off, Holmes's breath on the side of my face, Holmes stretched out beside me, the seriousness of Holmes's eyes. He's going to be so disappointed in me, I thought. And then I could hear Holmes's voice: *When they're close enough to grab you, they're also close enough to hurt. Go for the knee or groin. Headbutt them.*

I didn't have much range of motion because of how Burrows had had his arm across my throat, but I dipped my head forward and then brought it back as hard as I could. My skull connected with Burrows's face. His nose crumpled under the blow; I felt the cartilage give way. He screamed, and his arm loosened. I only had one leg free to move—the other was still supporting my weight—but I swept it outward, catching him in the inside of his knee. It forced his leg sideways, and Burrows, still screaming, moved with it. It was instinctive, his body trying to keep his knee from being broken. His grip loosened, and I twisted. I used my fist like a club, striking wildly behind me, aiming as best I could for his balls. I don't know if I got a direct hit, but after a few strikes, he released me, and I staggered to my feet.

When I spun around to face him, he was trying to stand. His face was a bloody mess, and his nose looked flattened. He was favoring his knee, and I thought maybe I'd done more damage than I'd realized. He took a step.

A chunk of the bookcase closest to Burrows exploded, filling the air with splinters, and a moment later the clap of the gunshot reached me. Burrows froze. I looked over.

Holmes stood in one of the narrow aisles, the salt-light like war paint. His chest and arm were drenched in blood. In one hand, he held Burrow's pistol—the one that had disappeared under the bookshelves.

"That was a warning, Headmaster," Holmes said. "Lie down and put your hands behind your head."

Burrows stared at him for a moment through the mask of gore. Then, without a word, he stretched out on the ancient carpet and laced his fingers behind his head.

"Jack," Holmes said, "would you take this please?" His knees buckled, and he tried to grab the shelf to catch himself, but something was wrong with his arm—he couldn't seem to move it. Instead, he ended up leaning against the shelves, slowly sliding down toward the floor. I darted over to him and caught him and helped him the rest of the way down. I eased the pistol out of his hand and checked that Burrows wasn't trying anything. Then I turned my attention back to Holmes.

"Aston is—" He stalled out and tried again. "Aston is—" He looked lost, and it was an expression I'd never seen on his face before. His eyes were the color of that salt-light. And then they widened, and his mouth moved, the hint of a curve at the corners, and his good hand came up to touch the side of my face, and in a tone of infinite wonder, he said, "Jack."

Chapter 30

Alexithymia

Holmes had his phone, so I called the sheriff's department. It would have been nice if we'd actually called them ahead of time, like we'd told Burrows, but apparently we weren't nearly as smart as we thought we were. That was one of the things Rivera told me — thoroughly — later.

The ambulance took Holmes first, and I stayed and answered questions from Rivera and Yazzie. I knew it was only the beginning of the ordeal. This would go on for a long time, as the detectives built the case against Burrows. Of course, they had a little help from me and Holmes — we had, after all, recorded the whole conversation in the library. They'd arrested Aston too, but I thought that prosecution might be a little trickier.

Finally Rivera drove me to Utah Valley Hospital. It was the same one I'd sat looking at from the Kneaders parking lot — towers of glass and stone the color of the desert. Inside, he got me into an ER exam room, where a doctor told me I had some scratches and bruises, but I'd probably live. I'd figured that out myself, but it's nice to hear it from an expert. I didn't think I'd feel as charitable when the bill finally came, but I'd worry about that another day.

Rivera offered to drive me home, but I refused. Then, of all people, he offered to stay with me while I waited to see Holmes. Maybe he felt bad about arresting my dad and almost ruining my life. I think, though, he was probably hoping I'd incriminate myself in some other murder. He had a major hard-on for arresting me, and it was going to take a while to go down.

The hospital waiting room was one of those places that could be empty and you still had the feeling that you weren't alone — probably because there was always somebody about to pass by in the hallway, or maybe because so many people had been in that space, and they'd left a kind of echo. The walls were painted muted blues and purples and browns. TVs hung on the walls next to watercolors of canyons and meadows and mountain streams. The TVs were all black. That was ok. I stared at the black for a long time. I could see a blurry version of myself. And I could see Rivera's blurry form next to me. Those were easy, indistinct things I didn't have to focus on. We sat on an oak-veneer bench with vinyl padding that sounded like a fart whenever either of us moved. The whole floor smelled like canned corn and the urinal cakes I dished up weekly in the boys' bathrooms at Walker; I wondered, in that blank space between thoughts, if we used the same distributor. After a while, a white woman with a bushy butch haircut came in and sat there too. She was wearing work boots covered in gypsum dust, paint-spattered carpenter pants, and an I'M WITH HER t-shirt. She looked like she'd been crying. And after a while, she left and didn't come back.

I'd read the Wikipedia page on traumatic brain injuries probably a hundred times over the last year. Some parts I had memorized word for word. I thought about Holmes, who'd been hit in the head twice over the last couple of days. I thought about edema, concussion, diffuse axonal injuries. I thought about focal lesions. I thought about alexithymia, a deficiency in identifying, understanding, processing, and describing emotions that occurs in 60.9% of individuals with TBI. I wondered if maybe the doctor had been wrong and maybe I was a little more banged up—I'd hit my head a couple of times too. I couldn't seem to feel anything. I just sat there, thinking about brain injuries and statistics and long-term symptoms, and then I'd think of what sunlight looked like on his eyelids, or how bad he was at scowling, or the little line that worried between his eyebrows. And then I thought less and less about anything, and after a while, when I came back from a vast, blank space, I remembered that in the ancient world, they had drilled holes in people's heads to try to help with head wounds. Trepanation. That was the word for it. Maybe that was why I felt like everything had drained out of me.

Rivera's hand was warm and rough and solid, and I blinked. He'd caught me; I'd been sliding off the bench.

"When was the last time you ate?" he asked.

I stared at him.

He shook his head. "Come on."

The cafeteria was closed, but he bought me a chicken salad sandwich and a Coke from a kiosk in the basement. They sold flowers and chocolates and get-well cards too. Then he took me back upstairs. I ate the sandwich in four bites. I drank the Coke. As soon as I'd tossed the trash, I sat down and started to drift again.

"You're wiped, kid. Let's get out of here. You can see your friend tomorrow."

I shook my head.

It was almost an hour later before a nurse appeared in the doorway and told us Holmes wanted to see me. I followed her to his room, nodding as she told me that I could only have a few minutes, that Holmes needed his rest, that I shouldn't excite him. Then she let me into the room, and wonder of wonders, Rivera didn't follow. He took up position at the door. I thought maybe he was hoping we'd give him a dual confession.

Holmes had gotten a private room, which made sense considering who he was and how much money his family had. It looked like most of the hospital rooms I'd been in, and I'd been in a fair share with Dad. Brown laminate cabinets lined one wall, covered with reminders and instructions printed on copy paper. A stainless-steel medical tray on casters was tucked into the corner. Soap and hand sanitizer and a sharps disposal were mounted by the sink. Near the bed, someone had written LETI on a whiteboard in blue marker. The nurse's name, I guessed. The monitor beeped steadily. Nobody had brought him flowers. Why hadn't I thought to buy him flowers?

I looked at Holmes last because I was a coward and because I knew how much it was going to hurt. He had a bandage high on his cheekbone, which was strange because I didn't remember a cut there. His eyes were glassy and half closed and ringed with exhaustion. One ear was still puffy where I thought Aston had hit him. His arm was swaddled in bandages. He was wearing a hospital gown, EKG wires snaking under it, and he looked so thin. He was thin. I mean, the kid had all sorts of crazy muscles, and he had that jack-in-the-box surprise ass, but mostly he was skin and bone. He didn't eat enough. I was going to make him eat three meals a day when we got out of here. I was going to make him eat so much soup until he was better.

"Quit talking about soup and how much he eats and whatever else you're mumbling about and get your ass over there," Rivera shot from the doorway.

I hadn't realized I'd been talking out loud. I stumbled over to the bed. Holmes's eyes followed me with sleepy contentment.

"Hold on," I said, and I went back to the door.

"Jesus God," Rivera said.

"Be quiet," I whispered and turned off the overhead lights.

Then the only light came from a bedside lamp, and it hung a soft, golden cone that brushed Holmes's cheek and temple and forehead, and it filled the hollow places with shadows. I sat. And then, because I couldn't stand it any longer, I reached out and took his hand. He made a noise, and I released him.

"Did I hurt you?"

He shook his head.

"Can I—H, I know we're just friends, and I know you don't—I mean, we aren't—I get it, but tonight—"

His hand found mine, the tips of his fingers threaded loosely between my own.

"Thanks." I wiped my eyes. "I, uh—it's been a long day. I just need this for a few minutes."

His pupils were big. He seemed to have trouble tracking my face. When he spoke, his voice was thicker than usual and even more detached. "They deactivated my pain sensors."

A laugh slipped out of me. It was that or sob.

"I like your laugh," Holmes murmured. "I like your smile. I like you. I thought Nick had a nice smile, but Nick wasn't nice. I don't know how to smile. Probably because I'm not human. I watch everybody, and they all know how to do things I don't know how to do. Maybe Nick was right. Maybe I'm not human. I don't feel human sometimes."

"You ate that Double-Double like it was nothing, and you move around like crazy in your sleep, and you don't even have a single laser-guided missile system built into your exoskeleton. Sorry to break it to you, buddy, but you are a real, authentic human."

"Nick said—"

"How about we don't talk about Nick?" My voice broke, but only at the end, and I thought I shored it up pretty well. "How about you tell me what we're going to do when we get out of here?"

Holmes was quiet. His thumb traced the side of my hand. He was crying, I realized. Or he had been crying. A tear leaked down the side of his face, only one, and then it glowed on his jawline, fell, and wicked away into the bedding.

"You are so fucking brave," I whispered. My throat was too tight for anything else. "You were amazing. And I am going to murder your ass if you ever do something like that again."

"Nationally, trained police officers have a hit rate below fifty percent." Holmes gave a one-shouldered shrug. "In some departments, it's below thirty percent, even when a suspect is less than ten yards away."

I stared at him.

"It was a calculated decision," he mumbled, chips of fire growing in his cheeks.

"And what was Burrows's hit rate tonight?" I asked.

Holmes tried to frown, but the meds must have been making it hard.

"A hundred percent, bucko. Jeez, H, I literally almost died when I realized he'd shot you. If you'd gotten yourself killed, I would have legit murdered you."

"You already said that. You said you'd murder my ass."

"That was in general. Now I'm talking about tonight specifically." He didn't say anything to that, and I rubbed my eyes with my free hand. I'd read the Wikipedia page on pistols because I still remembered him, that man from the accident, the glint of metal held low against his thigh. "God created men, but Colt made them equal. I guess whoever said that had never met a Holmes."

He opened his mouth to say something, and then his face twisted, and he shifted.

"Does it hurt?" I asked. "Do you need me to get a nurse?"

Holmes shook his head. After a moment, his features softened. His eyes were half-moons, the pupils black and swollen and trying to find me. I squeezed his hand. "Relax," I said in a low voice. "You need to sleep."

"When I get out of here," he said in a strange voice, "I want to eat chicken tenders. I want to eat them with all the sauce."

I stared at him.

"Because I'm Jack," Holmes said. "Because I love sauce."

"Oh my God. Oh my God!"

Holmes turned into the pillow.

"Are you talking shit? What the actual hell, H?"

He was giggling now. I had no idea what they'd doped him up on, but I loved it. I'd never heard Holmes giggle. I don't know if anyone had. Maybe we both needed to get hit in the head more often.

"That has got to be the weakest trash talk I have ever heard in my life."

If anything, that made him laugh harder, his face buried in the pillow. I fought the grin on my face and lost.

When Holmes had recovered, he lay on his back again. His face was smooth. He stared up at the ceiling, but he had a death grip on my hand. His voice was thready as he said, "I am very glad you're my friend, Jack."

"Well, good," I said. I watched the light on his face, how it highlighted the chiseled ridges. "Because I'm not going anywhere."

Not long after that, Holmes slept, and Rivera called my name. I slipped my hand free from Holmes's, and I made my way out of the room.

"He needs rest." Rivera frowned at me. "Both of you do. Here's the tricky part: do you want to sleep at the station, or do you want me to get some poor DCFS slob out of bed? And don't get started about how you're independent and that bullshit. Tonight is not the night."

"When will my dad—"

"We're working on it." In a softer voice, Rivera added, "But it won't be tonight, kid. Pick your poison."

"The station."

Rivera nodded, and we went to find his car.

Chapter 31

Blackfriar

I spent the night in an empty — and surprisingly clean — cell. I slept almost twelve hours, and when I got up, Rivera was still at his desk, in the same polo and chinos, the hair at the back of his head standing up from sleeping in the chair. After I badgered him enough, he agreed to drive me back to Walker so I could get some fresh clothes. He even bought me breakfast at McDonald's. Maybe he'd switched with Yazzie. Maybe he was playing good cop now.

Up the canyon. We had the windows cracked, and the air smelled like dust and stone and snow and the river. When we passed Bridal Veil Falls, the spray burned like magnesium, so bright it left an afterimage when I swung my head. In the draws, the morning shadows lay over everything like blue felt. A cottontail burst out of a crevice in an ancient slide, and he scampered into a clump of brush and disappeared.

At Walker, the campus seemed surprisingly normal, everyone going about their daily routine. A few of the students were out — some of them jogging, probably getting ready for cross country season; some of them scurrying toward weekend extracurriculars like robotics or chess or biodiesel; some of them dragging themselves toward the dining hall before they stopped serving breakfast. Apparently, word about Burrows hadn't spread yet. The scrub oak was starting to look bare; red and orange leaves drifted in the drainage ditches and stoppered the culverts. Whoever had this job next was going to have to get to work so a freak rainstorm didn't flood campus.

The cottage looked like it always did: the white siding, the old windows in their old aluminum frames, the impersonal curtains blocking out the inside. Rivera didn't bother with the carport; he pulled to a stop on the side of the street and shifted into park.

When he reached for the door handle, I said, "I'll be right back."

Rivera hesitated.

"Come on," I said.

"Jack, you're not thinking about doing something stupid, are you?"

"I'm going to pack some clothes. I don't want you breathing down my neck while I do."

"Because if you're thinking you can climb out a window, you ought to remember that I ran track in high school."

I smirked and glanced at him. "Twenty years ago?"

"I can still run faster than you, wiseass."

"Fine, come along. You can help me decide which undies I need."

"Jesus Christ. Will you go already? If it were me, I'd be packed already."

I slid out of the sedan and let myself in through the carport door. Then I stopped. The cottage looked the way I'd left it, the morning after that terrible fight with Holmes, when Burrows had come to try to kill me: the blanket lay where it had fallen, and in the kitchen, the dishes from our butter noodles were still stacked in the sink. The pile of mail from days ago sat where I'd tossed it. The air felt closed up, like nobody had been here in a day or two.

But the hair on the back of my neck went up, and I stopped breathing. I looked around, trying to figure out what had alerted me. The cottage was dusky, with the weak morning light filtering through the curtains and blinds. The only sound was my heart pounding in my ears. I reached for the door handle behind me. Rivera was twenty feet away, daydreaming about new misdemeanors he could slap me with. He had a gun. Maybe he had a few guns. He could stand there while I packed and pass judgment on all the holes in my trunks and hold his gun, and I'd be one happy clam. As my fingers found the brass of the handle, though, a voice came from the rear of the cottage.

"Don't be ridiculous, Jack. Come back here."

I didn't recognize the voice, but it sounded strangely familiar. It took me a moment to place it. The cadence, even the timbre, were Holmes's, but slightly deeper, slightly more resonant, and with that posh English accent I'd expected Holmes to have. A chill ran down my spine.

When I got to my bedroom, I stopped in the doorway to stare. Holmes's father was crouched over my desk, which had been pulled out from the wall, and he was currently prying off a panel on the back. It came loose with the pop of finish nails pulling free, and then he made a satisfied noise and drew out something rectangular and metallic. It took me a moment to recognize Watson's laptop, the one Holmes had taken from her safe, the one he'd insisted had been hidden somewhere no one would find it. I had a brief moment of wondering: how, why, and most clearly, what the hell was going on?

Then all my attention was absorbed by Blackfriar Holmes. He was taller than Holmes and me, with his long, dark hair combed back. He was white, that English kind of whiteness that looks conditioned by long winters or the moors or some shit like that, and he had a sharp triangle of a face. His eyes were the color of tarnished tin. He wore an expensive-looking black suit and mirror-bright oxfords. When he straightened from where he had bent over the ruins of my desk, even the movements were uncannily familiar and, at the same time, foreign to me. It was like déjà vu. I'd seen it all before on Holmes—my Holmes—but where Holmes was silk and water, this man was oil—even slicker, even smoother. Inhumanly so.

My brain tried to put together an explanation of what I was seeing before me. Holloway Holmes's father was in my bedroom. He had found Watson's laptop, which suggested that he had been looking for it. And then, everything tumbled into place, like those big, chunky pieces of a kid's puzzle, like it all should have been obvious the first time I laid out the pieces.

We'd never seen any sign that Watson had emailed Burrows. We'd seen an anonymous email to Watson, but nothing that went the other way.

We'd never seen any sign that Watson had contacted Burrows in any way.

We'd never seen any sign that Watson had known about Ellis Seward's murder, that she had suspected Burrows, that she had intended to blackmail him.

Moriarty had told us that Watson was onto something big. And Moriarty had also told us that Watson sold stories about the Holmeses, and now Watson was dead and a Holmes was standing in front of me. We had filled in everything else. We had gone from Watson to Campbell, and we had connected Campbell to Ellis Seward's death, and we had assumed that the chain had run in the opposite direction as well—that because Campbell had died to cover up the Seward murder, Watson had too.

"You did this." My voice sounded too loud in the small room. Fear gave the words a tremulous quality, and I didn't even try to mask it. "You killed Sarah Watson."

Blackfriar clicked his tongue and shook his head. He carried the laptop to my bed, sat, and opened the device. As he typed, he said, "I understand you accused Headmaster Burrows of the same crime. You're becoming a bit one-note, Jack. You'll want to watch out for that."

The sounds between us were the click of the keys, the whir of the laptop's fan, the unsteadiness of my breathing.

"Go on," he said. "I'm listening."

"You killed her. Not you personally. But you're the one who contacted Burrows, pretending that you were Watson, pretending to blackmail him." I stopped. Shook my head. "Was there even anything on that flash drive? How could there be? What could you have found?"

Attention still fixed on the screen in front of him, Blackfriar offered only a curled-up smile.

"It doesn't matter, I guess," I said. "Burrows freaked out. He emailed Watson. He asked her to meet. And he killed her. But you made it happen." Something else clicked. "She was blackmailing you. The email she got, the one asking her to meet at the maintenance building, she thought it was from you. That's why she went."

Blackfriar looked up. I wasn't sure he had blinked, not once since I had stepped into the room. The tarnish of his eyes froze me. Then he looked back at the laptop's screen and continued typing. "I have spent almost a week looking for this. I dare say that's the longest I've looked for anything since I was seventeen. I'm almost tempted to be proud of my son; he does, occasionally, show the rare flicker of potential. Of course, once Maggie told me about you, it was quite easy to figure out. My son has a sentimental streak that I cannot seem to cure him of." Then, in a murmur to himself, he added, "I did think that boy at Hewdenhouse would do it, but then, the best laid plans and all that." He looked up again. "I should have paid more attention to you, Jack. I won't make that mistake again."

Outside, a chickadee was singing. When Blackfriar shifted, the springs in the old bed groaned.

I swallowed and asked, "Why?"

"If you want my son to continue to find you interesting, you'll need to sharpen up a bit. That's a terribly vague question. If you mean, why should I have paid more attention to you, the answer ought to be obvious."

"Why did you kill Sarah Watson?"

"Good Lord. The only commendable element of my son's poor taste is that he usually prefers them smart. I see that he's made an exception."

"The IPO."

Blackfriar made a noise.

And then I understood. "He told Watson about what happened at Hewdenhouse, and she was going to sell that story right before the Zodiac IPO."

Blackfriar sat back, considered the screen, and then removed a piece of cloth from his pocket. He wiped down the laptop and then, carrying it in the cloth, returned it to the hidden space in my desk. He replaced the panel, pushed the finish nails back into place, and wiped every surface again, removing his fingerprints.

"Sarah Watson," he said as he worked, "was going to release a series of stories, Jack. All about my son. About his upbringing. Details of our family life. We do have a right to a certain amount of privacy, don't you agree? And so much of what she said would have been misrepresented in the media. You Americans have a flair for melodrama." He stood again. His eyes gave me myself back, like mirrors. "Why, they would have said the most outrageous things. They would have made it sound like I was breeding a sociopath."

He didn't smile. He didn't blink. If you'd taken a photo, he would have looked stoic, maybe even dour. But his amusement, his contempt, and something else—a thrilled happiness that I could only call glee—it all radiated out of him.

"You won't get away with this."

"Get away with what?"

"She was smart. She would have had a plan in case this happened."

"If we take your accusations and treat them, hypothetically, as if they were true, Jack, then I don't think Sarah Watson was terribly smart. No, not smart at all. Do you think she was smart?"

The chickadee had gone silent. The air in the cottage, so close, seemed too thick to breathe.

"Holloway will figure it out."

"Do you know, I honestly think he might? If he had the right data, there's certainly a possibility. But, of course, you aren't going to tell him, are you, Jack? You won't say a word about our chat. I wanted to meet you, and now that's sorted, and I think we can go our separate ways."

"You can't push him around anymore. You can't bully him. He's a good person, and he's smarter than you, and he's better than you." I licked my lips, which probably undermined it when I said, "And I'm not scared of you either."

Blackfriar laughed, the sound deep and rolling. He considered me for a moment with those tarnished, unblinking eyes. "I don't know why you should be afraid of me. I'm a paper-pusher, Jack. A glorified salesman, with a dash of an accountant. Why in the world should you be scared of me?"

"I know who you are."

Some of the glee was back. It made the tin of his eyes bright, although it didn't touch his face anywhere else. "I admire you, Jack. You and your father. You do such demanding work—the physical labor, I mean. And, of course, dangerous work. I've come to learn that every profession has its dangers, although I believe yours is more dangerous than most. Why, just the other day, do you know what happened?"

The silence dragged out, my skin prickling, his eyes steady on my face until I shook my head, and then it kept dragging until I whispered, "No."

"Just the other day, I needed my assistant to pick up my suit from the dry cleaner. Just down the block. And do you know what happened? The poor man got hit by a bus. He was gone." Blackfriar snapped his fingers, and I flinched. "Like that. I think about the sequence of events, so simple: I made one phone call, and the rest just…happened." He snapped his fingers again. "I feel responsible, you understand? It keeps me up at night, thinking about that, about what might happen if I make another phone call, about what might—" Snap. "—happen."

The blood in my ears sounded like the lake, like the water restless against the shore.

Blackfriar studied me for another moment, and then he walked toward me. I stumbled out of his path, and he headed down the hall. He didn't look back.

Somehow, I found my voice. "If you let him stay, I won't tell him."

Blackfriar stopped.

"Let him stay at Walker," I said, "and I won't say anything. Just leave us alone. Leave both of us alone."

He turned slowly. The triangle of his face was set in a frown. "And why shouldn't I do exactly as I please, Jack? Why shouldn't I guarantee your silence in some other, more secure way?"

"You can try."

His lips twitched in a smile. His silence seemed almost hungry. "Do you know, Jack, I think I like you? I think, in fact, you might be quite useful. Have a wonderful day, and give my best to my son. I'm afraid I can't visit him myself; there's no point in paying for discretion if I'm going to ruin the whole thing by showing up at the hospital. As you put it so clearly, Jack, I simply can't afford that kind of attention so close to the offering."

He left, one hand hanging at his side, snapping his fingers to music I couldn't hear. I heard the sound long after the door had closed behind him.

Chapter 32

Hole in One

They released Dad Saturday, and we went home to the cottage and both slept about sixteen hours. On Sunday, I spent the morning eating as many pancakes as Dad would make and trading stories. Jail hadn't been terrible, if I could believe my dad's version of events. In some ways, in fact, it had been good—they'd filled all his scrips, and for the first time in a long time, he'd had all the medication he'd needed. I knew that much had to be true because this Dad, the one who joked and made totally bullshit predictions about the Dodgers (like that Urias would have a better season than Buehler) and tried to flip the pancakes behind his back and dropped them on the floor every time, he hadn't been around in a long time. I hadn't realized how long, or how different things could be, or what my life used to be like—just this tiny sliver of it that I was getting to see again, now, for a moment before they evicted us and Dad's meds ran out. I was halfway through my thirteenth pancake when I had to push back from the counter and go to the bathroom and turn on the water and sit on the tile, my face against my knees, my shorts wet where I pressed my eyes against them, so he wouldn't hear me.

Eventually, though, Dad rapped on the door. "Jack? You ok?"

"Yeah." I snuffled into my shorts and wiped my eyes. They were hot. "Headache."

I could hear him on the other side of the door, shifting his weight, his hand scraping lightly over the wood. "Hey," he said in a different voice. "Open up, bud."

"Be right out." I splashed water on my face, cold against the fever there. I buried myself in the towel. I realized, yet again, I needed to do laundry, and that had a grounding effect. I could do laundry. I could find us a motel where they rented by the week and let you use a hot plate. I could find a part-time job. A grocery store. Or maybe two part-time jobs. A bakery would be good because I'd heard they let you take home the day-old bread. Hell, maybe I could work at Kneaders with Ariana, although she'd probably be my shift manager, and she'd ride my ass for sure—and not in a fun way.

When I couldn't stall any longer, I opened the door. Dad was standing there. He'd buzzed his hair again that morning, and he ran a hand over all that gray stubble and gave me a small smile. He didn't say anything. He hugged me. It had been a long time since he'd done that too, and I'd forgotten what it felt like, to have someone touch you, to feel safe. Then, after a while, he pulled back, and his face was wet. "Today's a good day. Today's a happy day."

I nodded.

A knock came at the door. Dad frowned.

I slipped past him. "I'll get it."

"Are you expecting—"

I wasn't expecting anything. I didn't know what to expect, not anymore. I didn't know what he'd think after the drugs wore off, I didn't know what he'd want, if he'd ever want to see me again, if he'd be glad that we'd caught Burrows but that was the end of it. But—a part of my brain insisted—maybe he's here, maybe he's standing on the porch, maybe he's knocking on the door first thing in the morning because, like you, he's been thinking about when he'll see you next and he couldn't wait any longer. I walked faster toward the door.

When I opened it, it took me a moment to recalibrate. The man on the porch was old—older than Dad, anyway. He was leathery and wrinkled like an old catcher's mitt, with his crisp, white hair in a businessman's cut. He wore a knit shirt with a logo I didn't recognize, pleated golf pants, and chunky Adidas golf shoes. He was smiling like a guy who wants to shake hands and do business and if you both play nice, he can still hit the back nine.

"Good morning," he said. "I'm sorry to impose so early. My name is Terence Pope—please, call me Terry. I'm the president of Walker's board of trustees." He hesitated, and when I didn't say anything, he asked, "May I come in?"

"Dad?"

Dad appeared behind me, stretching past me to shake Pope's hand. "Juan Moreno, and this is Jack. Come in, Mr. Pope."

We all shuffled into the cramped space between the living room and the kitchen. Dad put a hand on my shoulder. Mr. Pope glanced around. I was painfully aware of how little progress we'd made in cleaning up:

fingerprint powder still covered most of the surfaces, and some of my clothes littered the living room, and the breakfast dishes were still in the sink. Pope's attention returned to us, and he smiled.

"Nice day—" Dad began.

At the same time, Pope said, "Lovely home—"

They both broke off. They both chuckled. Dad was squeezing my shoulder a little too tightly.

"Mr. Pope," Dad said, "can we help you? If this is about us being evicted, you've got to give us more than a day's notice to vacate—"

"No, no, no. The contrary. Quite the contrary, I can assure you." Pope turned in place. Apparently he found the cottage fascinating. Apparently he couldn't get enough of checking it out. Maybe he was thinking of buying one for his lawn boy. "So much to say, Mr. Moreno. I feel the weight tremendously. I understand that the pain and grief that you've been through over the last week has been incalculable. In my position as president of the board, I feel it is my duty to handle this unpleasantness personally."

I wasn't sure if we were the unpleasantness or if he meant the whole bit about being framed, jailed, and almost murdered.

"The board, of course, condemns Mr. Burrows's actions. As I'm sure you would agree, the board—both as an administrative body and in terms of the individual trustees—is insulated from the day-to-day decisions of the institution. We had no idea, it goes without saying, what Mr. Burrows was doing. I told the board that you would understand that Mr. Burrows acted completely of his own agency. He was, we might say, fully liable for his actions."

Incalculable was a nice one. *Insulated* was another. And nice phrases too, like *this unpleasantness* and *fully liable*. I had to fight to keep the grin from breaking out. This motherfucker was good.

"In a gesture of goodwill, the board would, of course, like to cover any outstanding medical and legal costs resulting from this horrendous experience. There would be a small matter of some paperwork, and then we could begin to issue payments."

Dad's fingers bit into my shoulder now. He was trying to keep his face smooth. "Well, we'd need to talk to our own lawyer first."

"Mr. Moreno, I can personally assure you that is completely unnecessary. We all want what's best."

"But I want to talk to him first, Mr. Pope. That's what I'm telling you. Jack could have gotten killed. That maniac—"

"Dad," I whispered. "Do it."

He glanced at me.

"Tell him yes."

Pope was trying to pretend he couldn't hear me. He was actually looking up at the ceiling, which maybe he'd learned from *Looney Tunes*. I was surprised he wasn't whistling.

"Jack, with a good lawyer, we might be able to get more—"

"Just thinking out loud," Pope said in an artificially casual tone, "but, of course, there's the inconvenient fact that Jack has been working illegally at Walker—under false pretenses, if I'm to put it bluntly—and, of course, the rumors that he's been selling controlled substances to minors, totally unsubstantiated, I'm sure, but you never know what a jury will think, and then the fact that Jack was trespassing because he'd been officially removed from campus before he returned. These are the kinds of things a lawyer would say, Mr. Moreno. I'd like to keep this as civil as possible, and I'm sure you and Jack would as well."

"Mr. Pope, if you think you can come into my home—"

"Dad, please. Tell him yes." I caught his eye and mouthed, *Trust me.*

Indecision showed in Dad's face. Then it cleared, and he squeezed my arm once. "Mr. Pope, I think we can work something out."

Pope flashed white, capped teeth. "Excellent, excellent. You've got a very smart young man on your hands, Mr. Moreno. Very impressive. Quite the credit to you and your wife. The school's lawyer will draft the papers, and on—let's say Monday—on Monday, we'll be able to close this ugly chapter." He was nodding. He was so pleased with himself, I was surprised his heels were still on the ground.

He and Dad shook hands. And then he wanted to shake hands with me. And then he clapped me on the shoulder and told Dad again what a fine young man I was, and then he opened the door. I followed him out onto the porch. I couldn't remember the exact term for what I'd read on the Wikipedia page for negotiation—the phrase that had settled into my brain was slipping the salami, but there was no way that could be right. Still, I thought it would work.

"Mr. Pope?"

When he stopped and looked back, he had that big smile again. Maybe he was thinking about getting a birdie. Maybe he'd been working on his short game, and after that little coup inside the house, he was sure today was the day.

"When you say that the board condemns Mr. Burrows's actions, you mean all his actions, right?"

"Well, of course, Jack. What happened was a tragedy. A terrible tragedy."

"Uh huh. And will that be reflected in the paperwork? The specific actions you condemn, I mean."

Pope's smile faded. His eyebrows quirked. "I'm not sure I understand."

"Well, there was one significant decision that Burrows made, and I'm sure you'll agree, Mr. Pope, that it was a mistake: when he fired my dad."

"Jack, it's not... You understand that the situation is complicated. Walker does, after all, have a reputation. You know how it is. And I'm sure—yes, I think it makes perfect sense—I'm sure that you and your father want a fresh start."

"I don't want a fresh start. I like it here. And so does my dad. And we'd find it difficult to sign anything that didn't revoke my dad's firing. In fact, we'd find it impossible to sign anything that didn't clearly state that he'd continue to be employed. With back pay. And with full benefits."

Frowning now, Pope said, "The position does not currently include benefits—"

"I'm sure that's another decision you want to condemn. I'm confident of it, actually."

Dad had come out onto the porch now. Pope's gaze swung from me to Dad and back to me.

"Yes." He bared his teeth in a rictus. "Well, as you said, the board does condemn Mr. Burrows's actions, and, of course, I understand that you've done good work." He wavered. Then, in a rush, "Yes, I'll see what I can do. We can hammer out the details on Monday. Mr. Moreno, Jack." He nodded and practically sprinted off the porch.

Dad waited until we could hear Pope's engine turn over. Then he let out a shocked laugh. "Full benefits? Jeez, Jack." He pulled me into a hug and laughed again. "Are you kidding me?"

I let him hug me until it got annoying, and then I wriggled free. I smoothed down my hair and shrugged. "So you can stay on your medication. And so we have a place to live. And it's good insurance, Dad. I've heard the instructors talk about it. You could go back to PT. You could see specialists."

Grinning, Dad shook his head. "They are going to crap themselves when Pope tells them what he agreed to."

"They're getting two hard workers for the price of one. They ought to be grateful."

A tiny grin crept out onto Dad's face. He squinted at me.

"Why are you making that weird face?"

"Full benefits, Jack."

"Yeah, that's what I said. And even if we still have to pay out of pocket for some of the medication they don't cover —"

Dad waved the words away. The smile on his face got a little bit bigger.

"What?"

"Staff get free tuition for their children, Jack."

I stared at him. The words didn't make sense at first. Then I shook my head. "Even with medication and PT, you're still going to need help keeping up with everything. You don't want to overdo it, and Taylor can be such a bitch —"

"Jack," Dad said, "You're going to school."

"I don't need to go to school. I need to make sure you're ok and —"

Dad pulled me into a hug again. He was silent for a long time. When he spoke, his voice was thick with emotion. "Buddy, you're not supposed to take care of me. That's not your job right now. You get to take care of me when I'm old and when I need you to carry in my multipacks of Depends and when I get to turn up the TV until it's way too loud and when I get to scare the hell out of the neighborhood kids for getting on my lawn. Right now, you're supposed to be a kid, and you're so smart and so strong and so good, and if I let you, you'd keep throwing your life away. So, you're starting school."

"Ok, but Dad —"

He squeezed me tighter, and when I stopped trying to talk because I couldn't get any air, he whispered, "We haven't had a fight since your mom passed, and today is such a good day. If we're going to fight, can we do it tomorrow?"

That sounded like a good plan, so I nodded, and it took me a while to realize I was crying, my face pressed into his shoulder as he rubbed my back.

Chapter 33

Like That

Dad wanted to celebrate, and for some reason, he got it in his head that Ariana had to come. I'd made the mistake of mentioning her when Dad asked what I'd done after Burrows had kicked me out of the cottage, and no matter how hard I explained, Dad couldn't seem to understand one very simple concept.

"We're not, like, dating."

He was in the recliner. The Dodgers were playing the Astros. He was looking up steakhouses on his work phone. "You said she gave you a place to stay a couple nights."

"Yeah."

"And you like her?"

"I don't know." I was on the couch. I considered stuffing my head between the cushions. "I mean, yeah."

"And when she asked, you agreed that you were going to make things official?"

"I mean, like, more official than just, you know, whatever. But it's not like—I mean, she never said yes—"

Dad spoke over my stammering. "So, I want to meet her."

"She's probably busy."

"Ok," Dad said. "Another time."

I wanted to check my forehead. I was pretty sure I was sweating.

"And instead," Dad said, "we can have a chat about protection."

"Oh my God."

"Jack, you can think whatever you want, but I am not an idiot."

"I'll call her."

"Every time, Jack. No matter how much you think you like her."

"I'm calling her right now." I rolled off the couch and padded toward the bedroom. "Please stop talking."

"And her telling you she's on the pill does not count as protection."

"I thought today was a nice day!" It came out more like a scream than I wanted. "I thought we were having a great day!"

It was hard to tell over the Dodgers, but I thought Dad was laughing.

Unfortunately, Ariana was having a hard time understanding one very simple concept as well.

"You don't have to come," I said.

"No, it'd be fun. I want to meet your dad." Her voice got quieter, and she added, "And I miss you."

"He's going to be so annoying."

She laughed. Someone spoke in the background, and she said, "Jack," like she was talking to someone else. Then her voice came back, and she said, "Stop worrying about it."

"Tell her to come up to the cottage," Dad called from the living room, "so we can chat. We'll drive to dinner together."

"She doesn't have a car!" I shouted down the hallway.

"Jack, don't lie to your dad," Ariana said. "I can meet you at the cottage."

"Tell her she can come right now," Dad bellowed. "Tell her I want the tea on my son."

"Never mind," I said into the phone. "You don't have a boyfriend anymore. I'm officially dead."

She laughed. "I'll be up there in a little bit.

"You really don't have to—"

She was laughing again when she disconnected.

I stared at the ceiling for what felt like five minutes. Then I went out to the living room. Dad was still watching the game, so I stood in front of the TV. I held out both hands.

"What?" Dad asked.

"That's what I'm asking." I shook my hands for emphasis. "What the hell, Dad?"

"She seems nice."

"You didn't even talk to her!"

"I'm definitely going to like her."

"You like everybody! And now she's coming up here, and this place is a mess, and what am I supposed to do?"

"Well, son, if your sixth-grade gym teacher didn't tell you, and if your coach didn't tell you, and if your mom didn't tell you, then sit down, because I'm going to explain the importance of showering every day."

"This is not a nice day," I shouted over my shoulder as I marched down the hall. "And you're not funny!"

"Deodorant too, son. Apply liberally."

I slammed the door, which felt like giving him what he wanted.

The hot water did feel good. It unknotted some of the tension in my back, and it was weird how nice it felt to get clean in my own space after days of couch-surfing and running and hospitals and the sheriff's department. When I got out, I dried off and put on deodorant and wiped condensation from the mirror. I tried to fix my hair. Then I gave up, wrapped the towel around my waist, and headed to my bedroom.

I ditched the towel and began picking through my clothes. It was definitely time for laundry. Or maybe it was time to give up and just start over from scratch. A knock came at the door.

"Dad," I shouted.

No answer.

It had to be Ariana, so I shouted, "Come in!" I heard the door open, and I added, "Just come straight back. I'm in my room."

I was considering a pair of trunks printed with dachshunds when movement in the corner of my eye made me glance over.

Holmes was staring at me. He looked so much better than he had in the hospital: his color was better—although he did look a little flushed— and while he still looked worn out, he didn't look like death warmed over. His eyes were huge. His jaw dropped. And then I remembered there I was, buck-ass naked, with dachshund trunks hanging from one hand.

He was still staring.

It was nice—everybody likes a compliment—but I couldn't really enjoy it because I was too busy dealing with whatever the hell was happening inside my chest. It wasn't heat, or at least, not like any fire I'd felt before. In eighth-grade science, Ms. Tambor had done this experiment in front of the class, supercooling a rubber ball. When she dropped it, it hit the floor and shattered, and little wisps of smoke rose from all the broken pieces. Like that, I thought, his eyes on me. Today, the gray was lighter, and they reminded me of the first snow every year, the night you thought you'd get off school. A million smoking pieces of Jack Moreno all over the floor.

Then Holmes pivoted hard, shielding his eyes with one hand.

"H, oh my God," I said and yanked the trunks on. I was suddenly aware of the water beading at the nape of my neck, of a drop running down my spine, the sensation like someone drawing a finger along the vertebrae. My skin pebbled. "Sorry, I didn't—" I stepped, misjudged a pile of clothes—apparently there was a sneaker under there—and stumbled. Holmes whipped around and caught me, and I half-fell into him, and it turned into pulling him against me in a hug. "You're ok. Jesus, I was so worried."

His arms moved slowly, stiffly, to encircle me. He was warm. My world narrowed to the feeling of his hands against my bare back, riding over the sensitive skin there. He was wearing another oxford, the same gray as his eyes today, and I could hear the cotton rustling against the bandage hidden under the sleeve, marking the spot where he'd been shot. Then, with an urgency I remembered from before, Holmes released me and stepped back. Color painted bright circles in his cheeks, and his eyes skittered away.

A moment passed, and I said, "I'm sorry I didn't come visit again. I was busy Saturday getting my dad out of jail, and today—it's been so weird. I was going to call."

He shook his head. "There was no need."

"Of course there was. I thought you were going to die. You have no idea how happy I am to see you. You're ok, right? You actually are ok, and you didn't just break out of the hospital and walk through twenty miles of wilderness Terminator style again?"

After blinking, Holmes shook his head. "No, I—I mean, yes, I'm fine. A mild concussion. It has been...frustrating."

"Do you want to sit down? I want you to meet my dad." I pulled on jeans as I called down the hall, "Dad?"

"He's cleaning out the truck." Holmes said, the words neutral, but I could hear the question in them. "I didn't want to disturb him."

For a moment, neither of us said anything. It was late afternoon, and already a breeze was starting, the windows thrumming as it skimmed along them. The furnace kicked on. The corner of Holmes's mouth was quivering; he was trying not to bite his lip again.

"What's wrong?" I asked.

He shook his head once, severely. "Jack, I came today because I need to explain—"

"The laptop." It wasn't the first time I'd shocked him, but it was rare enough that I still enjoyed the sensation. "You hid it in my desk, right? After the police had already searched here, so everyone would assume that there was nothing left to find. The perfect spot where no one would look."

"Yes, but—"

I'd righted the desk, so instead of getting to the hiding spot through the back panel, I pulled out the drawers. Then I withdrew Watson's laptop and handed it over.

"Were you ever able to access whatever she has on there?" I asked.

He held it awkwardly against his body and glanced down, but I didn't think he was seeing it. "No. I'll continue to try, although it seems less urgent now."

He might try, but he wouldn't find anything. I was sure of that. I didn't know exactly what Blackfriar had done, but I knew he'd made it impossible for Holmes to learn whatever Watson had been hiding.

The tremor at the corner of Holmes's mouth was worse now, and then he broke down and bit his lip. When he spoke, his voice was so low that I could barely hear him. "Jack, I did not come for the laptop. I wanted to talk to you." He stopped. I could have drawn a long breath and held it in the pause. "About something." Another pause. "Something important."

"Oh my God," I said with a tiny smile. "We're really going to have to work on this. What's up? Are you mad because I let you get shot? Or because I didn't get shot myself? Or because I didn't hear Aston sneaking up on us?" He still hadn't said anything, and my smile flaked away. "I'm joking, H. What's wrong?"

He bit his lip again, and this time, he drew blood. His eyes were like silver, and I realized the shine was from unspilled tears. "I have wanted to—to explain why I reacted so poorly when—when—" And then he stopped, like he'd reached the end of whatever lifeline he was uncoiling. He stood there, trembling, his front teeth stained crimson.

"When you popped that massive boner and speared me in my sleep?"

His eyes got huge again.

I grinned. "God, don't get mad; it kills me to see your face when I say stuff like that. You don't have to explain anything, H. It's ok. I think you know how I feel about you. And I know you don't feel that way about me. It was just, you know, something that happened; we don't have to talk about it."

For a moment, that ferocious tension locked Holmes's face, his teeth digging into his lip. Then everything transformed: it was like watching locks undone and bolts thrown back, everything in his expression relaxing, opening up. He opened his mouth and started to shake his head.

Someone knocked.

"Shit," I said, "that's Ariana." I grabbed a sweater and pulled it on. When my head popped through the opening, Holmes looked like Holmes again.

"Who's Ariana?"

"Come in!" I shouted. I tried to smooth down my hair again. Then I snagged my Stan Smiths and a pair of socks. "Come on, I want you to meet her."

As I headed down the hall, Holmes trailing after me, Ariana came in through the front door. She'd curled her hair, and she was wearing jeans that matched mine and a gray heathered top. She smiled when she saw me, and I smiled back.

Then the door to the carport opened, and Dad came in and wiped his feet on the mat. He crossed the room to shake Ariana's hand. "Hello there. You must be Ariana."

"Yes, Dad, obviously this is Ariana." They were starting to chat, both of them saying how nice it was to meet each other. "And I want you guys to meet—H?"

When I turned around, he was gone.

"Just a second," I said as I jogged toward the carport door.

"Jack, it's rude to leave your guest—" Dad called after me.

"Seriously, one second!"

I slipped out of the house, and when I got to the end of the carport, Holmes was already thirty yards away, walking swiftly, his shoulders high.

"H!" He stopped, and when I caught up, I asked, "What the hell?"

He turned around slowly. He stared at me. The asphalt was cold and rough under my bare feet, the Stan Smiths and my socks dangling from one hand, the breeze freezing as it carded my damp hair. He was still staring. I folded my arms, the sneakers bumping my ribs, the laces swinging, their plastic ends clicking when they struck each other. I felt hot. I felt cold. He had put his arms around me, I thought. I had felt his hands on bare skin, his fingers fitting perfectly at the small of my back. Up the canyon, a cloud of starlings lifted, swooped, smoked away. Whatever was in me was like that, like the last still moment before the aspens quaked, like hot breath on a cold night. Say something, I thought. Say anything, and I'll say yes.

He said, "I'm happy your father is home."

The day was cold, the sun already dipping behind Timp, and the shadows drawing out across whitebark pine. I thought about Holmes going back to his residence, alone in his room, the door shut. The world kept out, and all the monsters kept in. I thought of my Holmes, the one nobody else knew.

I reached out. My fingers found his mouth. His lower lip was warm and slick where the blood hadn't dried. I pushed and prodded until his mouth relaxed into the right shape. And then I grinned. "Like that, dummy."

He put up with it for a moment, rolling his eyes at me, and then he pushed me away and bit his lip again.

"Go celebrate," Holmes said. "Your father is waiting."

At the door, I stopped and looked back, and there he was, still watching. The late light picked out the Ivy League cut, the shell of his ear, the blown-glass curve of his shoulder. And then, not really all that bad for someone who was such an all-around dork, Holloway Holmes caught my eye and smiled.

THE OLD WHEEL

Keep reading for a sneak preview of *The Old Wheel,* book two of The Adventures of Holloway Holmes.

Chapter 1

I Forgot

How to Break Up, the title of the article on my phone said, *and Still Be a Gentleman.*

"First thing you've got to remember," Dad said, "is go easy."

I barely heard him. One of the advantages of having a smartphone again—thank you, Jesus—was that I had access to, you know, everything. At least, most of the time that was an advantage. Times like this? When I'd spent the last four days reading articles titled "The No-Bullshit Break-Up" and "Be a Man and Do It" and even, kind of confusingly, "In Pursuit of the Carbon-Neutral Break-Up: Yes, It's Possible"? No, not much of an advantage. Not an advantage at all, really.

Dad jabbed me in the knee with an Allen wrench.

"Ow!"

He gave me a level look. People say Dad and I look alike, although I really only see it in our jaws, our mouths, maybe a little around our eyes. His hair is gray and buzzed (not like mine), and his skin is closer to bronze (I'm more of a dark olive), and he's built strong (so far, undetermined, but I think I'll end up somewhere between him and Mom). He tried to jab me with the wrench again, and I stepped out of reach. "Phone away." He waved the Allen wrench at the old mountain bike—technically his, although I was the only one who used it anymore. "I'm teaching you how to do this, buddy. I'm not doing it for you."

Sighing, I pocketed the phone. "How to Break Up and Still Be a Gentleman" had sounded like a lot of bullshit anyway.

Dad pressed the Allen wrench into my hand and pointed to the bike. It sat upside down on the cold concrete slab of the maintenance garage. The nice thing about working at the Walker School (one of the nice things, although to be honest, there weren't a ton) was that Dad had this huge, heated garage. In December, with the glass-block windows frosted over and the wind off Timp screaming against the cinderblock shell, it wasn't exactly warm. The ceiling heater rattled overhead, struggling to keep up, and the smell of hot dust mixed with the smell of two-stroke engine oil. But it was a hell of a lot better than doing this kind of work outside.

"Step one, get the lower forks off."

So, I went to work, and for a pair of quiet minutes, I didn't have to think about anything except disassembling the suspension fork. Dad rolled an oil-stained office chair over and sat; he was doing so much better since we'd gotten health insurance and he could get all his prescriptions and take them consistently, but he still got tired easily, and his balance got funny sometimes. Almost a year and a half later, we were still dealing with the effects of the car crash and the traumatic brain injury. I guess that's why they call them *long-term symptoms*.

"Did you ever break up with Mom?" I asked.

The question popped out before I realized I had formed it in my head. My face heated, and I kept my eyes on the bike as I tugged the lower forks loose. Dad rolled closer, and the sound of the casters on the concrete kept time with the heater's faint rattle.

"Put these on." Dad passed me a pair of nitrile gloves. Then he handed me a tiny screwdriver. "We're improvising here, so you're going to be careful. See those foam rings? You're going to get them out—and you're going to do it without damaging the seals underneath, understand?" He sat back, and his hands curled around the armrests. "And no, I never broke up with your mother. She probably thought about breaking up with me a time or two."

I nodded and kept my gaze on the bike. It probably would have been easier with a specialized tool, but it wasn't terribly difficult getting the foam rings out with the screwdriver. They were dark with oil and dirt, and they left smears on the gloves.

"Any reason you're asking?" Dad said in what I'd started to recognize as his I'm-so-carefully-neutral-I-could-be-Switzerland voice.

I shook my head.

The furnace rattled. The wind snaked against the walls of the garage. I turned the foam rings over in my hand and finally couldn't stall any longer and looked up at Dad.

He had his Switzerland face on. "Get the rubbing alcohol and a tub— we should replace those, but for today, we're going to clean them up as best we can."

So, I jogged over to the workbench, found the rubbing alcohol and an empty plastic tub, and carried it back over to the bike. I poured in enough alcohol to cover the pads, but when I went to strip off the gloves, Dad shook his head.

The chair creaked when he rocked slightly. "Do you miss her? That's a dumb question; I know you miss her. But…did something happen?"

"No."

The chair creaked again. "You just were wondering if I ever broke up with your mom?"

"I guess."

He rubbed a hand over his hair, and it made a soft sound.

"How do you know if something is serious?" I blurted this question like the last one. I heard myself, and I made a firm decision to get a lobotomy. "Like, if you should stick it out when you have a rough patch, or if that means you're not, you know, supposed to be together?"

Dad was silent for a long time. "Did you get her pregnant?"

"Dad!"

"Did you?"

"No!"

"Are you using condoms? Because I don't care if she tells you she's on birth control—you use a condom every time."

I blew out a breath and fished one of the foam pads out of the alcohol. "Jack."

"Yes, oh my God. Can we please stop talking about this?"

He didn't say anything to that, which was kind of an answer. He sat there, staring at me, legs spread, hands tight around the arms of the chair. I squeezed the pads to get the oil out and rinsed them in alcohol and repeated.

Finally, he said, "That's enough."

He stood and walked over to the utility sink. His first few steps were unsteady, but then he evened out. Water ran. When he came back, he had a bucket and a sponge. He worked the sponge around in the soapy water, and then, using the chair for balance, got down on his knees and started to clean the bike's frame.

"I'm supposed to be doing that," I said.

"You're sixteen, buddy." His voice was softer, and he kept his eyes on the sponge. "Why are you worried about sticking it out?"

"I don't know."

He moved the sponge in slow, careful swipes, and clumps of dirt fell away. Muddy water ran down to the concrete slab, and trickles of it curled inward along his wrist.

"It's just—" I hooked my arms around my knees. "There's a lot going on right now. And, I don't know." There wasn't a good way to tell my dad that I was feeling a little conflicted because of a gray-eyed boy who had made it painfully clear that he had no interest in me. "I don't know," I said again.

He paused, the sponge halfway up the bike's frame. "Do you like her?"

"This is the worst conversation of my life."

That got a tiny smile out of him, and he started scrubbing again.

"I don't know," I said. "Yes, I mean, obviously. Ariana is great. But sometimes I think maybe I—I rushed into this."

Dad made a noise that could have meant anything.

"What?" I asked.

He shook his head.

"Come on."

"Nothing." He smiled and tossed the sponge in the bucket. "I remember what it's like to be sixteen. You think you have to dip your wick into everything."

"Dad!"

He laughed. "It's not like you're the first teenage boy in the history of the world, buddy."

"That's not—it's not like that."

"Ok."

"It's not."

"I said ok, son. If you say that's not what it is, I believe you." One knee cracked when he got to his feet. "You like her, right?"

I groaned, but when he waited, I nodded.

"Well, why don't you see what happens? Take her to that dance. Winter—what is it?"

I squinted a dirty look up at him. "You know it's Wintersmash. And it's not a dance. And I can't go; it's invite only."

Dad frowned at that. "I'm sure you'll get an invitation."

Responding to that—telling him the truth—would only hurt him, so I didn't say anything.

After a moment, Dad cleared his throat. "It doesn't have to be the Winter-thing. I'm saying slow down. You feel like you rushed into this? Well, as an outside observer, I'm telling you I think you're rushing again. You've been dating—what? A couple of months?"

"But we've been hanging out longer than that."

"Well, it's a free country. You can break up with her whenever you want. But this is your first serious relationship; why don't you give it a little time and see how it develops?"

I thought about that. Then I looked up at Dad. "Do you like her?"

"It doesn't matter what I think."

I made a face.

"I like her," he said with a laugh. "She's good for you."

I made a different face.

Dad tried to flick me with a shop towel he pulled from his back pocket, and I barely dodged in time.

After that, it was easier to work than to talk. Everything Dad said had made sense. It had been — well, it had been what I'd been hoping he'd say, actually. And now he'd said it, and I hadn't died of embarrassment, and somehow...somehow I felt worse. Because what I wanted to say was, *But it doesn't feel right.* Or maybe, *But what if there's someone else, and even though I don't have a shot with him, I feel totally different when I'm around him?* Or maybe, if I were going to get agonizingly specific, *I know what love feels like, and this isn't it.* But, of course, all of those things were a fuck-ton scarier to say out loud, and sometimes, Jack Moreno was a coward.

With Dad watching to make sure I did it right, I replaced the rings, oiled them, and ran suspension grease around the inside of the upper forks. I was reaching for the lower forks when he said, "Run home and wash up. I'll finish here."

"I'll do it."

"You're going to be late." This time, he did get me with the towel, and even through my jeans, it stung. He grinned when I yelped. "Ass on fire, buddy. Run."

He was exaggerating; I had plenty of time before Holmes came over to help me study, and even if I was late, he wouldn't mind. Well, he would because he had this uncanny clockwork precision to everything he did, but he was nice enough that he wouldn't say anything. Going back to school had been awesome, an opportunity I'd never thought I'd get, but it had also meant coming face to face with the reality that teachers, unlike YouTube videos and Wikipedia articles, actually expected you to do something with what you were learning, and sometimes that was a hell of a lot harder than remembering the odd bit of internet trivia.

Outside, the Wasatch Mountains were blisteringly white with snow — so much snow that even at night, the canyon seemed bright. It furred the bare branches of scrub oaks and aspens, and it glazed the dark green of the pines. The wind bit at my ears and stole my breath in long steaming coils as I jogged home. The cottage wasn't far from the maintenance building, but I thought maybe Dad was right, and I should have worn a coat.

When I got home, I let myself into the cottage — we didn't bother locking the doors, not all the way on the ass-end of Timp — and turned on the lights. It was warm, which was one good thing you could say about it. It wasn't falling down; that was another. It was small, and when you first stepped inside, the thing you noticed was the smell from the three-quarters fridge, like something was burning. But it was ours, at least, as long as Dad stayed on at Walker, and that was enough.

I kicked off my Nikes by the door and was hopping toward the bathroom, peeling off my socks, when a knock startled me.

When I opened the door, Holmes was standing there. There's no good way to describe him: you start with one piece, like his eyes the color of starlight, and then you have to talk about the perfection of cheekbone, mouth, jaw, and then you're on to his neck, the breadth of his shoulders fanning out as he turned, the curve and line of arm until you reach that one knobby knuckle. The whole reason people started carving sculptures was because of guys like Holmes, where everything about him had the look of cold-chiseled perfection. He was wearing his usual getup: a wool driving coat, a pale oxford, dark chinos, chukkas wet with snow. He was gripping his school bag, and when he saw me, his hands relaxed. I noticed things like that with him; I liked noticing things like that, liked what they said.

"You left your socks on the floor," he said.

I shut the door behind him.

"Your dad has asked you several times not to leave them in the common areas of the house."

"Hi, H."

"It's eleven degrees outside. You shouldn't be barefoot in the winter."

"How was your day?"

He studied me, eyes like mercury beads. "My day was normal."

"You can do better than that."

Grimacing, Holmes passed me his bag and began working his way out of his coat. "I ate turkey sausage and scrambled eggs for breakfast. And I had a protein shake."

"But you didn't eat dinner."

"I had the protein shake late in the afternoon."

"That doesn't count."

"It most certainly does."

"Uh huh. One good thing?"

"I learned about a useful backdoor on a popular brand of doorbell camera, and I completed all my schoolwork."

"And one bad thing?"

"I already told you about the turkey sausage."

"Oh my God, ladies and gentlemen. A joke."

Holmes yanked the bag back. "You're a bad influence. We're beginning with chemistry tonight."

"No, please, I'll give you anything you want."

You couldn't tell, but Holmes ate this stuff up like candy. At least, that's what I chose to believe.

"I'll tell you where I hid the Nazi codebook. You can have my firstborn!"

"Your firstborn would doubtless leave socks everywhere."

"H!"

"Your room—"

"My room is fine! And for the record, I don't want to catch you sneaking in there to clean up again. If you find your present, I'm not going to give it to you. It's supposed to be a surprise."

You had to learn to read the microexpressions: the subtleties of mouth and eyes. He pretended to be busy hanging up his coat.

"If we are going to continue our arrangement—" H began.

The knock at the door stopped him. He glanced at me.

I shrugged and opened the door.

Ariana stood there. She looked cute. Scratch that. She looked fantastic, done up in a belted jumper dress that showed off her legs—and her curves—with her hair in perfect curls and boots she knew I liked on her. She smiled at me, gave Holmes a curious look, and leaned in. I kissed her automatically.

"Ready?" She glanced at me in my work clothes and bare feet and smiled uncertainly. "What's up? Are we still on for dinner?"

Dinner, my brain said.

"No, yeah, I just—"

Holmes ripped his coat from the hook. "It's my fault," he said, the words clipped and emotionless. "I'm sorry for keeping him."

"H, wait. I forgot—"

But he plunged out into the night, and the door clicked shut behind him.

Acknowledgments

My deepest thanks go out to the following people (in alphabetical order):

Justene Adamec, for catching my spoiler in the epigraphs, for spotting my continuity errors, and for helping me think more closely about Jack's negotiation at the end.

Savannah Cordle, for making me think more carefully about Aston—in many ways; for helping me fix the *vonkramm* email; and for spotting Manga Boy, who had survived from an earlier draft.

Fritz, for catching typos and errors that nobody else saw (channeling his inner Hazard with 'recur'), for spotting my slips from first to third (yikes), and even filling in my missing words!

Austin Gwin, for helping me with do acid right (it's true in a sense); for Macey's versus Macy's (another Utah quirk!); and for his kind, honest, and thoughtful response to Jack and Holmes, particularly Jack.

Steve Leonard, for giving me the correct title of the hymn, for perfecting my In-N-Out references, and for catching, among other things, my prepositional errors!

Raj Mangat, for fixing my fashion blunders (Louis Vuitton!); for helping me make the soccer scene clearer; and for catching so many errors (like Holmes's third hand!).

Cheryl Oakley, for reading the earliest version of this book, for being willing to give me her honest opinion, and then for helping me to make it so much better.

Pepe, for pointing out how much blood Olin would have lost; for careful reconsideration of Jack hiding under the bed; and for that absolutely gorgeous idea of the truck stop (even though I didn't end up using it).

Nichole Reeder, for catching Melissa (not Jessica), for pointing out that I had too many Sarais, and for reminding me about all the other ways Jack got himself hurt.

Tray Stephenson, for teaching me (how did I not know?) aggravating versus annoying; for teaching me (HOW, HOW DID I NOT KNOW?) taller than me, and for, as usual, his gentle encouragement as he caught a multitude of other errors.

Dianne Thies, for remembering Holmes's phone, checking out Doc Martens, and, on top of so much else, making me laugh about Dumpster Slut.

Mark Wallace, for catching dropped letters and missing end marks; for his honest feedback on Jack and Holmes's relationship; and for his insight into the timing of the mystery of Jack's background.

Jo Wegstein, for giving this story an infinitely richer texture and depth with her contributions to Burrows and Ellis in particular, as well as helping me with the trickiness of logistics and, as usual, my prose.

Wendy Wickett, for her patience with all things italics (and for my virtual cookie!); for helping me clarify my muddled writing; and for giving me (among other things) the correct plural for the Moriartys!

About the Author

For advanced access, exclusive content, limited-time promotions, and insider information, please sign up for my mailing list at **www.gregoryashe.com**.

Made in the USA
Las Vegas, NV
14 July 2023

74719470R00184